"The same elements t[...] romances into smash hit[...]ate romance with external conflicts threatening to tear apart the lead characters' unity) are incorporated with spectacular results in this novel."
—*Affaire de Coeur* on *The River's Daughter*

"A powerful, heart-rending, and unusual love story told with grace, authority, and compassion."
—Susan Wiggs, author of *Jewel of the Sea* on *The River's Daughter*

The Bear

Beside the stream crouched a grizzly, a magnificent monster with massive shoulders and rich brown hair painted silver at the tops.

Twana said nothing, but the tension in her body told Madsaw she'd spotted the bear and felt its great power.

How had she known it would be here?

The grizzly lifted its head and opened its mouth. Its roar, like something evil flung from a cave deep in the earth, echoed against the canyon walls and slapped at Madsaw's ears. Although he'd heard grizzlies bellow before, this was different, deeper, coldly savage. A chill raced down his spine.

"He knows we are here," Twana whispered, terror in her voice.

**Books by Vella Munn
from Tom Doherty
Associates, Inc.**

Daughter of the Forest
Daughter of the Mountain
The River's Daughter

DAUGHTER OF THE FOREST

VELLA MUNN

A TOM DOHERTY ASSOCIATES BOOK
NEW YORK

DAUGHTER OF THE FOREST

Copyright © 1995 by Vella Munn

Cover art by Royo

A Forge Book
Published by Tom Doherty Associates, Inc.
175 Fifth Avenue
New York, N.Y. 10010

Forge® is a registered trademark of Tom Doherty Associates, Inc.

ISBN: 0-812-53499-9

First edition: February 1995

Printed in the United States of America

0 9 8 7 6 5 4 3 2 1

PROLOGUE

Rain attacked great trees twisted and scarred by nature's violent hand, the relentless cadence as old as Salmon-Men, immortal spirits who lived in the underworld until called forth to replenish the rivers each spring. When the wind that drove the rain suddenly whirled in a new direction, the trees bent and recoiled, fought to shake off their sodden burden, prepared for another onslaught.

The battle had continued all day, spring storm against forest giants, and although some lay ruined on the ground, countless fir, spruce, and cedar remained standing, their heavy branches outstretched to protect their fragile children.

A young Nisqually woman, her thoughts as dark as the heavy, cloud-coated sky, huddled at the edge of the forest and breathed in the scent of salt spray, wet earth, and moss-draped trees. When the wind rocked her, Twana shuddered and ducked her head as yet more water cascaded down. Although her soft cedar bark cape and the hat that hid her gentle features were tightly woven, even her skilled handiwork wasn't enough to completely protect her from nature's fury. She should return to her people, to her tight, dry home. Only . . .

Thunderbird stood on the highest mountain peak, a lake on its back, lightning as its pet. Although she'd never seen the fearsome monster that was so much a part of her people's legends and would run in terror if she did, Twana didn't try to stop images of him flapping his massive wings to bring on the thunder, lightning, and drenching rain that isolated her from all others tonight. The shaman spoke often and fearfully of Thunderbird; her mother had first told her of the powerful spirit before she was old enough to truly understand.

Now she did. Thunderbird was part of her world. She, daughter of Saha and a man who had never held her, lived in a small village at the mouth of a river that cut its way down snow-capped mountains and through thick forests before feeding into the churning sea; her life always had and always would be dictated by the rhythm of great wings, seasons, the yearly return of the life-giving salmon.

Again she shuddered, cursed her slight body. She felt surrounded by rain, trapped by the night, unable to fight the forest-scented breeze that became an angry force whenever Thunderbird called forth a storm.

And yet she'd come to this lonely place where the river rushed savagely and endlessly to the mother sea—calling her to join it—because she'd felt even more trapped by the cedar walls and floor and roof of the plank house where she lived with the foul-smelling, hooked-nosed Tatooktche.

"It has been decided," he'd told her this morning while the clouds thickened and darkened. "You will become Quahklah's wife after the next dance to bring back the moon. Even though his rank is high and he could choose a chief's daughter, he has agreed to my bride-price. He has said he will use that which happens inside you for himself and it will make him a great trader with the sea-strangers, as I did with your mother. You *will* obey him. You will *not* shame me."

Twana pushed back her wet, waist-length hair and rested her hand on her shoulder, feeling a painful bruise through the thick cape. The mistake had been hers, but when she heard the name Quahklah, she'd recoiled in revulsion. The "No!" that escaped her lips had been as uncontrollable as her sight, the gift and curse that made her and her mother different from all others.

Tatooktche had given her no time to explain her reaction. She was his, his responsibility and right ever since her mother's disappearance. He had decided to trade the mysterious and sometimes frightening images that flowed through her mind for carved pipes, strong fishing tackle, even a sleek new dugout hewed from the straightest cedar.

She would have a husband.

Become as trapped as Saha had been.

Ignoring the rain, Twana lifted her head and shouted her despair into the night. Grizzly spirit was behind her in the mountains, hidden deep in his tight, dry cave, maybe able to hear her as clearly as she sometimes heard his mortal offspring when their foraging brought them close to the village. If Grizzly trusted his children's presence to her, maybe he would hear her desperate plea.

Maybe he would take her to live with him far from men like Tatooktche and Quahklah, far from all men who cared only that the gift passed from mother to daughter would make them rich.

The thought of finding shelter and peace with Grizzly spurred her, not deep into the forest where she might lose her way on a starless night, but to follow the river to where it emptied. She didn't stop until she stood at the edge of the cliff that looked down at the great and restless sea that both generously fed her people and sometimes brought storms one after another until a sunlit day became precious. Although she couldn't see the enraged waves that hurtled themselves against the rocks below and set the ground under her feet to shaking, the sound seeped into her, filled her with both courage and even more fear.

When lightning slashed its way through the clouds and momentarily exposed the rushing river and distant horizon, her fingers sought the fine gold necklace that circled her throat, but tonight her mother's gift offered no comfort or warmth.

Like Thunderbird, the sea had always been here. Both would exist long after she had given up her soul to a man twice her age and became like a spent wave slowly sinking into the sand.

"Please!" she called into the night. "Grizzly, please, hear me! I am set apart from all others. I truly belong nowhere except with you and others of your kind, the elk, mountain sheep, gentle deer, the silent fox. If I remain here, soon I will be like my mother, at the mercy of a man."

A powerful gust of wind threw her words back at her. Fighting the invisible strength, she touched her hand to her face, unable to tell whether the wetness came from more than the rain.

No. She wouldn't cry. Tears, like prayers to the beasts who ruled the forest, were for children. She knew where the wild creatures lived and slept and ate, even tonight "saw" the great gray whale feeding beyond the surf, but she wasn't one of them. She must face her future with courage and somehow survive.

Alone.

CHAPTER 1

The night told him everything. Owls called end-lessly to each other from deep within the forest, their voices echoing against the heavy silence. The wind played with thick treetops like a teasing child and not like the angry monster it had been the night before. Despite the never-ending dampness of his world, the scent of smoke touched his nostrils and warned him that he'd nearly reached the Nisqually village where a mur-derer lived.

Even crouched so low that he saw little more than the earth beneath his feet, Madsaw, Tilla-mook war chief of the Wolf Clan, knew all he needed to. His enemy was not about; Tatooktche had gone to his house to sleep and had left the night to the owls.

And to him, a man filled with the taste and heat of vengeance and loss.

Behind him crept his uncle Walkus, his younger brother Lukstch, and three others. They had come with him on this dangerous journey because his father, head chief of the Wolf Clan, had been murdered at Tatooktche's hands, and the death could not go unpunished. But although the others, all touched by the loss of their brother, father, and chief, insisted on accompanying him as he sought revenge, the true risk was his.

He didn't want it any other way. His thunder spirit had given him strength and speed and courage, a body and mind made for leading and fighting, for one day ruling his people. His eyes and ears would serve him well tonight and his spirit would not desert him. This he believed.

It was all that mattered.

"You are sure they have no dogs?" Lukstch whispered from where he crouched behind Madsaw. "If they do, you will never get close enough."

"I told you, I talked to a slave taken from here. He said the Nisqually had three dogs but lost them to a mountain lion. They have not yet had time to trade for more."

Lukstch snorted. "No one believes a slave. He could be lying."

Madsaw knew that but didn't bother agreeing with his brother. Instead, he slipped closer and then peered around a massive spruce. The moon had slipped behind a wisping cloud and now lacked the strength to light the night. He saw the distant houses as nothing more than indistinct shapes clustered together in a protected inlet within sight of the sea. Several taller shadows, he knew, were the totems that told each clan's history and deeds. Beyond that he could see nothing, could barely hear the now gentle waves.

With his mind clogged by what it had felt like to build a canoe to place his father's ruined body in, he signaled that he wanted the others to remain where they were while he continued alone.

"Madsaw, no," Walkus hissed. "When I said I would come with you, it was because I had lost a brother and share your pain. I do not want you fighting alone. You don't know how many there are. If you are overwhelmed—"

"Then you will have to take my body back to my mother. This is my war, my uncle."

"But—"

"The Wolf Clan has already lost one chief; it must not lose you who have taken his place." Madsaw wrapped his hand tightly around his stone slave killer, then held his body still so he could hear even more of whatever message the night might send to him. He'd hardened his body and spirit by bathing in an icy stream and carved a wooden image of Tatooktche, which he'd then clubbed until it splintered into countless pieces. His mother had begged him to wear elk-hide armor and a wooden breastplate as protection, but those things would only slow him when he might need to run like a deer. Run? No, he couldn't, wouldn't, do that.

Despite the wrenching pain of having lost yet another loved one, he had come here to avenge his father's death at Tatooktche's hands—not by killing him but by taking a hostage as tradition dictated. Only when ransom had been paid for the captive could he again truly walk like a man among his people. He knew that, accepted what must be.

"When I have her, I will return to you."

"What if her family wakes?"

"Then I will fight them," he said with his hand on his uncle's shoulder. "I am Nutlan's eldest son. It was I who found his body and carried it back to my mother, I who handed you the chief's crest."

"A responsibility I never thought would fall to me. If my brother had lived—Madsaw, this is too dangerous."

"I heard the thunder when I woke this morning," Madsaw tried to reassure his uncle. "Even now, I feel its strength in my bones, my muscles. I will succeed at this."

"Thunder, your spirit. You are sure?"

Madsaw stared at where he knew the top of the nearest mountain lay, remembering well the low rumble that reached him as he lay, alone, on his fur blanket while night surrendered to day. "Yes."

"That is good. Your spirit has been with you since you made your guardian search and has made you a worthy war chief. Only once . . ."

Madsaw glanced down at his uncle. Because of the dark, Walkus couldn't gaze into his eyes and find the truth in his heart, but maybe Walkus didn't have to. After all, his uncle had been there when Vattan was killed when the thunder spirit deserted him.

Vattan. His wife.

Madsaw took a deep breath, surprised by how hard it was to push the air from his lungs. He didn't want to feel any more grief, to struggle against the loss and pain that constantly lapped at him and made the nights last too long.

The lonely call of an owl sent claw prints of sensation down his back and briefly made him wish he'd worn a cape instead of leaving his body naked to the night. He shook off the feeling, focused on the house closest to them, pressed the slave killer to his chest, and slid silently away from the others. His bare feet dug into rock and damp sand, reminding him that he no longer had the forest to hide in. The air smelled of the sea and what lived in it, scents that were a part of him.

As he moved, still crouched low, eyes and ears straining, he heard his heart pounding. His arms and legs felt as strong as the sturdy canoes he built with maul and wedge. Surely if he was afraid, the fingers gripping his slave killer would be cold and numb, or hot and trembling. His heart, he told himself, had picked up its cadence simply because after days and nights of preparation, he was finally here. By morning he would be on his way back home with his captive, and all who lived in his village would speak of his courage and he would find peace.

The need to concentrate on his surroundings stopped his thoughts. The slave who'd told him about the dogs had drawn a sketch of the Nisqually village and pointed out where Tatooktche lived. In his mind he pictured the inside of the sturdy cedar-plank house with its double ridge-pole, high roof timbers, central fire pit, and separate sleeping quarters. Tatooktche was the house chief, and thus he and his family lived farthest from the entrance in the place of honor. Once he'd stepped through the oval doorway and eased his way along the edge of the open gathering area, it should be a simple matter for him to push past the woven screen that separated Tatooktche's family from the others. But making his way around sleeping bodies in that small, dark, private space would test his self-control. Clubbing his hostage into unconsciousness without alarming the others would take the greatest of skill. But it had to be done.

He would—

A sound froze him. For a heartbeat he thought he'd heard a dog, but when the sound was repeated, he realized it was caused by waves slapping against a canoe left on the sheltered beach. When he was close enough that the house he sought loomed ahead of him, he waited until the sliver of moon freed itself from the clouds, revealing that no dogs slept outside. But they might be inside; the slave might have lied. He didn't dare forget that.

A few more steps brought him to the opening. He pulled in cool, damp air and ran his free hand over his thigh. The muscle beneath flesh was rocklike, designed for stealth and speed. When he squared his shoulders, he felt as if he were expanding, becoming as powerful as the thunder. Tatooktche had broken the strongest of taboos, murdering not simply a stranger who had laid claim to a stretch of river boiling with salmon, but chief of the Wolf Clan. Tatooktche would pay for his crime, and a good man would sleep his forever sleep in peace, his death avenged.

It wouldn't be as it had when Vattan was murdered and helpless rage and grief ate at his heart.

Madsaw dropped to his knees and crept inside the large, high-roofed structure, then quickly stood. His feet slid silently over beaten earth and thin cedar planks. When he inhaled, his nostrils took in the smell of smoke, boiled clover root and giant kelp, seal blubber, dried cedar bark. Coals from the dying fire in the center provided enough light that he was convinced everyone was inside their sleeping quarters. They might not all be asleep, but if he was quiet enough . . .

A baby whimpered. As he pressed himself against one of the two carved posts that flanked Tatooktche's quarters, the sound intensified. He heard a woman say something but couldn't make sense of the words. Then he heard bare feet slap softly on wooden flooring, proof that the woman wasn't a commoner. The baby's cry became a shriek, then was almost instantly cut off. He imagined a milk-filled breast being stuck into the baby's mouth and waited, every nerve on fire, until he heard a masculine voice followed by a giggle from the woman.

He waited, trying to catch the sound of the baby's sucking. When he heard nothing, he realized that the screen that kept him from being able to see the baby and its parents muffled a great deal. If he remained silent, no one would know he had been here until they woke to find Tatooktche's daughter gone.

But if she let out a cry . . .

He shook his head, nearly hitting the thick knot of hair at the back of his head against the post. Tonight wasn't for question. Only action mattered.

When he was certain the baby had nursed its fill and had probably fallen back asleep, he slipped his hand past Tatooktche's elaborately decorated bark and fiber screen and eased his body into the close, unlit enclosure. He heard the deep breathing of two, maybe three people. The slave had told him that Tatooktche's wife had mysteriously disappeared several moons ago and he had not yet sought another. Tatooktche's mother lived with him, along with a sister who, it was said, could not hear or speak and thus would never marry. Tatooktche had only one daughter, the girl he sought.

Although he strained to make sense of the barely visible tangled shapes on the floor, they remained a mystery. When he lifted the covering a crack to let in a little of the firelight, he spotted a pile in one corner that he took to be blankets, and near it something with sharp edges that was probably a carved wooden storage box. The space was so crowded that he could barely move without touching something, or someone. His heart beat fiercely, and although he fought to remain calm, his breathing sounded to him like wind-lashed waves. On his knees now, he reached out tentative fingers toward what he took to be a head. He felt dry and tangled hair. This might be his enemy's mother, but there were rumors that Tatooktche's sister looked much older than her age and took no care of herself. When he'd assured himself that the woman still slept, he again searched by touching yet another mounded blanket. His fingers told him this person was larger than the other—Tatooktche.

Instantly, instinctively, he gripped his slave killer tighter and fought the heat that clawed at his throat. It would be so easy to bury his weapon into his enemy's skull. As Tatooktche's blood left his body, the man would truly and deeply know the meaning of revenge.

But Madsaw hadn't come here to murder.

Although he didn't think he'd moved, he must have brushed one of the sleepers with his foot. Even though he didn't have room to turn and see what he'd touched, he heard someone stir. Motionless, ready for fight, he waited out the sound.

It was repeated, stronger and less random this time. He now desperately needed to breathe and yet couldn't remember how. Barely able to contain himself, he scrambled silently around until he reached the screen. Then, as a figure sat up, he slipped back out into the main room.

As soon as he realized what he'd done, his heart filled with shame. He was a man, not a child hiding from danger. But if Tatooktche cried out a warning, the others would attack and his life would end with his blood seeping onto his enemy's floor, and his father's soul would never find peace.

The wind found its way through the house opening and pushed smoke around him. He choked down a cough, kept his eyes off the entrance and freedom, and waited out his thoughts.

The answer to what he should do came quickly. He had to return to Tatooktche's chambers for his enemy's daughter.

Although he was close enough to the screen that he could easily touch it, he didn't fully comprehend that it had moved until he heard a soft swishing sound. Instantly he gathered himself.

The screen was pushed aside, and someone stepped out, someone who handled herself as if sleep still held her in its grip. He saw her run her hand over the back of her neck, heard the faintest of sounds as she half yawned.

Then she froze, and he knew she'd spotted him.

The girl wore a sleeveless, beaten-bark mantle that had wrapped itself around her slender legs. Her hair, long and loose, half covered her face. Those things and her slight weight registered at the instant their eyes locked.

He waited in the red-tinged night for her to scream, held his slave killer aloft to let her know she would never make another sound. But although he saw her features contort and her body tighten, she remained silent. Instead, with a speed that took him by surprise, she leaned down, grabbed something, and held it high as if to protect herself with it. When he saw that she'd snatched a cooking basket, he wondered at the wasted effort.

"Go!" she hissed. "Go!"

He wanted to laugh. Despite the danger, he

nearly released the words that would tell her how foolish she was. Her eyes glittered. He couldn't tell whether terror or fury ruled her.

It didn't matter. Equaling her speed, he lifted his arm and swung the slave killer at her. She ducked and the basket caught the bulk of his blow. Still, he'd hit her with enough force that she was knocked off balance. She stumbled onto one knee, gaped up at him. For a heartbeat, their eyes again met. He didn't understand what he saw in hers, didn't want to feel anything for this girl. Then she started to rise and he hit her again. This time he felt stone strike bone.

She crumpled onto the smooth wooden flooring like a seabird settling onto an ocean swell. Her legs jerked, then became still. For a moment he stood looking down at what he'd done while his eyes and ears searched for danger and his heart struggled to free itself from his chest. When the house remained silent, he crouched beside her and touched the side of her head. His fingers became damp with blood, and he wondered if he'd killed her.

It didn't matter, not yet. He had to get her— them—out of here before the others woke. After sliding his arms under her, he stood with his burden clamped tightly to him.

She felt light, totally limp.

If this was Tatooktche's daughter, she now belonged to him.

CHAPTER 2

Madsaw hurried back through the narrow opening and stepped outside to let the damp night surround him. The girl in his arms still felt lifeless, but he couldn't allow himself to think about that now. After staring for a moment in the direction of the sea which bit lazily at the sand not far from the cedar-plank houses, he turned and headed toward the trees.

Although he wanted to look for his companions, he didn't dare take his eyes off the ground, because even though the sand was smooth, rocks and downed logs might trip him. He cursed the weak moon that was little more than a thin curve of silver-white. If Thunder was with him tonight, his spirit should have made the moon stronger. But maybe Thunder, in its wisdom, had decided he must rely on his own strength and courage.

Halfway to the trees, Madsaw stepped on something sharp and clenched his teeth to keep from crying out. He wanted to shift the girl so he could more easily see where he was going, but the thought that Tatooktche and the others might have awakened kept him going. Finally he felt himself being surrounded by cool bark and branches, felt soft, damp pine needles under his feet. Breathed in the forest that was, along with the sea, his life. A sense of power flowed through him and filled his muscles; he wanted to bellow his triumph to the sky.

"Madsaw, this way."

He looked around but saw nothing except shadow so deep it made him think of a great cave. Still, because he recognized his uncle's voice, he changed direction. "There were no dogs." He kept his voice calm and quiet. "And she came to me."

"Came? You've killed her."

"No," he said, although he wasn't sure. Even her long, thick hair which had slid over his naked shoulder blades felt too cool. "My weapon is surer than that."

Lukstch laughed, the sound a whisper. "You boast, my brother. Someday I will ask her what happened. When I do, she will say she tripped and hit her head."

"Just because you make so much noise tromping through the forest that even a hibernating rabbit hears you coming does not mean others are as clumsy." He stood with his legs widespread and his breathing heavier and louder than he wanted it to be. If Lukstch said anything about that, he would tell him the woman weighed as much as a full-grown elk, but the truth was, he was short of breath because he'd been unable to shake his mind free of what would have happened if he'd been caught. Tillamook and Nisqually might trade with each other; they might speak the same language, eat the same foods, and fish the same sea, but for one to sneak into the house of another was an act of war, and Tatooktche was a man who thought nothing of taking a life.

"We must leave." His uncle broke the brief silence. "Do you want me to carry her for a while?"

"You? You are Chief, my uncle, not a slave."

"I am also a man who has lost his brother."

Instead of acknowledging the faint words, Madsaw lowered the girl to the ground and propped her against a tree. She sagged to one side, an arm crumpled under her, the other trailing over her body. A memory surfaced in his mind, and he remembered the way his wife had looked when he pulled her body from the sea. Dragging his eyes off his captive, he handed his weapon to Lukstch. Only then did he touch the side of her neck, relieved to find her pulse strong. His thumb touched a thin, strange-feeling necklace. It belonged to him now, as did she. Filled with that thought, he grabbed her hair and pulled her head back, but the curtain of trees blocked out the moon so that he could tell nothing about her features. He pinched her nose; in a moment she began to struggle weakly and he let her breathe again.

Then, although maybe he should have tied her first, he gripped the girl around her small waist and threw her over his shoulder. As she settled limply against his chest and back, he became aware of warmth, of smooth flesh, of firm breasts pressing against his skin, and drank deeply of the moss- and salt-scented night to clear his senses.

"Did she fight?" Lukstch asked.

Madsaw told him no and then briefly explained what had happened. The others wanted to know everything, what the inside of a murdering Nisqually's house looked like, whether they were smoking many fish, if they had a great number of weapons. He answered as best he could, pointing out that he hadn't come to count fish and knives, then fell silent so he could conserve his strength— so he could, maybe, make sense of what he felt toward his captive.

It wouldn't be morning for as long as it took to skin the bark from a tall cedar. If he'd managed to get out of his enemy's house without waking anyone, they would be deep within the forest before the Nisqually knew a stranger had been in their village. Maybe Tatooktche would think Wolf Spirit had stolen his daughter. The thought made him shake his head at his own foolishness; surely Tatooktche knew who had taken the girl and why.

Lukstch led the way. As he followed his brother, his body slowed by his burden, Madsaw put his mind to the long journey here and the equally long one ahead of them before they reached their village to the north where great, solitary rocks rose from the surf to be endlessly buffeted by waves. Although he was at home in the dim, green forest and didn't fear its dense shadows, he would rather do his walking along the seashore where he could see nearly forever, where the trees didn't grow so close together that he had to follow thin, meandering deer and elk trails.

But if they followed the shoreline, their enemies could more easily track them. Deep in the forest, they were safe from everything except, maybe, evil spirits and a grizzly.

Madsaw clamped his arm more tightly around the girl and listened for his guardian spirit. Thunder had rolled only once this morning, the sound coming so soon after he'd wakened that later he wondered if he might have convinced himself he'd heard what he wanted to. Now, with his captive draped helplessly over him, he felt powerful.

"Could you tell?" Walkus asked after a few moments. "Is Tatooktche a wealthy man as they say? He will be able to pay much ransom?"

"It was dark, Uncle."

"But—"

"I saw his totem and the poles outside his sleeping place. They were as large as any I have ever seen. My fingers told me that the carvings had been done by a master's hand. Tatooktche had to pay a great deal to have a craftsman create them."

"What did they say?"

"He has three watcher guardians, a frog crest, but he has not had any potlatches."

"Three watcher guardians." Although they were

21

far from the Nisqually camp, his uncle kept his voice low. "This is not good."

Madsaw was about to tell his uncle he knew that, but just then the girl stirred and tried to lift her head. After a moment, she went limp again, but before he'd taken more than five steps, she began struggling.

Grunting, he lowered her to the ground. She lay on her back, her mantle still twisted high on her long legs, fingers stabbing at the air. Then she clamped a hand over her head where he'd struck her and rolled onto her side. He thought she might be sick, but although she breathed quickly and deeply, her stomach didn't surrender its contents. Neither did she cry out.

The men gathered around her. Madsaw crouched without speaking, his emotions dark and tangled as seaweed. This black-haired girl with a runner's legs was nothing to him, a hostage. If her father hadn't committed the sin of murder, if Tatooktche hadn't killed a man simply because he wanted that man's fishing place, this wouldn't have happened. But Tatooktche had broken an ancient law, and Madsaw was avenging his father's death.

She struggled to a sitting position, her hair seemingly too heavy for her slender neck. Because a little of the moon reached them here, he could tell when she stopped staring at his legs and lifted her head to look at him. Maybe a shudder ran through her at the sight of his strong, naked body. He hoped so. She should fear him, should know who he was and why he'd taken her. When she shrieked, he would teach her that he wouldn't allow her to call her people to her.

But she remained silent, one hand to her head, the other now near her throat as if she expected to feel a knife there. He thought about that, imagined himself cutting into the soft flesh, ending her as his father had ended.

"Don't," Walkus warned as if reading his mind. "That is not how it must be."

"My father never had a chance to defend himself. He was no more than a lowly candlefish to Tatooktche."

"So Tatooktche is an animal who bites and chews at his prey, who attacks the helpless. You, my nephew, shall show him how things must be. Before he has his daughter back again, he will be a poor man."

Madsaw could tell that the girl was listening intently. She now fully understood why she'd been kidnapped.

Suddenly angry at the delay, and at his near loss of control in the presence of those who meant the most to him, he grabbed the length of twined cedar bark he'd been carrying looped around his arm and dropped to his knees beside her. She shrank away, scrambling like a crab to escape his grip. When she stuck out her hands to defend herself, he grabbed them. Her strength surprised him. She twisted and pulled, tried to kick at his manhood, her small body as taut as the finest fishing spear. When a sharp toe almost found its mark, he flung her against the ground with such force that her head snapped back.

Before she could recover, he rolled her onto her stomach and lashed her hands behind her. She continued to fight even as he tightened the final knot. She acted more animal than human now, reminding him of a terrified deer caught in a trap. Still, she remained silent; he didn't understand that.

When he held out his hand, his brother placed a knife in it and he quickly sliced through the rope left dangling from her wrists. Then, although she shook her head rapidly from side to side, he looped the rope around her neck and tied a loose knot that settled against the base of her throat. Finally he pulled her to her feet. She tried to step away from him, her knee and thigh grazing against him. When her heat threatened to join with his, he grabbed the rope end that trailed down over her breasts and jerked her to him.

"You will not fight, slave. If you do, I will kill you."

"I am *not* a slave. I—"

Startled by her rebellion, he pulled back his arm to slap it out of her. Instead of cowering, she stood and stared at him, looking as savage as a cornered fox. The night kept her eyes' secrets from him. Still, her courage reminded him that until he'd captured her, she had been a wealthy man's daughter. He wanted to make her fully understand how much he hated her, but she was a maiden, barely tall enough that the top of her head reached his shoulder. If he attacked a helpless captive, he would be disgraced in the eyes of his people and he would lose pride in himself.

"Slave, hostage, the difference means little to me," he goaded her. Then, before she could say anything, he tugged on the rope, indicating she was to follow him. She resisted, then fell in line behind him. He thought she might let her head drop in defeat. It would give him great satisfaction to know she feared him, that she realized he held her life in his hands. Instead, she walked with her shoulders squared and her back straight. He thought she trembled slightly, but it might have been a trick of the wind. When he turned from her, he felt his back tingle and guessed she was glaring at him.

If she could reach a knife, she would try to bury it in him.

Dawn slipped under the thin fog that had come during the night and slowly, effortlessly, lifted it. The sun broke through clouds to warm the tops of trees. A warming mist rolled off the rich green matt, but the forest itself remained cool and damp. Still, the wilderness came to life as birds other than owls began calling to each other, their songs and cries a discordant note against the deep, silent background.

Several times Madsaw heard rustlings in the heavy fern underbrush and knew that animals such as mice and foxes were on the move. He heard nothing heavy enough to belong to an elk, but once he caught a sound he was certain had been made by a deer. When that happened, his uncle sent him a meaningful look. They had come with enough weapons for battle. That hadn't been necessary, but it would be a shame to return home without fresh meat if game was that close.

Madsaw hadn't once looked back at his captive. Despite her scalp wound and bound hands, she'd managed to keep up with him. After the first time, he hadn't had to jerk on the rope. That was all he needed to know about her, that despite her size, she was strong. Surely her father considered her valuable and would pay a great deal for her return, especially if what Sokolov, the Wolf Clan shaman, had said about her was right.

"It is light."

Madsaw didn't need his brother to point out the tree silhouettes against the now flame-colored sky. Still, he understood what Lukstch was trying to tell him. They'd walked through the night, and his easygoing younger brother was both tired and hungry.

So was he, Madsaw admitted as he searched for a spot with enough space between the nearly continuous wall of trees that he and the others could sit and rest. The night hadn't been that cold, but because it was always damp deep in the forest, they wouldn't be able to go without moving for long before they felt the chill. In a strange way, he wanted that. Maybe cold he would stop thinking about his father's lifeless body and the man responsible for the senseless murder.

"You did well," his uncle said once they were seated and Walkus had reached for his pouch of dried salmon. "You conducted yourself as a great war chief."

Madsaw accepted his uncle's offering. "Are you surprised that taking her was this easy?"

"Your courage and strength have never surprised me, but sometimes it is wise to say nothing until time has proven a man's beliefs to be true."

Madsaw thought about his uncle—his chief's—words. Although Walkus had only been alive for fifteen winters when Madsaw was born, the shorter man had always seemed far wiser, far more thoughtful, than he. A man like this should have children of his own so that his wisdom could be passed on to them. But Walkus didn't, which meant that leadership of the village would be turned over to Madsaw when his uncle relinquished the responsibility that had become his at his brother's death. "You have never been one to speak quickly," he told his uncle. "It is something I would be well to remember."

Smiling, Walkus jabbed a long finger at Lukstch. "You have always spoken with care, Madsaw. It is this one who opens his mouth before he knows what is going to come out."

"At least I have something to say," Lukstch shot back. "You, old man, remain silent for days because you are afraid your words will not have the wisdom of the ages."

Madsaw leaned his head against the tree behind him, only half listening to the good-natured argument. He hadn't told the men how much it meant to him to have them offer to accompany him here. He would have been within his rights to request their presence, and if he had, they would have had to agree. Instead, as soon as the time for mourning his father was over, both Lukstch and Walkus, as well as several others, had asked when he would be leaving for where Tatooktche lived, saying their hearts would find no peace until their chief's death had been avenged. He'd chosen these five because he felt most comfortable in their company and highly valued their friendship.

Friendship. The word settled deep inside him, pushed aside a little of the chill that had invaded him because two of the people who meant the most to him were dead.

"Are you going to feed her?"

Walkus's question pulled him out of his thoughts. He wanted to remind his uncle that it wasn't a warrior's way to be soft around a captive, but Walkus only meant to remind him that a dead captive had no value.

He straightened and slowly turned toward the girl, who now sat cross-legged as far from him as her tether would allow. He couldn't say what he'd thought he'd see. Maybe he truly hadn't cared until now.

That changed. His hands in the dark had told him right; there was little substance to her. Still, her straight carriage, and the steady way she still held her head despite the long walk, made him wonder what it would take to bring her to her knees.

She returned his stare, eyes glittering defiance and wariness. He opened his mouth to tell her that defiance from someone with a rope around her neck made no more sense than throwing rocks at an eagle. That's when her eyes caught and held his attention.

Not black, brown—a brown so deep that the color might have come from a winter-wet tree trunk. "What do the Nisqually call you? You are no longer simply Daughter of Tatooktche."

Her head snapped back at that. "What do you care? You called me a slave."

He felt his teeth clench; self-control was as elusive as a storm-tossed leaf. "I will again if you do not tell me what name you were given at your puberty ceremony."

Instead of responding, she briefly closed her eyes, her slender body swaying slightly. He guessed she was looking inside herself, as well she should since once he knew her name, she would no longer be a stranger to him.

"Twana."

When he heard her soft yet deep voice, he realized he, too, had been looking inside himself, although why that was, he couldn't say. "Twana. I have never heard that before."

"Did you think you would?" Lukstch asked. "We haven't traded with the Nisqually for a long time, not since the sea-strangers started coming. What the Nisqually call themselves is not our concern."

At the mention of the white men, Twana's eyes took on a new depth and darkness. "What is it?" he demanded. "What are you thinking?"

She continued to stare at him, her gaze now so intense that he might lose himself in her if he didn't fight the power in her eyes. "What?" he insisted when she didn't answer. He picked up the tether rope and jerked on it. Although he pulled her off balance, she managed to continue looking at him. "What is inside you, girl?"

"That you are a man who is full of himself. Who thinks himself a mighty warrior because he overpowered a maiden."

She was trying to anger him, push him to the edge of self-control. For a moment she nearly succeeded. Then he remembered he'd been asking her about her reaction to the white fur traders when she turned her words in a different direction. "Maybe," he said, "you are angry because you were so easily overpowered. If you were a shaman or witch as some say, you would not be trussed like a deer with an arrow through its heart."

His words had the desired effect. He saw their sting in her long blink and the pain now crouched in her eyes. Then, so slowly that he could mark the change, her expression changed until he swore she was smiling at him.

"I do not need a shaman's magic, Madsaw. Or a witch's dark powers."

She'd called him by name. As a captive, she should address him as Master. He again jerked on the rope to remind her of that. At first she resisted, but after a moment, she leaned forward so the twine wouldn't dig into her neck. "Remember your place, Twana," he warned. "If I decide to cut out your tongue, no one would stop me."

She didn't say anything, but then she didn't have to. Everything about the way she held herself, her shoulders slightly rounded now, nostrils flared, eyes wary on his body, told him she understood.

He didn't want to think about what it must be like for her to know she was at a warrior's mercy, but even as he made the decision to let her eat, his heart beat for her. He understood what it felt like to lose the most important person in his life. He'd raged at his father's death, but the pain of holding Vattan's lifeless body had nearly killed him, still made him feel half-alive. Maybe she felt as helpless as he had.

Without telling her what he was going to do, he got to his feet and stepped behind her. She twisted, trying to watch him. He crouched down, grabbed her arms, and untied the knots that held her wrists behind her. He waited for her to begin massaging her wrists; it might give him a feeling of power to see her do that. Instead, she sat with her hands now in her lap as if the discomfort he'd subjected her to was of no concern to her.

Irritated, he shoved a piece of salmon at her. She brought it to her mouth and chewed, still looking at him in such a way that for one of the few times in his life, he was aware of his nakedness.

"Madsaw, there are fresh deer signs."

He nodded to let his brother know he'd seen them. "Even the youngest fawn is safe from your arrow," he teased. "That is why they walk so close. They know you are here."

"What they know is that Madsaw, a man so clumsy he cannot carve a wolf's mask without cut-

31

ting himself, tromps through the forest like a bear drunk from fermented berries."

"It was you, not me, who sliced off his finger," Madsaw pointed out, his gaze fixed on Lukstch's shortened thumb. His brother had lost the tip to a beaver's teeth when the creature suddenly freed itself from Lukstch's trap, but he loved teasing him about it, just as Lukstch lost no opportunity to make fun of the less-than-expert wolf mask Madsaw had carved and painted to use during the Winter Ceremony. He shrugged. "If you want to chase fawns until their mothers attack you, I will not stop you."

"You will continue home?"

Madsaw glanced at his captive. Shaking off his reaction to those deep brown, doe-sized eyes, he nodded. "There is no way to know when Thunderbird might send another storm. I want to be home before that happens."

"You worry because you are old, Madsaw. I—" Lukstch tapped himself boastfully on the chest. "I am a true warrior, a brave man who has no fear of rain or lightning."

Madsaw could have pointed out that as a child, Lukstch had hidden behind their mother when thunder shook the earth, but the other men had already gotten to their feet and were checking their weapons. He kept several salmon strips for himself and his captive, then handed the rest to his uncle. With the others, he faced the rising sun and prayed that the day would be a bountiful one. The words, long part of him, easily rolled off his tongue.

"You have been two nights without sleep," Walkus reminded him. "A wise man does not let himself get so tired that he can no longer listen to his world."

"When my body demands rest, I will heed it."

"If the message is strong enough. Sometimes a man becomes so intent on what he is doing that he forgets other things."

"I will not forget."

"And you will keep your anger where it belongs, deep within you?" Walkus glanced meaningfully at the girl, then pulled his deer-hide apron from around his waist and handed it to Madsaw. "What you do to her at night will never be known by another, but I say this to you, my nephew. She is a hostage, yes, but still a maiden. To have her terrified of you, to treat her as a man treats a slave, is not worthy of a war chief."

Madsaw wrapped the soft hide around him until his manhood was hidden. The garment felt strange; he, like most Tillamook men, wore clothing only when winter chilled the air, or rain and wind drove them to seek cover. Still, his chief had spoken.

He waited until the others had disappeared into the giant trees that grew nearly as close together as hair on a dog's back. Then he grabbed the rope around his captive's neck. "There is a stream near here. I am thirsty."

Although he thought she might try to take advantage of her free hands, she fell into step behind him as he followed the debris-strewn path his tribesmen had taken. He'd told himself he didn't care whether she suffered physical discomfort, but obviously she was so thirsty that that was more important than resisting him—for now.

The creek, an old one that had cut deep into the soft earth, was so clear he could see the fish swimming in the shade cast by ferns larger than he could span with widespread arms. He stood over the water, listening to the laughing sound it made as it chased endlessly around rocks and exposed tree roots.

A fur trader had once told him about white men who built bridges over wide, deep rivers so people could easily span the water, not on foot but on creatures known as horses that sometimes pulled strange contraptions called wagons and carriages behind them. He'd wanted to ask what happened to those bridges when rain flooded rivers until they spread out onto the ground and roared their fury, but he knew no white words, and the trader hadn't understood the question.

Suddenly the ground beneath his foot sank away, nearly causing him to lose his balance. He straightened, looked around, disgusted with himself. He'd spent too much time inside his head both last night and this morning. That had never happened while he was a boy eagerly learning to become a warrior, but a boy hadn't seen death, hadn't felt the raw loneliness that came from sleeping alone.

Shaking off those thoughts, he grabbed the girl's arm and pulled her close. Her feet lost their hold on the slippery bank, but she managed to keep from falling in by grabbing a thin, gnarled trunk.

Looking at him out of the corner of her eye, she dipped her cupped hands in the cold stream and brought them to her mouth. She repeated the gesture several times, then rocked back onto her heels, her body still and yet ready. Now she looked at him boldly, and he wondered if she could see into him.

He returned her stare. "Maybe you are a witch," he challenged. "Your eyes are different."

"I cannot help their color."

"What made them that way?"

She started to push herself to her feet. He grabbed her tether, hauling her so close that she must feel his breath on her cheek. "Why?" he demanded, "are your eyes those of a stranger?"

"Not a stranger!" Her nostrils flared and her lips thinned. After a moment, she sighed, the sound drifting off to be swallowed by the trees. "Maybe I am kin to the grizzly."

Grizzly? He'd seen that deep, rich color on the fierce creatures' fur, but what she'd said couldn't be. "I think not, Twana."

"Are you sure?"

"Yes. What else would you be except a Nisqually?"

"I don't know." Her words sounded raw. "I don't know."

CHAPTER 3

He was too big. When he again tied her hands behind her, Twana only had to feel his fingers on her flesh to know fighting him would be useless. She hated being roped to him like an unruly puppy, and yet she understood why he treated her this way.

Tatooktche had murdered his father. Not only that, Tatooktche had returned with the man's harpoon, nets, and traps, and boasted of what he'd done. For once, his mother had raised her voice to question why he killed a man who was only fishing. Tatooktche insisted the other man threatened him with his three-pronged spear, but Twana knew greed for the man's salmon catch had been the real reason. Now custom dictated she belong

36

to the dead man's son until Tatooktche paid for her release.

Twana stared up at what little she could see of the sky through the matt of trees and pulled air deep into her lungs. She loved the cool scent of wet pines and ferns, the pungent smell of the sea. Even when she wondered if the only way she could escape Tatooktche was by letting the forest or great water swallow her, she didn't fear either of those things.

The man called Madsaw, yes. Tatooktche, certainly. Tatooktche's voice, his angry fists, never failed to send her heart to pounding. But she would always love this land. Only—she clenched her teeth to keep from shivering—she had never been this far from her village. She wasn't sure she could find it again; if she managed to break free, would she spend the rest of her life lost in the forest's vastness with only its animals and birds for companionship?

Madsaw lowered himself to the ground and tapped it to let her know she was to sit beside him. She did so, not because she wanted to be close to a man who had covered himself only at his chief's insistence, but because after a night of walking, her legs felt as weak as a newborn fawn's and her head throbbed from lack of sleep. The others said Madsaw had been without rest for two nights. Maybe he would fall so deeply asleep that he wouldn't be aware of her movements. She could get to her feet, gently draw the twine out of his hand—

No. With her hands behind her, she was helpless.

Feeling utterly trapped, she tried to make herself as comfortable as possible. While she walked, she'd been able to concentrate on the strength in her legs and tell herself that her speed was greater than his. As soon as he became careless or tripped, she would run.

But what good was speed when she couldn't use her hands? She would starve in the endless forest she both loved and feared.

Ignoring her, Madsaw stretched out on the ground with her tether wrapped around his wrist. With him so close, she couldn't make herself concentrate on anything except his lean hips, long, muscular legs, broad feet. His muscles contracted and then slowly relaxed like a mountain lion after a successful hunt.

No. She'd been a fool to think she could outrun him.

She lay on her side, her legs curled against her body, so she wouldn't have to put her weight on her hands. At least her fingers hadn't gone numb. He could have tied her so tightly that pain would now have her in its grip, but he'd taken care with the knots and she was grateful, trapped but grateful.

What was she thinking? She couldn't possibly thank him for a simple kindness.

"Don't try to run, Twana. You don't want my knife in your back."

"Dead, I'm worth nothing to you." She spoke with her eyes shut, not against him, but as defense against what she could no longer deny. Madsaw had become more than her enemy and captor. He was also a human being, someone she should fear but didn't; at least fear wasn't the only emotion flowing through her.

"A man does not lose face for killing an escaping prisoner," he said.

She knew that, just as, without his saying anything, she understood how little he cared about the ransom goods he believed Tatooktche would surrender. He'd captured her because it was expected of him, because his father's death must be avenged. That was all.

Still, she had to ask the question. "You would kill a woman with her hands tied behind her?"

"Your father murdered mine."

He isn't my father. Before the words could escape, she contained them. Her life was none of Madsaw's concern. She would wait and pray for— for what?

Twana felt herself being rolled over onto her back. Her trapped hands dug into her, forcing her to arch herself upward. Soft pine needles and moss brushed against her calves, and she wondered if she might become part of the earth itself. Eyes still blurred from sleep, she looked up at Madsaw. He was staring at her throat where her mother's gift lay. If he tried to take the necklace, she would kill him—somehow, someway.

"The sun is high," he said. "I want to be home before it finishes its next journey."

Home. Before she could ask herself what where

he lived looked like, he hauled her to her feet. For a moment she felt dizzy and had no choice but to let him support her. Then, angry at her weakness, she tried to wrench free.

"Don't fight me, Twana."

Simple words, powerful words. She wanted to warn him that he couldn't tell her how to act, but it would be a lie. "You think I should be like a deer being led to slaughter?"

"A deer knows when it is useless to fight."

She'd never seen a deer surrender as long as life remained in it, but she wasn't a simple forest animal. In her mind lived things that Madsaw knew nothing about but had taught her a great deal about her world and the people and animals that shared it with her. Those secret images—gift or curse—would remain hers as long as she could keep them from him. What would he think or do if she told him she had begun to sense they weren't alone in the forest? That there was something— not deer or elk or even wolf—out there.

He turned her from him, and she felt his fingers on her wrists. When he ran his fingers around her neck where his rope rested, she shivered. She tried to tell herself that her reaction came because she hated being touched by him, but it wasn't that simple. Looking into his eyes, feeling his strong fingers, nearly made her forget that they were enemies.

"I have never seen a necklace like the one you wear," he said. "So fine. And the color, like gold from the morning sun."

"Stop it," she warned when he pulled it tight against her throat. "You will not take it from me."

"I will do what I want, Twana. Where did you get it? You are spoken for? It is a gift from the man you intend to marry?"

The thought that old Quahklah with his rough, gnarled fingers might have slipped it on her made her stomach wrench. "Not from him. My mother."

"It is as thin as a few hairs woven together and yet strong. Where did she get it?"

"I don't know."

He grabbed her chin and forced her to look at him. "Do not lie to me, Twana."

"I don't lie! I never—" Breathing heavily, she fought for control. "She said it was a gift from a time before I was born."

"Your mother kept secrets from you?"

How dare he say that! He had never met her mother, knew nothing of her gentle kindness, the love that flowed through her for her child. "Whenever I asked her about it, she said there were things she couldn't talk about because she needed to forget. I came to respect that."

He stared at her for so long that she wondered if he could see to her heart, but that couldn't be. "Call it what you will. I say your mother hid things from you. We will walk until it becomes so dark that I can no longer see the way," he said after a long silence she didn't try to end. "Don't try to hold back, Twana. We have gone too far for your people to find you."

She took another deep breath, felt herself become both weak and strong, and decided to tell him the truth—at least a little truth. "I mean nothing to Tatooktche. He does not care what happens to me."

Madsaw had started to turn from her. He swiveled back around, speared her with his gaze. "He feels nothing for you?"

"No. What is inside him is not your concern."

"Not my—" he began, his tone as sharp as the edge of a skinning knife. Then a shadow passed over his features and lingered in his eyes. "You are right. Nothing matters as long as he does what he must."

Twana said nothing but nodded slightly so her captor would think she was agreeing with him. As she followed his lead down an elk trail, she struggled to close her mind to what her life would become when and if she was returned to Tatooktche.

When she dared take her eyes off the uneven ground, she glanced upward, thanking the spirits controlling the sky and earth that Tatooktche hadn't fathered her. Just knowing that what passed between him and her mother might have created her made her blood turn cold. Her mother's night cries, Tatooktche's angry voice—no, that violence should never result in a baby.

Was Madsaw married? Would she at least find some measure of kindness from the woman who shared her captor's bed? As she stared at his dark, broad back, she tried to imagine what his wife was like, what existed between the two of them, but the images wouldn't form.

She had heard of love between a man and a woman, but it had never been like that when her mother's family ordered her to marry Tatooktche. To love, one would have to first trust.

And Twana trusted no man.

As the weight of her thoughts pressed down on her, she felt her shoulders sag and couldn't think how to straighten them. She plodded behind Madsaw, listened to the faint sound her bare feet made on the soft-packed earth. Cool moisture from ferns, trees, and moss touched her skin and slowly worked its way inside her. The forest and mountains were places of renewal and peace. Alone in them, she had always felt quieted, but she wasn't alone today—might never again be blessed that way.

When an eagle briefly showed itself to her, she tried to put her mind on that. She should have been born one of his kind. Able to fly, she would spend her life cradled by the wind, her wings spread over the world.

She wasn't an eagle.

Tatooktche isn't my father. He gives me shelter only because his mother demands he do so. He has found someone who will pay a great deal to become my husband. He doesn't care. Has never cared for anyone except himself—his greed. Soon now she would have to tell Madsaw that. He would know how much Tatooktche expected to get for what took place inside her, and maybe greed would touch her captor as well. If she wanted to live, she would be forced to place her gift in Madsaw's hands.

Although she could no longer "see" the eagle, Twana continued to look for the great winged creature. A hunger as strong as any she'd ever experienced filled her, and it was all she could do not to cry. Hostage. Bartering goods. Wife to an evil-smelling old Nisqually who wanted to bend her to his will. Death.

Was that all there was for her? She would never fly, never again feel the wind on her cheeks and in her heart?

When she stumbled, she knew she'd allowed her thoughts to swamp her. Madsaw glanced back at her but didn't touch her. Instead, after a deep grunt, he started walking again. But even though she could no longer see his face, his midnight eyes continued to float before her until she couldn't remember where she'd lived and who had been part of that life before this man stole her.

The sun had begun its journey back to the earth when Twana finally pulled herself out of thoughts that ensnared her like a powerful whirlpool. For a moment she didn't know what had shaken her free of the never-ending dark energy. Then she did.

Body taut as a bowstring, she stumbled forward a few more steps as familiar and yet frightening sensations wrapped themselves around her. In her mind she saw *him*—a great, silver-tipped grizzly. The unseen beast walked at the bottom of a steep-sided canyon through which flowed a narrow stream, his nose constantly testing the air, sometimes rearing onto his powerful hind legs, mouth opened to reveal teeth capable of tearing apart anything else that walked in the forest.

A grizzly lay ahead of them. But not just any grizzly. Something about this one—something—

"Madsaw, wait!"

At her sharp cry, he spun around, his body ready for fight. She opened her mouth to tell him about the bear, but in the end could only stand there with words he would never believe shrieking inside her.

"Wait?" he repeated. "Are you giving me an order?"

"Not an order."

"What then?"

The grizzly had found a fallen log and was turning it over and over, looking for grubs, and yet when it should be intent on filling its belly, restlessness claimed it. How she knew such things, she had never been able to explain. Only her mother understood because the same happened to her. Many of the Nisqually shrank from what they knew lay inside mother and daughter and whispered that they walked with creatures from the underworld. Others such as Tatooktche, and soon Quahklah, thought only of using that sight for their own greedy end. If it hadn't been for Saha, Twana would still be terrified of the truth that existed inside her head. Today she feared only this bear—in a way she had never feared any of his kind. "We have to go another way."

"If you think to fool me—"

"You don't understand. We might not be safe."

"And you care about my safety?" His question ended with a harsh laugh. "I think not."

"We can make a large circle around it. Maybe it won't know we're here."

"*It?* Around what? You are talking crazy."

She was making him angry, but did she dare tell him what she knew about the world beyond his vision? "I have no choice but to go with you," she told him. "I have not fought you, have I? Please, just do this thing for me."

"Why?"

"Because—" Growling, the bear left its rotten log and lumbered toward a softly rounded boulder. Without breaking stride, it reached out a massive paw and swiped at a chest-high sapling in its way. The tree bent to the ground and slowly straightened. Angry, the bear bit the tree in two. When it reached the boulder, it clambered onto it, its body seemingly intent on driving the huge rock into the ground.

"Answer me, woman! You will not defy me."

His anger frightened her, but she still couldn't make the words come. Tatooktche had beaten Saha when her sight didn't please him or when she wasn't able to easily lead him to the fur-bearing creatures that made him a wealthy trader. She had spent most of her life hiding what she could of her sight from others, using it only when she had no choice. She would rather die than reveal it to her captor. But this grizzly frightened her in a way she didn't understand—a way she needed to understand.

Madsaw grabbed her, shook her so hard that tears sprang to her eyes. Enraged and frightened, she fought him as fiercely as she had when she first regained consciousness. For too long they struggled while her mind battled the grizzly's growing power over her.

Then Madsaw hooked his leg behind hers and bent her backward until she lost her balance. When he released her, she fell to the ground. Despite the deep cushion of soft earth and decaying vegetation, her teeth snapped together, causing her to bite her tongue. Pain seared her, but she didn't dare give in to it. Madsaw stood over her, legs widespread, hands folded into powerful fists. For an instant she saw, not him, but Tatooktche.

"You are my hostage, Twana. You will *not* defy me."

"You don't—I am ..." The grizzly was on the move again. Almost as if she existed inside the animal, she could feel its heavy limbs and body and something else, some dark emotion that sent a raw chill through her. She shook off the image and struggled to concentrate on the angry man above her. "There is a bear not far from here, a fully grown grizzly. He is angry, dangerous."

"A grizzly?" Madsaw straightened and stared at what he could see of the forest. "Here?"

"No. Beyond this hill. There is a canyon so steep and rocky that few trees grow there. The bear is in it, standing near a creek but not feeding on the fish in it."

"What is this? You see that far?"

See? "Yes." She wanted to blink, wanted to close her eyes so she could escape his intense gaze, but if she did, the grizzly would be waiting for her. "Yes."

"I do not believe you."

"I would not lie about this."

She waited for him to say something, to strike her maybe. As she did, she wondered if he could tell that she'd begun to shake, not from fear of him but something else. "Why should I believe you?" he asked in a voice so quiet that the forest nearly swallowed it.

"Do you think I say this because I want to make you angry? Madsaw, my eyes show me things no one else knows of. It is a-a gift. I—" Concentrating, she turned her thoughts to the direction the other men had gone. At first the forest kept its mysteries, but before long she sensed herself floating over a quiet pond, coming closer, settling near three recently killed deer with arrows still protruding from their bodies. "The hunters have been successful," she whispered. "They will return with three deer."

"This is impossible! You cannot see—"

"I know this thing, just as I know about the grizzly. Please, please believe me."

He squatted beside her and, although she couldn't understand the gesture, gently pushed her hair away from her temple. Maybe, she told herself, he simply wanted her to remember that he could do anything he wanted with her. "Three kills. Did my brother bring down one of them?"

"I don't know. I am one with animals, birds, and fish. Never humans."

"This grizzly, it frightens you?"

"Yes. I don't understand—yes."

"Why? You say it is in a canyon."

The grizzly lifted itself onto his massive hind legs and stretched upward, drinking in smells that would tell him everything he needed to know about his world. Suddenly, violently, he roared as if trying to wake those who dwell deep in the ground, and the hard sound vibrated inside her. Another shudder claimed her and yet she didn't want, didn't dare try, to close her mind to this beast.

"Tell me something, Twana. You hate me, don't you?"

"What? You have taken my freedom."

"I asked you a question. You hate me, don't you?"

What good would it do to lie? "Yes."

"And you don't care whether I live or die."

"Your life means nothing to me, Madsaw. Just as mine means nothing to you."

He continued to stare at her, and she could see in him doubts that Tatooktche and others of the tribe no longer had. She couldn't think what else she might say to make him believe her and prayed her plea had reached him.

"You believe he would not let us pass in peace?"

Did she? Another "look" at the grizzly gave her not enough of an answer. This powerful young male was filled with a dark energy that seemed to flow far beyond it—far enough to touch her. But did it go beyond that? "He is different from others of his kind, somehow different."

Madsaw stood and again looked out at his surroundings. A breeze caught a strand of his night-colored hair and pressed it against a thick eyebrow.

He pushed it away. He'd cocked his head slightly to the side, and she knew he was trying to hear more than rustling trees and calling birds. But the grizzly was too far away for Madsaw—for anyone but her—to be aware of.

"I do not lie about this. He carries much anger inside him."

"You say you know he is angry. Do you take me for a fool, woman?"

"If he attacks, you will be a dead fool."

For an instant she thought he might laugh and wondered despite herself what his laughter would sound like. Then his expression became so stern that she lost the question. He jerked his head, indicating he wanted her to join him. Although she struggled to bring her feet under her, her lashed hands made her awkward. When he reached down and steadied her, his fingers were gentle in a way she hadn't expected.

"I want to see this bear of yours."

"No!"

"Yes. A bear can smell any scent the wind brings him, but his eyesight is weak. We will use the wind to keep our smell from reaching him. Then I will know whether you have told me the truth."

Wondering whether she had taken leave of her sanity, she struggled to control her gnawing fear. She tried to tell herself she'd stopped arguing because Madsaw would only bend her to his will, but maybe the reason had more to do with his brief, gentle touch than dread. That and a powerful need for answers of her own.

Not understanding herself, she told him she would take him to a high place overlooking the canyon where they could hide and watch. He placed a finger in his mouth to moisten it and then held it aloft so the breeze revealed its direction to him.

He took a few steps, then stopped and looked at her. Grunting in that deep way of his, he turned her from him and untied her hands. "It is a good thing only you and I are here, Twana. Otherwise, I would not listen to your nonsense."

"But you are. Why?"

He didn't answer, and she wondered if he couldn't. Silent, they started climbing. Twana shifted her weight to her toes so she could dig into the soft earth, feeling both weary and filled with limitless energy. Soon Madsaw would no longer doubt her, and she would know if she should have remained silent. But she had to take the risk; something about this grizzly called to her as no other creature ever had. If she didn't look at him now, study him, understand him, the time would come, maybe soon, when she had no choice.

When she felt certain they had chosen a safe path, she turned herself over to the inroads the bear was making on her thoughts. He continued to stay by the creek, but fishing still didn't interest him enough. Instead, led by his nose and maybe more, he wandered aimlessly, restlessly, as if searching for something—or someone. But that was impossible, wasn't it?

After they'd traveled perhaps half the distance, she stopped and stood crouched over with her body utterly still. She felt Madsaw's eyes on her but didn't return his gaze. She didn't dare allow herself to become any more distracted than she already was. After a moment, the bear "spoke" to her again. Called to her.

She pointed with an arm that seemed strangely heavy. "He remains beside the swift stream," she explained. "He will have to turn around and go back when he leaves the canyon. It is not an easy route, not fast."

Madsaw stared in the direction she'd indicated. Although she couldn't place herself inside him as she'd done with the bear, she knew he still doubted her. But then she didn't blame him. Except for her mother, no one understood.

"I have been there before, many, many moons ago," Madsaw explained. "It is not a good place, a safe place. I left because the shadows and cold rock walls may be home to Beak Bird."

Madsaw's words sucked the warmth from her fingers and toes. Beak Bird, a fierce man-eating monster, had such a sharp beak that it was said he could tear the flesh from a whale before the great creature could seek safety in the sea's depths. Maybe that was what she feared.

"Do you hear me, Twana? If this is a trick—"

"If it is a trick, then you will kill me."

He stared at her in that strong, probing way of his but didn't say anything. Barely aware of what she was doing, she rocked forward and focused her entire attention on what lay beyond the living green and brown mass that surrounded them. She felt herself being absorbed by trees and mountains, becoming one with them. "There, now. I see

52

him, dark against the rocks that surround him. He rises to sniff the air, then shakes his head and bellows. The sound—like that which is said to come from Beak Bird."

Madsaw laid his hand on her shoulder. She felt the weight and control of him, but didn't try to wrench free. Strangely, his fingers allowed her to weather the fear that invaded her simply because the grizzly had growled. "Tell me more," he said, his voice free of judgment or ridicule.

"Sunlight seldom reaches this place," she began softly. Nausea crawled up her throat, and she had to fight it before she could continue. "It is as you said, filled with shadows and cold stone. At the far end the stream flows so swiftly over boulders that not even a grizzly would survive if he fell into it. Deer and elk seldom venture here. I think it is because there is only the one way out, and a deer knows he may become trapped."

"I want to see your grizzly."

"You want—no," she gasped, although she'd come here for that very reason. "The danger—"

"He is in a deep hole, while we will be far above him. If it is as you say, we will be safe. And if this is a trap—"

"Then he will kill both of us. Madsaw, a grizzly knows nothing of gentleness. Because he lives, he kills. That is why I warned you."

"Is it?"

"What are you saying? You think—"

"I know only what I see, Twana. You tremble; you want to flee and yet you do not. What is ahead? What is it you fear?"

She had no answer for him, and none for herself.

Despite the cool that never left the forest floor, Madsaw was sweating by the time he joined Twana where she lay staring down at the world below them. He was glad the others weren't here to see his folly. This captive telling him what she had—and him not shaking the lie out of her—

But he hadn't seen a lie in her eyes. Instead, she'd trembled when she told him about this grizzly only she could see. In the end, all argument had gone out of him and he'd followed her because he wanted to know the truth about her.

But now—if she'd somehow placed him under her witch's spell—

The canyon below was so deep in shade that at first he couldn't see anything except the faintest of outlines. Even the wind seemed unable to reach this place, leaving it so quiet that it was as if he stood at the edge of the land of the dead. But as he continued to concentrate, he saw the great boulders that clung to steep sides, the tall yet sparse trees that had found a foothold by taking life from the bodies of those that had fallen. Finally the stream itself became a pale, swift-moving ribbon.

And on a low stretch of earth beside the stream crouched a grizzly, a magnificent monster with massive shoulders and rich brown hair painted silver at the tips.

Twana hadn't said anything, but the tension in her body told him she'd already spotted the bear and felt its great power. He heard her suck in her breath, holding it for so long that her lungs must ache, and knew they shared many of the same emotions. Below them was the one animal that didn't run from man, who turned spears and arrows into useless splinters.

How had she known it would be here?

He needed the answer, wanted to demand it of her, but didn't dare since all but the faintest sound might alert the grizzly. Only, more than caution kept him silent. Unless he'd learned nothing about his captive, he believed she was caught so deep within her thoughts that she was incapable of responding to him.

Because he hadn't taken his gaze off the grizzly, Madsaw saw it push itself to its feet with lazy and yet powerful strength. Then it lifted its head and opened its mouth. Its roar, like something evil flung from a cave deep in the earth, echoed against the canyon walls and slapped at his ears until he wanted to clamp his hands over them. Although he'd heard grizzlies bellow before, this was different, deeper, coldly savage. He had no control over the chill that chased itself down his spine.

"He knows we are here," Twana whispered. She sounded awed and frightened, and yet no muscle moved.

"How can he?" he whispered back. "His eyesight is weak, and we are too far away for him to catch our scent."

When she didn't answer, he stared at her, but she didn't seem aware of him. Instead, she continued to scrutinize the beast now pacing along the stream bank, its head constantly moving as if searching for answers in the inadequate light. Only occasionally did it look down at the water that should have held its attention. As a young boy, Madsaw often went with the men of the village to fish while the salmon fought their way upstream to spawn. During those times, even the smallest child could spear more fish than he needed. While he and the other children competed to see who could catch the most, several men always stood watch for hungry grizzlies. More than once, the guards had ordered everyone to run, leaving their catch behind. Even today he remembered the childish mix of awe and fear and excitement he'd felt the time a grizzly lumbered so close that he could smell its fat-laden body. This grizzly was too far away for it to make that impact, and yet Twana acted as if it could reach out and touch her.

After continuing its restless, searching movements for several more moments, the bear finally lowered its oversized head and peered at the water rushing past him. When he saw the bear's shoulder muscles tighten, Madsaw knew it had spotted a fish. Suddenly lazy bulk turned into graceful speed. As smooth-moving as any deer, the bear launched itself at the water. A moment later it lifted its head. Water streamed from its mouth, and Madsaw could just make out the wriggling outline of a small fish. As he waded back to shore, the bear turned so that it seemed as if it was looking straight up at them. Then, inexplicably, the bear dropped the fish and walked toward them until stopped by a moss-caked boulder.

Beside him, Twana shuddered. Her gasp was so soft that he might have imagined it. "What's wrong?" he asked, but wasn't surprised when she didn't answer. He repeated his question, his tone firm this time.

"He—he has only one ear."

Madsaw glanced down and saw that she was right. "Maybe he lost it in a fight with another of his kind."

"Maybe."

Maybe. The word was little more than a sigh, weak like a small child begging for comfort. He didn't know what to do with her emotion, wanted to order her to lay herself open to him so he would understand everything about her, and yet he sensed that might never happen.

"Why do you care whether a grizzly has one ear or two?"

She hadn't taken her eyes off the bear who continued to stare, its attention fixed on where they crouched. "There was—two winters ago—a cub with a missing ear."

"I asked you. Why does this matter to you?"

"Matter?"

The bear reached out sharp claws and dug at the thick moss as if that, too, like everything else, angered it. "It is in your voice," he finally thought to say. "In the way you look at him. This beast frightens you."

Yes. Although she hadn't spoken, he was certain he'd been given her answer. When she shot him a glance, her brown eyes begged him to understand that she wasn't able to give him more. She had no right; she was his, and even her thoughts belonged to him. But the words to remind her of that remained tangled inside him.

This woman knew where grizzlies walked. Feared one that had had its ear torn from it.

They watched the bear until sunlight no longer slid through the trees to warm their backs with thin fingers. For a long time the grizzly stared up at them, occasionally clawing at the sheer wall that separated them. When it bellowed, the air itself vibrated and Twana's knuckles turned white. Finally the beast seemed to grow tired of trying to make sense of what its weak eyes couldn't find and caught another fish. Then it drank deeply and slowly stretched out on the ground. Twice it lifted its head, its attention trained on where they watched, but at length sleep claimed it. Only when it hadn't moved for a long time did Madsaw sense Twana relaxing.

Still not believing what had happened since she'd told him of the grizzly's presence, he touched her shoulder to let her know he wanted her to follow him away from this too silent place. She nodded and waited for him to lead the way. He thought she might be thinking of how to escape and wondered if he'd made a mistake by not taking the rope around her neck. But she'd warned him of the one-eared bear. Maybe she didn't want him dead.

When, finally, they were back on level ground, he took a moment to study his surroundings before gripping her wrist. She flinched, then relaxed as if reluctantly accepting his control over her. Her mouth still looked pinched and her eyes held a depth and darkness he didn't understand.

"When you said you knew where a grizzly walked, I called you a liar. I no longer do. But I still don't understand."

"I know you don't."

"And—" he increased his pressure slightly. "—now I want to."

"Maybe you won't believe me."

"I can't decide that until you tell me certain things."

"Sometimes . . ." Her voice hung on the afternoon wind. "I am as one with the animals who share this land with me."

What he'd expected her to say, he didn't know, but it wasn't this. "As one?"

"Their thoughts are mine."

"Their spirits—you believe you hear their spirits?"

"I don't know." She moaned. "I don't understand. For a long time I fought what lives inside me, what I have no control over. But my mother carried the same mysteries within her. She said I shouldn't hate or fear what is."

The maiden was speaking nonsense. He nearly told her that when he remembered the shaman's warning. Sokolov had reminded him of the stories about a Nisqually woman who knew where to hunt for deer and elk, even when winter sent them far from their usual feeding places. It was said she could track beaver and fox and knew to the day when the salmon would return to spawn, but that her husband kept her gift for himself. Because he had never seen that woman and knew the Nisqually to be tellers of great tales, Madsaw had laughed at the stories, but Sokolov hadn't. His tone sober, the shaman insisted that the stories were true. He had seen her magic, her witch's gift, and believed.

It was also said that the woman had a daughter, a maiden with powers that rivaled her mother's. That girl, Sokolov told him, was Tatooktche's child.

"Your mother taught you her tricks?" Madsaw asked.

"They are *not* tricks. If they were, I would have nothing to do with them."

"Why?"

She gripped her elbow and began rubbing it. The gesture seemed to give her a measure of comfort, and in a little while, her eyes began to lose their depth. "These tricks, if that is what you believe they are, made my mother a prisoner of what went on inside her, and of great value to Tatooktche."

"Where is she?"

"Gone. I don't know—gone."

He sensed there was much more to what had happened to her mother than the little she'd told him. Soon, because she belonged to him, he would insist on more. He didn't want to believe she shared thoughts with animals; it was impossible, a shaman's trick or a witch's evil. But when he looked at her, he saw neither a powerful shaman or dangerous witch. She was a girl, his hostage.

And she had led him to a grizzly.

CHAPTER 4

A one-eared grizzly.

Although the beast slept far behind them, Twana continued to fight waves of terror that sucked the strength from her and sent her head to pounding. She tried to hold on to her thoughts, to understand why she'd had this powerful reaction when always before the sight of a grizzly had left her with nothing except a mix of awe and respect, but for that to happen, she needed silence inside her heart and mind. As long as she followed her captor through the forest, that wasn't possible.

She'd told him too much. By letting him see her fear, she'd exposed herself to him and made herself vulnerable in ways that went far beyond his rope around her neck. She should have remained silent; she knew that, but the grizzly's power over her had been so great that she'd been incapable of anything except trembling before it.

As she sidestepped a half-buried root, she forced herself to cast aside the lie. True, the one-eared grizzly touched her in ways she didn't understand, but so did the man called Madsaw. Even now in the whispering light that signaled the beginning of night, she could see enough of his outline to be aware of his great strength. His smooth flesh was that of a young man, and yet he carried the honor and responsibility of war chief. No wonder he'd had the courage to sneak into Tatooktche's house. A man like that wouldn't run in fear from a distant grizzly; maybe he felt nothing except ridicule for her.

And maybe his emotions toward her slid in another direction.

Her mouth went suddenly dry, and Twana swallowed repeatedly in an attempt to return moisture to it, but the world around them was growing dark and she was unable to keep dark memories from surfacing.

Men wanted certain things of women. When she reached puberty, she'd been taken to the menstruating house and made to stay there for five long, hungry days and nights, not just so she wouldn't spread bad luck through the village but because Tatooktche wanted her kept pure so she would have even greater value as a wife. When she finally stepped outside the little hut, she became aware of male eyes following her. If her ears hadn't rung from her mother's warning, she might have lifted her head to search for gentleness in a man's face.

But men knew nothing of gentleness when it came to what they wanted from a woman; hadn't she learned that from Tatooktche? And the faint scars on her mother's legs and back—wounds from a time before Twana had been born—

"We will stop here for the night."

Madsaw was pointing at the base of a tree so tall that from where she stood, she couldn't see its uppermost branches. Its roots spread out in all directions as if determined to take every bit of nourishment from the ground. Some of these spruces, it was said, were older than the ancestors of the oldest Nisqually, and although she found that impossible to believe, she knew it had taken season upon season for this one to grow to its present size. When Madsaw urged her forward, she felt the tree reach out to embrace her. Still, maybe because the quiet of night had taken over the forest, she found little comfort in its massive trunk. At night men's thoughts and deeds turned to—to what? Some called that hard joining of bodies love, but how could what Tatooktche had done to her mother be the same as what she felt when she held a baby in her arms?

"Sit," Madsaw ordered, and although she wanted to scream and fight and run, she did as he said. For a moment he stood over her, reminding her of how he'd looked in Tatooktche's darkened house when she saw him for the first time. He'd been a terrible force, a nightmare monster thrusting himself into her world, and yet crying out for help

hadn't occurred to her. How could it when Tatooktche had never lifted a finger to ease her life?

Madsaw reached into the pouch tied around his
waist and pulled out several strips of dried
salmon, but although she hadn't eaten since
morning, Twana wasn't hungry. He'd covered his
male parts, but it would take little effort for him
to change that.

She nodded. His mother, not a wife but his
mother. When she bit off a piece of salmon, she
had to force herself to chew. He should sit; that
way his strength wouldn't seem so great. But once
he was beside her . . .

"Have you ever been to the village of the Tillamook Wolf Clan?"

"No," she whispered, then, because tension
coated the air like a heavy layer of whale blubber,
she told him that she had never been allowed to
accompany the Nisqually when they traded. She
had, she said, long wondered what other villages
looked like, but Tatooktche always ordered her to
remain behind.

Instead of saying anything, Madsaw dropped to
his knees so quickly that she couldn't stop herself
from shying away. He stopped her by wrapping
his fingers around the rope that now hung between her breasts. After pulling until she was
slightly off balance, he caught her chin with his
free hand. His thumb bit into her flesh, but she
forced herself not to fight him. For a long time
he studied her in the growing dusk, and what she
saw in his eyes took her back to the first time

she'd stepped out of the menstruating hut to find the village's men watching her.

"You say you have never been to my village. Then you never saw Chief Nutlan."

"Chief Nutlan?"

"My father. The good and peaceful man your father murdered."

She recoiled, but he allowed her no more freedom. When she stopped resisting him, he slowly, teasingly, reached out and took her necklace between thumb and forefinger. Her eyes now stinging from unshed tears, she waited for him to yank it off her. If he did, somehow, someway, she would kill him.

"Where did you get this?"

"I told you. My mother gave it to me."

"Where—" his nail brushed her throat "—did she get it?"

She was losing control over her emotions. If Madsaw continued to loom over her like a powerful grizzly, she would forget the difference in their strength and claw and kick until he beat the life out of her. Didn't he understand—

"I asked you a question, Twana. How did your mother get such a strange necklace? It is unlike anything I have ever seen."

"From a man. Before I was born."

"What man?"

"I don't know!" The words burst from her, splintered against the great tree she sat under.

"Your mother keeps secrets from you?"

"No! Yes. What does it matter?"

It was now so dark that she could no longer find

the light in his midnight eyes, and yet by the way he held his body, she knew he was giving her question serious thought. She didn't want to talk about her mother, and if she could put her mind to anything, she would have tried to pull him in that direction. But his knees pressed against hers, and his fingers were slowly moving closer to her breasts. When he grabbed her, she'd been wearing a short dress that covered only one shoulder while dipping under the other arm so she could move freely. She'd been proud of the care she'd taken in creating the garment out of the soft inner layers of cedar bark, but the mantle was meant for sliding easily over her body, not resisting a man's insistent hands.

"You are right, Twana." His voice became a deep growl that belonged on a night creature. "I do not care about your mother. She is nothing to me. Only Tatooktche—did he tell you what he did?"

"Tatooktche says little to me."

"He murdered my father, drove a spear through his heart and pounded a rock against his skull until I could no longer recognize him. I found him, held his lifeless hand, carried him back to the village so he would find peace among his family. My mother cried as if her heart were being torn from her." He released the rope only to fasten his hand around the back of her neck. Now his face was so close that she felt the heat of his breath. He clamped his other hand over her breast.

"I know what it is to lose someone I love. I would have killed Tatooktche if it hadn't been for my mother. She made me promise to seek vengeance in the Tillamook way, not in that of a mountain lion or wolf."

The forest had been stripped away. A few moments ago it had been settling itself for night, turning itself over to the creatures of the dark, but now it seemed that even the wolf and mountain lion had retreated before Madsaw's fury. "I-I never met your father, Madsaw. Never—"

"Your father killed him. Destroyed—"

"He isn't my father!"

Isn't her father? Waves of emotion as powerful as the sea surged through Madsaw, making it nearly impossible for him to take hold of what she'd just said. He was aware that he still had his hands on her body, but the lust that had brought him to her side had been stripped from him. "You lie."

"I do not! Tatooktche is *not* my father."

"No! It is said—I questioned a slave who had been traded from your village to mine. He said Tatooktche's wife had disappeared and no one knew what had happened to her. He also said you had just become a maiden and still lived under his roof. Tatooktche boasted, even to a slave, that he could get a fine bride-price for you. No one except a father can make that claim."

Twana was breathing heavier and quicker by the time he finished speaking, but he cared nothing for her thoughts—only that she spoke the truth. "He *is* your father, Twana."

"No."

Instead of slapping away the word, Madsaw slackened his hold on her. In a disquieting way, he

67

was still aware of how her young breast had felt in his hand, but then it had been so long since he'd slept with a woman, so long since he'd wanted to. "Tell me," he ordered.

When she remained silent, he heard a distant wolf begin to howl. It might be a supernatural wolf from the dark canyon where they'd watched the grizzly, one with the power to steal a man's soul, and yet he couldn't turn his thoughts to what he might do to protect himself should it come closer. "Tell me," he repeated.

"What difference does it make? He has assumed a father's responsibilities. A father's rights."

"It matters because I say it does."

"I—Tatooktche married my mother when I was a child. He—he was not a kind husband. At first he wanted my mother to send me somewhere else to live, but she refused and then—then my worth grew in his eyes. He has no love for me, and I none for him."

Twana's voice became so void of life that he wondered if she had fallen into a trance, but when he concentrated, he heard her shallow breathing and knew she was struggling to keep her emotions under control. "Your birth father is dead? That is why Tatooktche married your mother, because she had lost her husband?"

"I don't know."

"What don't you know?"

"Anything about my birth father," she whispered.

"Your mother told you nothing about him?"

"No."

Why not? he wanted to ask, but before he could, she continued. "It—I . . . Tatooktche is a greedy man. That is why he married my mother, why he keeps me under his roof. Because he forced her, my mother made him a wealthy man."

"What did he force her to do?"

In a voice now taut with emotion, Twana explained that Tatooktche had used her mother's sight to guide him to many fur-bearing animals. Because the shaman had already told him that, he didn't try to hang on to her every word. Instead, he pushed his way past the simple telling, seeking despite himself a greater understanding of what Twana's childhood had been like. What he heard was the story of a fatherless girl who only wanted to be the same as all others. But she and her mother were different, and the village leaders distanced themselves from the two women. Although Saha had gone to the chief several times asking for protection, she had been sent away.

"Your mother's family knew nothing about what kind of man Tatooktche was when they accepted his bride-price?"

"I don't know. I was so little. It doesn't matter. Nothing does except that she is now free of him."

Such melancholy draped Twana's words that Madsaw nearly touched her in concern. "Free? You know where she is?"

Madsaw didn't know how long he'd been waiting before he realized she wasn't going to answer him. He sat close enough that he was able to sense when she wrapped her fingers around her necklace, and guessed she was taking comfort from it.

He wanted her to speak; he'd demanded words from her and she'd given them to him. But before he could think what to say next, he heard the wolf howl again. He didn't believe it had come any closer, and yet the sound held a warning note. If Twana could lead him to a grizzly, maybe she could command a wolf to attack.

Unable to free himself from his sense of unease, he slid around until the spruce he'd chosen protected his back. "You say Tatooktche has assumed a father's rights and responsibilities."

"Y-Yes."

"Tell me, Twana. Does honor mean anything to him?"

"Honor? He cares only that he become more and more wealthy. It is never enough. No matter how successful he is at trading, and his success grows beyond anyone's belief, he is never satisfied."

"Maybe he plans a great potlatch."

The sound Twana made might have been a laugh. If it had been louder, he could be sure. "He would never willingly give his possessions to another," she said.

"Why not? A great man shows his greatness by what he relinquishes."

"Tatooktche seeks to become the wealthiest man in the village, wealthier than the chief. That way, he says, he will become chief."

Madsaw could have pointed out that a man could only become chief because his father was chief before him, but Twana was simply telling him about the man she lived with, not defending him. "Will it happen?"

"Maybe. Already many look at him with awe. He has so many blankets and weapons, masks and feast bowls, elk-horn purses and dentalium money strings, even iron bracelets and neck rings from the sea-strangers. He made his slaves build him a hut to keep them in."

"Hm. Then I will demand a great deal from him to avenge my father's death."

"You can demand, Madsaw. But maybe he will not hear you."

"He will; he must. If he doesn't, he will bring great shame upon himself."

"Shame or greed. I cannot say which means the most to him."

He wanted to tell her that no man dared ignore the ridicule of his people, but a man consumed by the desire for wealth might try to find a way to both keep what was his and continue to hold his head high. When they reached his village, he would send his brother to Tatooktche. Lukstch would wait until all the men of the Nisqually were assembled and in a loud voice issue Madsaw's demands. Tatooktche's reaction would tell him a great deal about his enemy.

In the meantime, Twana would remain with the Tillamooks—inside the house of the man who had kidnapped her. The thought of her sleeping at his feet as tradition dictated instantly made him hungry in that way only Vattan had been able to satisfy.

Twana was a beautiful maiden worth a great deal in bride-price. He wondered if any of the village's young men had led her into the forest, then decided Tatooktche wouldn't have let her out of his sight long enough for that to happen. If that was so, then Twana had never slept with a man.

"Come to me."

When she sucked in her breath, he knew she'd been waiting to hear that from him. It had always been said that a man's hostage was his to do with as he wanted, and Twana wasn't strong enough to fight him.

"Come to me. It is my right."

By way of answer, she scrambled away from him, but before she could get out of reach, she backed herself against the spruce. Instead of going after her, he listened to the night for a moment. The wolf had been silent for a long time. Now it howled again, only he could tell it was farther away than it had been earlier, that it was no creature sent from the underworld. "You are not to fight me, Twana. You know that," he told her. "As long as I have claim to you—"

She jumped to her feet so quickly that she was nearly past him before he realized what she'd done. He lunged at her, the force of his weight knocking her against the ground. As soon as she landed, she began trying to push herself out from under him. He fought to gain control of her elusive wrists, but her hands slapped both at the air and him, making it all but impossible for him to pin her. Finally he grabbed one wrist and forced it against the earth. Before he could reach for the other, she raked her nails against his neck.

Cursing, he tried to jerk away. He must have released the pressure on her trapped wrist; either that or she was much stronger than he'd guessed. When he felt his fingers biting into dirt, he quickly forced his knees under him.

Angry—or maybe another emotion ruled him—he leaned into her as she tried to scramble away from him. This time when he lunged, he caught her body fully under his. She bucked like an elk fawn playing on a spring morning.

"No! Please—no!"

He'd never seen a woman fight like this, never suspected she would risk broken bones to free herself from him. For an instant he simply and insanely wanted to let her flee into the night. He would tell the others that she had cast a spell over him and he'd been unable to move. But he was a Tillamook war chief, a member of the feared and respected Wolf Clan, and Tatooktche had greatly wronged him.

"Stop fighting!" He now sat with one leg over her hips while she tried to fight her way out from under him. Her body was turned so she couldn't reach behind her to tear at his flesh again. His slave killer was still tied to his waist. He could easily smash it against her head and—

And kill her.

"Stop it! You can't fight me." To give weight to his words, he leaned forward and fully covered her body with his. Under him, he felt soft heat. For so short a span of time that maybe it hadn't been, she stopped fighting. He felt a little of her flowing into him, a woman silently speaking to a man in that way that didn't need words. Then the sensation died, and although she must have known it was useless, she began struggling again, whimpering like a frightened child.

She was his; she knew it. He was a man, son of the Wolf Clan head chief, and no man worthy of taking his father's place would allow his hostage to defy him. Despite her resistance, he rolled her over onto her back and pinned her arms above her head. He sat with his legs straddling her waist and his chest nearly touching hers. She heaved great breaths that pushed her breasts upward, her body always moving, always seeking freedom. The frightened-child whimper continued.

"You are mine. Remember that, Twana," he said when she stopped to take a breath.

She whipped her head from side to side. "No. Never . . ."

Her body was drenched in sweat, and her arms and legs trembled as if she were a leaf caught in a strong wind. Through his chest he felt her heart hammering as his had when he carried Vattan's body from the sea, and he remembered what it felt like to be utterly helpless. "Twana, listen to me. I am not a mountain lion who has come across a newborn fawn. Do not think of me like that."

"You—let me go."

He couldn't do that, but neither did he want to so frighten her that she might seek death because she believed she had no other way. Still holding her wrist, he slid off her and pulled her up and against him. Her back from where it had pressed against the earth felt cold and damp. He forced her to place her hands on his chest, hoping she could feel his heart beating and understand things that spoke without words. "I want you to know something, Twana. I have not slept with a woman for a long time. My body wants yours."

"I have never—"

"Never lain with a man?"

"No."

"And that is why you so fear me?"

"Y-Yes."

He knew it was a lie.

His bed under the spruce tree felt as soft as the fur he slept on at home, but even if it hadn't, Madsaw would have had no trouble falling asleep; he was that tired. Now, deep in the middle of the night, a dream slipped past his body's exhaustion. He became aware first of a thin, silvery light that slipped through the trees to reach for him. He was crouched on the ground with his hand on something that felt warm and alive. Fascinated by the light and the sound that had joined it, he paid little attention to the warmth until its movements suddenly became violent. His thoughts now wrenched from the light, he stared down at what he'd found.

His wife's features stared up at him, and yet her face seemed to be covered by a sheen of water that both frightened and angered him. He tried to speak to her, but instead of reaching her arms out to him, she began sliding away from him like a beaver gliding across a river. He grabbed her, pulled her back, surprised by how violently she fought him.

Then he was no longer touching Vattan. Her features faded away as if they'd been nothing more than rain spreading itself over a leaf. He stared, body rigid, waiting to see what would happen to her. Other eyes, another's mouth, began to form, and soon he saw little except eyes as dark and rich as a grizzly's fur. This woman opened her mouth, screamed silently. Her arms and legs thrashed with such fury that he thought she might hurt herself. As he tried to pin her to the ground, the dream left him.

Beside him, caught to him by the rope he'd tied to his wrist, Twana fought some unseen enemy. Although her movements unsettled him, he lay with his arm propped under him and watched. She struck the air, twisted her body until it seemed her spine would snap, then, unexpectedly, fell still. Just as he was about to touch her, she began attacking the air again. This time her thrashing took her farther from him until the twine that held them together became taut.

Not wanting her to strangle herself, he slipped closer and laid his body over hers as he'd done earlier. He felt even more heat than he'd remembered from his dreams, and now slick moisture from her sweating flesh. Her long, loose hair lay tangled over her shoulder, and he clamped his hand around as much of it as possible so she could no longer throw her head about.

"Twana! Twana! Wake up. It is the night spirits, nothing more."

He felt a burning sensation on his chest and took that to mean she'd opened her eyes and was staring at him. "Twana, let them go. They can't follow you into the morning."

"Madsaw?"

Her breathy plea made him all but forget who they were to each other. "Let them go," he repeated. "They are nothing but spirits."

"Not spirits. One Ear."

The grizzly? "Twana, listen to me. You were having a dream about the bear we watched today."

"He's evil."

Wondering if she had truly awakened, he felt until he found her cheek and then pressed the back of his hand against it. He thought she leaned into him, then told himself that couldn't be. "He is only a grizzly," he said softly. "Young and powerful, but not a spirit bear. If he were, he would have climbed out of the canyon and attacked us."

"No," she whispered. "You don't understand."

"Then tell me."

Tell me. If only Madsaw had said something, anything else, but he had freed her from her nightmare, and instead of being angry at her for disturbing his sleep, he'd touched her with a gentleness she'd only felt from her mother. With her eyes hot and dry, she stared at him in the dark and, despite the risk, opened herself to him.

"I know that grizzly, first saw him when he was a cub. I—his mother attacked a boy."

"How do you know this?"

"I—heard the sounds. I shared everyone's fear for the child."

"Tell me, Twana. Tell me everything."

Wondering if she'd regret this, she looked into

the past and let it absorb her. "The boy was so young, still a small child. He was following a deer trail hoping to bring home a deer so his father could boast of his skill. When she attacked, Son of Palkma climbed a tree, but before he could get high enough, she clawed his leg. The tree was too slender to hold the bear's weight. Maybe that saved his life, but he was forced to spend the night in it until the bear finally left. When he climbed down and started home, she returned."

"You were there? Are you sure the bear had a cub?"

She was leaving too many questions unanswered, but with the past tumbling inside her, she didn't know how to make him understand. "Palkma and other relatives were looking for him. My—my mother led them; I was with her. We heard the boy scream and came running. Although the men carried weapons and attacked the bear before it could reach Son of Palkma again, she didn't leave. Instead, she took out her fury on the hunters. One, the boy's grandfather, was killed."

Madsaw didn't say anything, and yet his silence somehow served to give her the courage to continue. "For a long time, it was feared Son of Palkma would die. He no longer runs, and his mother still cries. The men's weapons were as nothing against the grizzly. It left only after it had vented its anger on everyone. A few days later, she returned. My mother watched and warned, but she couldn't stop—anything."

"The grizzly came into your village?"

"Yes. Our shaman said someone had broken taboo and that was why she and her cub tore apart the fish-drying racks, but others said the grizzlies simply took what they wanted. Even when someone's hatchet sliced through the cub's ear, the mother remained until she had eaten everything. After they left, the village chief said the two had to die; everyone agreed to that. But some of our braves were wounded and the shaman's magic was useless against them."

"It is one thing to decide to kill a grizzly, quite another to put a spear through its heart."

Although it was so dark that Madsaw was nothing more than an unseen presence, Twana closed her eyes so she could better concentrate on what she needed to say. And yet the words fought to remain inside her because once they were said, her captor would know so much about her.

"All lived in fear that they would return. That was when my mother again offered her sight. She agreed to lead the men to the bears so they might kill them. Tatooktche—he ordered the village to pay him for her services—but this time she defied him, as before, taking me with her so Tatooktche couldn't vent his anger on me. Later, when she returned . . ." Twana gulped in night air, but even with that inside her, she couldn't tell Madsaw what had happened when Tatooktche's temper exploded.

"The hunters succeeded. My mother found her in a place where she couldn't quickly escape and—"

"You saw the killing?"

She should have known he was going to ask

that. Still, several heartbeats passed before she was able to answer. "Yes. It—it had to be."

Now it was Madsaw's turn to remain silent for so long that the night sounds circled around them. She heard the wolf's distant cry and let her thoughts catch on the way it spread softly over the air before fading into nothing. Unlike most of her people, she had never feared a wolf, only found peace in their solitary howl. "The men of your village killed the mother bear but not the cub?" Madsaw asked. "Even without her to feed him, he lived?"

"He was not that small; she had already taught him how to fish and search for grubs. He must have left for a time. Otherwise, I would have known he was still here."

"But he has returned; you are sure it is the same grizzly."

"Yes. Madsaw, there is more," she said without understanding why she wanted to reveal this to him. "It took a long time for the mother to die. She fought; although badly wounded, she refused to give up her soul. Maybe she told her cub to hide. Instead of remaining by her side where he would be easily killed, he ran. The men were unable to find him. But I— He watched us."

"Watched?"

"I saw him," she whispered. "Felt his eyes on me."

It seemed that she lay near Madsaw for a long time before finally falling back asleep, and even when darkness overcame her again, some part of her remained aware of his presence. As she was waking, the wolf howled again, the sound melancholy and distant, but he only spoke that one last time, and she knew he was turning the forest over to the day creatures.

The rope had enough slack in it that she was able to sit up without disturbing Madsaw. She slid around until she rested her back against the cool tree trunk and shivered in the morning chill. Mist had not yet begun to rise from the ground. Instead, dampness lay heavy all around her as if it alone were powerful enough to keep the forest silent and still. More times than she could count, she'd walked into the wilderness as night became morning so she could be part of the ageless, quiet awakening, but today her surroundings didn't interest her.

She had spent the night beside this man, and with darkness wrapped around them, she'd told him many things. He hadn't forced his way on her; for that she was grateful. But even though he hadn't, his presence alone had been so powerful that he'd caused her to have a nightmare.

As she studied his long, strong body, a feeling unlike any she'd ever had spread over her. In her mind she imagined herself touching his muscular legs, brushing her lips over his chest. He would look up at her with lazy, knowing eyes and her face would flush, but she wouldn't run. Instead, she'd continue her exploration of him—hands on shoulders and ribs and waist, his leg resting on

her lap as she traced the fine, dark hairs coating
his calf. His gaze would become darker, hotter,
and when she could no longer do anything else,
she would untie the garment he wore and gently
take his manhood into her hands.

Gasping for air, Twana drew her knees up to her
chest and held them there, rocking slightly. Her
face still held a strange heat that shouldn't be, and
the breeze wasn't strong enough to cool her arms
and legs, or that newly discovered place deep in her
belly.

Madsaw stirred, and she was almost glad because now they would return to his village and
she would be seen as his hostage and never have
those feelings again.

To her relief, he said nothing to her beyond
what was necessary and seemed lost in thought.
He watched her work the tangles out of her hair,
and although she couldn't understand why, his
eyes remained on her while she ate the salmon
he gave her. Finally he took hold of her tether
and drew her toward him. "My mother's name is
Apenas," he said. "She will be responsible for
you."

"Your mother? Tatooktche killed her husband."
"Yes."

"She must hate him as much as you do."
"Yes."

Fighting to remain calm, she forced herself to go
on meeting his eyes. "And she will hate me."

"I cannot say what lives in my mother's heart,
Twana."

She didn't need to be told anything more. The

way he held himself when he spoke about his mother, the way his voice quieted and became even more serious, told her that the bond between mother and eldest son was a powerful one.

Because she had no choice, she didn't resist when Madsaw headed back into the forest. At least he'd left her hands free, she thought as her gaze fastened on his shoulders. At least he no longer treated her like an animal being led to slaughter.

Morning had slid down massive trunks, and in places sunlight reached the ground itself, making the rich, deep green carpet seem to dance as light and shadow flickered over it. It had rained a little during the night, but the heavy top branches had absorbed most of it.

Madsaw could walk forever. With his hunter's legs and instinct, he could live out his life in this unpeopled place. Rain and wind, sunlight and summer harvest, he would know all these things and they would nourish him.

Frightened by thoughts she didn't want, Twana tried to imagine what his village looked like. Did the Tillamook live close to the sea as the Nisqually did? Maybe they'd chosen to build their houses in the forest where the storms couldn't so easily reach them.

Maybe . . .

Her head snapped back. Her ears rang and her vision blurred until she barely saw the man walking ahead of her. She strangled on a sob and nearly called out to him, but even if he held her in his arms, he wouldn't be able to protect her. One Ear was no longer in the ravine. He had spent the night there, but had found his way out and was on the move.

His lumbering gait was bringing him closer to her.

CHAPTER 5

Looking like patient old men, the sturdy wooden houses of the Tillamook stood grouped around the edge of White Whale Beach, the village sheltered this morning by fog little more than waist-high. Last night's tide had thrown several logs so far up on the shore that two nearly reached the broad walking planks the members of the Wolf Clan had placed near the entrances to their houses. Behind the long line of large structures stood several casually constructed huts used by menstruating women. Other huts, Twana knew, held the ashes of the dead. The largest of these had a great wooden wolf figure on its roof. The wolf's head was lifted toward the heavens; its mouth hung open, revealing sharp teeth, and its stone eyes seemed to follow her. Twana had no doubt that

that was where Madsaw's father rested, and sent his spirit a silent message; she'd had nothing to do with his death.

As many smoke racks as she had fingers on one hand sagged with the weight of countless small candlefish, and a large number of painstakingly created canoes with ornately carved prows were beached just above the tide line, but those things didn't long hold her attention. Instead, her eyes were drawn to the tall totem poles before each house. Most included carvings of Thunderbird, Crow, and Sea Grizzly, and all but one also depicted Raven. Four totems had potlatch rings carved into them, proof that those who lived there were wealthy enough to hold the lavish feasts and gift giving that took as much as a year to prepare for. The largest totem, so new that the wood had not yet begun to dry and crack, depicted a menacing and yet somehow protective-looking wolf at the top. Certainly Chief Walkus must live here. Although she didn't tell Madsaw this, she was impressed by the skill of the carvers who had made their work look so alive that she almost believed the watcher guardians now had their eyes on her.

From what she could tell, there was a canoe for each house, proof that no fishing parties were out. Maybe there was a river nearby that provided the Wolf Clan with all the salmon they needed. If so, she might be put to work tending their weir. She hoped so, because checking the fencelike enclosure's strength would give her something to do. But maybe she would be forbidden to come anywhere near the village's main food supply. Could she survive having to spend her days trapped inside with nothing to occupy her hands?

Although she and Madsaw had started walking as soon as it became light enough to see, except for several tangle-haired children playing with a puppy, no one else was outside. The totems and carved figures on the burial huts looked lifeless under the heavy clouds, as if they might easily disappear into the dark forest waiting behind the long-settled village. Because of the fog, everything had taken on an unreal quality; that was how she felt this morning, unreal.

Beside her, Madsaw stopped. Without looking at him, she knew he was watching the children. After a moment, she heard his deep and easy chuckle; the sound nearly distracted her from something else—something dark nibbling at her senses. Should she have told him about One Ear? But if he thought the grizzly was stalking her, he might kill her to keep the village safe. She would wait, watch.

"If the Nisqually had dogs," Madsaw said softly, "I might not have been able to enter Tatooktche's house."

She didn't reply because it made no sense to talk about what hadn't been. She hadn't resisted when he told her they would soon reach where he lived, had faltered only briefly when they came close enough to the village that she could smell smoke and fish. It wasn't because she'd resigned herself to her fate; that would never be. But a strange darkness which she believed had nothing to do with One Ear had begun to grow inside her even before she saw the village, and she'd been unable to shake herself free from that.

Would she die here; was that what she felt—her death?

"My mother waits for my return."

Twana struggled to concentrate on what her captor had just said. "She will be proud of you," she told him as the children left their play to stare at her. One, a boy maybe as old as nine winters, had painted his face red as if prepared for war. When he smiled up at Madsaw, she saw that his tongue was stained from eating cranberries. "To have taken an unarmed woman—"

"You weren't unarmed, Twana. You tried to protect yourself with a wooden box."

She'd forgotten about that. Besides, he was making fun of her. Although she guessed he lived in the house with the smaller of the two wolf totems, she waited for him to lead the way. Instead, he ran her tether through his fingers, his eyes now steady on her. "You will not run, Twana. It is a long way from here to your village, over a mountain you say you have never climbed before. If you try to return to your people, I will be waiting there for you."

"You have much pride, Madsaw. Maybe I can run faster than you."

"Can you outrun an arrow?" he asked as the red-faced boy laughed. "If you don't stay where I place you, that is what I must do. Do not forget, your people will not welcome you back until Tatooktche has paid for your return."

She knew that. She also knew she would rather

be lost in the forest for the rest of her life than return to Tatooktche, to his fury. Before she could decide whether she dared tell him that, pain stabbed at her head, making her instantly sick to her stomach. Half-frantic, she tried to concentrate on the curious and somehow friendly boy, but his features blurred and she couldn't hear what he was saying. Unable to stop herself, she clamped her hand against her temple and concentrated on keeping her breathing calm. She forced her eyes to remain open, but even so, she felt as if she were traveling as fast as a diving eagle through the dark forest, going farther and farther, stopping above a massive moving form.

She had found One Ear. He was still far from here and intent on ripping apart a log so he could get at the grubs hidden inside. In her dreams he had become a fearsome monster, but this morning he was simply a bear with an empty belly, and she told herself she had no need to fear him, at least not now.

She didn't, she realized as she pulled her thoughts from the grizzly. What she felt, the fear that churned her stomach and slicked her flesh with sweat, came from another source.

"What is it?"

"I—nothing."

Madsaw grabbed her elbow, and she felt herself being torn between his presence and what was happening inside her. "Is there a grizzly?" Near here?" he demanded.

"No."

"You do *not* lie to me."

"I am *not* lying! Madsaw, believe me, I see One Ear, but he is far away, feeding. Simply feeding."

Madsaw didn't say anything, and without his words to distract her, she felt herself again slipping away from him. Although nothing seemed to exist beyond what was happening inside her, she somehow remained aware of her surroundings. The heavy house walls, great totems standing like stern sentries, the sound of the sea lapping lazily against wet sand, even the silent forest beyond, was familiar—familiar and yet totally new and terrifying.

What did she fear about this place?

A child's shout tore her free from the dark and swirling sensations inside her. When she blinked and stared in the direction the sound had come from, she realized the cranberry-eating boy had called out that the war chief had returned. After shaking his head at the boy, Madsaw increased his grip on her arm and turned her toward him. "I do not understand what happens inside you."

"Neither do I."

"What are you saying?" He sounded confused. "Your sight belongs to you. It is yours to control."

"No. It is not that simple," she admitted. "It is I who belong to it."

Madsaw's mother, who stepped out of the house Twana guessed belonged to Madsaw, was a slight, straight woman with glittering eyes that missed nothing and a slow way of moving her hands that made Twana think of a meadow flower patiently reaching for the morning sun. Apenas wore a soft, exquisitely made cedar-bark cape dyed red and black, and her long gray hair was caught at the neck in a rawhide thong. Although she barely came to Madsaw's shoulder, there was a presence to her that demanded respect. As mother and son hugged, Twana felt a shaft of pain for what she and her own mother would never have again.

Madsaw had barely acknowledged his mother's greeting when others, alerted by the children's cries, emerged from their houses and hurried to him. Surrounded by men, women, and children who stared at her in silent curiosity, Twana felt utterly alone, but at least the noise and confusion kept the nightmare inside her at bay.

Madsaw wasn't quick to boast how he'd captured her, but as several elderly men asked seemingly endless questions, the story unfolded. When the others heard how she'd fought Madsaw inside Tatooktche's house, several women shook their heads. Their words weren't about her courage, but how skillful Madsaw was to have overpowered her without waking any of her people. Madsaw didn't tell them that her struggle had been a silent one, or that the man he'd taken her from wasn't her birth father. He said nothing about following her to a one-eared grizzly. He also kept silent about the things the two of them had done and said last night, her frightening dream—his gentleness. If she found the courage to tell him about today's unfathomable fears, would he keep that to himself as well?

What was she thinking? This man was her captor.

"You must be hungry," Apenas said to Madsaw when Twana thought the questions would never end. "And in need of sleep."

"Not sleep so much, Mother. But my belly wants more than dried salmon."

Apenas laughed and punched her son on the arm. "This one," she announced, "has always been impossible to keep full. Maybe he thinks his mother has done nothing except pick salmonberry shoots for him since he left."

Madsaw chuckled and draped his arm around his mother's slight shoulder. "Salmonberry shoots. Maybe after I have some of them, my uncle and brother will have returned with the deer they were hunting."

News of the possibility of fresh meat caused several children to squeal with delight. Before they'd settled down, the cranberry-eating boy stepped boldly closer and touched Twana's tether. Obviously he wanted to be put in charge of her. Although there was nothing hostile in the boy's manner, Twana clenched her fists, feeling degraded.

"Not now, Vasilii," Madsaw said. "Until I am sure she can be trusted, she will stay with me."

"She is a hostage, my son," Apenas said. "Surely she knows what is expected of her."

"Maybe." He glanced at Twana, his black eyes both serious and appraising. "Maybe not. There are things you do not yet know. Things I dare never forget about this woman."

Apenas looked upset but only led the way into their house. With Madsaw still holding on to her neck rope, Twana had no choice but to follow them. Blinking to accustom her eyes to the loss of light, she took note of the dark but spacious main room with its wooden floor, high storage shelves, lowered fire pit area surrounded by filled berry baskets and roasting fish, stacked wood, a large weaving loom, and five separate sleeping quarters. The largest bedroom at the rear also had the biggest carved figure in front of its ornate curtain, that of a strangely peaceful wolf head on one side and a man holding a fine spear on the other. Without being told, Twana knew that was where Madsaw, Wolf Clan war chief, slept.

Like the totem figures had, the wolf silently regarded her, and she felt trapped inside the heavy walls and massive ceiling beams with only a little light coming through the door opening. If she'd been entrusted to Vasilii, she'd be outside and surrounded by childish voices. At least One Ear and the other—whatever it was—hadn't yet followed her inside.

When Madsaw's mother directed her to do so, she stepped down and knelt near the smoldering fire, watching as Apenas handed her son a fresh-picked basket of sweet-smelling shoots. Her stomach rumbled, but she wouldn't ask for a bite. What if she was refused? When she dared, she glanced at the others in the room with them, trying to determine who were the parents of the two young children watching her from a corner. Madsaw had told her that Lukstch and his wife, his two younger sisters, and a cousin and her family lived with him. The sisters were both married, but only one had a child, a baby. The youngsters, then, must belong to Madsaw's cousin.

Apenas watched, amused, as her son grabbed a handful of shoots and popped them into his mouth. Only after he'd swallowed did she turn her attention to Twana. Instantly her expressive eyes became hard, and Twana nearly flinched under the relentless scrutiny. "She is young, strong, worth a great deal to her father."

"That remains to be seen. First Lukstch must take our demands to Tatooktche."

"I tremble at the thought of your brother entering the Nisqually village. He *must* not go alone."

"He's not a child, Mother, someone who wanders unthinking into danger."

"You do not have a mother's heart, Madsaw. Until you hold your own child, you cannot know what it is like."

"No, I don't know that," Madsaw whispered, and although she didn't understand the reason behind his melancholy tone, for the briefest moment, Twana's heart ached for him.

"There is something you must know," Apenas went on when Madsaw trained his attention on the low fire, seemingly oblivious to the others. "Sokolov insists this girl carries evil within her; he will not be quiet about that. He says you must pay him to work the magic that will protect the village from her."

"Pay?" Madsaw's eyes narrowed. "How much does he want?"

"He will not say, not until he speaks with you."

"Until he is sure everyone believes as he does,

you mean. That way he can hope I will not refuse him."

Apenas glanced around the room, then leaned toward her son and spoke in a whisper. "I do not know what lives in the shaman's heart. Last night he walked out into the sea until only his head remained above the surface. When all were watching him, he prayed to Tekajek to protect the village from her."

"Did the spirit of the water hear his prayer? Maybe Sokolov dove to the bottom of the sea looking for Tekajek. It is a shame he did not drown."

"Don't speak like that!" Apenas warned sharply. "Sokolov is the son and grandson of great shamans. Why you do not believe in his powers—"

"I don't believe because his medicine doesn't work. And I will *not* be by cowed by him."

Despite the faint firelight that had painted Apenas's features in red hues, Twana could tell the woman was deeply upset. Still, her thoughts remained with Madsaw. "You asked the shaman to bring back a woman who had drowned, to put life back into your father," Apenas said. "No shaman can take away death."

"It's more than that, Mother." Although Madsaw still held the food basket in his hands, he made no move to eat. "I spoke out of anguish those times. I was filled with anger and pain, not thinking. Sokolov does not have his father's power; I have always said that."

Apenas scurried to her feet and hurried to the opening. After peering about, she turned her back toward her son. She didn't speak until she was close enough to him that the others couldn't overhear. "You have the strength and courage of youth, my son. What you lack is the wisdom of age. The day will come when you will fully accept what has always been for the Wolf Clan."

"And maybe the day will come when the clan must learn to walk in a new way. The sea-strangers—for too many, they are nothing more than newcomers willing to trade trinkets and weapons for as many furs as can be brought to them. But these are greedy men, killers."

"You don't know that, Madsaw. Vattan's death could have been an accident."

Madsaw spat into the fire, his features so dark that not even the flame-light could touch them. "I will *never* believe that. This, too, I say: "The sea-strangers' greed knows no end." He jerked upright and stared at Twana until she felt herself being pulled into his intensity. "If they continue to come, the sea otter, beaver, and mink will one day be no more."

"Madsaw, please!" Apenas gasped. "If nothing else, keep your thoughts to yourself when the traders are here. The piles of fur grow daily. Soon all will be ready. There is no way you can stop what will be."

"Soon? There has been word?"

Apenas nodded. "The strangers camp upriver; they will be here in three days, maybe less."

"Three days." Madsaw's jaw clenched, and in the gesture Twana read helpless fury. Strangely, she wished she could free him from that emotion.

"I prayed they would come and go while you were gone," Apenas said. "But that is not to be."

Suddenly Twana could no longer hold on to the conversation between mother and son. Although she was struck by how strange it was to see two people disagree and yet continue to show their love for each other, the dread she'd felt earlier had found its way through the wooden walls and was beginning to press itself against her.

She hated this Tillamook village, not just because she'd been brought here against her will, but because something—some dark and horrible thing—waited for her. It might be One Ear. If his brain held on to memories of the day his mother died, he might remember the girl who had been there. But if it was something else, something as elusive as mist, how would she ever understand?

Fighting, she brought her thoughts back to the moment, maybe because Madsaw had just told his mother that Tatooktche wasn't his hostage's father. Lips tight, Apenas demanded a full explanation. When Madsaw finished, Apenas scooted closer to Twana, and Twana felt the older woman's strong, thin fingers bite into her chin as she turned her face toward the cooking fire.

"Who is your birth father?"

"I don't know."

"Don't know? I have never seen eyes like this, not black but brown. Madsaw, can you trust brown eyes?"

"Trust?" Madsaw stared, his thoughts far from her and yet not far enough. She didn't want to be touched by what lay inside his head and heart, didn't want anything to do with this man who had captured her. Did she?

Apenas's head snapped back and she stared intently at her son, then at Twana. "If you do, I believe you are a fool," she said. "Think on this, my son. If the shaman is right and this girl has evil powers, perhaps she has already used them on you."

Madsaw held up his arm and turned it around as if searching for something. "There is nothing different about me, Mother. No monster has tried to consume me."

"You laugh when you should not. Have you slept with her?"

For so long that Twana cringed under the weight of the silence, Madsaw said nothing. Finally: "No."

"A man alone with a strong, healthy girl who cannot run from him?"

"I did not take her."

Apenas, still holding Twana's head, continued to gaze at her son. "I believe you," she said finally, "because you are of my body. But I tell you this. Sokolov has warned me of what she might do; when he speaks there is hate and fear in his voice. Her eyes—they are not Nisqually eyes. Maybe they come from Beak Bird."

"Maybe." The corner of Madsaw's mouth twitched and Twana stopped breathing while she waited for him to laugh and call his mother foolish. When he didn't, she felt lonely.

Madsaw remained with his mother until he'd filled his belly and given Twana permission to eat.

Then, not looking at his captive, he walked over to the opening and stepped outside. He could feel not just his mother's eyes on his back but Twana's as well and was unable to deny a certain truth. His house felt different with his hostage in it, less dark, less filled with memories of loss. She'd said little, done nothing except watch him, and in the watching must have learned a great deal about him. He couldn't say whether this was bad or good.

The morning fog had retreated to the sea, revealing the massive rocks with water constantly pounding around them. All but a few of his clan were outside. The children still played with the puppy, and several women were separating spruce roots that had already been soaked and dried into thin strips while his sister-in-law and another woman had taken some of the strips and were rolling them between palm and thigh for use in matting. Another time he would have reassured Lukstch's silly young wife that her husband had been healthy and happy the last time he saw him and should be home before nightfall, but today he had too much on his mind and there were too many eyes on him.

Vasilii loped over to him, again asking if he could be put in charge of the hostage. When he explained that his mother was doing that, Vasilii sighed elaborately and scratched his cheek where the dye was particularly thick. "I'm *never* going to be a warrior. I'll be a child *all* my life."

Madsaw reassured Vasilii that he'd never heard of that happening, shared an indulgent grin with

Vasilii's mother, Kitlote, who had once told him that Vasilii was more trouble than all the puppies in the village, then turned his attention toward the sea, reassuring himself that the canoe he'd been working on remained above the tide's reach.

Although the thought of having the sea-strangers here made him wish he held a hatchet in his hand, he started toward his uncle's house thinking to ask Chief Walkus's elderly aunt for more details since there was nothing the old woman didn't know. He'd just skirted a trio of wrestling puppies when he sensed more than saw Sokolov step out of his house. The short, wild-haired shaman straightened and stared at him, but instead of approaching him as Madsaw expected, Sokolov simply folded his thick arms over his leathered chest and rested them on his fat belly. Madsaw returned his gaze, returned the challenge. When the buzz of conversation around him suddenly all but ceased, he knew the others had taken note of what was happening between war chief and shaman, but he didn't try to acknowledge anyone.

Only Sokolov mattered, only his poor magic and hatred for a girl brought here against her will.

When Apenas yanked on the capture rope, Twana scrambled to her feet and stumbled behind the older woman, blinking at the sudden light when they stepped outside. Almost as one, the villagers turned to watch her, and Apenas called out to several of them. Laughing, Apenas boasted of her son's courage in walking into the Nisqually camp and taking a hostage.

Head high, Twana suffered the curious stares. A young boy tiptoed over to her and quickly rubbed his dirty hand over her leg. Then he laughed and hurried back to his friends before announcing that he had touched a witch. The other children hooted like owls and began arguing about who would be the first to cut off her hair and weave it into a magical bracelet. Twana could only stare and wonder if she would ever laugh again. Still, when a little girl peered at her from behind her mother's legs, she smiled and felt rewarded when the girl waved shyly at her. Madsaw was nowhere around.

"They are my eyes," Apenas told her, indicating the others. "My friends, my family, they all watch you. If you try to run, they will stop you. You will bring no shame to my son."

Twana glanced over at the brooding woods that grew so close, they probably always cast a shadow over the village. Something—maybe nothing more than dark trees—seemed to be waiting for her. Until she understood better, she didn't dare surrender herself to the wilderness.

"It is time for you to bathe yourself," Apenas ordered unexpectedly. "I will be careful not to let you walk near our fishing weir. That way no one can ever say I broke a taboo. It is one thing for my son to speak harshly of the shaman within the privacy of his own home, but to take a witch to a salmon place—"

"Will we be alone?"

Apenas gave the tether a jerk. "Do not interrupt me, hostage. It is not your place."

"I meant no disrespect," Twana offered as she forced herself not to rub her neck where the rope had bit into it. She looked around hoping to see the cranberry-eating boy, but couldn't spot him. A kind face, even on a boy painted for war, would have comforted her. "But to be naked while others watch . . ."

"You live with the man who murdered my husband. I can never forget that, Twana. What your heart feels is no concern of mine. I will do with you what I wish, and you will not fight."

Twana opened her mouth, but nothing came out. This bustling village with its brooding totems, angry shaman, curious children, and watchful adults would never embrace her. She might know which spirits and wild creatures had been carved on the sides and fronts of canoes and be able to do her share of weaving and food gathering, but she had been brought here against her will so the Wolf Clan war chief could have his vengeance. She was a hostage, nothing more.

When Apenas led her away from the houses, Twana forced herself to concentrate on her surroundings as a way of stilling her heart's lonely beating. A well-worn path cut through the trees, but before she'd gone farther than the length of three totems, the forest closed in around her and Madsaw's mother, separating them from everything except the wilderness.

She glanced upward but was able to take little comfort from the thin ribbon of cloudy sky overhead. She told herself it was only her imagination; surely the trees grew no thicker here than where the Nisqually lived, and yet her thoughts weren't strong enough to keep her unease at bay. Although she wanted to see what One Ear was doing so she would know if he stalked her, she was unable to put her mind to the task.

That other emotion—dark and cold as a cave—tried to suck her into its depth, and it was all she could do to keep from falling in.

Finally she heard a sound like deep, distant laughter and knew they were nearing the river. "There is a place where a small creek feeds into White Whale River," Apenas explained. "Except for when the young men are preparing themselves for their spirit quest, everyone bathes there. I will take you downstream so you cannot poison our cleaning place."

Despite what Apenas said about her undesirability, Twana was eager to lower herself into cold, swift-moving water. There was dried blood in her hair from where Madsaw had struck her, and she wanted to rid herself of that memory. Still, she hesitated.

"We are the only ones here," Apenas said impatiently. "No one else will see."

"What if someone comes?"

"Then they will know you are bathing yourself for my son."

"For Madsaw?"

Apenas's eyes traveled down Twana's body; she said nothing.

"But I'm a hostage, not a wife, not even a maiden in his eyes."

"If you believe that, you are a fool. My son has needs of the flesh. For a long time those needs lay still within him because the pain in his heart was so great. I wondered—wondered if he would ever heal. But I have seen the way he looks at you, the look of a man with no one to warm his bed." Apenas pressed the heel of her hand against her temple as if defending herself against some deep anguish. "He will want you; I cannot stop that. But after he remarries—"

Remarries? Then Madsaw had been married before; what had happened to his wife? And why should it matter to her? "You have chosen a bride for him?"

"The daughter of another chief as is befitting him." Apenas threw out the words as if eager to be done talking. "Now that his time of mourning is over, it is time for him to prepare to take his rightful place at the head of the Wolf Clan."

"A chief's daughter. They know each other?"

"Kukankh and my son have seen each other, but in their hearts they are strangers. That does not matter. It is enough that she is worthy of him." Apenas's gaze sharpened. "This is not your concern, Twana."

"I—She is of the Wolf Clan?"

"What is this? You are filled with questions when you should simply accept. There are no other unmarried women in our village worthy of a war chief, but I have chosen well, a quiet, gentle girl from the village of the Raven Clan. Her parents have been careful to keep her secluded from men and she remains pure. Soon Wolf and Raven will be one."

Twana wanted to know more about this girl who would soon share Madsaw's bed, more about the nameless woman who had once been part of his life, but Apenas would only tell her it wasn't her concern. It wasn't; why couldn't she make herself understand that? Once again she looked at the creek, still reluctant to pull her dress over her head.

"I will not allow you under my roof until you are clean," Apenas snapped. "Do as I say. Do not defy me or my son."

"That wasn't my thought."

"Wasn't it? Listen to me. My son's heart has known much pain. I have seen him walk into the forest and stay there for many days and nights. When he returned, I knew he had not slept in all that time; his grief was too strong. Once, he took his canoe far out in the sea and I didn't know whether I would ever see him again."

"Alone out to sea?"

"He went there seeking peace. And then to have to carry his father's broken body— Enough! I cannot talk about that." Apenas wrapped her arms around her middle, face tense and pale. "It will give my heart peace to see Madsaw happy in a man way. It is your place to give him that happiness."

Fighting tears she didn't want or understand, Twana pulled her dress over her head and stepped into the creek. Icy water bit at her ankles and then her calves. As soon as she was sure of her footing, she headed toward the deepest part of the creek, teeth chattering. Her legs felt numb; the shivers now controlling her left her no room to think of anything else, not even the darkness that waited for her return. She lowered herself until water lapped at her chin, then leaned back so she could wash her hair. As she rubbed sand through it and worked at rinsing the long, straight mass, her fingers occasionally brushed the hostage rope.

Apenas no longer held on to it. If she let the creek's current sweep her away, she would soon reach the river itself and be swept into the sea. Maybe she would keep on swimming until a shark found her.

But she didn't want her life to end that way.

Twana had slipped back into her dress and was trying to squeeze more water from her hair when her fingers once again caught in the twine around her neck. Gathering her courage, she walked over to where Apenas crouched at the water's edge. She waited until Apenas looked up at her, then slowly untied the knot at her throat and handed the wet twine to Madsaw's mother. "I will not run."

"Why should I believe you?"

Her answer seemed so complex that at first Twana wasn't sure she could find the words. Then: "I have no place with the Nisqually now. I have no choice but to wait until the debt has been settled."

"And then?"

Sharp pain sliced through Twana's forehead. For a moment she thought One Ear might be trying to claim her thoughts, but when she remained rooted next to Apenas instead of being spirited through the forest, she knew that wasn't it. "Then I will be given to an old man whose greed rivals Tatooktche's."

"What if this man, your intended, learns that you slept with your captor?"

Slept with? Apenas spoke as if she believed Twana would willingly spread her legs for Madsaw, but that would never be.

Never.

"I don't know," she answered.

CHAPTER 6

It had begun to drizzle by the time Twana and Apenas returned to the village. Accustomed to rain since birth, Twana barely acknowledged its presence. Although her every move was still scrutinized, she soon realized Madsaw's people had more to do than watch her. The pit oven near the central fireplace was being enlarged, and a number of large rocks had been piled near it to be used to line the underground oven. The thought of eating clams or mussels steamed in their own juices made her mouth water. She caught enough snatches of conversation to understand that the refinement was being done to accommodate the appetites of six or seven sea-strangers—and that the prospect of generous traders had everyone anticipating a successful gathering. One woman was finishing work on an elaborate abalone-shell pendant so heavy Twana didn't know how the wearer could stand it around her neck. Maybe she thought the pendant would make her stand out from the others. Laughter, rich and full, accompanied much of what the women were saying, and she felt cut off from the companionship the others took for granted.

Apenas had stopped to speak to an elderly man, but before she could say more than a few words, her fingers clenched and she caught her breath, capturing Twana's attention. Apenas was staring at a short, big-bellied man striding toward them. From his long, wildly tangled hair, Twana knew he was the village shaman. He wore an elaborately decorated cape over his narrow shoulders, and his long, thin legs stuck out below the hem like the hollow stems of giant kelp. In his right hand he carried an ornate ivory and abalone soul catcher, which, when he was close enough, he stuck in front of her. "Evil!" His deep voice bounced off the surrounding trees to capture everyone's attention. "The evil one must not walk among us!"

"I have been careful," Apenas protested. "She did not bathe where we do."

"It is not enough. Land Otter Man has taken your son's senses; he told me so in a dream. If Madsaw refuses to protect those he will one day lead, I must." The soul catcher, designed to portray a double-mouthed sea lion's head, began to shake as if Sokolov had been taken by a fit, and his eyes became so large that they dominated his face. "My power is great, but no one can say how much evil this creature carries inside her. If she looses—"

"Be quiet, shaman! You sound like a child afraid of the night."

Startled, Twana stared behind her until she spotted Madsaw pushing his way through a group of gawking children. Moisture, a gift of the gentle rain, clung to his broad chest, arms, and legs. He still wore the garment his uncle had given him, but except for that, he was utterly naked—and looked utterly fearsome. "Do you hear me, Sokolov?" he asked in a commanding voice. "I am responsible for the hostage. Only me. I know what I must do."

Sokolov shook his head, matted hair slapping from side to side. "She is not like others." He jabbed at her with his soul catcher. "This is no mere hostage, Madsaw. She is exactly like her mother, a powerful witch."

How Sokolov knew of her mother, Twana couldn't say, but maybe every shaman in all the forest villages had listened to stories of a woman with the power to look deep into the wilderness, to see the depths of the ocean.

"You know nothing, shaman." Madsaw now stood close to her that she could feel his body's heat. Sokolov's unexpected and menacing presence had terrified her; now she felt strangely protected. "You have heard that her father is a wealthy man and want some of that for yourself," Madsaw challenged. "Is that what you want, for me to turn the ransom over to you?"

"A true chief knows that magic must be paid for." Sokolov pressed the soul catcher against his chest and stared up at the rain-filled clouds. Slowly his eyes closed. When he opened them again, only the whites showed. "Land Otter Man, I entreaty you to return Madsaw's senses to him. Otherwise, he will bring ruin upon his people."

"Ruin the Wolf Clan? I am only one man doing what I must to avenge my father's death."

Hands lifted to the sky now, Sokolov continued. "The sea-strangers come. They carry great bundles, but if they see the witch, they will not trade."

Twana wanted to scream a denial; there was nothing about her that could possibly make the white men fearful. But if others believed Sokolov, maybe they would order Madsaw to return her to Tatooktche. Maybe they would insist she be killed.

"You have the ear of the sea-strangers?" Madsaw asked in a sarcastic tone. "Maybe they call you when one of them is hurt or injured. Yes, that must be it. You are so powerful that when they go back across the sea, the traders will take you with them so no witches can reach them."

Twana heard Apenas suck in her breath at her son's outburst, but the older woman didn't say anything. Although several children giggled, most of those now pressed around them simply waited to see what the shaman would do. "You are too full of yourself, Madsaw," Sokolov warned, then again closed his eyes, chanting so low that she couldn't understand what he was saying. He began rocking from side to side, his arms outstretched as if he was in danger of falling. At length a shudder tore through him. Spittle formed at the corner of his mouth; he spat loudly, then pressed the heels of his hands against his eyelids.

When he finally opened his eyes, he stared at her, the anger inside him taking her back to what she'd felt when she and Madsaw looked down at One Ear. "She smells evil," he asserted. "Her eyes—different. When the sea-strangers see her, they will hate all Tillamooks. Maybe they will fire their weapons at our chief. Listen to me, Madsaw. Listen well. I speak out of fear for success in trading. You do not believe me because Land Otter Man has control of your senses, but you are the only one."

Was that true? But no matter how desperately she needed to see how the rest of the village was reacting to what Sokolov had said, Twana didn't dare take her eyes off him. His soul catcher was heavy and well made. In a heartbeat it could become a weapon. If he swung it at her, she would fight; she had no choice because the will to live was that strong. But to oppose a shaman?

Madsaw folded his arms over his chest, threw back his shoulders, and spoke nearly loud enough for a fox kit hidden deep within its den to hear. "You have said a great deal, shaman, and I have listened, but now it is my turn. My hostage is mine, part of me until I decide different. You say her presence would make the sea-strangers run in fear, but I do not agree. These are men who travel far from their own lands. They would not be frightened by a mere girl."

"She is not a girl; she's a witch."

"A witch!" Madsaw swung toward her, raked his gaze over her. He seemed so powerful today, more cougar than human. "If she is a witch, why didn't she know I was coming for her? I struck a blow that rendered her unconscious. When I put a rope on her, she was unable to free herself. Is this a witch? No."

"She is biding her time, Madsaw. When she seeks her vengeance, she will destroy the entire village."

Even before Madsaw clamped his fingers around her hair, Twana knew he was going to grab her, but something, some silent warning from him, stopped her from trying to escape. Instead, she allowed him to drag her beside him. "I have no wish to be part of the trade, shaman," Madsaw said. "I would rather let a sea serpent swallow me than to sit down with those men. What I would not do myself, I will not allow my hostage to do. I have spoken. Neither she or I will look into the eyes of those I hate."

"It is not enough. She—"

"Silence, shaman! When you become village chief, maybe I will listen to you. Until then—" he jerked Twana even closer; the gesture ground their hips together "—she is mine."

As the day gave itself up to a cloud-draped night, Walkus, Lukstch, and the others walked into the village carrying three deer carcasses. When Madsaw asked, his brother proudly informed him that it had taken a lengthy hunt by skilled hunters to bring down the elusive deer. Walkus only shook his head at his nephew's boasting before admitting that the deer had been down on their knees drinking from a rain-fed pond and were easily killed. The effort had been in carrying them back to the village. Madsaw said nothing beyond warning his brother that if he continued to tell great stories, no one would believe him.

When Lukstch's giggling wife wrapped her arms around her husband's waist and began pulling him toward the house, Madsaw made his way to the great fire and stood staring into its blackened depths while rain drizzled down around him. No one had tried to keep the fire going in the rain; if anyone was still outside, they would look at him and remember that Sokolov had said Land Otter Man had stolen his senses.

Maybe he had, Madsaw admitted as he turned his back on the fire and reluctantly stepped inside his home. Here a fire burned brightly, flames and shadows dancing on the walls and illuminating the wolf head that stood guard in front of his sleeping quarters. He could hear Lukstch and his wife giggling behind their curtain, and although he fought his reaction to the sounds of lovemaking, his belly tightened in remembrance. Once he and Vattan had laughed like that. Now—now he slept alone.

Someone was sitting silent and still in front of the fire, and although he continued to stare at shadows and remember when Vattan had laughed with him, he knew Twana shared the room with him. The impulse to turn and walk back outside seized him, but he fought it because if he left her now, he would only have to face her later.

114

"Where is my mother?" he asked.

Twana spoke without looking up at him. "She didn't say; she only told me to wait here."

"Did she?" Her voice drew him, pulled him away from the night and closer to her. She seemed vulnerable and small with his silhouette looming over her. At any moment the rest of his family might return from Walkus's house, where they were surely telling the chief about the confrontation between war chief and shaman, but for now there was only her and him and the two people making love. "You were right," he admitted. "Three deer were killed. Tell me, Twana. Do you speak with the animals? If you asked them to lie down before my weapons, would they do so?"

"No. No. I see, but that is all."

"All? You say you know what lives inside One Ear's heart."

"He's different." For the first time, she looked up at him. The movement brought her features into shadow, made her seem more spirit than woman. "Madsaw, why does your shaman hate me?"

"He doesn't understand you. What he feels is fear, but he cannot say the word, so he strikes out."

She shifted position, a movement that was both graceful and silent. She should have been a deer, he thought, a swift, cautious creature who survived thanks to its keen senses and strong legs. Wondering if she was thinking about what Lukstch and his wife were doing, he came closer until the fire touched his flesh and began to dry the rain lingering on it. "Don't speak to Sokolov. That is for me to do."

"Because I'm yours."

She sounded both defeated and defiant, a combination he would be wise to never forget. His mother had told him that Twana had promised not to try to run back to the Nisqually village, and from what she'd told him about Tatooktche, he believed her. But if she felt as trapped as she looked, she might bolt into the forest like a terrified deer—where One Ear could be waiting for her. "You hate that, don't you?" he asked. He looked at the space beside her, questioned the wisdom of sitting near her, and then did so. The heat felt greater now, but whether it came from the fire or her, he couldn't say.

"Hate what?"

"Being mine."

"I am not a piece of property!"

"Aren't you?" If she asked, he wouldn't be able to tell her why he'd attacked her; surely he wouldn't let her know he felt as uneasy as a man alone in the sea when he was around her. "If I decided to kill you, no one would stop me."

"You've already said that!" She started to lift her hands, then clamped her fingers around her knees until the trapped flesh turned white. "Does it make you feel like a powerful chief?"

He should shake the defiance out of her. If anyone heard, he would be shamed. But it was just the two of them with the dark outside and rain on the roof and his brother making love. Despite himself, he listened for sounds from the other room, but he could hear nothing now and could only imagine that Lukstch had pulled his wife's naked body against his and was whispering words meant for them alone.

"Madsaw?"

Her voice was morning mist, the whisper of a raindrop gliding over a broad fern leaf. All it had taken was that gentle sound and he'd forgotten his anger—or maybe he finally admitted he'd never been angry at her. "What?"

"Why won't you trade with the sea-strangers?"

Why? The answer lay tangled in his belly, and he would rather face a stormy sea than tell her anything, but she'd shifted her weight so she now sat cross-legged with her hair falling over her shoulders and her lips slightly parted as if she were pulling the fire's heat deep inside herself. He could bury himself in that heat, forget everything except warmth. "It was a long time ago."

"What was?"

"When—they will be here soon. When they come, I will leave."

"What happened, Madsaw?"

He wanted to drag her outside and order her to leave; if he never looked at her again, maybe he would be safe from the past. But her voice, her gentle woman's voice, had found its way inside him and he couldn't remember how to move. Neither could he think how to speak.

She remained beside him, reds and blacks glinting in her grizzly eyes, her breathing slow and easy and yet already a part of him. "Your mother said you once had a wife. She—she also said that you will soon marry again. It is good that the Raven and Wolf Clans become one; the marriage will strengthen the Tillamooks."

"Why do you speak of that? It is none of your concern."

"Why?" She rocked forward as if wanting to embrace the flames. Her gaze remained fixed on three logs that snapped and shot seemingly endless sparks. "While we were alone together, I told you of the pain of losing my mother, things about my sight that I thought I would never tell a man who had captured me. When my dreams attacked me, you held me until I found freedom. We are enemies, Madsaw. Strangers and yet not strangers."

Not strangers. Maybe she was a witch; where else would her wisdom come from? "Tell me something, Twana. If you could kill me, would you?"

Her body became so quiet that he thought she might have turned to stone. Still, his flesh continued to be touched by her warmth, and he knew how much life she carried within her. It was as if he had never spoken to a woman before, never had the thoughts he did tonight. He wanted to cast them from him and throw them into the fire. He also wanted to wrap them around him and drown in a darkness that beckoned as much as a sunlit morning.

"I don't know," she whispered.

"But maybe?"

"Maybe. Madsaw, I will not have been returned to Tatooktche by the time the sea-strangers come. Maybe I will be ordered to remain where they can't see me; I want to know why. I also want to know if you would kill them if you could."

Her words awakened a long-buried image. He saw, as clearly as if he had been there, Vattan frantically running along the beach while the white traders pounded after her. He felt her fear, heard her desperate cries for him, saw his canoe with its fine-carved paddles propped on its side. With her, he sweated and groaned as she dragged the craft to the surf and waited for the tide to draw it out to sea.

Mostly he heard her silent prayer for him.

"If they were here, my knife would run red with their blood," he said.

"Why? Please tell me, why?"

He wasn't going to speak. He'd spent moon after moon trying to escape the past and only wanted the pain to end, but he became aware of a warm weight on his forearm and realized Twana had touched him. It had been so long, so incredibly long, since he'd felt a woman's touch. Something close to terror chased through him, but the emotion was gone so quickly that maybe he'd imagined it. He felt himself being gentled by her, a fierce forest creature freed from the violent storm inside him. His mind filled with thoughts that went nowhere, and although he tried to hold on to them, nothing mattered except that she had brushed her fingers over his flesh.

"They killed my wife," a stranger using his voice said.

"The fur traders?"

"They wanted her; I told them that would never

be, but they found her when I wasn't there. My canoe—she thought she would be safe in it." The nightmare lapped at him, and he nearly lost himself in it, would have if it hadn't been for the warm and gentle presence beside him.

"How did they kill her? Can you say the words?"

No! he wanted to yell, but if he did, it would be a coward's cry, and he was a man, a chief, a warrior. The fire didn't hold his attention, and except for them, the great house was silent. He wondered if even their whispers might echo, if the walls would forever hold what he said. He didn't want to be sitting next to this woman, but his arm held the feel of her fingers, and nothing else mattered.

"She drowned."

"Your canoe sank?"

"Yes," he said in anguish. "I was not finished with it; it was not yet watertight. She ran to what I had made thinking she would be safe in it; instead it killed her. I killed her."

His hands were clutched by his side, two fists as tightly knotted as wet leather, and yet she drew the one closest to her onto her knee and ran her nails gently over his knuckles until some of the pain went out of him. "It was an accident, Madsaw. Not your fault."

"She shouldn't have died."

"No, she shouldn't have. To leave life before one's time is a terrible thing. Sometimes those who are left behind spend their lives blaming themselves."

How did she know that? He should ask her, and

yet words remained knotted inside him, trapped there by anguish.

"Listen to me, Madsaw," she whispered. "What you feel, this guilt, is turning you dark inside. You hate the sea-strangers and you hate yourself because Vattan is dead, but I ask you this. When are you going to put down your hate, your guilt? Your life should not be spent this way."

She hadn't released him, and through the thick mist of his mind he was aware that his other hand was no longer clenched. Her question washed through him like a warm bath, and yet he fought its cleansing. Not a night had passed that he didn't remember what Vattan looked like when he finally pulled her from the sea. He had screamed, the sound inhuman, and if Walkus and Lukstch hadn't held on to him, he would have attacked the traders. He hadn't cared whether he lived or died; only ending the pain had mattered.

But his uncle and brother refused to release him, and soon his father joined them. While he stared down at Vattan's body, his father had ordered him taken deep into the forest, where he was made to stay until the traders left. Then the three men he loved most in life helped him prepare Vattan's body to meet the spirits.

"I loved her," he muttered, anguish rubbing his throat raw. "She—she had just told me she was carrying our child."

"Oh, Madsaw. I'm so sorry."

His mother had told him that, used those very words, as had his father, brother, and uncle, and yet it was as if he were hearing them for the first time. "Why should you care?" he asked in an attempt to protect himself from this woman's power over his emotions.

"Because I understand." After spreading her fingers over his broad hand, she lifted it off her leg and brought it close to her mouth. For a moment, he thought she might kiss it. "I know what the pain is like. When my mother disappeared, I spent days and nights praying for her return. There was a hole in my heart; that hole has never gone away. I know what it must feel like in another."

But he had more than a wounded heart; he also carried the guilt of not being there when Vattan needed him. His canoe had failed her; he hadn't heard her cries.

"I have been thinking about something," she whispered. "You may not want to hear the words. If you believe I have no right saying them, I will understand and be silent, but I cry for you because you have felt loss not just once but twice. Before one wound can heal, Tatooktche inflicts another. Sometimes, Madsaw, a wound kills."

His heart had felt dead for so long; he couldn't tell her she was wrong. What she'd just said spoke a great truth about him and made him ask if there was anything he could keep from her. The thought of being utterly vulnerable before her filled him both with resentment and a strange peace.

"I would hate to feel like that," she continued. "But maybe that is what it is to be a man. Maybe a man's heart is different from a woman's. He cannot let go of a wrong, even if it destroys him inside."

"You are truly a witch, Twana."

"No. I'm not. What I am is a woman who may never again see her mother—the one person I could truly open my heart to. I look at Tatooktche and in my heart I know he is responsible, but what can I do? If I bury a knife in him, will I be free? Will my mother return?"

Once again he wanted to pull free; once again he lacked the strength. "What are you saying, that I should lay down my weapons and be like a rabbit hiding from an eagle?"

"You are a warrior, Madsaw, not a rabbit. You have shown me that a warrior can have a heart, and it brings me pain to think that that heart is not allowed to heal because it has been wounded, not just by loss, but by ceaseless thoughts of revenge. If you kill Tatooktche or me, will your father come back to life? If you cut the throat of a fur trader, will you hear Vattan laugh again?"

He couldn't let her continue. Each word she spoke twisted him in a new direction and left him in awe of her wisdom when she should be nothing to him. When he pulled free, she didn't try to stop him, but neither did she shrink from him. Instead, she sat as still as a deer testing the air for danger, and yet there was a soft light in her eyes, a new-found wisdom that told him she'd learned something about him—something he himself didn't understand.

* * *

Madsaw had remained silent after she was done speaking, and yet in his silence she sensed the struggle going on inside him. If she had been wise, she would have known what he was thinking, but all she could put her mind to was that she'd held his hand and rested it on her knee and now knew, truly knew, that his flesh was rough and strong, his muscles powerful enough to heave a hunting spear or carve a fine canoe. There'd been lightning and thunder in his hands, unseen and yet part of him. That thunder and lightning had reached her, entered her, taken over until some of him flowed through her veins.

Before she could prepare herself for the loss, he'd gotten to his feet and walked over to the high storage shelf. He'd gotten down a cedar chest and taken out a fine carved ceremonial wolf's mask with teeth and eyes made of abalone shells. For a long time he held it in front of him, turning it one way and then the other as if looking at it for the first time. She wanted to ask him if it had been his father's, but the silence was too great and she couldn't think how to break it. Finally he'd put it back and picked up a beautiful dancing shirt woven from cedar-bark fiber and mountain goat wool with ermine trim at the neck and sleeves. She hadn't been able to make out all of the intricate design but was certain symbolic wolf claws had been woven into the shoulders. The workmanship was exquisite; if this was Madsaw's, he'd had to pay his wife a great deal to make it for him. She all too easily imagined Vattan sitting in front of the weaving loom while she worked the many soft strands together into a garment that would bring honor to both her and her husband. It had been a labor of love; the way Madsaw held it against his chest told her that.

By the time the others entered the house, Madsaw had been in his sleeping quarters for so long that she'd twice had to add wood to the fire. The contrast between conversation and the silence that had surrounded her jarred her, and if she could, she would have found a dark corner to hide in. But it was bedtime; she was expected to sleep at Madsaw's feet.

When she was slow to stand, Apenas stalked toward her. "Your master waits for you."

"Maybe he is asleep. I don't want to disturb him."

"Don't argue with me, Twana. You know what must be."

Apenas was right; she'd been stalling. She stood and walked behind Apenas as the older woman led the way. One of Madsaw's sisters watched openly.

The room was utterly dark, forcing her to drop to her hands and knees so she could feel for where Madsaw lay. Because she'd stood here earlier with the curtain pulled back, she knew Apenas's bed was on the opposite side of the room. Still, if Madsaw took her, Apenas would know.

Madsaw didn't move, and yet because she couldn't hear him breathing, she guessed he wasn't asleep. Reaching out with tentative fingers, she briefly touched what she believed was his hip. She crawled a little farther, then curled herself into a tight, uncomfortable ball on a bark matt. Tense, she waited for a sound, a movement, but he remained still. When her knees began to protest the cramped position she'd forced them into, she stretched out a little. As she did, Madsaw moved and she caught her breath. If he reached for her, she would have to obey.

But she'd never given her body to a man; the thought terrified her.

Something touched her belly. Madsaw had stretched out his feet, and they were now resting against her. She felt speared by him and wondered if he'd brought himself into contact with her for no reason other than to let her know he controlled her and could turn that control into reality whenever he wanted.

"Madsaw?" Apenas whispered. "I can take my sleeping blanket into the great room."

"Stay here. I don't want her."

"But—"

"Listen to me, Mother. I don't want her."

It was a lie. How she knew that, Twana couldn't say, just that she'd seen something in his eyes earlier tonight, heard something in his voice, that told her he was thinking like a man who'd been too long without a woman. Surely he wasn't afraid that joining his body with hers would risk his soul; hadn't he told her he didn't believe the shaman's threat?

And yet he was keeping himself from her when his body wanted hers.

Why?

The rain increased in strength, and for the first time tonight, she listened to the wind. It seemed a lonely sound like lost children crying out for comfort. For a long time she clung to the sound, fighting to keep anything else from entering her thoughts, but it was an impossible battle. Madsaw's heel pressed against her middle, and she couldn't escape it. It was more than a man's foot taking control of a woman's belly, more than two people trying to fall asleep to the song of rain and wind. She'd completed her puberty ceremony; she should be ready to leave childhood behind. But to become a woman at his hands—

The wind made a sharp whistling sound, then changed to a deeper tone, briefly capturing her attention.

Maybe she was afraid of the storm.

And maybe she was afraid of herself.

The question rocked her, and in a attempt to distance herself from it, she concentrated on relaxing her entire body so sleep might claim it. She managed to uncurl her fingers and, by moving her head, was able to decrease the tension in her neck. Still, her belly continued to feel imprinted by Madsaw.

Rain and wind had quieted the night creatures. They'd sought their caves and dens or huddled under sheltering trees to wait until the storm had spent itself. She would become one of them, a forest animal curled deep inside its home until it was safe to emerge again, lulled by sounds spawned by Thunderbird.

Thunderbird. The beast, it was said, was so immense that it could carry off whales as easily as an eagle carries a trout. Thunderbird didn't care about a small woman. Didn't . . .

No! Although her scream remained trapped inside her, Twana's body vibrated with it. Tonight was for her, for thoughts of Madsaw, for trying to understand—

No!

There was no fighting One Ear's power over her. She had no choice but to send her mind out into the stormy night on a fearful search. For too long the grizzly hid from her, his presence as elusive as what she felt for Madsaw, but she had to know— had to try to understand.

Finally she found him, the only creature moving tonight. Rain ran down his sides, and if there'd been a moon, his fur would have glistened, but his heavy body remained dry under the thick coat. When thunder rolled, he barely slowed. A slash of lightning made him roar, not in fear, but anger. In the sudden, short light, her mind filled with the sight of that great, mutilated head.

He wasn't looking for food. Instead he circled the village. Nearly paralyzed by fear, Twana searched until she understood how much distance separated One Ear from the home of the Tillamook Wolf Clan. A strong man could walk out of his house at dawn and reach the grizzly before afternoon.

If One Ear began to charge, he would run out of breath before he burst from the forest, but if he held himself to a trot—

He wasn't charging, wasn't coming closer. Like a wolf testing a prey's strength, the grizzly kept a steady distance between himself and what he was stalking.

Still, he continued to walk, continued to defy the storm. And Twana wondered if she was his prey.

CHAPTER 7

When Apenas crawled out of bed, Twana wanted nothing more than to try to lose herself in sleep, but Apenas insisted that she'd been in bed long enough and needed to see to the fire. Body aching, Twana tentatively straightened her legs, discovering that Madsaw's sleeping mat was empty. She stood and followed the older woman into the great room to greet the morning light already reaching inside. As she went about the task of breaking branches into small lengths so they would easily catch fire, she struggled to clear her mind, to reclaim her thoughts.

It seemed as if she hadn't fallen asleep all night, but she must have dozed off several times; otherwise, wouldn't she remember fear that stretched forever? Instead, what came to her were bits and

129

pieces, muscle-cramping tension that slid off into nothing only to slam back into her with such force that she thought she'd scream from it.

When Lukstch and his wife stepped out of their sleeping quarters, for a few heartbeats she surrendered to the tender looks they gave each other, but before she could ask herself how a man and a woman could so easily weave their lives together, last night regained its hold on her.

One Ear might be stalking her. It shouldn't be possible; a grizzly owned its world, took what he wanted when he wanted. Only creatures who needed caution in order to stay alive remained in the shadows. One Ear was instinct, muscle and fang and bone ruled by his belly's demands; a grizzly thought nothing of the past, harbored no grudges. Did he?

The back of her neck prickled, causing her to apprehensively glance over her shoulder at the door. It was morning, the world already warming. There was nothing to fear in a soft, damp day— one no different from all others.

Except that One Ear was out there, maybe waiting for her. Remembering?

"Did you hear me?" Apenas interrupted her tangled thoughts. "There is work for you to do today." She handed Twana a large number of red cedar strands and a small pile of mountain goat wool and in clipped tones told Twana she wanted Twana to weave her a new rain hat decorated with the scarce wool. "Tell me, did your mother teach you a woman's skills? Maybe what you make will be so loosely woven that every raindrop will reach me."

Holding her temper in check, Twana assured Apenas that she'd learned how to cook and sew at her mother's side. What she didn't tell her was that although her mother had taught her basic skills, Tatooktche's demands on Saha hadn't left her enough time to turn her daughter into a master weaver. Saha. Even now thoughts of the woman who'd given her birth filled her with both love and grief.

She waited until everyone else had helped themselves from the boiling pot which this morning held large chunks of salmon generously flavored with fern and clover roots, and then ate herself. She'd just begun untangling the wool when Madsaw stepped inside. He looked, not at her, but at his brother, who was patiently grinding a deer bone into an arrowpoint.

"I would hate to ask you to travel as far as the home of the winter wind," Madsaw said. "If you were gone from your wife much longer than when we went to the Nisqually village, I fear you would be like an elk at mating season."

Instead of blushing, Lukstch puffed out his dark chest. "It is a heavy burden to be a young man full of energy and need. Perhaps you remember what it was like before you became so old."

Glaring, Madsaw folded his arms over the faint outline of his ribs. "At least I have gained the wisdom of age, something that may forever elude you. You have a little energy left? You are ready to make another trip?"

Lukstch sighed. "Can't it wait until tomorrow? My arrows need repairing, and I promised Oyai I would go fishing for otter with him."

Madsaw gave his giggling sister-in-law a sideways look. "Fishing? Maybe you think you have the strength for another night with your wife."

"Oh yes, ancient brother, I believe I do."

Even Madsaw's shy youngest sister laughed at that. After promising Madsaw that he would do his bidding tomorrow, Lukstch announced he was going to bathe and that if his wife wanted to accompany him, he might be talked into searching for moss for making yellow dye. Because she'd seen a large quantity of moss in the storage area, Twana knew that wasn't what the two young people had in mind. As they started for the entrance, she nearly begged them to remain inside where they would be safe.

But it was the way of the Tillamook to go into the forest whenever they wanted to hunt or gather. Who would listen to a hostage's warning? But if she said and did nothing and two people who'd done her no harm were killed—

Could she? Always before, her gift had simply happened; she'd never had the courage to see if she could direct her mind's journey. But One Ear all but demanded that she search for him; today she felt strong enough—compelled enough—to answer that challenge.

Breathing deeply, she forced herself to float out over the treetops. The effort made her half-sick, but like a newborn fawn learning to run, she embraced her growing skill. Imagining herself an eagle hovering over the treetops, she concentrated on anything that moved. She first spotted a family of foxes, the sharp-toothed kits nipping at each other as they waited for their mother to bring home a dead mouse. Not far from the den, an owl slept in a dying spruce. Farther on a bedded elk rose on long legs and shook his head as if he wanted to free himself from his heavy antlers. After a moment, the elk lowered its head and began feeding on ferns that had just pushed their way to the surface. Twana wanted to remain with the elk, to watch it tear endlessly at leaves and roots, but she didn't dare.

Floating, waiting for the inescapable signal, she opened her senses to the wild. Fear nipped at her, but she forced it aside. Slowly, like thunderheads building on the horizon, she became aware of the one presence she didn't want but had to understand.

Although she knew it wasn't possible, she half believed she could smell the oily grizzly, hear its heavy breathing. One Ear was sleeping, his body curled in around itself in a way that reminded her of how she'd spent the night. A breeze rippled the beast's rich coat, and a small bird hopped close hoping to find vermin buried in the thick fur. The beast's mouth hung slack, but even in sleep, his teeth were awful to behold. Whether he was closer than he'd been last night, she couldn't say; the only thing that mattered was that he hadn't left the land of the Tillamook Wolf Clan.

"Twana."

She started and looked up. It took a moment for Madsaw's features to come into focus, but it didn't matter because she'd already recognized his voice. "What?"

"Take your work outside with you. Follow me."

"Outside?" Where One Ear might more easily find her?

Madsaw's voice became impatient. "I have work to do on a canoe and want you near me."

Because he would only force her to go with him if she resisted, she nodded, then waited while he ate and took a maul and wedge from a storage box. If he knew the grizzly was within an easy day's walk, he might call the hunters together and order her to take them to the creature. She wanted that to happen, wanted to watch while Madsaw drove a spear deep into One Ear's heart and put an end to her fear of the great creature, but she'd seen an old man killed by One Ear's mother and had to stand by helplessly while Son of Palkma sobbed in pain.

Today she only wanted to sit with the wind in her hair while Madsaw worked on his canoe and One Ear slept.

The boys she'd seen when she was brought into the village were playing in the surf this morning. One of them pretended to be a sea monster while the others ran around him slapping him with giant kelp. As she separated strands of wool from the soft mass and laid them on some bark to keep the sand off them, she couldn't help but laugh at their antics. Madsaw, who was working nearby, glanced at them frequently, his mouth easier than it had been when he ordered her to follow him. Finally the boys grew weary of the game and several wandered back toward their houses. When one ran so close that he kicked sand on her work, she glared at him, then nodded in recognition; it was the war-painted boy from yesterday.

"Vasilii," she heard a woman call out. "Be careful! You are like a whale caught in the surf, thrashing until the tide takes you back out to sea." The woman came closer, stabbing with her finger to tell Vasilii to take his energy elsewhere.

"It's all right." Twana held up the wool and shook it to show the woman how easy it was to remedy Vasilii's carelessness.

"I will never be able to make that one slow down. I wish I had never told him he could haggle with the sea-traders this time. He is so eager; waiting is so hard for him. He keeps saying he wants to go to meet them; he barely listens when I tell him no."

"Maybe he has a great deal to trade," Twana said when the woman leaned down to study her work.

"Not so much. A discarded elk antler, some black stones he says the trader's will want. He has to learn what has value and what doesn't."

Vasilii's mother seemed to be a very wise woman, a woman who didn't look at the war chief's captive as if she were beneath notice. "Sometimes that is a hard lesson."

"What would be harder is to believe success comes without work. A boy does not become a man until he understands that." Sighing, the woman sat down near Twana. "I am called Kitlote. I was born a Chinook, but my mother and I were brought here after a raid. I tell you this so you will understand why you have been on my mind. I know what it is like to be thrust into a strange world."

Her eyes burned, and it took Twana several moments before she felt enough in control of her emotions to speak. "Your son plays with the Tillamook children. They think of him as one of them."

"We are both now Tillamook, ever since I married Stokim. Only once in a great while do I think about what I knew as a small child. But you are a woman; your memories of home are much stronger."

She wanted to tell Kitlote that although she'd grown up in the Nisqually village, she'd never run as freely with the other children as Vasilii did—not from the time of her fifth summer when she first spoke of the strange images inside her. Instead, she let her attention wander back to Madsaw, who was chipping wood from the canoe's interior, his naked back taut from strain. Every once in a while he stopped and checked the sides' thickness with sure fingers. "It is different for me," she said finally. "I will never marry a Tillamook. The time will come when I will be returned to the man I belong to."

"You don't want to?"

How many times had she dreamed of fleeing Tatooktche with her mother? But she'd been a child then, and her mother had told her there were worse things than living with a greedy man—like wandering the wilderness alone, forever alone. "I don't know what I want," she whispered, thoughts filling her, boiling over. "To never again hear an angry voice, to live in peace ..." Madsaw leaned into the canoe and scooped out cedar shavings. Then he took a backward step and cocked his head to one side, studying his handiwork. She could almost reach out and touch his sense of satisfaction, almost lose herself in his mood.

"It is good to see him doing that," Kitlote said, indicating Madsaw. "For too long he would not touch a canoe even though his skill is greater than any other."

"Because of Vattan."

"He told you about her?"

"Only a little."

"My husband says he speaks to no man of her." She didn't know what to say, could hardly tell this woman that she'd held Madsaw's hand last night while words and emotion poured from him.

"He is to remarry soon. Did he tell you that?"

"We didn't speak of it, but his mother said—"

"That canoe is part of the bride-price. When he is finished, he will present it to Kukankh's father."

The canoe wasn't for him? Even though he'd turn it over to another, he was working as if possessed to transform a massive red cedar into a thing of beauty and use. "I—didn't know."

Kitlote started to say something, but just then Vasilii ran up to them. "Mother! Mother!" He held out a small clump of gull feathers. "You could dye them red; the traders would think they are wonderful!"

"Vasilii! Enough!"

Vasilii looked crestfallen. His lower lip sticking so far out that he was in danger of tripping over it, he slowly let the feathers drift to the sand. After a moment, Twana scooped them up and handed them back to him. "Keep them," she said. "When you have a few more, they will make a fine decoration for a blanket."

"I can't make a blanket; that's women's work."

"But if you ask in a gentle voice with smiling eyes, maybe some girl will make one for you."

Vasilii looked unconvinced but held on to his feathers. He glanced at Madsaw, frowning. "Why can a man make a canoe but not a blanket? I don't understand."

"Because that is the way it is, curious one." Kitlote patted her son's skinny leg, then stood. "Go. I will see if there is a basket you can put the feathers in. If I do that, will you leave me alone?"

"If you make me some red dye, I'll stay in the forest until the salmon spawn again."

"I wish." Kitlote laughed. "It is not good for a person to be alone, Twana. That is why my mother wanted me to marry, so I would have someone to share my life with. I saw you sitting here and remembered her words."

Somehow Twana held back her tears until Kitlote was gone. The woman hadn't said much to her, and most of it had been about Madsaw or her son. Still, she was grateful for the simple kindness. If there was any way she could let Kitlote know how much she appreciated her gesture, she would gladly do it. Maybe, someday, she would tell Kitlote about the loneliness that sometimes boiled inside her until she thought she would explode from it.

And if she did, what would Kitlote say?

What would Madsaw say?

Like the surf pounding at a rock, Madsaw slowly and patiently chipped excess wood from the sides of his canoe. In his mind he'd already filled it with the boiling water that would soften the wood and make it easier for him to force the sides apart. He'd always enjoyed that part, for it was then that his creation stopped being a felled tree and began to look like a canoe, but because he'd bent himself to his craft countless times since he was old enough to pick up a maul, what his hands were doing didn't claim all of his thoughts.

Twana had been talking to Vasilii's mother, but Kitlote had left, and now, except for the sound of the sea, it was quiet. Without looking at her, he knew she was watching him and wondered at the insanity that prompted him to have her near him today. He should have learned his lesson last night when sleep came no easier than trying to find his way through a strange forest on a moonless night. Twana had touched his body with lightning and filled him with thunder until his need to join his body with hers had been stronger than any need he'd ever known.

But he hadn't dared reach for her. His mother's presence had had nothing to do with it. Even the possibility that Twana might fight him wasn't what had kept him staring at the ceiling until he thought his mind would splinter.

If he made her his in the way of a man and a woman, for even one night, would he ever be able to free himself?

Sweat ran down his back, and his shoulders had begun to ache, reminding him that he'd been at his work since early this morning. Dropping his maul to the sand, he rose and strode toward Twana, unmindful of a cramp in his right calf from having knelt for so long.

She sat cross-legged on the sand. Tiny grains clung to her toes and ankles, but she'd been careful not to let any get on the wool, which lay in straight strands near her. Her hands were busy with the task of weaving cedar strips together; they fascinated him, strong fingers working with a sureness that rivaled what happened when he focused on a canoe.

She shouldn't be this graceful, shouldn't be capable of taking over his thoughts the way she had. "Go inside," he told her. "I was wrong; I don't want you here."

"What have I done?"

"I feel your eyes on me; I don't want that."

"I didn't mean to make you uncomfortable." Unexpectedly her mouth softened, and her eyes looked less wary. "I like watching you work, Madsaw."

She liked watching him work. For reasons he didn't want to understand, her words warmed him. Vattan had often said that, teasing that she was exhausted from endlessly studying him as he went about the task of creating the elaborate wolf carving that adorned the prow of every canoe he made. Twana didn't speak with Vattan's voice, didn't look at him with his wife's eyes, and yet he felt less alone simply because his hostage admired his skill. "I have a great deal to do before this one is finished," he said when she continued to look at him instead of obeying his command.

"And then you will give it to your intended's father?"

"Yes."

"You—I hope you will be happy with her."

"Happy?" He turned to watch the sea. Almost instantly the unrelenting gray captured his thoughts, his mood. "I barely know her. She's a child."

"A child? But—"

"Kukankh will come to live with me once the bride-price has been paid, but I will not sleep with her until she has reached puberty."

"The Nisqually would never do such a thing. To marry a girl who has not yet become a woman is not how it is done."

He'd grown weary of this conversation, or maybe the truth was, he shared her belief. "She is the daughter of the chief of the Raven Clan. Her parents and my mother have decreed that we should wed. There is no other who equals my rank."

"I know." Twana gathered up her work and then stood, the way the muscles in her arms and legs moved fascinating him. "It is the same for me,"

141

she said softly as she turned to leave. "In my village, there are no others like me."

Twana's words stayed with Madsaw for most of the afternoon as he filled the canoe with water that he heated with hot rocks from the fire. To help with the softening, he set several small fires around the canoe and then shoved strong poles into place to hold the sides apart. It was nearly dark and his stomach had begun to complain by the time he let the fires go out. Still, he was reluctant to leave.

He was proud of what he'd accomplished today, proud and tired. He hoped he would fall asleep the moment he lay down tonight. If not, the quiet time with Twana within his reach would test him as no spirit search ever could.

As soon as he stepped inside his house, his mother handed him roasted salmon. Because he was still hot from tending his fires, he sat near the opening where the evening breeze could reach him and studied his surroundings. Last night the house had been all but empty, but tonight every one of the thirteen people who lived here were inside, the children playing lahal with bone cylinders while most of the adults joined in the nonsensical songs that were part of the game. His mother sat near him and started telling him about an argument between cousins living in one of the other houses, but he barely listened.

Twana had already spun the wool into yarn and was concentrating on the hat, using as her frame a pole caught between two pieces of flooring wood.

Every once in a while, her fingers ceased movement and her body became quietly tense. It wasn't until she'd done that for the third time that he understood.

Ignoring his mother, he walked over to Twana and waited for her to look up at him. When she did, her loose hair slid away from her face, leaving her features exposed. "Where is he?"

"He?"

"Don't play games with me, Twana. You know of what I speak."

She nodded, her fingers once again working automatically. "He slept for a long time today, and when he woke, he easily found fish to fill his belly."

"And now?"

"Now he lies beneath a great cedar tree but is not sleeping. Instead, he listens."

"Maybe he is listening for you."

"Maybe," she said, her voice calmer than he thought it would be. "It has rained. My scent no longer clings to the ground, and he may not know where I am. Maybe he doesn't care."

"The traders are to the north. Is that where One Ear is?"

"No. He's closer to where the sun rises."

"Hm. Maybe he will head north in the morning, find them. Attack them."

"I think not. Even a grizzly knows to weigh his strength against others. If he sees many loud men, he will not want to be near them."

He didn't know whether to believe her. Certainly no other wild creature would walk into a fur trader's camp, but a grizzly didn't understand the meaning of fear, and One Ear seemed like none other. "Maybe he is a spirit bear. Maybe he will find you no matter where you hide."

Her fingers jerked spasmodically, but she didn't drop her gaze from his. "A spirit bear doesn't lose his ear to hunters, Madsaw. And yet I still believe he holds memories of his mother's death."

"So you say. He is close?"

"No."

"If he comes closer, you will tell me. Do you hear me? I will not have my people's safety jeopardized because of you."

"Yes," she whispered. "I hear."

The night had beat around and inside Twana, a great heart slowly measuring the time until morning. Madsaw hadn't been asleep when Apenas ordered her to bed, and she curled herself as far as possible from him, but the sound of his breathing had slowly lengthened out until she'd envied his escape.

Now it was morning and she was back at work on the hat. As he'd done the day before, Madsaw went outside almost immediately after rising. She wanted to join him, wanted to listen to the sea and watch him work; instead she had nothing to look at except sheep wool and the large, thick beams that formed the house's framework—beams that prevented sunlight from reaching her. Even when One Ear's aimless movement snagged her attention, a part of her continued to study the overlapping side and roof planks, and she asked herself over and over again how much of the work Madsaw had done.

She didn't want to think about him, didn't want him to be a part of her life.

When she thought she might go mad from having to remain inside, Apenas told her to leave her weaving and help the women thread dried candlefish with wicks for burning when the traders arrived. She was so grateful at the change of scene that it wasn't until she'd begun removing the oily fish from the high racks that she realized none of the woman had acknowledged her presence. She looked around for Kitlote, but the young mother was nowhere around and she was left feeling both surrounded and isolated. Because Apenas was never far from her side, she concentrated on her work, telling herself she didn't care where Madsaw was or what he was doing.

The children were beside themselves with excitement over the prospect of having the traders arrive. Even those too young to understand were trying their mothers' patience by constantly getting underfoot.

"I wish you had gone with your brother," one woman admonished her toddler who'd just tripped and landed on a pile of candlefish. "If you were out looking for the traders, I wouldn't have to give you another bath." Sighing, she planted the little one on her hip and headed for the trail that led to the bathing place.

"Looking for the traders?" Twana blurted before giving herself time to test the wisdom of her words. "Where did the boys go?"

"They are children; who knows where their legs take them?" a mother answered. Her comment was met with laughter, but Twana's heart felt frozen. The prickling on the back of her neck warned her that Apenas was glaring at her. If they were alone, she might have told Apenas that the thought of having the children in the forest filled her with fear, but if she spoke of a one-eared grizzly foraging far from the village, the others would only be further convinced that she was a witch—or thought herself one.

She tried to fill her mind with the slow task of readying the candlefish, but a huge dark cloud threatening rain hung over the village this morning, adding to her unease. The women laughingly assured each other that if there was a downpour, the children would soon return. Otherwise, the sun—hidden though it was—would be high overhead before their empty bellies drove them home.

An argument rose over whether the trader's would demand their time with the tribe's female slaves before agreeing to sit down with those who had goods to trade. She had no say in what happened to them, no say in what happened to her.

Sokolov's wife, a tall woman with large breasts and feet as broad as a man's, insisted that her husband had had a dream in which Twana had been presented to the traders. "The hostage fought, but that only excited the sea-strangers more. They had their way with her, all of them. Their energy was inexhaustible, and in the end the hostage was rendered unconscious."

"A dream?" Apenas asked. "Was it an ordinary dream or one brought by the spirits?"

"The spirits, always the spirits speak with him. My husband heard Thunderbird just as he was finishing with me. He immediately went to sleep and this morning told me what he had seen. He also saw the trading. He says the Wolf Clan will be blessed if the hostage satisfies the whites. Before the sea-strangers leave, they will heap great riches on us."

That brought an excited chorus from the other women, and although a few glanced at her, Twana felt all but invisible. The dream might be real and it might simply be part of Sokolov's determination to prove his superiority over her.

"You are sure?" Apenas asked, sounding awed. "The trade will bring us much wealth?"

Sokolov's wife nodded and repeated her husband's dream, in such great detail this time that Twana wondered if she was adding her own embellishments to it. Sokolov had to be wrong; hadn't Madsaw said that his medicine was so weak, he shouldn't call himself a shaman?

But if he was right . . .

Although it threatened rain all morning, the air simply remained heavy and damp, and by the time the youngest children started to complain that they were hungry, fully half of the candlefish had had wicks threaded through them. Apenas told her to finish a few more before returning to her hat weaving, then left, heading toward the beach. Working quickly, Twana did the rest of her work, but when she left the few remaining women, it wasn't to go inside.

Instead, knowing she was risking Apenas's wrath, she walked over to a group of boys who'd just emerged from the forest. From the snatches of excited conversation, she learned that they'd decided to head in different directions, with honor going to whoever found the traders first. Although none of the boys would admit it, it was clear that talking about walking, alone, farther into the forest than they'd ever been before was much easier than actually doing it. How, one boy after another asked, could they spend a day searching if they hadn't brought anything to eat?

"Vasilii? Where is he?"

Suddenly tense, Twana watched as Kitlote rapidly approached the boys. They looked around, confusion darkening their already dark eyes. "He wouldn't say where he was going," one of them finally offered. "When we tried to make him tell us, he laughed and boasted that his guardian spirit had told him where to look."

"Vasilii doesn't have a guardian spirit yet." Kitlote clamped her hands over her elbows. "You know that. Didn't you wait for him?"

One of the boys explained that when Vasilii didn't return to the gathering place at the lightning-struck spruce tree overlooking the river, they assumed he'd already returned to the village. "He isn't here." Kitlote's voice took on an edge that tied Twana's stomach into a knot. "Think. What did he say?"

"He boasted that he had been given the sight

and speed of a deer and could cover ground much faster than any hunter."

Twana waited for Kitlote to say something; she needed to hear Vasilii's mother laugh and express confidence that her son would soon be back. Instead, the young mother stood with her hands now pressed against her stomach, her attention fixed on the forest.

Twana breathed deeply twice, three, finally four times. Eight boys had returned safely from their journey; one hadn't. Closing her eyes, she surrendered herself to the wilderness. Almost immediately she felt herself being pulled away from her body with such dizzying speed that it made her half-sick. Treetops whipped past her, some of them standing straight and still, others waving erratically in the grip of the whimsical wind. In her mind she climbed up and over the closest hill and then another. She frantically searched for signs of movement that would tell her she'd found a young boy—a boy hurrying back to safety—but although the forest was alive with mice, fox, deer, birds, even a foraging small black bear, she saw nothing of Vasilii of the smeared war paint and adventurous spirit.

She knew she wouldn't; her gift brought her to wild creatures, not humans.

CHAPTER 8

"**I** hate this fear."

Twana looked around to see if anyone else was within earshot, but although the boys who'd gone out with Vasilii were still mumbling among themselves, she and Kitlote were the only adults standing near Kitlote's house.

"You told me he is full of courage," she said, wishing her words carried more conviction. "Perhaps he simply decided to go farther before returning. Maybe he has found the traders and is with them."

"Maybe." Once again Kitlote's attention was drawn to the dark and endless forest. "A mother feels certain things. We know when a boy is afraid or angry. When our children are content, that enters us as well. My son is not at peace with himself; I feel it."

So do I. Not sure where her thought had come from, Twana could only stand and listen as Kitlote questioned the boys further about what they'd seen and done, what her son had said. Maybe because they now sensed Kitlote's anxiety, the boys answered as thoroughly as possible, but instead of giving Kitlote a clear idea of where Vasilii might have gone, they contradicted each other. One was certain Vasilii had said he was going to follow the river far upstream because the traders often followed the waterways. Another had heard Vasilii boast he was going to climb Cougar Mountain so he could see forever. A third was adamant that Vasilii was going to try to trace the path of an eagle he'd seen flying from the direction of the winter wind. The eagle, Vasilii had told his friend, had shown him the way.

"He says—he told his father that he has seen Eagle in his dreams. But there is much distance between here and the land of ice." Kitlote spoke slowly and deliberately, and yet there was a breathy quality to her voice that made Twana even more anxious. Without thinking, she held out her hands, and Kitlote placed hers in them.

"He is hungry. He will be home soon," Twana told her. "A child's stomach is stronger than his boastfulness."

"Vasilii would rather play at being a mighty hunter than eat. When I remind him of his belly, he always looks surprised."

The boys, still muttering that Vasilii would soon

be back, began shuffling toward their respective houses. When they'd all left, Twana keenly felt the loss of their youthful presence and guessed it must be even more so for Kitlote. If Apenas saw her holding a woman's hands instead of tending to her tasks, she would risk Apenas's wrath, but if she left, Kitlote would be alone.

"My husband will call me foolish," Kitlote muttered. "He says I must give our son more freedom, but Vasilii does not yet join wisdom with his courage. I wish—" She looked up at the dark cloud, then again turned her attention to the forest. "I just want . . ."

She wanted to place her arms around her son. Twana didn't need to be a mother to know that.

"I must consult the shaman."

"Sokolov? He will want payment."

"I know." Kitlote took a shaky breath. "And Stokim will be angry, but he does not have my heart; he doesn't understand."

Twana was still staring after Kitlote when she heard her name being called and turned to find Apenas striding toward her. She clenched her fingers in her skirt and hurried to meet her captor's mother.

Apenas folded her arms and glared up at Twana. "Your master wants you. I said I would send you to his side, but you are not where I ordered you. Instead, you are bothering Kitlote."

"Not bothering. Her son is missing."

"Missing?" Apenas's lips thinned, then she demanded an explanation. By the time Twana had finished, irritation had faded from the older woman's eyes. Now she looked nearly as anxious as Twana felt. "That boy. He had just learned to walk when he tried to run into the sea. Many say he would make a great chief because he is fearless, but a chief must think as well as act."

"That's what his mother says. She's going to consult with Sokolov."

"Sokolov. He will demand a fine blanket, but maybe he will tell her where to find her child." Jerking her head, Apenas indicated she wanted Twana to follow her back to the house. Although Twana thought she might berate her for not obeying earlier, Apenas remained quiet.

Except for Madsaw and his brother, the house was empty. As soon as she entered, she realized Madsaw and Lukstch were deep in conversation. Waiting to be recognized, she walked over to her unfinished basket and picked up the soft strands. She was trying to decide whether to remain where she was or slip closer to Madsaw when dread slammed into her. Fearing what she'd see if she followed her instinct, she concentrated on her fingers, willing them to begin weaving.

It was impossible. The darkness, tinged red today, called to her, challenged her to look into the center of the darkness—a cloud-draped wilderness that held a small boy, and a grizzly.

One Ear, closer than he'd been this morning, had climbed onto a boulder and was now standing on his massive hind legs, front legs hanging loose and yet deadly near his belly. In her mind she saw herself crouched in front of the beast, her arms and legs so close to the killing claws that she could easily reach out and touch them.

She felt heat, smelled the oily, long-unwashed body, listened with his ears and smelled through his nostrils and saw what little his inadequate eyes perceived. There was something out there, whether prey or simply a random movement that had caught his attention, she couldn't say. What she did know was that One Ear wouldn't rest until his small brain understood.

A boy—a little boy was out there.

"Twana."

Madsaw's voice shattered her concentration. He was motioning her to join him and his brother, his features stripped of all emotion. Aware that Apenas was watching her every move, she was careful not to stand too close to Madsaw. Still, his heat—so different from One Ear's—touched her senses and made her vividly aware of both their bodies. He tapped the floor near him, indicating he wanted her to sit.

"I do not have to tell you this; there are many who say that what I do is none of your concern. But it is your life, and I want you to know what I have decided."

One Ear— No. She couldn't concentrate on the grizzly with Madsaw demanding her attention. "Decided?"

"My brother will leave for the Nisqually village at dawn tomorrow. He will take with him my demands for your ransom."

The thought of Tatooktche's reaction to being forced to pay to have her returned to him filled her with dread, and yet from the moment she'd learned that he'd killed another man, she'd tried to ready herself for this. She struggled to bring forth an image of where she'd lived for her entire life, but the tall totems and solid houses, even the narrow beach leading to the sea and the mountains that both sheltered and trapped the village, remained only faint images.

"Because I will not trade with the sea-strangers, I have little use for furs. However, I have heard that Tatooktche possesses a white man's weapon."

She'd seen the rifle herself, a heavy, frightening piece of metal and wood that spit flames and sent the birds to squawking with its mighty sound. Tatooktche had fired it twice right after it came into his possession, but since then, he'd kept it wrapped in blankets, saying he was saving its powerful medicine. "He won't give it up," she insisted. "He says it makes him stronger than any other."

"Does it mean more to him than his reputation?"

Because she'd never understood Tatooktche, she couldn't answer Madsaw. "Is that all? His rifle for my return?"

"No." Apenas spoke for her son. "Madsaw may have no use for trading furs, but I do. Because it was my husband who was killed, I am asking for a man's weight in beaver and mink."

"A man's weight? I have never—"

"And an engraved copper plaque. The slave who told us about the rifle says Tatooktche was given one in trade."

"It means too much to him," Twana blurted. "There is only that one piece of copper in the village. When he brings it out of its storage place, he boasts that only a chief should have such a thing."

"It is more important to him than his daughter?"

"I don't know," Twana admitted, not bothering to point out that she was no birth kin to Tatooktche. "And if he refuses?" She glanced at Lukstch. "What will you do then?"

"Then I will stand before the entire village and announce that Tatooktche is a man without honor."

"You can't! Please, you can't!"

Madsaw grunted. "Why not?"

"Because . . ." She didn't want to think of the fun-loving Lukstch throwing insults at Tatooktche. If she did, she might be swamped by the fear that had consumed her when she thought of Vasilii, surrounded by trees and mountains and endless shadows. "You don't know his anger; I do."

Lukstch expanded his chest and folded his arms over it, looking for all the world like a boastful child. "I am not afraid of an old man with a rifle wrapped in blankets. I leave now, Twana. Is there any word you wish me to take to him?"

She shook her head. "Tatooktche and I are two people forced to live together; there is no love between us."

"Love? Only honor matters in this, Twana," Madsaw said softly. "That is why you are here."

Madsaw's terse words pounded at Twana, adding to the drumbeats already vibrating inside her head, and for a long time after Lukstch left, she couldn't think about anything else. She ate a little fish and tried to go back to her work, but she kept making mistakes in the twining of warp and weft. Madsaw and Apenas continued to talk to each other, speaking so low that she couldn't hear what they were saying. She guessed they were talking about her, wanted to ask Madsaw how he could show her kindness one moment and act as if he hated her the next. She'd just begun to unravel her latest error when Lukstch's wife hurried inside and grabbed Madsaw's arm.

"Come outside, please! Kitlote is begging Sokolov to look for her son, but the shaman refuses. She asks for you now."

Not thinking what she was doing, Twana jumped to her feet and ran for the opening, unmindful of Apenas's disapproving glare. Kitlote and her husband were standing in front of Sokolov, Kitlote's high and frightened voice a sharp contrast to the shaman's terse but soft-spoken replies. Twana eased her way through the crowd, careful not to impose her presence on anyone. Although she had to stand so far from Kitlote that she didn't believe the woman had seen her, she easily sensed Kitlote's fear and wished she could help.

Wished she knew if Vasilii was safe from One Ear.

"He has been gone so long. How can you—"

"He is missing because you stayed the boy's uncle's hand when he needed to be beaten with alder boughs," Sokolov insisted. "You argued that he should not bathe in the winter water even though you know he will never become strong and hard if he continues to be treated as a small child."

"He was sick from having eaten bad fish. It was only one day, shaman, only one day."

"A good mother doesn't stand between a boy and his uncle's training."

Kitlote continued to protest that Vasilii had been so ill, he could barely stand and that the boy's uncle had allowed Vasilii to go back to sleep instead of ordering him outside in the predawn frigid air, but Sokolov only waved off her arguments, saying over and over again that the boy was paying for his mother's transgressions.

"You won't help me?" Kitlote asked, her voice tight with panic.

"No one can help your child. The forest dwarfs have him."

Shocked gasps followed Sokolov's statement; one young girl wrapped her arms around her mother's legs and began crying. "No!" Kitlote gasped. "No! Please say it is not so."

"I tell you only what is," Sokolov declared. "Vasilii is a foolish child unschooled by his elders. He walked where it is unsafe and the dwarfs grabbed him; they have taken him beneath the ground with them."

White-faced, Kitlote reached for her husband, who looked just as horrified. They clutched each other, two people who had just heard that their child was worse than dead, but although Twana's heart went out to them, she couldn't make herself concentrate on what Sokolov was saying now. *Unsafe*. Vasilii had ventured where it was unsafe.

Only, the danger didn't come from a malevolent dwarf.

"Twana, come with me."

She jumped at the sound behind her, but didn't have to look to know who it was; maybe she would always know the sound of Madsaw's voice. Feeling as if she'd been surrounded by a river's whirlpool, she backed away from Kitlote. She desperately wanted to offer comfort to the young woman, but if Sokolov saw her hug Kitlote, he might insist that she and not a dwarf was responsible for Vasilii's disappearance.

"This is not your concern."

"What? Madsaw—"

"Did you not hear me, Twana? A Tillamook child is not your concern."

"He's a little boy, venturesome and brave, not yet filled with wisdom."

Madsaw folded his arms across his naked chest, the gesture momentarily tearing her thoughts from a child in danger. Although the day was cool, he wore only the covering his uncle had given him. He looked magnificent, all wild strength and courage. "Then it doesn't matter to you which tribe a child comes from?" he asked.

"Oh no, never."

A faint smile touched his mouth, and with the gesture, she realized he's been pushing her, not because he was angry with her but because he wanted the truth from her. "Can you see him? Can you say whether the dwarfs have him?"

"I have never seen such creatures. And neither did my mother."

Madsaw rocked back on his heels as if absorbing what she'd just told him. She knew what was coming next, should have made the first move herself, but with him standing before her like the strongest tree, she couldn't put her mind to anything except him. Where a moment ago he'd spoken as if he could barely stand to be in her presence, he now seemed content with himself—and with her.

"I looked," she whispered after what seemed both a long time and only the briefest moment. "I tried to find Vasilii, but my gift makes it possible for me to find animals, not people. You know that."

"When you went into the forest in your mind, what did you see?"

Suddenly light-headed, she fought the need to run from him, from the words building inside her. And yet he'd asked a question they both needed to face. "Many creatures; a small black bear."

"And?"

"One Ear is out there." She forced the words. "Close?"

Instead of answering, she surrendered to the demands inside her, demands Madsaw had made on her. One Ear was on the move. From the way he plowed through the forest, nose to the ground, she guessed he'd picked up a scent. Ferns, small trees, thick grasses, were crushed beneath his paws, and when he ran up a slope, his claws dug deep into the soft earth. She all too easily imagined what those claws could do to a small boy.

"Twana?"

Had Madsaw ever spoken her name so gently? She struggled to open her eyes, surprised to discover that he'd taken her arm. "He is closer than he was earlier."

"Has he found Vasilii?"

"I don't think—no. He—he would still be with the body if he had."

"Then there's still time."

How long had she known he would say that? Maybe from the moment he'd heard Kitlote beg Sokolov to save her son's life; maybe before. "I don't know where Vasilii is. The forest hides him."

"Twana, I can't stand here and do nothing. Sokolov lies, but the others believe him; no one will look for the boy for fear of defying the shaman. There is only us."

Us. Even though her legs were firmly under her and she was in no danger of swaying, Madsaw hadn't released her arm. Something of his, some energy or strength or courage, flowed from his hand and into her until she wondered if the same blood coursed through both of them. Only a few moments ago he'd said he wanted to send her back to Tatooktche in exchange for a rifle, but that no longer mattered to him.

Or to her.

"I'm afraid," she whispered. "I have to tell you that; I'm afraid."

"So am I."

His words sliced through her, brought him into ever sharper focus. "You are the war chief; you are afraid of nothing."

"A man who does not fear a grizzly is a fool, Twana. Will you go into the forest with me, let me know if One Ear comes too close? I will not force you on this."

She didn't have to go with him. She could remain within the house he'd built, weaving his mother a new hat while he carried the risk on his shoulders alone. But if she did that, One Ear might kill both him and a frightened little boy. "It's afternoon," she whispered. "It will be dark all too soon."

"Then I will spend the night out there. I ask it again, is this something you can do?"

"Yes." *Because you are touching me and I feel a part of you.* "Yes."

Madsaw told his uncle what he and Twana were going to do. Because his mother would beg him to stay in the village, he asked Walkus to say nothing until he and Twana were out of sight.

"You risk a great deal, my nephew," Walkus said. "Maybe more than your life if it is as your hostage says and there is a grizzly nearby."

"My reputation; I know. But if you knew where to look for Vasilii, would you be standing here?"

"You know the answer to that, Madsaw. My heart is with the boy, but if I went with you now, everyone would say I was defying the shaman."

Madsaw could only nod at his uncle's wisdom. He prayed that when his time to lead came, he would be guided by his head and not his heart. Today, however, his concern for a little boy was stronger than anything his head tried to tell him.

If he returned with Vasilii in his arms, all would believe him great, and if he failed—if he failed, his brother might have to gather what was left of him and carry his bones back to their mother.

"Tell me, Twana," he said once they'd slipped into the shadows at the back of the village. "Are you still afraid?"

"Not now. Children play here all the time; sometimes young people come here when they want to be alone. But soon . . ."

"Soon fear will wash over you?"

"Maybe he hates me. If he senses my presence, maybe he will come after me. Madsaw, I might not be the only one in danger. You understand, don't you?"

He did, but as he looked at her with shadows dappling her features, protecting himself against a grizzly seemed far less a danger than spending the day and maybe a night alone with her. She still wore the dress she'd had on when he captured her, but her hair was no longer tangled from sleep the way it had been then. Most of all, her eyes were no longer full of fear of him. It might be a trick of the deep purple cloud overhead, but it seemed that there was a peace to her he hadn't been aware of at the beginning. Despite what he might be leading her into, what she could be leading him toward, she was comfortable in his presence.

No, not comfortable. Something strong and warm and alive—the same emotions coursing through his body.

Because the other boys had told him where

163

they'd last seen Vasilii, he led the way to where the river flowed at the base of Cougar Mountain. Several times he pointed out where the boys had left their mark on the thick matt of leaves and needles that made up the forest's soft floor. When he did, she nodded and smiled a little at the children's carelessness but said nothing.

Finally he stood where the river rushed between great rocks with such force that he could barely make himself heard and stared up at Cougar Mountain, an imposing mass of boulders and the few sparse trees that had somehow found a foothold in what little soil existed there. The top of the mountain was blanketed by the cloud that now enveloped their world. The wind had built in strength and carried with it a powerful scent of rain.

Twana joined him, her arms dangling at her sides, wind-whipped hair slapping across her face. With her toe she pointed out several footprints. "They spent a long time here walking about, probably trying to decide what to do."

Madsaw squatted and placed his hand over one of the prints. Although the ground was cold, he wanted to believe that Vasilii had left a little of himself behind. When he stood, Twana placed her foot beside the print. "This one is so small, smaller than Vasilii."

"Most of the boys are. That might make it possible for me to find his tracks."

"I pray you are right."

Although he'd glanced up to study the rain cloud, the emotion in her voice turned him toward her. She'd caught her hair at the back of her neck with her hand, a gesture that thrust her breasts against her dress and made him even more aware of her as a woman. His mother refused to see her as anything except someone who lived with the man who'd killed her husband. But Apenas was a woman in mourning, not a man who had slept alone too long—a warrior with a restless body.

Clenching his teeth, he forced himself to return to his study of his surroundings. Upstream, the river became even more pinched by boulders. It hissed and screamed and threw spray high into the air. He'd come here with his father and uncle before going on his spirit search and remembered how awed he'd been by the river's anger. If his relatives hadn't been with him, he would have run away.

"I don't think he went that way." He indicated the river. "There are limits to Vasilii's courage."

"I was thinking the same thing," Twana said, her words nearly lost beneath the river's call. "It is not a place I would want to be near if I was alone."

She didn't want to be here; if she weren't so concerned for Vasilii, she would be sitting inside his house. And maybe— Thunder rumbled, rocking the world around them and momentarily drowning the sound of the river. Twana withstood its onslaught without moving, but her eyes remained locked on him and the thought he'd had before the thunder returned. Maybe it was he who gave her the courage to walk where One Ear ruled. Awed by the trust she'd place in him, he touched the club and dagger he'd tied around his waist.

Lightning streaked the sky. He watched, not its path, but what it did to Twana's eyes. They momentarily became bright and innocent without depth or seriousness, and he wished they were two children free to play and laugh. Before he could ask where the insane thought had come from, she turned from him and stared up at Cougar Mountain. When she lowered her gaze to the river again, he knew what she was thinking. Although a man or woman with long legs could jump over the river here to get to the base of the mountain, the span was too great for a child. That left only the direction of the winter wind.

"To the north, the trees grow so thick that the sun never touches the ground," he explained. "The last time, when the sea-traders had finished with the Makah, they followed the shoreline until they reached us. They are doing the same this time; why didn't the boys listen to the words of their elders? Every boy in the village could search here until they grew old and they wouldn't find the traders because they aren't here."

"Who can explain the thinking of a child? All that matters is that Vasilii and the others were here, and he went—he went deep into the forest."

"Then we must follow him."

"I know," she said with her hand now at her throat. "Madsaw? That is where One Ear is."

Trees and ferns that thrived on heavy moisture and little sun grew so thickly that Twana didn't dare take her eyes off the ground. Still, because there was so much for a careless boy to brush against, Madsaw was able to follow Vasilii's tracks with little difficulty. When she flicked a spiderweb off her shoulder, Twana nearly told him he didn't need her here; he would find the boy all the faster if he didn't have to shorten his long strides to match hers.

But that wasn't why she'd agreed to accompany him. Time and time again, she shut out her surroundings and focused on the deadly presence. The grizzly hadn't once stopped moving and was lumbering, not toward or away from them, but in a huge circle. He seemed compelled by some force inside himself to climb one hill after another, not to search for food but out of a primitive restlessness. She sensed his agitation, his dissatisfaction with himself.

Madsaw didn't ask about One Ear, and she believed he trusted her to tell him if the grizzly came too close. Knowing that gave her a sense of pride and responsibility and made it possible for her to clamp a hand over her simmering fear.

Thunder and lightning played with her senses. The wind had become angry, beating at the treetops until they bent low before its onslaught, and still it didn't rain. If it hadn't been for the threatening storm, she might have been able to better concentrate on her enemy, but the electric air confused her senses. She knew One Ear was awake and deadly; she couldn't tell how close they were to that deadly power.

"There." Madsaw stopped and pointed. "Vasilii

sat and rested here for a while. You can't tell how he is?"

"No." She forced the word, frustration at not being able to tap into Vasilii's emotions gnawing at her. "I wish—I have been trying, trying so hard. Madsaw, when my mother disappeared, I stared first out at the sea and then into the forest until my eyes ached, concentrating as I never have before, but she had no message for me. If I can't reach my own mother, how can I find a boy I barely know?"

He didn't say anything, and in the silence punctuated by complaining trees, she realized how much of herself she'd given away. He now knew about the dread that had clawed at her heart, her helpless tears, her unrelenting fear for her mother's life, her desperate loneliness.

"She left no sign? No one had any idea what happened to her? Maybe One Ear—"

"No!" she interrupted, the image he'd conjured up making her shiver. "There were no grizzlies around that day; I'm sure of that."

"No bears? But what else could it be?"

"I don't know. Madsaw?" Frightened and yet fascinated, she watched herself stretch out her hand to touch his elbow. His flesh felt cool from the wind, and yet his ropelike muscles would never surrender to the elements. He glanced down at what she'd done, then stared deep into her eyes until she wondered if he'd somehow climbed inside her.

There was only the two of them, only this great

teasing storm and a lost boy waiting for them to find him.

Only One Ear.

Madsaw stepped closer, or maybe she was the one who made the first move. A shower of needles knocked loose by the wind floated over his head, a couple of them resting briefly on his black hair. She wanted to take the needles and clutch them to her, to always have something that had touched him. Again the sky bellowed, made her feel alive in a way that had only a little to do with the great power behind the sound.

Madsaw had brought her here, his compassion and concern for a little boy more important than her fear. Touching him now, she knew that Vasilii's need had only a little to do with why she'd said yes. Madsaw had taken her beyond dread of a grizzly, given her the courage to walk where One Ear ruled.

I want—want you, Madsaw. Want us together. You turning me into a woman.

He reached for her, wrapped his hands around her forearms and drew her near so that she felt his breath warm her upturned face. She was a leaf in the river's grip, a tiny bird pitting its strength against a storm's gale. She should run, flee her captor's power over her, but how could she fear a man who made her feel this alive? If there was nothing left of her when he was done with her, did it matter?

At least she would no longer be alone. She would have become a woman.

He pulled her so close to him that his features

blurred and her breasts were pressed against his chest. The tips hardened and she wondered if he could feel their thrust. He pulled in a deep but ragged breath and she had her answer.

Take me. Make me part of you.

"Twana. Twana." Her name seemed ripped from him, a soft whisper immediately captured by the wind and tossed skyward. In her mind she followed the words in a desperate attempt to snatch back the sound of his voice.

He ran his hands over her back, strong fingers exploring her body. Then he touched her forehead with his lips, the gesture so exquisitely gentle that she thought of the feel of a butterfly. Only, no butterfly left a molten imprint behind when it flew away.

Madsaw . . . What . . .

Now his fingers were in her hair, slowly drawing the strands away from her scalp, and she clamped her hands around his hard waist in an attempt to keep her legs from giving out on her. There was so much to him, all power and courage, a man destined to be chief, a brave fighter and skilled canoe maker—a man who had slept alone too long.

A man wanting to put an end to that.

When she felt his belly grind into her, she shuddered, but the thought of escaping never entered her mind. Instead, she pressed with equal strength, thinking only that her body had turned into something she didn't understand—something far stronger than any other force.

"Twana."

"Wh—what?"

He didn't answer; maybe he didn't know he'd spoken. Her breasts throbbed, feeling heavy and hard, needing his hands, his body pressing against them. She wanted to bury herself against him, to feel his strong arms around her, to have him fling her dress into the underbrush and take her down and lay her out on the damp-smelling carpet. She'd—what? She couldn't simply wait for him; doing nothing was like being dead.

But what did he want from her? What did he deserve?

He shifted his weight, a thigh pushing against her until she felt off balance. She reached for his shoulders, thinking only that she needed to hold on to him when—when . . .

No! No! Not now!

"Twana?"

"One Ear!"

CHAPTER 9

Every line of Madsaw's body felt as if it had been yanked tight as a bowstring. In a single heartbeat he'd gone from thinking of nothing except the woman he held in his arms to unseen danger.

"Where?"

"I don't— Wait."

She didn't say anything else, and her tension warned him not to distract her. When she pushed against his chest, he released her. Still, he stood close enough that he believed he could hear her heart beating, so he could defend her if need be. She now stood on tiptoe, her head slowly turning as if fighting the wind for a better understanding of her world. She breathed slow and shallow, the act reminding him of how right she'd felt in his arms. He would give a great deal to know what was happening inside her, to look at the wilderness with her eyes, to understand—

"He smells something."

"Us?"

"I— No. The wind is blowing from his rump to his head. He can't be following his nose. Maybe a sound. Maybe— He stops. Rears onto his hind legs, lifts his head high, opens his mouth. His teeth . . ."

A shudder coursed through her, and thinking only to give her a measure of courage, he took her hand and squeezed just enough, he hoped, that she would be reminded of his presence. "He's angry," she went on. "Something is out there; he knows it but cannot find it. Madsaw? What if it is Vasilii?"

"Twana," he whispered. "Do you know what direction One Ear is looking?"

Again she fell silent, and he waited for her, feeling her every emotion through her fingers. Her nails dug into the back of his hand, and if he hadn't been afraid of disturbing her, he would have pulled free. Instead, he suffered the discomfort, waiting for answers.

"He has stopped looking."

"Maybe it was nothing."

"No. I know how a grizzly acts when he searches for prey. There was something out there. But the storm keeps secrets, and One Ear knows not to fight the wind and thunder."

Madsaw felt both keen disappointment and relief, but before he could say anything, Twana began speaking again.

"There. He is leaving, turning and looking over his shoulder, then walking again. I . . . Madsaw, I searched in the direction he was looking. There are no animals there."

"No animals but maybe a small boy?"

"Maybe."

Her word hung on the air. He continued to hold her hand, wondering at his growing understanding of her. Another might become impatient with her long silences, but he understood she needed time with the images inside her head. When they'd revealed themselves to her, she would share them with him. This, he believed.

"No," she said with more assurance this time. "There is nothing nearby, nothing that belongs in the forest. And yet his reaction—I can take you there."

I can take you there. At that moment he ceased to think of her as his hostage and studied her with the eyes of one hunter staring at another. Their prey wasn't a deer or elk but a small boy, and their weapons no greater than her comprehension of her world. "Is it far from here?"

"We will be there before dark."

"And One Ear—"

"We must pray for the wind to protect us. Otherwise, he will know we are here."

Madsaw allowed her to lead the way, and when she stopped to reassure herself that she was going in the right direction, he waited for her to continue. Still, no matter how much she had to concentrate on where she was going, a part of her remained acutely aware of him. They seemed to walk with the same legs, sharing the same goal, thinking of nothing except bringing Vasilii safely back to his parents.

Only, it was more than Vasilii this late afternoon. True, she never once dared let her thoughts stray from One Ear, who had found a grub-laden tree and was tearing it apart, but Madsaw claimed more of her thoughts than she'd dreamed possible.

By the time they were only a short distance from where she believed One Ear had been looking, the storm clouds had lost a little of their deep purple hue, and yet the air's wet smell remained just as potent. It became harder to see, and she was aware that the day was losing its energy. If they didn't soon find Vasilii—

Weary of the heart-heavy thought, she cast it away and concentrated. Her legs were fatigued from walking and her right instep ached from where she'd slipped on a tree root, but if she stopped to tend to her bruise, her legs might stiffen and it would be nearly impossible for her to start walking again. Hunger gnawed at her.

Madsaw was with her; that was all that mattered. She wasn't alone, and the one man she couldn't dismiss hadn't left her side.

A sound, so faint that the whistling trees nearly stole it, jarred her nerve endings. She paused, not sure she'd heard something, and saw that Madsaw, too, had been brought up short. She opened her mouth to ask a question, but he silenced her with a warning finger. When she took a sideways step, he followed her, his body as alert as a deer smelling for danger. He pointed, then silently indicated he wanted her to follow him. She did, crouching low in imitation of him, struggling to keep her thoughts split between where she was heading and One Ear.

Madsaw stopped so abruptly that if she hadn't been looking at him, she might have run into him. Still crouching, he pointed toward a hemlock stand. For a moment she saw nothing, then a random movement caught her attention. There, nearly dwarfed by the trees, sat Vasilii. He was rocking back and forth, his knees pulled tight against his body. When he ran the back of his hand under his nose, she understood; they'd heard him crying.

Suddenly weak with relief, she grabbed Madsaw's arm. "He's alive. Alive."

"One Ear didn't find him," Madsaw whispered, his voice thick with the same emotion that filled her. Turning, he clutched her to him, and his heart beat like a ceremonial drum, beat in time with hers. He held her with a strength that spoke of relief and dying fear, and she felt blessed because he'd given her his raw reaction. "He wasn't— Where is the grizzly?"

Clinging to him, she closed her eyes and sought. Beetles had built themselves a home deep in the earth, but One Ear had found it and was tearing at the loose soil, flinging it between his legs as he dug with single-minded purpose. She felt the great body ripple with effort—with the animal joy of venting his energy on helpless prey. And then she knew; only a single hill separated the grizzly from them. If the wind gave up its hold on the wilderness or turned in another direction—

"We have to leave," she whispered. "Now. Vasilii. He has to know—"

"If he sees us, he may cry out."

Madsaw was right. A high-pitched squeal might carry to the grizzly's one ear. "What are we going to do?"

"Stay here," he ordered. "I need to get behind him and cover his mouth. I would rather he be frightened than dead."

Sobered by Madsaw's comment, she knelt behind a tree while he began a wide circle around Vasilii designed to bring him out behind the hemlocks. She divided her attention between Madsaw's slow progress and Vasilii's silent weeping. When he again wiped his nose, her heart went out to him. How frightened he must have become when he realized he'd lost his way. What had begun as a boastful promise to find the sea-strangers had turned into a nightmare. She sent a silent message of reassurance to Kitlote that her son was safe.

She could no longer see Madsaw, but she imagined him moving like a well-trained hunter, his presence known only to owls waking from their day sleep. When she'd seen One Ear's killing teeth, her fear hadn't been for herself. Madsaw's weapons were little defense against fangs and claws, but he was war chief, a fearless man who would face death rather than run from it. If One

Ear attacked, if Madsaw was torn apart, she would see.

She would rather sacrifice herself than have that happen.

Suddenly Vasilii jerked up and back as a large hand clamped itself over his mouth. She felt the boy's fear, felt his futile battle, then relaxed as he stopped struggling. When she saw Vasilii turn and embrace Madsaw, her heart swelled and tears blurred her vision.

Holding Vasilii to his chest, Madsaw quickly returned to her. She stood, thinking to touch Vasilii in love and relief, but before she could stretch out her hand, her gaze locked with Madsaw's. She'd never seen that look on him before; all day he had kept his deepest emotions hidden from her, but now raw relief more powerful than a grizzly's strength etched itself on his features. There was nothing she could say or do, no words that would kill the residues of his long tension. In understanding, she laid her hand over his and squeezed. She blinked back more tears but felt no shame.

He simply nodded, his attention slowly traveling from her eyes to where her hand still pressed against his, and she knew she would never forget that his eyes, too, glistened.

"We have to hurry," he whispered. "There's a shorter way back."

He hadn't asked if she had the energy, but then she didn't expect him to—didn't want him to. As she helped a shaky Vasilii reach the ground, pride swelled her chest. For now at least, she and

Madsaw were one, and their only goal that of getting a boy safely out of the forest. Twice Vasilii started to say something, but his squeaky voice alarmed her and she held her finger to her mouth to silence him.

"Soon we'll talk," she reassured him. "But first we have to get to where it's safe."

Vasilii's eyes widened with fear at that, and he stared out at the forest, mouth trembling. If she hadn't been so uneasy herself, she might have laughed at the way he kept gnawing on his lower lip.

Madsaw squatted, indicating he wanted Vasilii to climb onto his back. When she saw that the boy had settled himself too low on Madsaw's hips, she gripped Vasilii around the waist and helped him into a better position. Madsaw stood, stared in the direction he'd indicated they were to go, then glanced over his shoulder at her.

Once again she was filled with the belief that they were equals—and that looking for a missing boy had shaken him deeply.

There seemed to be no end to the strength in Madsaw's legs. As she struggled to match his pace, she kept her attention trained on the effortless way his hips moved, his bunching and relaxing thigh muscles, his dark, naked buttocks. Although he walked soundlessly, she felt deep inside her the solid contact his feet made with the ground. He'd looped his arms around Vasilii's legs, which caused the muscles in his arms to remain tight. She wanted—she wanted nothing except to feel his body against hers. Rest? That could come later when the restlessness inside her had been satisfied. Sleep? Who could think of shutting out the world when Madsaw filled that world? She had to breathe deeply to keep her emotions from swamping her and was glad Madsaw couldn't look into her and guess what she was thinking.

Once he stopped to let Vasilii stretch his legs. He seemed not at all concerned with his own comfort, only asked with his eyes for her to tell him about the grizzly. In short, terse words that captured Vasilii's attention, she explained that One Ear's nose had brought him closer to where they'd found Vasilii. She didn't think he'd yet caught their scent, but if he did—

"Come on, Vasilii," Madsaw ordered. "We need to get going again."

Vasilii stood on tiptoe and stared at the underbrush that all but held them prisoner. "What bear? I don't see anything."

"Only Twana does," Madsaw said. "It is a gift."

"Then she's a witch like Sokolov says."

"She is a woman who helped find a lost boy."

Warmed by his words, Twana found the strength to once again keep up with Madsaw. Night was settling around them, coming early today because the storm clouds brought their own darkness. She was lost, utterly lost, and yet because Madsaw continued to walk with purpose, she knew he would lead her to safety. Over and over again she took her thoughts to One Ear, who was now so close to where Vasilii had sat that she shuddered. If the grizzly had found the boy before they did—

Madsaw didn't say anything, didn't ask what knowledge she held inside herself, and she understood he still put his trust in her. Despite herself, despite the warning hammering in her head, her heart formed an impossible image of how the day could end. They would return Vasilii to his parents, watch as a sobbing Kitlote clutched her son to her breasts. Then while the village buzzed with talk of what they'd accomplished, Madsaw would take her hand and lead her into their sleeping quarters. Apenas would take herself elsewhere. Once they were alone, Madsaw would pull her against him, whisper words of admiration and love—

Love? From Madsaw?

Shaken by her thought, she blinked furiously and concentrated on his powerful back. How could she be so foolish as to think that her captor might have such feelings for her? He was promised to another, was building a canoe as part of the bride-price. He'd taken her with him because she alone could tell him whether he would remain alive. That was the only reason.

"Madsaw?" His name rasped against her throat, and she had to swallow before she dared try again. "He has found where Vasilii stood. He is smelling the ground, roaring, pushing himself onto his hind legs and sniffing the air, dropping back down again."

"Has he found our trail?"

"He will. There is no way he won't."

Madsaw stopped and swung around toward her. "If he follows us, we will lead him to the village."

At that her blood turned cold. "The braves can stop him. Their weapons—"

"And he may kill some before we kill him."

She already knew that, but having Madsaw reinforce her worst fears made her legs feel like limp seaweed. She clamped cold fingers around her necklace. "It's me he wants. I will wait for him."

"No."

"It has to be, Madsaw," she insisted. "Better one childless woman than an entire village."

His night-shadowed eyes told her everything; he hated what she'd just said, wanted to fling the words from both of them. But he couldn't deny their honesty. Before he could speak, her body spasmed, taking her from him. She closed her eyes, concentrated.

"What is it?"

"He has found our trail."

If he had the power in him, Madsaw would have folded Twana against his chest and carried her to the beach, where he could place her in his finest canoe. It would be better to send her far out to sea than to face what they were facing right now. But he was no shaman; he could only deal with the reality of what she'd just seen. "Tell me," he hissed.

"He—had his nose pressed to the ground as if he could pull something from it. Then his body went rigid and he didn't move. Now—now he is pushing through the forest."

"He is coming our way?"

"Yes, but slowly."

Slowly. Maybe there was time for—time for what? Anguish swamped him as his thoughts dead-ended in a tangle of nothing.

"Listen to me," she was saying, her voice hauntingly calm. "Vasilii *has* to live. With its children dead, the Tillamooks will have no future."

She was right. Agony ripped into him, agony heavily mixed with a greater helplessness than he'd ever known. Thunder shook the earth and sky, but he could take no strength from his spirit. Shifting Vasilii's weight so he would have one free hand, he reached out and touched Twana's cheek. She leaned into him and warmed herself on his hand.

"I have no words," he whispered. Another thunderclap nearly stole what he was trying to say.

"I know." She seemed to shiver, but it might have been a trick of the lightning once again piercing the clouds. "Go, now!"

With Vasilii's innocent weight making its impact, he turned and took a step. When he looked back over his shoulder, she'd already begun to walk away from him. She looked so proud and straight, a woman bravely facing her death—a woman given courage simply because he'd touched her? Even before she spun around and stared at him, he knew she was going to do it. He should close his eyes, black out her image, run toward the safety of his village.

But Twana was willing to give up her life for those who should be her enemy; he would go to his death with that knowledge.

Feeling dead inside, he wrapped his arms securely around Vasilii's cold little legs and bent his back to his task. He could no longer hear Twana, was becoming less and less aware of her physical presence and guessed that she was once again walking away from him, maybe once again clutching her necklace. Lightning split the sky; he was still waiting for the thunder when he smelled rain. Almost immediately, fat raindrops began hitting the tops of the trees that surrounded him. He stopped and listened, felt the first wetness hit him. The trees buckled and waved as the wind picked up strength and Vasilii wrapped his arms even tighter around his neck. "Madsaw!" the boy gasped. "Thunderbird is angry. He throws lightning at us."

Madsaw understood Vasilii's fear, but what he felt was far different. Ignoring the rain now pelting both him and the ground, he cried out for Twana. The wind screamed, as, it seemed, did the forest itself. He tried again, straining to hear a sound that wasn't part of the storm. Frustration whipped at him, making it nearly impossible for him to concentrate, and then he heard—or thought he heard—her soft yet strong voice.

"Twana! Come to me!"

Just as he'd decided to go after her, she appeared, her hair already sodden with water, head bent to protect her face from violently driven raindrops. He was unable to see into her eyes, but it didn't matter. Little did except knowing that she wasn't walking to her death tonight.

"He can't find us in a storm," he said when

they'd covered the distance that separated them and she stood looking up at him with one hand shielding her face. "He will seek shelter."

She nodded but said nothing, and he knew she was searching for One Ear. He waited out her journey until he sensed that she'd returned to him.

"He has found a tree with a hollowed-out place in its trunk. It is just large enough for his body, and he is curling himself into it, tucking his nose under his leg to protect it."

She'd delivered her words without emotion, but he couldn't believe she felt nothing. When she covered his wet arm with her equally wet fingers, he understood what mere words could never tell him.

"Let's go home," he whispered. As he started toward where he'd spent his entire life, he knew that before the night was over, he would tell her that he'd never known anyone braver than she.

He might even tell her that she'd touched his heart in a way it would never forget.

No one was outside when they reached the village, but because the rain continued to cascade down, Madsaw hadn't expected to see anyone. By now he was cold and tired and hungry, and guessed that Twana's discomfort matched his. Still, she would want to see the boy reunited with his parents before tending to her own needs. When he paused, she stepped beside him. She no longer tried to protect her face from the rain; he felt the same way. The storm had won and they were simply exhausted survivors. "I sent Kitlote so many thoughts," she told him. "I prayed that her heart would find peace, but I knew it was a hollow hope. Only holding her son will give her rest."

"It is not an easy thing being a parent; my mother has said that often."

"Living, being part of someone else, is not an easy thing."

She was thinking of her mother, and maybe remembering that he, too, had felt the keen pain of losing someone he loved. For a moment he simply stood where he was as the knowledge that he would never forget this day and night with Twana became part of him. Their lives might cease to be as one, but they would always have this.

For as long as they lived, they would both remember that they'd saved a boy's life and revealed a little of their hearts to each other.

Twana stepped inside Kitlote's house first. He followed, Vasilii now walking beside him instead of being carried as befitted a future brave. He saw Kitlote and Stokim leap from where they'd been crouched before the fire, heard a woman's sharp cry, watched Kitlote run to Vasilii and clutch her son to her breast. Beside her, her husband touched his son's back with a trembling hand.

"You found . . ." Kitlote swallowed and tried again. "You found him."

"He's fine," Twana whispered. She wanted to say more, but her throat tightened until she could barely breathe. How long had she waited for this moment? It seemed that thoughts of seeing Vasilii back with his parents had filled her forever; it would be a long time before she was done looking at three people holding on to each other, mother and child crying unashamedly, father shaking.

Madsaw stood beside her, his body now steaming in the heated room. Her own legs threatened to collapse under her, and yet he seemed capable of standing forever.

"He's a brave boy," Madsaw told Stokim. "And wise to remain where he was instead of running. If he had, he might have injured himself."

Kitlote finally released her grip on Vasilii and, on legs that looked no stronger than Twana's, stumbled toward Madsaw. She stared up at him, tears streaming down her cheeks. "You saved my son. You brought him back to me."

"Not just me, Kitlote."

Still trembling, Kitlote faced Twana. Her body swayed; she looked incapable of taking another step. Not waiting, Twana pulled the other woman against her. She'd thought herself beyond any more tears, been proud of her ability to concentrate on the search instead of giving in to emotion, but the moment Kitlote hugged her back, she felt as if she'd been caught in a wild river's grip. Sobs racked her body and she clung to Kitlote with a strength she thought beyond her.

"I prayed—" Kitlote took a shaky breath. "I prayed until my heart failed me."

"It doesn't matter," Twana soothed. "He's safe; that is the only thing."

"I thought—I thought I would die with the pain."

She'd felt that way when her mother disappeared, but her mother had been a woman and not a small boy—not someone who had come from her own body. In that moment when there was no sound except for the rain pounding on the roof, she knew what it was to be a mother willing to lay down her own life for her child. Emotion washed over and through her, and without knowing she was going to do it, she found herself looking at Madsaw. Her arms were still around Kitlote; she still shared the woman's tears and trembling, but now her thoughts went to Madsaw.

In his eyes she learned how much they shared.

CHAPTER 10

Twana had no idea how long she and Madsaw remained with Vasilii's family. She didn't sit for fear she wouldn't be able to stand again, and when Madsaw finally told her they needed to go home, she followed him back out into the storm on feet that felt as if they weighed as much as two boulders. Rain continued to slash its way to the ground. It was as if the torrent and wind were at battle with each other, each fighting for dominance. The central fire had gone out, and without a moon to guide her, she might have lost her way if it hadn't been for Madsaw's silent form ahead of her.

His feet, guided by a lifetime of walking the path between one house and anther, made a soft plodding sound on the wet ground, a sound like so many others that came from him and instantly became part of her. When lightning briefly bathed the village in white-gold, his body was sharply outlined and she knew she would never forget what he looked like at this moment.

They were nearly to his house when she stopped, letting him go in ahead of her. Utterly alone now, she allowed the night to envelop her. She was aware of wet cold, the wind's howling song, forest smells that had existed since before the first Indian set foot upon this land. The traders came from a place she couldn't imagine, would never want to see. She'd heard of the Tlingit, who lived in the frozen land of the winter wind, and the Yurok, who made their home where the summer sun dried the earth, but this rainy place was her home. She shared it with her people and now with the Tillamook and their war chief.

And with One Ear.

Although she had to spread her legs to keep from collapsing, she took the time to send her thoughts out through the night to the sleeping grizzly. *Thank you. For a small boy's life, I thank you. Do you hear me, One Ear? Vasilii is just beginning his life. He has done no wrong to anyone, lifted his hand against none of your kind.*

It seemed as if One Ear stirred, but she couldn't be sure. Not fully understanding why, she continued.

I, too, have lost my mother, One Ear. Maybe we share something, you and I. Share the same heart.

The great mound that was his body moved. She waited, touching him with her heart and mind, fearful and yet not afraid. He lifted his head and stared out at the night. Then—then he blinked and looked into her eyes.

She couldn't move; even the blood in her veins seemed to cease its journey. The little eyes so inadequate for the rest of him gave out a message different from what she'd received from any other animal. She didn't understand the difference, didn't know what to do with it. All she knew was that he was looking at her and something passed between them.

The grizzly stretched his head even farther as if he, too, was trying to make sense of something beyond his comprehension; she told herself it couldn't be, a bear simply existed. He knew nothing except satisfying his body's demands.

But this wasn't the first time she and One Ear had looked at each other.

I don't hate you. I can't. Do you understand that?

Not blinking, One Ear continued to stare at her.

Madsaw had begun to grow concerned by the time Twana entered. When he saw the look on her face, he stopped in midreach for something to eat so he could turn his full attention on her. She seemed different somehow, as if something beyond his understanding had touched her. When he handed her a piece of salmon, he had to speak her name before she stirred herself enough to take it from him, and when she started to shiver, he led her to the fire.

"You found Vasilii?" Apenas asked for the second time. "How can that be?"

Madsaw put his mind to answering his mother, but as the telling slowly emerged, his thoughts continued to be split between Apenas and Twana. The mysterious look slowly faded from his hostage's eyes to be replaced by exhaustion so deep, he wondered if she might fall asleep where she sat. The rain had plastered her dress to her body. She looked smaller than he remembered, more child than woman tonight. Because he'd spent the day with her, he knew how much strength there was to her. At first it worried him to see her like this, but then he realized he'd been given something precious. Always before she had kept a barrier between them. Tonight she was nothing except naked exhaustion and relief.

And something else.

Halfway through a bite, she stopped chewing to stare over at him. Her grizzly-colored eyes had become like deep pools of water. They shimmered, waited, touched him. He reached out in the only way he knew how, too spent himself to have any defenses against her. With his mind he answered her unspoken message. Yes, today they had saved a boy's life. Yes, today they had been equals, two people driven by the same fears and hopes and determination. Yes, she had been willing to sacrifice herself for his village. Yes, he would always remember.

"Madsaw. How did you know where to search?" his mother prompted.

"Her gift." If the others became aware of the invisible ropes that held him and Twana together, so be it. "She found Vasilii. Without her, the boy wouldn't be alive."

"You don't know that. Maybe he would have found his way home in the morning."

"Not if the grizzly reached him."

Apenas's mouth sagged and her eyes suddenly looked stricken. He wished he had the energy to hug her, because no matter how much she was ruled by her family's place in the village, she was under it all a mother with a mother's instinct to protect a child.

"You saw a grizzly?" Chief Walkus asked.

"Not me. Her. Her magic, her gift, warned her of the bear's presence and she told me."

"What are you saying? Lies, all lies! Madsaw, you are war chief! To let the witch throw a spell over you! It makes me sick."

Madsaw jumped to his feet and faced Sokolov. "You have no right," he warned the intruding and unwelcome shaman. "This is my home. You enter it only when you have permission."

"Permission!" Sokolov spat. His tangled mass of hair lay in wet, plastered clumps against the sides of his face, its condition telling him that the shaman hadn't taken time to put on a rain hat after hearing what had happened. "When a chief falls under a witch's spell, a shaman does what he must. She is evil! She walks with Land Otter Man, has taken your hair and buried it near a grave house."

"Stop it!" Madsaw felt his mother's eyes on him begging him not to anger the shaman further, but neither her plea or what his chief might think meant more at this moment then possible danger to Twana. "You didn't walk with us today," he told Sokolov. "You did not see what happened, didn't carry Vasilii back to safety."

Sokolov lifted his arm out from under his cape to reveal his soul catcher, which he shook in Twana's direction. She stared back at him. "She has taken your soul, Madsaw," Sokolov continued. "Made you so blind that you cannot see."

"Blind?" Madsaw taunted. "What I saw was a boy so lost that only a woman with magical sight could find him. She could have left him there, left me at the mercy of a grizzly. But she didn't."

A low murmur told him that others were weighing what he'd just said. Twana's exhaustion was no more. Like him, she'd become alert, cautious, angry, and he silently thanked her for having the wisdom not to confront the shaman. He'd spent his life around Sokolov and knew how closely the man guarded his pride. If a hostage challenged him, her life would be at risk.

"It is a trick, Madsaw," Sokolov continued, his attention now darting between Chief Walkus and Apenas. "A witch's trick."

"What witch walks back into her captor's village?"

"One who flaunts her black powers."

Madsaw knew he should say something, but momentary weakness washed over him, reminding him of how much energy he'd expended today.

"Listen to me." Sokolov directed his speech to the entire room. "I have made medicine today, medicine that made it possible to look into the witch's heart."

"You lie, shaman."

"Never! You are a fool for not believing, Madsaw, a fool. Listen to me and listen well. It is she—" he jabbed the soul catcher in Twana's direction "—who sent an innocent boy deep within the forest. You think Vasilii only became lost? If you do, you are blind. What child doesn't know to remain close to his village? Are they not taught that from the moment they learn to walk? But Vasilii's feet did not belong to him today. *She* claimed his senses and forced him to walk until he no longer knew where he was. *She* found him, not because of this thing you call her sight, but because she knew where she had sent him."

Someone whispered, "Is it possible?" and Madsaw thought he recognized his mother's voice. He wanted to shake her, and yet he understood why she might believe the lie; Sokolov, and his father before him, had always been part of her world.

Weariness continued to assault him, making it nearly impossible for him to form the words he needed to battle the shaman. "You speak nonsense," he challenged. "Words with no weight behind them. You say you made magic, but no one saw you work it. You fear her sight; that's why you refuse to acknowledge it."

"Fear?" A bubble of spittle formed at the corner of Sokolov's mouth. "I have no need of fear; my magic is too strong. It is you who should shrink from her, but it is too late. You are under her spell."

From out of the corner of his eye, Madsaw noted that Twana's fists were clenched. He couldn't let her attack the shaman; if she did, Sokolov's hate would know no bounds.

"Leave!" he ordered Sokolov. "This is my home. You have no right to enter. I will not say it again."

"What will you do, Madsaw? Kill me?"

At the moment he believed himself capable of doing just that; if his body hadn't felt weighted with rocks, he would have shoved the shaman back out into the storm. "Do not tempt me, shaman."

"Madsaw, no!" Apenas gasped.

"Madsaw, careful," his chief and uncle warned.

"Listen to them." Sokolov jabbed the soul catcher at him. "They speak words of wisdom, words you would heed if she hadn't stolen your soul. Listen to me, all of you!" His voice rose until it echoed off the walls and nearly blocked out the sound of the rain. "I say it! The witch has worked her powerful spell today. She is responsible for what happened to Vasilii. She is! Today she tests her strength on a boy, on the war chief. Tomorrow she will turn her evil on the entire village."

"Leave!" His legs, which a moment ago had been limp, suddenly filled with strength and propelled Madsaw toward the shaman. The smell of old fat hit his nostrils, and for the first time he noticed that Sokolov had covered his face with seal blubber as protection against the weather. Fine! Being thrown outside wouldn't bother him. "I say it. This is my home and you have no place here."

Head pounding, Twana stared at Madsaw. Long after Sokolov backed out of the opening, muttering over and over again that she would destroy the entire village if not stopped, Madsaw continued to pace from one end of the great room to the other. The little children hid behind their mother's legs when he came close, and even Chief Walkus remained silent. Apenas gaped at her son as if she'd never seen him before, her face pale. She muttered a warning, but Madsaw paid her no mind, and after a moment, Apenas fell silent, her attention now fixed on Walkus as if she expected her chief to end Madsaw's anger.

Walkus didn't try, and Twana guessed the older man understood that some emotions simply needed to run themselves out before a warrior regained his senses.

"Madsaw, stop," Chief Walkus finally warned when Madsaw stalked over to the opening and stared out into the night. "It is over."

"It isn't over. You know that."

"It is for tonight. You and I will talk in the morning."

Madsaw spoke with his back to his uncle. "I will not take back what I said. He's wrong. Dangerously wrong."

"Sleep, my nephew."

Walkus slipped past Madsaw without touching him, but as the rain reached out to claim him, he turned back around. "Say no more," he said softly. "First sleep."

Sleep.

Twana fought off the word, but it returned to sap her arms and legs of what little strength remained in them. Madsaw hadn't given her permission to go to bed; if he didn't, she would cover herself with a blanket and fall asleep where she sat. In truth, she would rather do that because if she was out here, she wouldn't have to spend the night next to him.

Him.

Him . . .

She became aware of someone pulling her to her feet, but it wasn't until she felt a man's hard body along her length that her mind fastened on what Madsaw had done. At his prompting, she took a stumbling step toward the sleeping curtain, but when she could barely drag her other leg forward, he lifted her in his arms. Clinging to his neck, she breathed in his wet, warm smell, felt his trembling muscles, listened to his heart beating. Apenas hissed something, but what Apenas thought didn't matter.

Only Madsaw did.

The night was spent in bits and pieces of dreams, sometimes ruled by One Ear but usually filled with Madsaw. Twana stirred several times to reassure herself that he was sleeping beside her. She should be at his feet; that was how it had been before. But either he'd placed her beside him or, in her sleep, she'd sought him. In the end, she stopped questioning and simply surrendered.

Madsaw was next to her; they'd survived a day together in the wilderness and brought a boy safely home. She'd looked into One Ear's eyes and felt something that defied understanding.

And somewhere in the middle of that day, she'd wrapped her arms around Madsaw and he'd held her close and there'd been nothing else.

Now, as the house began to stir, Twana forced herself to put sleep behind her. Madsaw sighed, his rough hand dragging over her arm. She touched his thumb, not surprised to find that even her fingernail was capable of absorbing his heat.

"Don't touch him, Twana."

"I didn't mean— There was nothing—"

"I know what I see," Apenas whispered. "I will not let you take his soul; before that happens—"

"Mother!"

Although scant firelight entered the quarters, Twana saw Apenas flinch from her son's outburst. She wanted to tell him that Apenas was simply speaking with a mother's heart, but it wasn't her place to stand between the two of them.

"I have to say it," Apenas protested. "Her hold on you is so strong. If I don't protect you from her, you will be lost."

"I'm not a child, Mother. I know my own mind."

"Your mind! She has touched your body, your man's body. Don't you see that?"

Grunting in exasperation, Madsaw stood and stalked out of the room. Not giving herself time to think, Twana hurried after him. It continued to

199

rain, but gentler now as if the storm were trying to pace itself. The two young children were seated in front of the fire watching their mother add hot rocks to the boiling basket. Twana did what she could to straighten her twisted and still damp dress, then walked outside and into the nearby forest to relieve herself. That done, she closed her eyes and looked for One Ear, easily finding him where she'd left him last night. He looked as if he hadn't moved, his great body slowly rising and falling as he breathed, and she wondered if she'd only imagined what had happened between them last night.

By the time she returned to the house, the children were standing at the entrance, staring out at the rain. Madsaw sat near the fire eating dried herring eggs. He seemed oblivious to his surroundings, and she moved slowly so as not to draw his attention to her.

It seemed that Apenas's eyes never left her, and although twice Twana boldly returned the older woman's hard gaze, she didn't want to confront Apenas. She'd discovered that her right instep was deeply bruised and was glad simply to sit. She'd just finished examining it when Kitlote slipped through the opening and hurried over to her.

"I didn't say it enough last night," Kitlote blurted, ignoring everyone else. "There aren't enough words to thank you."

"None are necessary. I understand."

"Do you? Can you?"

Twana couldn't answer that. She thought she

knew what it meant to feel as if she were drowning in fear, but Kitlote was speaking with a mother's heart—something beyond her comprehension.

"The terror I lived with—all night I kept reaching out to touch him, to assure myself that he really was back with me. He said you and Madsaw had to walk a long way before you got him back to the village."

"Vasilii's energy had taken him far into the forest."

Kitlote shuddered at that, then dropped to her knees beside Twana. For a moment she simply stared at Twana's foot, then gently touched the bruised area. "You hurt yourself. What about Madsaw? He carried my son so far."

"I don't know."

"He didn't tell you how he feels?"

"No." Twana dropped her voice to a whisper. "We have not spoken to each other this morning, or during the night."

"Oh." Kitlote glanced at Madsaw, who was now talking to one of his brothers-in-law. "That's not right."

"He was exhausted. And—Sokolov was here last night."

"He came to us, too, warned us not to be fooled by you, that you were simply testing your strength. I can't believe that."

Twana was grateful for Kitlote's belief in her, but one woman's words against a shaman's anger wasn't enough. Because she didn't want to burden Kitlote with her thoughts, she asked about Vasilii and learned that the boy was still asleep. "He hasn't moved since he went to bed. A few times he muttered something. When he did, I held him against me and he quieted."

Madsaw was getting to his feet. Twana struggled to think of something to say to Kitlote, but just knowing that he was heading their way stripped her mind of all other thought. He walked with the sureness she'd come to expect from him; if he still felt the effects of yesterday's long journey, he hid it well.

For a moment his eyes raked over her. She struggled against the impulse to shrink from him and from the equally powerful need to wrap her body around his. Still standing, he asked Kitlote about her son. Kitlote answered in detail, explaining that the other children were anxious to talk to Vasilii about his adventure but were learning a lesson in patience.

"I know I thanked you," Kitlote went on, dividing her attention between Twana and Madsaw. "But those words seem so inadequate." She ran her hands restlessly over her dress. "That is why I came here this morning. I have my husband's blessing in this. He may say little, but he was as frightened as me, and his relief is the same. We—we offer the two of you everything we have in gratitude."

Twana barely suppressed a gasp. Although not one of the wealthiest men, Stokim was a skilled trapper, and no one had a larger pile of furs than he. "You can't—" she began.

"Possessions mean nothing when a child's life is at stake."

Tatooktche would never believe that. Casting off unwanted thoughts of her stepfather, Twana again tried to tell Kitlote that she hadn't once thought of being rewarded when she set off to find Vasilii.

"It doesn't matter. You returned life to my heart. Both of you," Kitlote added, nodding at Madsaw. "Whatever you want, whatever we have, it is for you."

"No. Not for both of them."

Twana hadn't seen Apenas approaching. She stood beside her son, body tense, thin mouth working. When she looked down at Kitlote, her expression softened a little. "I share your relief. To be frightened for one's child's life is a terrible thing, but your gratitude must be extended to my son, not her." Apenas glared at Twana, then again focused her attention on Kitlote. "The woman is a hostage. She is not worthy of accepting gifts."

"Mother," Madsaw warned. "This is *not* your concern."

"It is," Apenas insisted. "You are of my body, Madsaw. Do not ever forget that."

"Have I? Kitlote, listen to me. Your offer means a great deal to me. I know it comes from the depth of your heart, but I cannot accept."

"But—"

"In that my mother is right. Neither Twana or I want to reduce you to poverty."

"It wouldn't be poverty, not as long as we have our son."

A smile touched Madsaw's lips, and for an instant his eyes seemed less dark. "I understand," he continued patiently. "But I will say it again. Twana and I didn't search for your son because we were filled with thoughts of wealth. What we did was done out of love and concern and is not something that can be rewarded with furs."

Although Kitlote continued to stare up at Madsaw, she remained silent. Clearly this wasn't what she'd expected to hear. Twana, too, couldn't take her eyes off Madsaw. He had been right, utterly right, to turn down Kitlote's offer. Without having to consult her, he'd known she felt the same way, that the only reward she'd needed was finding Vasilii alive and safe.

Still, Apenas had voiced a truth. She was a hostage, subject to the whims and decisions of the man who'd captured her.

Kitlote started to stand, then sank back down beside Twana. Awkwardly she reached out to embrace Twana. Finally, aware that both Madsaw and Apenas were watching them, Twana took a deep, unsteady breath. "Return to your son," she whispered. "Tell him—tell him I love him."

Madsaw had left with Kitlote. Because he hadn't said anything to her, Twana could only guess that he wanted to talk to Stokim. She remained where she'd been sitting, her thoughts both tangled and dark. She wanted Madsaw here with her, and yet she was glad for his absence. She had been with him for an entire day and night, and needed time alone—time to bring her emotions back under control.

She was absently rubbing the flesh around her

bruise, thinking about how tightly Madsaw had clutched Vasilii to him last night, when a shadow enveloped her. Thinking Sokolov might have entered without her having seen him, she looked up, but it was Apenas. With a sharp jerk of her head, Apenas indicated she wanted her to join her in the sleeping quarters.

"I will say this to you only this one time," Apenas began tersely once they were alone. "You are not to touch my son as if you are equals. You are his responsibility, his possession, not a true woman."

"I didn't—"

"Quiet! If he takes you, you will submit. I cannot stop my son from being a man. But if you try to take his heart, I will kill you."

Kill you. Apenas's warning echoed inside her, making it nearly impossible for her to think. "Would you rather I hadn't gone with him?" she asked. "Maybe you believe a boy's life is not such a terrible thing to sacrifice as long as I remain apart from your son."

Apenas slapped her, the blow snapping her head backward. Before she could recover, Apenas grabbed her shoulders, bringing her face so close to hers that the older woman's breath pressed against her flesh in an unsteady rhythm. "I would lay down my life for my son," Apenas hissed while Twana fought the impulse to free herself. If she struggled, she might injure Apenas, and no matter how she felt about Madsaw's mother, she couldn't do that. "Did you hear me?" Apenas continued. "My life is a small thing to give in exchange for my son's freedom. If you are truly a witch, I may have sung my death song. And maybe—maybe I will kill you first."

"Why?"

"Why?" Apenas repeated. "Because that may be the only way to stop your evil."

CHAPTER 11

The day after Madsaw and Twana returned with Vasilii, a scout brought word that the traders would reach the village before nightfall. Madsaw sat inside his uncle's house saying little as Chief Walkus conferred with other clan leaders about how to insure a successful trade. The others kept glancing at him, but they knew why he refused to have anything to do with the sea-strangers. His brother had been gone since the day he and Twana went looking for Vasilii. By now Lukstch should be at the Nisqually village presenting his demands to Tatooktche.

Not for the first time, Madsaw felt uneasy. Still, Lukstch wasn't afraid of anyone or anything and had promised he would make sure Tatooktche listened to everything he had to say. Because

Lukstch intended to present his demands in public, Tatooktche wouldn't dare ignore the command to compensate Madsaw for their father's murder. How Tatooktche reacted to that command, Madsaw couldn't say.

Around him an argument raged about whether it was better to present the traders with the female slaves after the trading had been completed or offer them as soon as the sea-strangers came into the village. Chief Walkus insisted that the utmost goodwill was necessary and could only be accomplished once the men's physical needs had been met. Others argued that the sea-strangers might be a long time satisfying themselves, thus delaying the trade until it was nearly time for them to leave for the Nisqually villages.

"Speak, Madsaw," his uncle insisted. "What do you say on this?"

"It doesn't matter. I won't be here."

"Can you say that for the rest of your life? What about when you take my place?"

"You are right. I'm sorry. My mind was on other things."

"Maybe on your hostage," an older man teased. "If you grow weary of looking after her, I offer my services. She will have no complaints about my treatment of her."

Madsaw laughed because it was expected of him, but he knew that as long as there was breath in his body, he wouldn't let Twana step inside Maquinna's house. Maquinna had worn out two wives and was trying to arrange a marriage with a girl no older than his daughter.

A girl. Soon he, too, would take a child under his roof and call her his wife.

With an effort, he forced his mind onto the matter at hand, telling the others that he believed the traders should first be given what they'd come to expect. Once they'd been in the woods with the slaves of their choice, cooking should commence. As soon as the smell of smoked salmon, steamed clams, fresh berries, roasted elk, and sun-dried salalberry cakes filled the air, the traders would have more than sex on their minds.

Even Chief Walkus laughed at that. "It is a shame your brother isn't here. He would show the sea-strangers how to eat."

Thinking of Lukstch's love of food, which rivaled his interest in his wife, Madsaw smiled. "He and I talked long about when to carry my demands to Tatooktche. I thought he would want to wait until after the trading; if he did, I would say nothing."

"He is growing up, finally. He knows Tatooktche won't take your demands seriously if they don't come for a long time. Besides, if he waited, the sea-strangers would have reached the Nisqually village and his words would go unheard there. Lukstch has asked me to do his trading for him. I hope I will be successful."

Madsaw had no doubt of that. Although not the oldest man in the village, his uncle had a presence about him that made others respect him. He continued to sit, contributing what he believed he needed to, until everything had been decided and the others left. Chief Walkus reached into a small basket and removed a pinch of tobacco mixed with lime, which he placed in his mouth. Then he handed the basket to Madsaw.

"You have not changed your mind?" Walkus said thoughtfully. "You truly cannot bring yourself to look at the traders?"

"My anger will only jeopardize the trade. You know that."

"I know what you believe. I just needed to hear it one more time from your lips."

Madsaw nodded and placed a tiny amount of tobacco between his teeth and cheek. He'd never acquired a taste for tobacco, but his uncle considered it a rare treat and offered it only when he was in a particularly generous mood. "I thank you for agreeing to stand in my place," he said. "By the time you have haggled for both me and my brother, you will be exhausted, unable to demand a good price for your furs."

"How little you know me, nephew. I intend to think of myself first. If I still have energy, I may try to get a few glass beads in exchange for all your hunting."

"If I believed that, I would not leave." Still smiling, Madsaw grew suddenly serious. "Some say I have lost my senses. If anyone else were chief, or if I had already taken on those duties, I would put that first."

"I understand. Madsaw, I loved Vattan, and I saw your anger, your grief, at her death. Those things remain inside you. A wise man does not knowingly open old wounds, especially when the welfare of an entire village must be considered."

Madsaw simply nodded. Still, what his uncle

had said meant a great deal to him, and with his thoughtful silence, he hoped to let Walkus know that.

"Tell me something," Walkus said after a short silence. "Is it as Sokolov says? Your hostage can indeed see animals hidden from all other eyes?"

"I believe in her gift." Since leaving the forest, he'd said nothing to Twana except to ask her about One Ear. She'd assured him that the grizzly had found so much to eat where he was that he roamed little. That, they both knew, could change. "Sokolov is wrong. She's not a witch."

"Maybe she would use this gift to help you with your hunting."

Madsaw shrugged, his thoughts going to Twana, whom he'd told to stay inside so she could finish work on his mother's hat. She, too, seemed to want to have as little to do with him as possible; he just wished he were comfortable with that. "She won't be here that long," he finally thought to say.

"Maybe. Maybe not. Your demands may be such that Tatooktche can never meet them. Perhaps you wish her by your side forever."

Did he? Right now he didn't dare look deep enough inside himself to uncover the answer—or maybe the truth was, he already knew.

Madsaw remained with his uncle awhile longer, then, driven by restlessness, he left the chief's house and stepped out into the foggy, misting day. The traders would soon be here. Even now he felt himself being torn between his desire to leave and fear for Twana's safety. He'd told both her and his mother that he wanted her to remain inside as long as long as the traders were in the village. She was a beautiful woman; if one of the sea-strangers chanced to see her . . .

Half-angry at himself, he wrenched his thoughts free. He was already late in leaving for the Raven Clan village. If he didn't hurry, he would be considered rude, and both he and his future father-in-law would be shamed. But instead of turning his steps in that direction, he continued to stare out at the forest, admitting to himself, if no one else, that he had no wish to sit down with Cleaskinch.

"Madsaw! Stop!"

Sokolov's strident voice instantly splintered his thoughts. "You are leaving?" the shaman asked, his tone accusatory.

"What I do is none of your affair."

"These are the words of a leader?" Sokolov spat. "I think not. To run away—"

"Not running. I have business elsewhere."

"With Cleaskinch. Yes, I know all about that, have consulted the spirits, who say it is good that the Wolf and Raven Clans be united. But this cannot be done another time, when no one will miss the war chief?"

Sokolov's role was to heal; he had no right expressing himself on tribal matters. Because he didn't want to waste time in an unnecessary argument with Sokolov, Madsaw stepped around the shorter man. Sokolov grabbed his arm with dry fingers, pinching into his flesh. "Listen to me,

Madsaw! She isn't with you now. Her hold on you weakens when she can't touch you with her evil. You *must* listen."

Madsaw jerked free, the urge to strike Sokolov so strong, it took all his will to battle it.

"I speak the truth. She will only bring destruction to us if she remains here. Return her to Tatooktche, now. If he won't take her, you must kill her."

"Why do you hate her so?"

Sokolov said nothing, but then he didn't need to. Even before he met her, the shaman had spoken against Twana. Now everyone knew Twana had done the impossible by finding Vasilii. Sokolov had insisted that Vasilii's parents would never see their son again because they had broken a taboo; Twana had proven him wrong.

The shaman would never forgive her for that.

Should he take Twana with him? The thought died almost as soon as it came to life. He was going to see the girl he'd soon marry. How could he face Kukankh and her father with Twana beside him—still inside him?

"I say this to you, shaman," he said forcefully. "Twana has been ordered to remain inside my house while the traders are here. If you so much as look at her, I will make war on you. Do you understand?"

"What a great war chief you are, threatening to murder a shaman because of a hostage."

"I'm not that foolish. If your medicine failed and a member of my family died, I would be within my rights to spill your blood, but the hostage is not a

Tillamook. I simply give you a warning; touch her and you will live to regret it."

The air felt close and stale, as if it had been in too many lungs before reaching hers. Heat from the fire had spread throughout the house, and if she hadn't been so tense, Twana might have grown sleepy. Outside, she heard excited voices as the villagers called out in greeting to the traders. On the few occasions when the strangers bartered with the Nisqually, the trading had been done at nearby Beaver Dam, a sacred place full of good luck. Twana and her mother had always remained in the village, Saha quietly obeying Tatooktche, Twana filled with curiosity about men who lived on the other side of the sea.

Today she was hidden because that was what Madsaw wanted.

Madsaw. Despite the distracting commotion outside, her thoughts clung to the last time she'd seen him. Not long ago he'd stepped inside, picked up a basket full of seal oil, a fish-oil dipper, and a miniature wooden carving of his canoe—all gifts a man might take to his future in-laws. Although his words had been for his mother, he'd stared at her for a long time as if wanting to remember a great deal about her. He hadn't come close enough to touch her, and yet he'd somehow left a part of himself lingering on her flesh. His eyes had been dark but without the shine she was used to; confused, she'd absently fingered her necklace, and he'd studied the gesture.

He didn't want to leave, didn't want to sit in a

near stranger's house and talk about taking a girl for his wife. But he knew his duty, knew and obeyed.

A shrill laugh followed by a woman's high-pitched squeal shattered Twana's thoughts. Despite Madsaw's orders, she hurried to the doorway and peered out. From where she was, she couldn't see much, just that everyone, it seemed, was gathering in front of Chief Walkus's house. She caught glimpses of several men dressed in heavy furs with fur hats on their heads, but because they were in the middle of the growing group, she couldn't be sure how many of them there were.

All she knew was that suddenly her heart felt as if it had been touched by a dead man's finger.

Shocked, she stumbled backward and reached for a wall to steady herself against. Her vision blurred, and her head pounded until she thought she might be sick. She desperately wanted to look out again so she might better understand, but it was easier—safer—to remain where she was.

Could she somehow have glimpsed One Ear just beyond the village? If her thoughts had been so full of Madsaw that she'd lost touch with the grizzly, maybe One Ear had found her without her knowing. When she could trust her balance, she closed her eyes and took herself beyond Madsaw's house. Her attention was first drawn to a doe and her twin fawns bedded down not far from the river, but they didn't long hold her interest. Several mice were about, and on the opposite side of the river from the deer, an elk grazed. The river itself was full of fish, and far upstream from where the Wolf Clan bathed, a beaver had begun work on a cottonwood. Up the feeder stream she went in her mind until the banks became jagged rocks and water tumbled loudly over a series of small waterfalls. She'd been here many times in her thoughts, loving the contrast between steep hillsides and protected meadows where the stream flowed wide and slow and shallow. It was in one of those meadows, with sunlight nourishing tiny white wildflowers, that she found One Ear. He was all but sitting in the stream, his rump crushing some of the flowers while he swatted playfully at whatever he'd found in the water.

No, this was not a dangerous animal.

Then what—

Gathering her courage, she'd started toward the opening again when she spotted Sokolov and Apenas walking her way. She shrank back, then held her ground. Apenas didn't look at her; it was as if Madsaw's mother wanted nothing to do with her. Sokolov's glare was so intense that it was all she could do not to scream. Pushing ahead of Apenas, Sokolov boldly stepped inside. Knowing that if she showed fear, Sokolov would take advantage of it, she continued to stand where she was.

"You are a beautiful woman, Twana. Beautiful like a poisonous snake."

"What do you want?"

"The witch is not a fool," Sokolov told Apenas. "Your son does not see the danger; he will never see it as long as she spins her web over him."

"What do you want?" Twana repeated. Sokolov

smelled of old grease, making her wonder if he ever washed himself.

"That is none of your concern, Twana. A decision has been made." He jerked his head in Apenas's direction. "You will accept it."

No! But until she knew what Sokolov was talking about, she would be wise to remain as quiet and calm as possible. A sharp squeal came from the gathered villagers, this one tinged with panic, and she guessed a trader had selected a female slave for his use.

"You heard," Sokolov chortled. "Soon you will know that woman's pleasure."

"What are you talking about?"

He moved just enough to block the entrance. "I have talked to Madsaw's mother." He again indicated Apenas. "She agrees that the traders will find favor with you."

"No! Madsaw said I was to remain inside, out of sight of the sea-strangers."

"My son does not know his own mind."

"How can you say that? Did he not bring Vasilii safely home?"

"Because he was under your spell," Sokolov answered, eyes narrowing until they almost became lost in his fleshy face. "I did not come here to argue with a hostage. I have spoken with the spirits. I." He poked his undersized chest. "They told me the truth, the truth you keep hidden from Madsaw."

"You waited until he was gone," she challenged. *Escape!* "Is that a brave man?"

"A wise and cautious man," Sokolov said with a

smirk. "Look at her, Apenas. I have watched her with a man's eye, seen the way she carries herself, how her body calls to your son."

"He wants her," Apenas muttered.

"Because she has captured his soul. But you are not as powerful as you believe, Twana. I dare you; fly to freedom."

"I can't fly; no human can."

"Ah! The witch admits there are limits to her powers. Limits—" his hand snaked out so quickly to capture her wrist that she didn't have time to evade him "—that all others will see once the traders are done with you." He began pulling, his weight and punishing fingers more than she could resist.

"No!" she gasped. "Madsaw—"

Sokolov slapped her with such force that her head snapped back. Dizzy, she only half heard him order her to be silent. When he tried to grab her other wrist, she kicked at him, but he evaded her foot. He hit her again, this time using his fist.

"Stop it!" Apenas shrieked. "You will not treat her like an animal."

"I do what I must. Otherwise, she will try to escape."

Escape was very much on Twana's mind, but until she could clear her head, she didn't trust her legs to take her to freedom. Sokolov now had hold of both of her wrists, gripping them so tightly that her fingers had begun to turn numb. His strength frightened her. Apenas stepped closer; in the older woman's features she saw too much of the son, remembered the way Madsaw had looked at her earlier today—remembered their time alone.

If she ran now, she might never see him again.

"Listen to me," Apenas insisted. "Listen and understand why I am here with Sokolov. I am a mother; a mother wants nothing more than her children's happiness. My son has mourned long enough; it is time for him to find peace with a new wife."

"He doesn't want—"

"How dare you say what he does or doesn't want! You are not one of us, Twana. You will never be. I will *not* have him walk your way; I will *not*."

How many times had she heard Apenas say that? "You think turning me over to the traders will change what your son feels?"

"What she knows," Sokolov interrupted, "is that there is a way to prove to all that you are not even worthy of being called a witch. When the traders are done with you, they will see you have no more value than a trade trinket. Do you think they would ever let their war chief share his bed with a piece of property? A nothing."

That was why Sokolov wanted to hand her over to the traders, so she would be humiliated and his power reasserted. If only Madsaw were here, he would—would what? Defy his mother, the shaman?

"I will not have my son twisted by the daughter of the man who killed my husband, his father," Apenas said, her tone weary yet determined. "He *must* have a worthy wife, deserves that. You will *not* take that from him."

"Tatooktche isn't my father."

"Silence!" Apenas ordered. "You will not speak again!"

Twana was hauled out of the house. If she struggled hard enough, she might be able to free herself, but all eyes were on her now. A single command from either Sokolov or Apenas would propel any number of the Wolf Clan into action; she might be dragged on her belly before the sea-strangers, and this, if nothing else, she wouldn't allow to happen.

When they were close enough that she could see an already naked slave woman being led into the forest by a thick-shouldered trader, her body went numb. Terror had overcome her earlier, terror that had nothing to do with One Ear. The emotion surged back again, so strong that she could do nothing except try to survive it. Although there'd only been a light rain earlier and nothing but occasional showers remained, the world was becoming darker as if she'd been thrust into a deep cave—a cave with One Ear at the other end.

No, not the grizzly.

"What have we got here?" a thickly accented but understandable voice asked in Tillamook. "What a pretty one. Hold up there, Jacquet. You sure you ain't interested in this one?"

"Too late," the man heading for the forest with the slave hollered over his shoulder. "I've got me a powerful hunger."

A third man laughed, then said something Twana didn't understand. "Apenas, what are you doing?" Chief Walkus asked.

"I cannot let her destroy my son's life," Apenas replied in the same shaky but determined voice Twana had heard earlier. Sokolov was barely holding on to her now, but why should he? Tillamooks and sea-strangers alike had surrounded her; she had nowhere to flee. "She is weak. Otherwise, would she be standing here now?"

Twana heard a number of people mutter among themselves, but it was impossible to make out what they were saying—not that it mattered. Her head still felt as if a storm were taking place inside it, and her stomach had become tightly knotted. Afraid she might be sick, she sucked in as much air as she could, grateful that at least she was outside instead of in the close, tight-feeling house.

"I offer her," Apenas said with new strength, "to be used as if she were a slave." She stared at Sokolov, the gaze holding for so long that Twana wondered if Apenas was speaking with the shaman's mind.

"This is not Madsaw's wish," Chief Walkus countered.

"Whoever this Madsaw person is, he'd better show up in a hurry or I'm going to start spreading her legs." The trader's comment was met by loud laughter from his companions, the harsh sounds chilling Twana. She wanted, needed, to send Madsaw a message on the wind, but how could she when she had to concentrate on what was being said about her?

Apenas was telling Walkus that because Madsaw wasn't here, she had to speak for him. After consultation with the shaman, they had agreed that offering Twana to the traders was necessary so they could prove she was nothing but a helpless captive. Because she'd heard those words before, they swirled around her, then faded into nothing.

Danger! The emotion stabbed through her, left her weak.

"Let me get this right. You're handing her over to us for a little fun and games?" A big man, his chin and cheeks matted with hair, grabbed her and swung her toward him. He smelled of sweat and dirty hides. "She's a beauty, boys. A real beauty."

"Get your dirty paws off her, Phillip. You go shoving your dried-up dingus into her and you'll probably kill her. You let a real man—"

"Real man? Ha! Ever since that Tlingit squaw took after you with her cleaning knife, you've been sounding like an old lady."

They were saying horrible things nearly beyond her comprehension. All she knew was that she feared and hated the bearded man, yet knew he wasn't the source of her terror.

"Apenas! This is not right," Walkus protested. "Madsaw—"

"My son is not himself. He must see her as she is, a nothing."

Twana prayed Chief Walkus would order the trader to release her and send her back to Madsaw's house. Instead, he remained silent, and when she forced herself to look around, she understood. There was something dark and dangerous in the sea-strangers' eyes. At any moment they might attack, killing all who stood in their path. Chief Walkus was unwilling to sacrifice his clan's safety for her.

"I've got first shot at her," her bearded captor insisted. "Once I'm done with her, if there's anything left of her, the rest of you can fight over her."

"The hell you say."

Twana couldn't understand why the sea-strangers were speaking the language of the Tillamook. If it was because they wanted to further terrify her, they had succeeded. She expected her captor to shout down the man who'd just spoken, but he didn't. Instead, he became strangely still the way an elk does when he senses danger.

"You heard me. I want a look at her."

Before she could focus on whoever had spoken, her captor shoved her at another man. She was free, then a prisoner again so quickly that she couldn't react. This new man was no larger than the others but maybe a little older, a little harder around the mouth and eyes and—

The eyes.

He stared down at her as a wolf studies a rodent trapped under his claws. Head cocked to one side, he held her firmly at arm's length. His gaze started with her face, then traveled slowly, boldly, down her body. She fought off a shudder, but there was nothing she could do about her terror. This—he—this man was what she'd feared.

When he pulled her around so that her face was no longer in shadow, she willed herself not to struggle, He smelled no better or worse than the first man who'd grabbed her. His skin looked as if it had long been attacked by sun and wind and storm, aging his flesh but not the muscles underneath. There were flecks of gray in his hair and beard, and yet she couldn't call him old. Around his neck he wore a heavy bear-claw necklace.

How many bears had he killed so he could display his trophies? The question was still forming inside her when he let go of one arm. She blinked, realizing too late that he was reaching for her throat. She felt his rough fingers scrape against her neck and knew he was reaching for her necklace.

His eyes—his grizzly-colored eyes—widened and then became slits as he almost gently fingered the necklace her mother had given her. She willed herself not to move and prayed he wouldn't destroy it.

He didn't; instead, he let it fall back against her throat, then gripped her chin, pulling her even closer to his unwashed body. He stared at her until she wondered if their eyes had become one, if either he had lost himself in her gaze, or she in his.

"You aren't Tillamook, are you?" he asked.

"No." She forced the word, hated him, hated herself. "I am Nisqually."

"So. So Saha *did* have my child."

CHAPTER 12

Head throbbing, Twana could only stare into eyes too much like her own. She saw everything, the grotesque necklace around the thick, hairy neck, glimpses of an unwashed throat, long hair matted and oily but thin at the forehead, a nose wider than her own, surprisingly well-shaped lips half-hidden by the fur between nose and lip. The man stared back with shocked and yet coldly appraising eyes that told her not enough of what was going on inside him. She wanted to run and yet she didn't; needed to scream and remained silent.

Around them, the villagers and traders had all but ceased talking, but she didn't care what anyone else might think or say. She now knew why her mother had refused to let a child's curiosity take her near the traders, understood why Saha had refused to speak of the man who'd given her daughter life.

Her mouth went dry. She swallowed, but it was of little help. She tried again. "What is your name?"

"Conrad. Just Conrad."

"I never knew."

"She never told you?"

Twana shook her head, then stopped when the movement increased the turmoil inside her.

"Too bad. That way the two of you could have hated me together."

She waited for him to ask her her name, but he didn't. Instead, he slowly increased his grip on her shoulder. This life-hard man, this stranger, had lain with her mother and brought her into being. The knowledge weakened her knees and emptied her heart.

Abruptly Conrad whirled away, his hand firmly clamped over her upper arm. He dragged her with him a few steps until they were standing in front of Chief Walkus. "She's my daughter," he announced, his voice once again full of strength. "My own flesh and blood. Look at her eyes; you can see they're the same."

Lips clamped together, Walkus folded his arms and silently met the trapper's gaze.

"Ever since her mother ran out on me, I've been wondering, thinking one day I'd come back and look. What's going on here? How come a Nisqually's living with the Tillamooks?"

Although Conrad repeated his question, Walkus

didn't answer. Twana thought he looked both uneasy and strangely accepting of what the trapper had just told him. When Conrad continued to insist on an answer, Sokolov pushed forward and, his chest swelled with self-importance, explained.

"A hostage? You're the chief, right?" he asked Walkus.

"Yes."

"And you make all the decisions around here." Walkus nodded.

"That's what I figured. Look, the brave who grabbed her, Madsaw, he isn't here, right? Course he isn't. Otherwise he'd be after me defending his property. Only, Twana isn't his property anymore. She's my daughter."

The word "daughter" made Twana's stomach lurch. Some of her earliest memories were of her mother thrashing in her sleep and crying out in panic; this man had to be responsible.

"I'm taking her with me."

"No!"

Ignoring her outburst, Conrad indicated his companions, who'd come closer as if to protect their fellow trader. "I've been thinking about her mother for years now," Conrad continued. "Wondering what happened to her, if I left her with a little reminder of me. Now I know. Did you hear me, Chief? I'm taking my daughter with me."

Eyes narrowed, Walkus explained that Twana must remain in the Wolf Clan village until ransom had been paid for her release. "The man she lives with murdered my brother. My nephew *must* have his revenge."

"Tatooktche killed a village chief? I have heard of some pretty stupid things in my life, but that about beats all. Never mind," he said with a wave of his free hand. "That's between Madsaw and Tatooktche, none of my concern. I have a right to my flesh and blood. A man's child belongs with him."

"The Tillamook say a child is part of her mother." Walkus looked at Twana for the first time, but although his stare lasted a long time, she didn't know what he was thinking.

"Her mother ain't here; I am."

Twana had thought herself numb, but Conrad's words sent a chill surging through her. *Madsaw!* she sent into the wind. *Please, help me!*

Conrad was speaking; she struggled to understand. "I've got use, need, for this girl. She's mine by right. Who's going to claim her? Tatooktche? He gave up all claim to her when he killed your chief. Madsaw? All he wants out of her is a chunk of revenge. Me, I'm kin. When we leave, she leaves with me."

"No!"

For half a heartbeat, Twana believed Madsaw had returned, but it was a woman's voice. "No," Kitlote repeated as she pushed herself through the mass of people. "You can't think such a thing, my chief. She saved my son's life. One does not throw away someone who brings a child back to his village."

Walkus stared, not at Kitlote, but at Twana, the flesh between his eyes now wrinkled with concentration. "She is not being sent to her death." He

228

stepped closer to stare first into Twana's eyes and then up at Conrad. "They are the same."

"Not just the eyes," Conrad insisted. "You see that necklace she's wearing? Pure gold. Valuable as hell. I put it on her mother, and when she ran away from me, she took it with her. Looks like she gave it to our daughter—maybe so she'd always have a reminder of me."

Twana wanted to yank the now-hated necklace off her, but when she felt it against her fingers, all revulsion went out of her. This was a gift from Saha, all she had of the woman who'd carried her inside her body.

Conrad started to argue again that he had claim to Twana, but Chief Walkus silenced him with an uplifted hand. The chief then jerked a finger at Apenas, indicating she was to come with him. When the two disappeared into his house, the other traders crowded closer, asking Conrad seemingly endless questions. Smiling thinly, Conrad explained that he and Saha had once lived together, and as long as she was around, he'd had no need for another woman. Since she ran away, he'd never found anyone who satisfied him like she had.

Twana felt dirtied and sick, desperately wished she could say something to defend her mother's honor, but she couldn't force herself to speak to Conrad; his unrelenting fingers on her arm were all she could stomach of him.

Her father.

Now, finally, she understood why her mother had told her she could never speak of the man.

It seemed as if Apenas and Chief Walkus were gone forever, and yet when they returned, she hadn't been given time to prepare herself for what they might say. Apenas kept her eyes on the ground; she seemed somehow shrunken and older, locked within herself.

"It has been decided," Chief Walkus declared. "There are ties between a man and his daughter that can never be broken, blood ties. I do not know why Saha turned her back on him; that is not for me to say. What my heart tells me is that Twana is part of this man."

"No!" Twana gasped. She whirled, but the traders pressed close around her, trapping her.

"Silence!" Walkus warned. "You do not speak! It is my turn. What I say," he continued when Twana, overwhelmed, fell silent, "is that the hostage is no longer a baby in her mother's arms. She has a woman's mind, a woman's heart. It is right that she learn who her father is."

No!

"But I cannot simply turn her over to the trader."

Twana's heart took a quick, hopeful lurch, but before it could be repeated, Walkus cleared his throat and went on. "She is here as a hostage, until my brother's death has been avenged, I cannot allow her to simply leave. It was my thought to have the trader force Tatooktche to pay the required ransom, but that is not a quick or easy matter, and the traders will not long be here. I have decided, therefore, to allow Conrad to act in Tatooktche's place."

Her body both cold and numb, Twana could only gasp while Walkus's words sunk in. Before she'd been given enough time, Conrad placed himself in front of Walkus. "Let me get this right, Chief. You want *me* to fork over for her ransom?"

Walkus nodded.

"What the hell for? She's my daughter. What's to prevent me from simply taking her with me?"

By way of answer, Walkus nodded at several braves, who quickly, silently, flanked their chief.

"Don't mess up this trade, Conrad," one of his companions said. "Give them their damn trinkets for the girl. It's nothing compared to what we're going to miss out on if the Tillamooks decide they ain't going to trade with us."

"Damn you, Mitchel. They're going to want more than a few trinkets, don't you get that? All right, Chief. You tell me, just for argument's sake, what you were hoping to get for her."

Even as she heard Walkus mention the rifle and a man's weight in furs, Twana felt herself slipping away from the village, desperately looking for Madsaw, sending him a wordless plea for help.

Surely he wouldn't allow her out of his life.

A hard bellow broke her concentration. "I don't give a damn about your complaining, Conrad! You want the girl, you're going to have to pay for her."

"I'm not *paying* for my own blood."

"The hell you ain't. It's different here. Ain't you the one who's been telling us that for weeks now? We're playing by their rules, you kept saying. Well, you want to be part of the game or not?"

Conrad was fairly trembling with anger, and his

hand rested dangerously close to the knife at his waist. Twana noticed that the braves around Chief Walkus hadn't once taken their eyes off that hand and that they, too, had weapons at the ready. If fighting began—

"All right, all right, damn it! You win, Chief. I'm not about to risk my neck over this. But I want your word that you're not going to change your mind. She's mine; the Tillamooks don't want nothing to do with her anymore, right?"

"The ransom has not yet been paid."

"I'm getting to it. Don't hurry me. Do I have your word?"

Chief Walkus nodded, and in the light cast by the meeting fire, Twana thought that he looked as if he had aged. Her own arms and legs felt as if they belonged to someone who had been alive since the beginning of time and only wanted to rest.

Conrad didn't have an extra rifle or furs he was willing to get rid of, but with prompting from his companions, a pile of knives, iron pipes and kettles, cloth, tobacco, and finally rum, grew slowly yet steadily. Twana couldn't make herself focus; these items had nothing to do with her, meant nothing to her.

When Conrad finished, he stepped back, hands turned into fists by his side, and glared at the Tillamooks. "She'd better be worth it. If she turns out to have her mamma's sight, you get her back and I get what's mine, understand?"

"She has the sight."

Apenas had been silent for so long that Twana had all but forgotten her role in this. Now she stared at Madsaw's mother, begging with her eyes and thoughts for Apenas to spare her from this fate. Instead, speaking in a barely audible whisper, Apenas reassured Conrad that she'd seen Twana's curse with her own eyes. "This is right," she finished. "The hostage's power over my son frightens me. I do not want her here."

"So he's got an itch for her, does he? It doesn't surprise me. Look—" Conrad addressed his companions. "I'm taking her back to where we camped, get a few things straightened out, make sure she understands."

"Whatever suits you," one of them said. "After all, she belongs to you now."

Belongs. Why had it taken her so long to comprehend that simple, horrible fact? The look in Conrad's eyes, the power in his fists, suddenly terrified her. Unthinking, Twana whirled and ran. She'd gone no more than a few feet when someone grabbed her arm and jerked with such force that she nearly lost her footing. Still off balance, she struck out. Her hand became tangled in a mass of greasy hair.

"Stop it, witch!" Sokolov insisted, jerking her again. She fought him with all her strength and took momentary pleasure in his cry of pain as her nails dug into the flesh under his eye. He tried to slap her hand away, and in so doing, released his grip on her enough that she was able to free herself. Again she whirled.

This time she collided with Conrad.

"Grab her!" he ordered. "Get some rope. Damn it, you're not getting away!"

She was surrounded by unwashed, hide-clothed bodies, and no matter how hard she fought, there were too many of them. Someone forced her arms behind her and looped a rope around her wrists. She kicked at whoever was tying her. The man cursed, but because others were holding on to her, she was unable to take advantage of his momentary distraction. Hands now lashed behind her, she looked about wildly. Sokolov pushed his way through the crowd, and with a grimy hand clamped over his bleeding cheek, pushed her toward the waiting Conrad. "Leave with her, now!" he ordered. "The witch is not wanted here."

Smiling, Conrad slowly and deliberately grabbed her hair. His fingers lingered on her necklace; she waited for him to yank it off her, but he didn't. Instead, he pulled her so close that his features blurred. "At last," he breathed into her face. "At last, Twana."

No! Madsaw, please, no!

But Madsaw wasn't here, only Apenas, who wouldn't meet her desperate stare.

Guided by instinct, Madsaw walked out of the night forest and onto the large, peaceful stretch of sand where his people had always lived. As he neared the Wolf Clan village, he'd listened for the sounds that would warn him that the traders were still around, but except for the ancient call of owls, the forest remained silent. The meeting fire still burned, making him believe the whites hadn't left that long ago. If they'd still been here, he'd planned to simply reassure himself that Twana was all right before spending the night in the woods.

He should have remained in the Raven Clan village; Cleaskinch had expected it. But he couldn't sit across from his future father-in-law while the man talked about how a marriage between Madsaw and his young daughter would make the Tillamooks far stronger than they'd ever been—not with concern for Twana tightly wrapped around him.

He didn't want to care for her; didn't want her in his thoughts. Wished he'd never laid eyes on her.

Feeling nearly as tense as he had when he and Twana searched for Vasilii, he started toward his house. The village dogs trailed after him for a while, then dropped to the ground, where they almost immediately fell asleep. One's belly was so fully rounded that it looked pregnant, proof that there had been much to celebrate today.

The moment he stepped through the opening, he knew something was wrong—missing. He breathed in the fire-warmed air, but although his eyes hadn't yet adjusted to the greater light, he knew he wouldn't find Twana here. The room felt empty and hollowed-out, stripped of an essential essence.

Lukstch's wife sat bent over the fire, looking half-asleep. Next to her the two young children squabbled over a small mound of beads. Their mother admonished them to be quiet, then went back to packing something in her storage box. Both of his sisters and one brother-in-law were about, but he barely acknowledged them. Not finding his mother, he strode across the wooden boards and entered his sleeping quarters.

"Where is she?" he asked, not caring whether his voice carried to the others. "What happened?"

"She is gone."

Gone. "Where?"

"With the traders."

"What? No. That cannot—"

"It is. Madsaw, please let me speak. You have to understand."

There was no explanation, nothing that could possibly make any sense, and yet as his mother told him what had happened, numbness and denial washed away to be replaced by reality. Why had he left? Why had he allowed his hatred of the whites to rule him? "You are a wealthy man, my son," Apenas finished. "The owner of many fine knives and kettles."

"Why did my uncle ask for so much?"

"The trader was willing to pay it."

"Willing?" Something about his mother's voice set his nerves even more on edge. "Did you tell him about her gift?"

"No. He already—already . . ." He could hear his mother breathing. For a moment he worried about the strength of her heart, but fear for Twana was too great for the emotion to hold. "Tell me," he managed. "How did he know about her?"

"He— Isn't it enough that we have been paid for your father's death?"

He didn't see it that way, couldn't justify in his mind that Tatooktche would never have to face the consequences for murdering his father, or that his mother's grief and loss had been compensated for. "Your heart is at peace?" he asked.

"Your uncle's is. And Sokolov says—"

"Do not speak of him to me!"

"I have to," Apenas insisted. "He said—he offered . . ."

"Offered what?" Madsaw pressed when his mother fell silent.

"Her to the traders."

"He what?" None of this made sense. "He had no claim to her, no right."

"He is responsible for the clan's safety, Madsaw. His belief was that once everyone saw how helpless she was before the sea-strangers, no one would ever speak of her witch's powers again."

"You allowed this?"

"Don't hate me, Madsaw. My heart beats only for you and the rest of my children. I have no other reason for living."

"Don't say that."

"She is like a spider who has spun her web over a victim," Apenas insisted. "You are that victim. I—I fear her."

Maybe she did; he couldn't say. "Sokolov offered her to the sea-strangers? And one offered to buy her?"

"Y-Yes."

Although Madsaw continued to question his mother while his heart screamed that he should be searching the night forest for Twana, he was unable to get Apenas to say more than she already had. Her only response was that he could find peace and walk into his future now that Twana was out of his life. Finally she fell silent, and exhausted himself, he did the same. He'd been pacing in the dark room, his foot occasionally brushing both his and Twana's sleeping matts. This time when his toe touched his bed, he ordered himself to lie down and accept his chief's wisdom, but before he could turn thought into action—if that was possible—pain stabbed through him.

Twana. To never see her again?

Not saying anything to his mother, he walked out of the sleeping quarters. He needed to hear from Walkus's lips that Walkus believed he had avenged his brother's death by selling Twana to a stranger. Madsaw stared, not at the still-glowing meeting fire but toward the woods. *She* was out there somewhere, the property of a man who might take her far from here.

How could he abandon her?

How could he defy his chief?

"Madsaw."

He stopped in midstride, dark anger surging through him at the sound of Sokolov's voice. Still, he forced himself to head toward the shaman's house. Sokolov stood outside it, arms folded over his ample belly, and Madsaw wondered if Sokolov had seen him enter the village and had been waiting for this moment. "You had no right," he told the shaman, careful to stand far enough away that, maybe, he wouldn't be tempted to strike him. "She was not yours to barter with."

"That is not for you and me to argue, Madsaw. What is done, is done."

"It can be undone."

"You would defy your chief?"

"Don't tell me what to do, shaman," he warned, wondering how many times he'd said that to Sokolov since Twana became part of his life. "I will speak to my uncle, and what he and I decide—"

"Madsaw, please, don't."

His mother's cry startled him, making him wonder how he could have been so focused on Sokolov that he hadn't heard her approaching. "You had nothing more to say to me," he reminded her, carefully watching the interplay between her and Sokolov. The shaman was staring openly at his mother, but she didn't once look at him. "Why did you follow me?" he asked.

"To see where you were going. Don't go after her, I beg of you. It is done. Done."

Was it? His heart didn't, couldn't, believe that. "My uncle—"

"Your uncle only did what a wise chief must," Sokolov interjected. "He rid the village of a witch and saw that you received compensation for your father's death."

"Come back with me, please," Apenas pleaded. "See what the trader gave for her and you will understand. My son, you are wealthy. Wealthy beyond what Tatooktche would have given you. When you marry and unite the Wolf and Raven Clans, no one will be more powerful than you."

Powerful? At the moment he felt nothing except helpless fear, impotent anger.

"Tell me about him."

"Who?"

"The sea-stranger who bought her."

Mouth working silently, Apenas grabbed his arm and tried to pull him back to the house, but he ignored her, staring instead into the shaman's small, bloodshot eyes. There was a look of victory in those eyes that chilled him as a winter storm never had. "Madsaw, please," his mother begged. "Forget her. Think of your tomorrows. When you see how many—"

"What did you say to him, shaman?" Madsaw pressed. "What words did you use to convince the trader to give up his wealth for a woman?"

"I had to tell him nothing."

Nothing. Shaking off his mother, Madsaw stepped toward Sokolov and forced himself to grab the shaman's filthy hair. He pulled him close and, despite Sokolov's struggles, easily fastened his other hand over his throat. "If you wish to see the morning sun, you will tell me everything."

"Everything? Gladly." Sokolov laughed. "The sea-stranger is the witch's father."

"What?"

"Are you deaf, Madsaw?" Sokolov taunted. "His name is Conrad; he placed his seed within Twana's mother's belly."

"No!" Memories of the little Twana could tell him about the man her mother fled so many years ago flooded through him. "That cannot be!"

"I do not lie on this, Madsaw." Sokolov jerked

free. "Do you think your chief would sell your hostage to anyone? No. But if that man gave life to the witch . . ."

Despite the blinding headache now pounding at him, Madsaw felt his mother's hand on his arm. He tried to look at her, but she remained a dark blur, like his thoughts. "Please, listen to me," she whispered. "I would die for you. Twana is with her father; your father's death has been avenged."

"Her father bought her?" he asked, unable to force his thoughts beyond that point.

"Who better, my son? I have found peace; the same will happen now for you."

"No."

"Yes," Apenas insisted. "Cast her from you. I beg you. Find in your heart the same quiet I now know."

CHAPTER 13

The other traders were camped downriver from where Conrad had taken her. Twana could hear the men talking and laughing among themselves. An occasional higher-pitched voice told her that they'd brought some of the slave women with them. Although she listened intently, she didn't hear a woman cry out, and guessed that the slaves had willingly submitted to the men, and as a consequence, hadn't been treated harshly.

It hadn't been like that for her mother.

Conrad, who'd been rummaging through his belongings, finally gave his heavy pack a kick and walked over to his own small fire. From where she sat tied to a tree, she watched warily. Having to pay for her had enraged him; even now, with the day long spent, he continued to mutter words that made no sense to her.

As soon as he'd gotten his fire started, he'd pulled a heavy jug of rum out of his pack and had been drinking steadily. Now he dropped heavily before the fire and took another deep swallow. He'd barely glanced at her earlier as he'd forced her to walk with him. Now, however, he fastened his eyes on her.

"You look a hell of a lot like her," he muttered. "So much that even without that necklace, I'd have known you were her kin. The same high cheekbones, little waist, woman's hips. You got any babies?"

"I am not yet married," she told him. If she remained silent, he would think she was terrified of him, and she refused to let that happen.

"That's not what I asked. Looking the way you do, I'm thinking some buck would have spread your legs by now. You ever slept with a man, Twana?"

Anger, not fear, closed her throat. He may have paid for her, but he didn't own her.

"I asked you a question, daughter. Have you had a roll on the ground with some buck?"

"What does it matter?"

"What?" His laugh caused an owl to fall silent in midhoot. "Because I'm your pappy, don't you understand that? How does that make you feel?" He upended the jug and again swallowed. Despite his heavy beard, she imagined his throat moving up and down. Her arms ached from being tied behind her, but she wouldn't tell him that. Madsaw had once placed a rope around her neck, but she'd never felt rage and hatred toward the Tillamook war chief. She'd known why Madsaw captured her, just as she knew why Conrad kept her a prisoner—only their reasons were far different.

"I asked you a question, Twana. How does it feel to know you're mine?"

"You do not own me."

"Ha! I beg to differ with you, girlie. I paid for you fair and square, paid for my own kin, damn it. That damn chief and the woman with him—what was her name?"

"Apenas," she said, forcing out the word.

"Yeah, Apenas. She sure wanted you out of there, maybe more than the shaman did. She really hate you that much because of what Tatooktche did to her husband?"

If Conrad wanted to know those things, he would have to talk to Apenas and Sokolov himself. All she cared about was Madsaw—Madsaw, who had spent the day with the girl he was going to marry and might now be looking at knives, pipes and kettles, a rum-filled jug.

Madsaw had been compensated for his father's murder; he had no more use for her, and she was trapped here with a grizzly-eyed man whose features danced with black and red shadows, whose deep voice frightened the owls into silence.

"Hey!" Conrad kicked at her leg. "I'm talking to you, Twana. From now on, whenever I say something to you, you either answer or jump right to doing what I want. Do you understand?"

She glared at him, praying he couldn't hear her heart's erratic beating.

"Damn you, just like your mother. Thinking you're better than me."

"She hated you."

"Not at first, she didn't." He laughed. "Way back when we met, I offered her things none of the braves in her village could. Hey, why wouldn't I, seeing as what went on inside her head was unlike anything I'd ever heard of before? She thought I was something wonderful, specially when I started talking about how I was going to take her home with me. You don't have any idea what my world's like, do you?" He sounded almost wistful. "Neither did she, but she was sure as hell curious. Telling her about being able to go places on horseback—hearing about horses liked to drive her crazy with curiosity—thinking about not having to haul wood to keep herself warm, no more cutting up stinkin' fish and watching it rain day after day. She believed me, wanted to hear everything I could tell her about England. Your mommy had a curiosity about her, that's for sure."

Although she wanted to hear more about what her mother had been like before she was born, Twana remained silent because she guessed that somewhere in the telling would come things she didn't want to know.

"She was a smart one, I'll give her that. Learned English a hell of a lot faster than I picked up her language. She left her village to live with me; did she tell you that?"

Twana didn't speak, didn't move; what she and

her mother had talked about was none of this man's concern.

"She did all right. Her folks all but disowned her, saying she was promised to someone else, maybe some chief. I don't rightly remember, but I wouldn't be surprised because she was worth more than any other girl around. I'll tell you something, daughter. Your mother was crazy about necklaces and bracelets." He leaned forward, nearly losing his balance and toppling sideways, then straightened and again reached for her necklace, but he was sitting too far away. "Damnation. Gotta stop drinkin' that stuff. Yep, all I had to do was give her something pretty to wear and she thought the sun rose and set in me. At least she did for a while—until I started pushing her."

"You beat her! I saw." The words exploded from her before she could stop them.

"I did what I had to, *daughter*. You've got the sight same as her; you know how damn easy it is for you to find something other folks don't have an idea about. I was looking thirty years of living in the eye when I came across her, and all I had to show for those thirty years was the clothes on my back. I figured every beaver and mink she could lead me to, I had a right to. After all, she was my wife."

That was a lie; Saha had told her she hadn't had a husband before Tatooktche. Whatever Conrad had done, it didn't include paying a bride-price for her. Strengthened by reassurance that her mother had never sat down at a bridal feast with this man, she was left to wonder how he'd convinced Saha to leave her family and live with him.

Maybe her scars told the story.

"She hated you."

"What do you know? You weren't even born then. All right. All right." He laughed bitterly. "So she wasn't too crazy about me there at the end, but it didn't matter none to me—not as long as I had the upper hand. She was making me rich, Twana, finding so damn many beaver, I didn't know how I was going to get all the pelts out of there."

The image of Conrad slaughtering beaver that Saha had led him to made her ill. If she had the use of her hands, she would have wrapped them tightly around her stomach—or around his throat. "You forced her."

"Yeah, Twana, I did."

She waited for him to say more. All the while she thought she might scream, wondered if he would care. Wondered if Madsaw might somehow hear. But Madsaw was with his wife-to-be.

When Conrad took another drink, he began choking; she prayed he would die, not caring how she would free herself. But although his eyes bulged and his nose turned red, he finally brought himself under control. "Good stuff," he wheezed. "Makes me crazy, but maybe that's better. You got it figured out, don't you, *daughter?* You know why I paid a king's ransom for you."

He stared at her with such intensity that it was all she could do not to drop her gaze. If she hadn't been determined not to let him know how afraid of him she was, she would have.

"Your mommy was on her way to making me a rich man before she took off. I'm not going to let that happen again."

She's gone. You can't touch her.

"Maybe you're as good as she was, maybe better. And—" He scooted closer, one hand still holding his jug, the other snaking out to capture her ankle. She shoved violently and managed to free herself, but because she was tied to the tree, she couldn't scramble away.

"Stop it!" He slapped, meaning to hit her leg but striking the ground instead. That seemed to enrage him, and when he pulled his knife out of his belt, she wondered if his anger would turn him into a murderer. "You don't fight me! That's what your mommy did, fought me. I couldn't have that. Wouldn't put up with it. She learned; damn it, I figured she'd learned her lesson. But soon as she'd healed up enough to crawl—" He carefully set down his jug, held out his free hand, and drew the blade lightly over the back of his arm. Despite the uncertain light, she could see that the blade was sharp enough to slice away the graying hairs there. "I didn't even know she was carrying my kid," he mumbled. "All these years never knowing for sure. But now . . ."

After nearly knocking over the jug, he managed to get his hand around it again and fastened his lips over it. She listened to him drink, her nose wrinkling at the unpleasant smell. Although she'd once seen Tatooktche turn into an angry, stumbling stranger after drinking some rum he'd gotten from a sea-stranger, she couldn't concentrate on what it was doing to Conrad. He'd laid his knife on the ground within easy reach. Any time he wanted, he could pick it up and kill her.

If she could, she would let his blood run onto the ground.

"Been thinking about those slaves the boys been fooling with," he slurred. "Not much fun being a slave, but you'd better get used to it, *daughter,* 'cause that's what's going to happen to you. I get what I want out of you. You do what I say. That's all there is to it. It's going to be different this time, different."

He looked as if he was falling asleep. Surely, with his eyes all but closed, he could no longer see her. She tried to stretch her feet closer to the knife, but he'd tied her too close to the tree. What did it matter? Her hands were numb. A slave? She would rather be dead.

Madsaw!

With a belch, Conrad forced himself to sit up straight. Still, he blinked so rapidly that she was sure she was little more than a blur to him. "All these years," he muttered. "All these years of waiting for my chance to come back and look for Saha. If the Hudson Bay Company hadn't been paying me such damn good money to help them establish some forts north of here, I wouldn't have let so much time pass. But hell, I figured I was going to get rich. That's what they told me; do their dirty work for them, and they'd heap gold on me. Ha! A man starts showing a few gray hairs and they can hardly wait to discard him like a bunch of old bones. Well, they was wrong. There ain't nothing wrong with this man's body. Nothing at all."

Had the rum loosened his tongue? When Tatooktche drank, he'd first vomit and then sleep until the sun had set twice.

"Well." He swallowed, a little of the liquid dribbling from his mouth onto his beard. "Well, soon as I figured out what them bastards was planning to do with me, robbing me, I grabbed everything I could get my hands on and hightailed it for Nisqually country."

She didn't care. Didn't he know that what he'd done with his life before this moment mattered not at all to her?

"I asked questions. Asked them until I went hoarse. Finally someone told me about a woman with strange powers who was living with a Nisqually named Tatooktche." He grinned, showing rotting teeth. "I knew it was her. And when I heard she had a kid, well . . ."

Something about what he was saying froze her thoughts. She struggled for understanding but could only wait for him to continue.

"I knew where the village was; should, all right. It weren't all that far from where she grew up. I thought about grabbing her, just grabbing her and taking off with her and her kid. It wasn't like I owed this Tatooktche anything; after all, I'd had his woman long before he did."

I hate you; don't you feel my hatred?

"But I'm a cautious man. I wouldn't still be

kickin' if I wasn't. I figured, this Tatooktche would have to be three kinds of a fool not to know how valuable she was. He wouldn't just let her go, probably wouldn't even let her out of his sight."

Conrad was right, not that she'd tell him.

"So I bartered. Tried to get two for the price of one."

"Bartered? When?" Twana gasped, her body burning and frozen at the same time.

"Last winter."

Winter. When her mother disappeared. When she'd spent desperate and endless days searching for the woman who'd vanished while she was in the menstrual hut. "You—took her?"

"Catching on, are you?" he slurred, a dead smile splitting his mouth into a hard line. "Yeah, Twana, your mother went with me. I had her, again."

She was going to be sick, to scream her horror and despair into the night. Instead, she somehow held on to her sanity and waited him out.

"It weren't easy, believe you me. One look at me and I thought your mamma was going to tear my throat out. Fortunately, I'd told Tatooktche what to expect. We were both ready. Grabbed her while she was off by herself so no one could hear her screams, we did."

Both of them shoving her mother back into a nightmare so vile, she'd never told her own daughter about it. "You killed her." Although a whisper, Twana's voice echoed, and in her mind she imagined Conrad's knife in her hand, plunging it into his heart. She'd never doubted that Tatooktche

251

was responsible for her mother's disappearance. But to now know that Conrad had been part of it—

"You think I'm crazy?" He laughed and tried to take another swallow, but tipping his head back caused him to nearly lose his balance. "I paid dearly for her. I wasn't going to risk losing my investment."

"A rifle," she blurted. "You traded a rifle for my mother."

"You saw it, did you? Tatooktche, he said he'd just tell people he'd done a little private trading and no one would have the guts to ask him too many questions. I figured that was his problem. Me, I had enough to do trying to beat some sense into that woman's head."

Beat. She didn't want to hear any more, only wanted to watch blood flow from Conrad's chest, but she could only will herself not to scream as he went on. At first Saha had fought like a wildcat, Conrad said. Looking at Twana now, he figured her to be a lot smarter than her mother had been. At least she wasn't going crazy like some trapped animal. "Finally Saha got it through her head that she wasn't going to get anywhere fighting me. She started listening to reason, even did what I told her to. At least that's what I thought."

Madsaw, please!

"Then she tried to stick me." He looked around, finally focusing on his knife. When he tried to pick it up, it slipped out of his fingers. "But let's just say she was in a weakened condition. By the time

the dust had settled, she was the one with a knife
sticking out of her."

Madsaw, please!

"I think she wanted it that way," he muttered,
seemingly to himself. "She chose death over me."

And I choose to kill you. Only, she was as helpless as her mother had been and could think of
nothing except her mother's last day. She prayed
her mother had died quickly, that she hadn't tried
to cling to life because of her love for her daughter.

"I tried to trade for you, too; guess I told you
that," he said after a long silence. "What do you
think of that? Even before I was sure you was my
kin, I knew I wanted the daughter as well as the
mother."

"I—I never saw you."

"Because Tatooktche and I did our dealing
where no one would overhear. Like I said, I didn't
want your mother seeing me before I was ready.
That's why I never set foot inside the village." He
stared at her for a long time, mouth trembling
slightly. His eyes had become so glazed that she
could no longer be sure of their color. "I offered a
hell of a lot for you, but it didn't do me a damn bit
of good. Tatooktche said—said there was some old
man willing to hand over a lot more for you than
I could offer. Otherwise, you'd have been working
for me a long time ago."

She didn't want, didn't need, to know any more
and now understood that the fear she'd felt when
Madsaw first brought her to the Tillamook village
hadn't been because of One Ear. Somehow she'd

known she'd learn what had happened to her mother.

And look into the black hole of her own future.

Mouth dry, her head feeling as if it had been split in two, she could only watch as Conrad clamped his lips around the bottle. The sound of his noisy swallowing sent her stomach to churning again, but she didn't dare be sick. She needed her strength, all of it.

"There's never been any woman like her," Conrad muttered as he struggled to get to his knees. "Most beautiful— People back in England, they point to those powdered ladies saying how they're beautiful, but they've never lain with your mother."

"Don't say that! Don't *ever* say that again."

"You going to stop me?" On his knees, he scooted closer. Lurching forward, he grabbed the front of her dress. She felt his knuckles on her throat and forced herself not to recoil. If he brought his hands close enough to her mouth, she could bite him. No matter what punishment he inflicted, she would have that satisfaction. "Come here, you," he muttered as he pulled on the dress. "Don't you be fighting me. Come here!"

He'd tied her to a tree; didn't he remember that? But when he yanked with such force that several of the strips of bark that made up her dress were torn apart, anything she might have been going to say fled her mind. She would *not* be stripped naked. She would not!

Somehow.

"You think you know what it's like being different? Hell, you don't know nothing." He continued to pull on her dress, but not with enough strength that he did any more damage. "You try getting old out here. Can't keep up with those youngsters. And when the company you've been working for for most of your life throws you out like yesterday's fish— I'm not dying broke and alone, Twana. Not while I've got me a daughter."

"I am not your daughter. Not in my heart."

"Oh yeah," he taunted. His hold on her dress tightened. Fear lapped at her, fear and a maddening sense of helplessness. "Think we're not kin, do you? I'm telling you something right now, Twana. Something you damn better listen to. Before I'm done with you, you're going to do everything I want you to, when I want. Now . . ." He tried to smile; at least that's what she thought he was attempting. "We're going to start off simple." His words ran together. "You know what I am, don't you? I'm your pa. Call me that, call me Pa."

Pa. The strange word sounded horrible to her ears. She would rather die than say it.

"You hear me?" He was trying to stand but couldn't because his fingers were still caught in her dress's fibers. "Pa! You call me Pa!"

"No." She kept the word low and controlled, never once took her eyes off him. "No."

"The hell! I say—I say . . ."

He'd started to swallow; the flesh around his mouth was turning pale. It seemed that he was looking inside himself now instead of at her. When he flung himself away from her and began retching on the ground, she simply stared. His vomiting went on and on, exhausting him. His arms shook, and when he briefly glanced over his shoulder at her, the shadows weren't strong enough to hide his deadly white face from her. He began muttering something, but she couldn't make sense of the words.

It didn't matter. At least he was no longer ordering her to speak to him.

"Damn stuff. Makes me—belly ain't as good as it used to be—makes me . . ."

She watched, totally fascinated by what was happening to him. It was as if his body were underwater. Every movement he made took great effort, strength he didn't have. When he tried to push himself away from his vomit, she almost felt sorry for him. With a second effort, he managed to slide far enough away that his long hair no longer dragged in it. "Sick. So sick." He started to wipe his mouth with the back of his hand, then, slow and nearly graceful, he pitched forward, his face flat against the ground.

"Conrad?" his name on her tongue tasted vile, and yet she forced herself to call out again. He might have moaned; she couldn't be sure. But he didn't move, and in a short while she heard him begin to snore. Tatooktche had done that when he drank too much, and she guessed it would be a long, long time before Conrad woke. Still, she watched him for several more moments until the burning in her wrists pulled her attention off him. She scooted backward until she'd taken the pressure off them, but when she tried to wiggle her fingers, she knew he'd so securely tied her that she could never free herself.

Not thinking, at least trying not to, she slid around until she'd stretched her legs out in front of her. She flexed her legs over and over again, then concentrated on her fingers, slowly returning circulation to them.

She was alone. With only the dying campfire and moon to light her world.

Breathing deeply, she waited until Conrad briefly stopped snoring and then strained to hear what she could of the night. The owls once again called to each other, and in the distance she could hear some small creature moving about. Concentrating, she learned that the sound belonged to a young mouse and wondered whether it would survive the night or feed one of the owls.

She was as helpless as a mouse in an owl's claws.

Alone with the drunken Conrad.

Madsaw . . .

Once again, she spread her thoughts, her heart even, over the wilderness, but although she came across several deer grazing on the moss that clung to a recently fallen tree, the warrior didn't miraculously show himself to her.

Why should she pray that Madsaw was looking for her? He had no need of her, no reason for wanting to free her from a man she hated enough to kill.

Conrad. Forcing herself to remain calm, she again stared at the inert trader who'd bought her mother and, with Tatooktche's help, spirited her far from her home—who'd made Saha so desperate that she'd risked death. As yet another owl joined the others, she made a silent vow. Someway, somehow, he would pay. She—

A movement touched her senses and immediately claimed her entire being.

One Ear. Far away and yet coming closer, nose constantly testing the air.

"Never. I ain't never going to do that again," Conrad muttered. He sat cross-legged on the ground, his head held in his hands. He hadn't moved all night and even now couldn't do more than speak in slow, disjointed sentences. The white of his eyes looked blood-soaked; his hands trembled. After repeating several times that he was getting too old to drink, he pushed himself to his knees and stood.

Twana watched his every move, her exhaustion from having spent a nearly sleepless night forgotten. One Ear shared this deeply forested mountain with them; if either she or Conrad spoke loudly, the grizzly might hear. He'd seemed content to remain deep in the trees all the time she was with the Tillamooks; she could only guess that the traders' sounds of celebration had captured his attention. And now he sought her?

A self-satisfied smile spread over Conrad's features, pulling her attention from One Ear. "No reason putting it off, *daughter*. Now's as good a time as any to start working you. Those so-called friends of mine aren't going to be of a mind to head for the Nisqually village for at least another day, and I sure as hell ain't going to get drunk with them."

She didn't care what the other traders did; didn't he know that?

"Damn, I'm hungry," Conrad muttered, a grimy hand pressed to his stomach. "You, too, I bet. All right, I got me a proposal for you. Show me you've got the sight and I'll let you eat. Play stubborn on me and you're going to starve."

Vowing to say as little as possible to him, she watched as he walked over to her and, grunting, lowered himself to his knees. He pushed her forward so he could look at her hands, all the time muttering in that language she didn't understand. "Those hands look all right, not swollen. Still, it ain't good keeping them behind you." When he suddenly patted her cheek, she didn't have time to react and could only suffer his control of her. "Got to protect my investment, you know. Tell you what. I'll make you more comfortable. Won't let you free, though; I know better than that. Then you're going to lead me to a beaver."

He pointed in the general direction of the river. "Beaver, land otter, marten, I don't care which as long as he's got a fine pelt. Then when you're finished, I'll let you do it all over again." He laughed and patted her cheek again. "You got that, Twana? From now until the end of your life, if you want to eat, you does what I say—what I want."

Lightning bolts of fear threatened to sear her. She'd spent the night looking at his limp body and telling herself she would be able to escape him, made herself strong with the thought. But it was

morning now, a lightly overcast day with a breeze
that smelled faintly of salt and seaweed, and she
was nothing more than a dog tied to a pole. Only
by filling her mind with thoughts of Madsaw was
she able to keep terror from taking over.

"You hear me, girl? You want to eat, you lead me
to a beaver this morning."

Could she sacrifice an animal's life so she would
have the strength to fight Conrad? If she didn't,
she would weaken and die.

Conrad began fiddling with the rope around her
wrists. She held her breath, waiting for that moment of freedom, but he quickly yanked her hands
in front of her and tied them together again while
painful spasms shot through her arms. Blinking
back tears, she tried to order her arms to move,
but they'd been in an unnatural position too long.

If only One Ear would burst from his hiding
place. Maybe he would attack Conrad instead of
her. And maybe—

"This ain't no ball, Twana. We ain't here waiting
for some prince to ask you to dance. You're going
to work." He reached for his knife, slipped it into
his belt, then pushed himself to his feet, grunting
loudly. The sound seemed to hang on the air, and
she prayed One Ear would hear.

And maybe Madsaw—

She felt a jerk on her wrists and realized
Conrad was trying to get her to stand. Because
she couldn't use her hands as leverage, she struggled for several moments before she made it to her
knees and then onto half-numb legs. A glance at

Conrad told her he enjoyed seeing her awkward and helpless.

"You know what we're about, don't you? Either you start paying me back for everything I had to surrender for you, or you're going to be sorry you're alive."

Her throat went dry, and although she swallowed several times, it did little good. Painful pricks attacked her legs, causing her to stumble. Still, she kept her eyes on him and reminded herself over and over again not to give in to panic and despair.

She would live, would free herself from this man. Somehow.

"Don't like it much, do you, Twana?" He indicated her bound hands. "Neither did your mamma. Once she told me she'd rather be dead than be treated like a slave, but I figured that was just talk. Anything's better than death."

Was it? At the moment, with hopelessness and fear lapping at her, she couldn't say.

"Concentrate, *daughter*. What's out there? Any beaver near the river? What about a marten? They're sneaky as hell. Show me one of them and I might give you everything you want to eat."

The thought of food made her sick, and yet she needed to eat; maybe that was the only way she could clear her mind. He continued to lead her away from the ashes of his fire and deeper into the woods. Although he carried his rifle over his shoulder, he'd left his pack behind, telling her he intended to return here.

"Come on, Twana. I ain't going to wait forever."

He was waiting for his chance to murder an animal whose only crime was that his fur was considered valuable. Only, she couldn't think about that now. She had to—

Conrad propped his rifle against his leg and pulled her closer; she smelled the residues of last night's vomiting. "It is not always easy," she said softly. "Animals hide; it is their way."

"Don't give me that. If you're anything like your mother, you can find newborn mice buried under an old log."

He was right. "You frighten me; I can't think."

"Do I? Well, that's just too bad."

Forcing herself, she lowered her eyes until she was staring at the ground in what she hoped was a gesture of defeat. "Give me time, please. I want—I want—"

"What the hell is it you want?" Still holding the rope, he reached out to grab her necklace. Or maybe it was her throat he wanted to run his fingers over. It didn't matter; she *wouldn't* let him!

Grunting, she shoved herself at him. The instant she pushed her shoulder into his chest, she grabbed for his knife. Her fingers closed around it and, ignoring the pain of rope cutting into her wrists, she yanked it from his belt.

"What the—"

She didn't give him time to finish. Screaming now, she drew the knife back as far as she could and plunged it into him. She felt it sink into flesh, imagined it cutting into the muscles along his side. Finally the knife hit bone. He cursed and staggered away from her; ripping the blade out, she came at him again. He turned away, protecting his wounded side. She aimed at his belly, but he managed to deflect the knife with his arm, and this time it hit his hip, its invasion on his body quickly stopped by bone. She struggled to free the weapon, but he held on to her rope and used it to jerk her off balance.

"No!" she screamed, not caring that she sounded like an animal fighting for its life. "No!" She struck out with her foot, kicking him in the face. She felt his head snap back but was afraid the blow hadn't been powerful enough. As she strained against him and readied herself for another kick, he sank to his knees.

He released the rope, not because he was beaten, but because he'd reached out for his rifle and was pulling it toward him. Blood stained his shirt; his eyes looked dull with pain—dull and yet sharp with anger.

"Damn you, Twana! I'll kill you!"

"Will you?" she gasped. She lurched back, the knife clutched in her numb fingers. He'd lifted his weapon and was pointing it at her. She knew little about a white man's rifle, just that she could never outrun its deadly power. Staring at it, she forced herself to think. "If you kill me, you will have nothing."

He blinked, and she guessed that what she'd said was sinking in. She could repeat herself, but she didn't ever want to speak to him again—only wanted to see him dead. He seemed unaware of his wounds, and yet his rifle trembled and she knew strength was leaving him.

"Like your mother. Just like her. You're willing to die over this?"

"Yes." She took a backward step, and had just begun another when he thrust the rifle forward and rested the end against his shoulder. His breathing became labored and loud; still, she couldn't say whether he was dying.

"Fine," he hissed. "You wanna die, you get your wish."

"Do it," she challenged. "Put an end to me."

"The hell—" Cursing, he struggled to his feet and stood there, swaying, trying to look at his side and her at the same time. "Put down that knife or I'm going to make you sorry you were ever born."

He'd barely been able to hold on to the rifle, but now as she stood frozen by fascination, fear, and hatred, he aimed it at her chest. Suddenly nothing mattered except that her mother had died at this man's hands and she wasn't going to let him do it to her.

Nearly drowning in panic and the will to live, she whirled and ran, silently begging the forest to envelop her.

A rifle blast shattered the morning quiet.

CHAPTER 14

Twana felt a rush of air over her head and knew the shot had missed. Whether Conrad had meant to hit her or not didn't matter. All that did was getting away from him.

At first she ran with the terror of a fawn pursued by a mountain lion, but before long, she forced herself to slow enough that she could look around her. The forest was thick but not impenetrable here, and if she could keep from tripping on the tangle of ferns and roots, she might reach safety. She jumped over a decaying log that nourished spruce and hemlock seedlings, glanced up long enough to take note of the endless greens and browns, prayed the forest would shelter her. Would protect her from Conrad.

She could hear him cursing, absorbed the heavy

thud of his feet on the thick moss carpet, wanted to scream at him that he was destroying the fragile life underfoot. But so was she; it couldn't be helped. Acting on instinct, she began heading toward the river, where she might eventually find her way back to Madsaw.

Madsaw? He had no need for her.

Legs churning, she scrambled up a slight rise and risked a glance behind her. To her horror, she saw that Conrad with his longer legs was holding steady with her, maybe even gaining. The loose end of rope from her hands kept tangling around her legs, but if she stopped to grab it, she might drop the knife.

He yelled something she didn't understand, the harsh shout propelling her back into action. She felt her feet begin to slip on wet moss and dug in with her toes. When she held her breath, she heard the river. One Ear! Where was he?

Struggling with each step, she began the steep downhill slide that would end at the river's edge. She prayed it was narrow enough there that she could jump to the other side and find a hiding place before Conrad overtook her. If not—

A sharp jerk yanked her hands downward. Fighting for balance, she reached for the closest tree. As she did, the knife fell from her fingers to be immediately swallowed by the thick growth. Sobbing in frustration and fear, she sank to her knees and yanked at the rope wrapped around her ankle. She managed to free herself, but she'd lost precious time. When she looked behind, Conrad was so close that she thought she could see the sweat on his forehead.

"You'll never make—never."

She had to get away, had to run. But without the knife? She wasted even more time in a frantic search for the weapon; then, with Conrad drawing dangerously close, she scrambled to her feet. She'd taken only a few steps and was trying to find room between two close-growing trees when someone grabbed her arm and pulled her against him.

Traders! How—

It wasn't a trader.

"Hide," Madsaw hissed, his magnificent body all but naked, black eyes digging into her.

Madsaw. She wanted to scream his name to the heavens, to collapse against him, but that would have to wait. He'd already pushed her away from him with such urgency that she slipped on the uncertain ground. Landing on her hands and knees, she whirled around. "He has a rifle!"

"I know."

In his hand, Madsaw carried the slave killer he'd used to capture her. But now, instead of aiming it at her, he was using it to defend her. Sweat glistened on his back and chest, and his breath sounded as ragged as hers, but where she was nearly spent, he looked as strong as the largest tree.

He was staring at the man standing farther up the hill, the man now reloading his deadly weapon.

"Get away from her!" Conrad ordered. "She's mine."

"You're wrong. She is mine."

"Yeah. Who—the hell—are you?" Conrad had bent forward while readying his rifle. Now he leaned back and took a deep breath. As he did, his face contorted with pain.

"Madsaw."

"Madsaw? Wait—I paid for her, fair and square. What are you doing here?"

"I reject the barter."

Barter. Mesmerized by the argument between the two men, Twana told herself Madsaw hadn't followed her simply because he wasn't ready to release his possession, but his words confused her.

Conrad was trying to tell Madsaw he couldn't reject a bargain struck by the chief, but with each word, he sounded more and more out of breath. His side and hip were bleeding freely, and when he tried to clamp a hand over his ribs, the rifle all but slipped from his grasp. Madsaw stared at Conrad, reminding her of a wolf waiting for its prey to die. "You can't have her," Conrad whimpered. "I paid for her fair and square."

"I returned the goods to your companions. Then I came looking for you."

"Returned? You can't . . ."

"I will not allow my hostage to leave with you." *Allow. Hostage.*

Conrad's mouth had begun working. He spread his legs and managed to lift the rifle to his shoulder, the effort stripping what she could see of his face of all color. "Get away from her, or I'll kill you."

"Will you?" Madsaw held the slave killer high,

his powerful arm cocked to throw it. "And maybe I will kill you first."

"The—hell—you will. My men will hunt you down."

That might be the truth; she couldn't say how white men dealt with revenge. If Conrad died from his wounds, would his companions kill both of them?

What did it matter?

Madsaw left her side and slowly, cautiously, began climbing toward Conrad. The trader's eyes never left him, and yet they seemed clouded and his mouth hung open. Once again, the rifle trembled. "Back off," Conrad whispered. "You heard me; back off."

"You do not tell me what to do, trader. Put down your weapon."

"The hell—" With an effort that nearly brought him to his knees, Conrad straightened. In horror, Twana saw a finger tighten, imagined the rifle shooting fire and death at Madsaw.

He never had time. Even as the flesh around his knuckle was turning white, Madsaw lunged and swung his slave killer at the rifle, smashing it toward the ground. Cursing, Conrad made a move as if to resist, then pitched forward, trapping his weapon under his weight.

Madsaw stood over him, legs widespread, the slave killer raised and ready. Despite the distance separating them, Twana understood Madsaw's every emotion. She wanted to order him to kill Conrad, waited for the words to burst free. But they remained locked within her.

"Listen to me," Madsaw said. "The goods you traded for her are with your companions. Return to them, take what is yours. And if you ever walk into the Wolf Clan village again, you will not leave it alive."

Conrad muttered something, the words lost in the gentle breeze.

"I spare your life because I do not want your companions to seek vengeance on my people. There has been enough killing; it must end."

"The hell . . ."

Twana waited for Conrad to move or speak again, but the trader remained motionless, and she wondered if she'd dealt him a fatal blow, if he would bleed until none was left inside him. She stood on shaking legs and slowly made her way toward Madsaw. The forest had enveloped him, a dance of shadow and light turning him into something both magical and unreal. She tried to concentrate on his size and strength, but all she could think of was his words.

He'd called her his hostage, his possession, and then in a gentle, almost weary tone told Conrad that the killing must end. Which was he: fearless war chief or the wise leader of a large clan?

When she was close enough that she could have touched Madsaw, she forced herself to look, not at him, but down at the trader. His eyes were nearly closed, and his chest rose and fell in an unsteady rhythm. He was so much less today, no longer the fearsome man who'd robbed her of her freedom and murdered her mother. Although not an old man, he'd lost the strength and bearing of youth.

Whether those he worked for had cast him aside or not, he believed that, saw himself as a man alone against the world who'd tried to possess a woman and then her daughter, who may have never known the meaning of love or kindness.

She hated him.

"Leave him," she whispered when Madsaw leaned over to pick up the discarded rifle. "Please, just leave him."

For the first time since he'd heard a distant rifle shot and started running toward the deadly sound, Madsaw felt capable of rational, calm thinking. Twana didn't say anything; her breathing had nearly returned to normal. Even with her tangled hair and ruined dress, she looked in control of both her body and her world. Pulling out his knife, he indicated he wanted to cut her bonds. She held out her hands and waited while he cut through the loops. Not trusting himself to look at Conrad again, he began walking away from the unconscious trader. He could no longer hear Conrad's breathing when he realized Twana wasn't following him. His feet sliding a little on the morning-damp ground, he looked back at her.

She returned his stare, deep brown eyes shining with life and maybe unshed tears. He wanted to know what had happened to her since Conrad took her, needed to hear what she'd endured. She looked so small, so vulnerable, and yet she'd been the one to inflict the wounds on Conrad—her father. Had she struck him during a desperate battle for her life or had she been ruled by revenge?

The answer could wait. First he needed to truly

believe that she was alive, and that he no longer had to be terrified for her.

Because she still hadn't moved, he retraced his steps and settled his arm over her shoulder. He expected her to collapse against him, but although he felt her shudder, she remained erect and strong.

"He's my father," she whispered.

"I know," he replied, hoping the words would help. "My mother and Sokolov told me everything."

"Not everything." She was staring at the ground, absently rubbing her reddened wrists. "He killed my mother."

"When? Why?" He didn't dare look back at the trader.

She told him a little, speaking softly and quickly, sounding like a lost child and yet holding herself like the bravest of men. Rage against Tatooktche flooded him, but the emotion lasted only as long as it took Twana to take a deep breath. He wanted to tell her that he admired her as he never had another human being, yet something stilled his words.

He wanted her, not just because he'd thought of nothing except her for days and nights now, but because he might not be complete again unless he possessed her. When she shifted her weight, he realized they'd been standing motionless for a long time.

"It's time to go home, Twana," he whispered as he again began leading her away from where they'd left Conrad.

"Home? To the Wolf Clan village?"

"Yes."

"Nothing has changed, then, has it?"

He wanted to tell her she was wrong, that everything had changed between them, but he didn't. He couldn't.

Her feet made no sound on the forest carpet. Her hair, tangled and limp, lay over her cheeks and shoulders like a protective cape. Once she glanced up at him, and he saw in her eyes a depth that reached to her soul—told him she had very little reserve left. Her torn dress set his teeth on edge. If Conrad had forced himself on her— The thought that a man would have his way with his daughter made him want to bellow in rage.

"Tell me, please. Did he hurt you?"

"Just my hands." Her voice was dull. If she hadn't been matching his pace, he would have picked her up and carried her. "He got drunk and became unconscious."

"He tore your dress."

She picked at the frayed strips. "He— Why are you here?"

Because I couldn't do anything except look for you. "Did you think I wouldn't come?"

"I didn't know what to think. Conrad paid for me; Chief Walkus said—"

"My uncle does not look at this through my eyes." They'd reached a place where tiny white flowers grew in a thick mass that reached clear to the water's edge. The flowers seemed to fascinate Twana. Slowing, she stared at them until he

273

reached down and picked one for her. She stopped, held it up to her nose and inhaled.

"Wonderful," she whispered. "There was a time when I thought I might never again smell the forest."

Because she was afraid she would be killed. He'd tucked his weapons back in his belt, and yet it would have taken very little for him to rush back to Conrad and smash the man's skull.

"You rejected Conrad's offer." She was still staring at the tiny, perfect flower. "Because it wasn't enough?"

Because without you, nothing matters. "You told me what he did to your mother. I couldn't let that happen to you."

"You saved my life, Madsaw."

For a heartbeat, he felt as if he were staring into a deep, dark cave. The thought that she might have died today was enough to steal the strength from his limbs.

"I told myself you wouldn't come, that you could step toward your future without me."

"Did you?"

"Your chief accepted goods in trade for me. The debt has been paid. Your father is at rest."

That wasn't for him to say. The others agreed with his uncle's decision, but they hadn't lain beside her at night, hadn't searched for a missing boy with her concern matching his, hadn't heard she'd been taken by the man who beat her mother until she fled in terror. "Would you rather I'd stayed in my village?"

"Your village, Madsaw. I don't belong there."

"That is not where we are," he told her. "Here, there is only you and me."

"'Here.'" She breathed the word. "Will he die, Madsaw? Did I wound him so much?"

Because he'd seen a number of injured men, he was able to tell her that, although the stabs had stripped Conrad of his strength, he believed the trader would recover. "I wish I'd killed him," he finished. "After what he did to you—"

"He bought me, Madsaw. I belonged to him."

Just as she belonged to him until the debt caused by a man's murder had been paid. His head throbbing at the thought that she was right and nothing had changed between the two of them, he asked if she wanted to stop and rest. She looked around her, seemingly surprised to discover how much distance they'd covered, then stumbled to a stop. The tiny flower fell from her fingers. She tried to straighten her dress, but too many fibers had been ripped apart, and there was little she could do to cover herself. "He said so many things," she muttered. "Horrible things. But he'd had so much rum that little of it made sense."

"Did he hurt you?"

"No, but . . ." She pulled free, but instead of walking away from him, turned in a small, uneven circle. "I don't know what he wanted to do. Maybe he didn't either."

He didn't care what went on inside Conrad's mind; if Twana hadn't been there, he would have killed the man.

"What if he can't return to his companions? They might leave him behind."

"None of them speak our language as well as he does. They need him to trade with all who live here."

"With my people." She'd stopped pacing and now didn't seem to know what to do with her body. Although he wished she'd rest, he was grateful for the restlessness in her because it made it possible for him to believe she was healthy and strong—and very much the woman he wanted to sleep with.

"Are they still my people?" she asked, her eyes darkening until they looked no different from his. "Will I ever belong with them again?"

"Is that where you want to be?"

"Want?" She lifted a hand to her hair, then started raking her fingers through it, slowly easing away the tangles. He wanted to do that for her, that and much more. "My life isn't mine anymore."

He'd known she was going to cry before the first tear pooled on her lower lashes. She stood beyond his reach, maybe because she didn't want him touching her, but he couldn't be content with that. With a single step, he covered the distance separating them and pulled her against his chest. She sobbed, pulling in great shuddering breaths that shook her body until he believed that without him holding her, she would have collapsed.

In a way, he envied her release. When he lost Vattan and then his father, he'd had to hold his head high so no one would question whether he was worthy of becoming chief. Alone in the middle of the night, he'd stared into the darkness, his heart heavy and yet empty. He didn't know how to cry; he'd been taught that a man shed no tears.

But maybe tears would have soothed his pain.

"I-I never got to tell my mother good-by," Twana whimpered. Her wet lashes fluttered against his chest and he reacted instinctively, his manhood instantly hard. If he moved at all, she would know.

"Maybe she can hear you."

"I miss her so!" A fresh onslaught of tears silenced her, and as he continued to hold her, muttering sounds with no meaning behind them, his need retreated. She was a woman fighting her way through grief, not a woman wanting to join her body with a man.

"I'm sorry," she whispered, then leaned away so that the breeze instantly cooled the hot tears she'd left on his chest. "I shouldn't have—I didn't want to cry. I kept telling myself I wasn't going to, but—but . . ."

"I know, Twana, I know."

He did. Hadn't he lost, not only his father, but the woman he loved as well? She blinked away the last of her tears, slowly bringing her world back into focus. There was only Madsaw. She'd expected him not to know what to do when she broke down, to step away from her and maybe even order her to be silent. Instead, he'd enveloped her in his arms and, with his weight and warmth, shown her that she wasn't alone after all.

Not alone; with Madsaw.

I'm done, she wanted to tell him. *There aren't any tears left inside me.* But when she tried to form the words, they slipped from her like mist under a warm sun. He stood with his feet half-buried in the soft, deep carpet, a thin shaft of sunlight settled over his left arm, the rest of his body muted by cool shadows. She remembered how the tiny flower had looked caught in his large, strong fingers and knew he'd been seeking to touch her heart when he handed it to her.

Why didn't matter. Whether he regretted the gesture didn't either.

When she breathed, she felt her breasts push against what little fabric still covered them. Always before she'd been careful to hide her nakedness from him, but that no longer mattered. They were surrounded by wilderness far from all others. If she looked—if she could tear her thoughts from him—she would know what animals shared the forest with them, but that didn't matter.

Only he did.

He had black eyes, midnight eyes that she quickly lost herself in. She felt as if she were flowing into him, even without touching, becoming part of him. Why he'd come looking for her didn't matter; neither did what he would have to say to his chief and mother and shaman when they returned. There was only the two of them with the river singing behind him and a couple of small birds calling to each other from the top of a nearby tree. There were a few of the small white flowers on the ground behind him, strong tree roots covered by pale green moss, ferns that took their strength from the never-ending moisture, all of that part of the wilderness that sheltered them.

"Thank you," she whispered, "for stopping him."

"Don't think about that. You're free; that's all that matters."

She wasn't free, but the bonds that held her heart had come into being because he'd looked at her and touched her; she couldn't tell him that. He was wonderful, wild and magnificent and wonderful. Mouth dry, body hot, she searched for words to tell him, but there weren't any inside her. There was only sliding close and pressing the flat of her hand against his warm chest.

"I thought I'd never see you again," she whispered.

"Apenas begged me not to come. I have to face my chief."

"Why did you defy them?"

He didn't answer; instead, when she started to back away, he caught her hand to him and held it there, trapped between chest and palm. She'd heard his heart beating more times than she could remember, but never had she felt as if she held it. When she glanced up at him, she saw that his eyes had taken on a smoky haze. There were too many secrets in those depths, great loss and courage, a man who'd always known his place with his people but was now looking at his world in a way he never had before.

She was responsible for the change.

When he enveloped her hand with his fingers and slowly drew it to his mouth so he could brush his lips over her knuckles, her legs weakened. If standing before him hadn't been the most important thing in her world, she would have collapsed.

Instead, she stood both brave and frightened before him and accepted the strange new feelings now flooding her body.

She hated her ruined dress, not because it reminded her of Conrad, but because she wanted no barrier between her and Madsaw. He'd always been careful to cover himself when he was around her; she wanted to tell him she no longer wanted that. Instead, she rose onto her toes and, feeling far bolder than she'd ever believed possible, touched her mouth to his. He groaned from somewhere deep in the center of his being, his warrior's body shuddering.

After a long, silent moment, he gripped her shoulders and pushed her away from him. "This shouldn't be," he groaned. "We shouldn't . . ."

"I know," she whispered back. Tears welled in her eyes; no matter how hard she fought, she couldn't kill the pain of his simple words. "I know," she repeated, trying to make herself believe.

"My chief—I didn't care. All I could think about was that I might never see you again."

"And—that meant more than his words?"

By way of answer, he spread his hands over her back and slowly, so slowly, drew her against him. She turned slightly, easily pressing her cheek against his chest as her breasts tightened and hardened. Her entire body felt as if it had filled with hot liquid; she was overcome by a sense of restlessness so deep that it knew no end—none except his body silencing her lonely cry.

He'd begun running his hands over her throat

and shoulders, covering her arms, the back of her neck, lighting a fire. At first she could only cling to him as waves of sensation washed through her, but soon that wasn't enough. She needed to touch him in return, to share her restless heat. Gathering her strength, she drew just far enough away from him that she was able to run her hands over his ribs, along his side, finally to the hard, dark nubs of his breasts. She heard him suck in his breath but now lacked the courage to look into his eyes. Instead, she stared at his warrior's chest, not quite believing that they'd come together like this—that they both wanted the same thing.

He'd begun pressing the heels of his hands against the swell of her breasts, the gesture both sensual and possessive. This morning, under Conrad's control, she'd believed she never wanted a man to touch her again. But Madsaw was different; her heart beat for him and she could never fear him. Never hate him.

What she felt was far, far different, overwhelming, wonderful.

When he gripped her dress's neckline, she didn't understand what he was doing. She heard it tear a little more and then he was guiding it over her shoulders and down her arms, to her waist, over her hips, letting it slide to the ground.

She stood naked before him.

Naked except for her mother's necklace.

He was staring at her now with such intensity that she couldn't ignore his gaze, couldn't pretend the man look wasn't there. "What . . ."

"I see a beautiful woman, full and ripe."

A woman. "Tatooktche calls me skinny."

"Don't speak his name; I don't want to hear it. Listen to me, Twana." He placed his hand under a heavy breast and pushed it upward until the pulsing nipple jutted toward him. "You are beautiful with a body that calls to me. I can't ignore the call; I won't."

I don't want you to. I want—you. Silent, she stood before him and watched him bend forward to cover her breast with his mouth. When he sucked her into him, her lower belly began to pulse with a life of its own, a life that knew and wanted nothing except him.

The sensual contact didn't last long enough, but before she could protest, his hands again encircled her breasts and he began kneading them. The heat inside her grew until she was afraid she might explode. In an instinctive gesture aimed at self-preservation, she gripped his wrists and tried to pull him off her. Ignoring her, he continued his sensual message, taking her further and further from self-control.

Fear shot through her, a lightning bolt of alarm. Made weak by it, she could only fight her way through it, try to make sense of it. Was she afraid of Madsaw?

Maybe it was something else.

"Twana, Twana. I won't hurt you."

"I—know that."

"Then what?"

What? The question spread out over the forest and seemed as large as the wilderness itself. She needed to concentrate, to call on her gift, but

Madsaw's very breath was inside her. "I—don't know what you want." She sounded like a whimpering child and hated what she couldn't change about her voice.

"You."

You. His hands fully covered her breasts and he pressed their weight against her, pressed past a lifetime of restraint to where a woman waited. Her defenses were nearly gone; there were only words left. "I belong to you; you can do what you want with me."

Even before she'd finished speaking, he rocked back onto his heels, his hands now knotted by his side. Her breasts felt instantly cold and cut off from what they needed as much as life itself. "Is that how you see this? I'm forcing myself on you?"

No! "I-I don't know."

"You don't know?" His fists tightened and he half turned from her. Still, his gaze snared her and demanded that truth. "You don't know your own body?"

Around you I don't. "I've never—you know that."

"And this isn't the time and I am not the right man."

There'd never be another man like him; didn't he know that? Forcing herself to go on meeting his hard and honest gaze, she turned her thoughts inward, cast off the lingering residues of whatever had tried to claim her.

"I want us to be equals," she told him honestly. "But if Tatooktche refuses to pay ransom, I will become your slave; you will have the power of life or death over me."

"Do you think I would kill you?"

No! Why had she said that? "You frighten me. I am afraid of what I feel around you."

He ran his gaze slowly, tellingly, down her naked body. "What do you feel now?"

It was a quiet request, a simple need for understanding. "I am not ashamed to be standing before you like this." She glanced down at her swollen breasts with their hardened tips. "What you have done to me—I am not afraid of that."

"Do you want me?"

Tatooktche had never asked her mother that; she was sure of it. The same must have been true with Conrad. But Madsaw was neither of these men; instead, he stood before her as war chief of the Wolf Clan, a courageous warrior, a man. "Yes." The word pushed past her lips. "Yes."

"Yes," he breathed. He started to reach for her, then stopped. "But it is more than that, isn't it?"

Did he know everything about her? Agitated, she raked her hand through her hair, too late noticing what the gesture did to lift and define her naked body. "I have never lain with a man."

"And you never expected to become a woman in the arms of the man who dragged you from your home." His voice sounded tortured. "Neither did I. But what I believe now is that the time for talking has ended. We want each other, Twana. Your body has told me the truth about what is in your heart, and I know what I need."

Her body had told him the truth? Maybe all he'd needed was to hold her breasts in his capable hands, breathe in air that had been inside her lungs, for honesty to be revealed. Looking at him, she realized he'd sucked in his belly, that his upper body was hard and taut as if he had to fight himself to keep from touching her—that his loin covering couldn't hide what had happened to his manhood.

"Don't think back or ahead, Twana. Forget everything except us. Your heart knows what it needs."

His simple words were so beautiful, so honest. She began trembling again, not because the wind briefly chased across her naked flesh, but because he was looking at her—simply looking. His eyes said it all; he thought her beautiful.

Beautiful in the way of a woman.

CHAPTER 15

She was liquid strength in his hands, a pulsing life force far stronger than anything he'd ever touched. He didn't remember lowering her to the soft carpet at their feet, barely remembered casting aside his loin covering. All that mattered was that she hadn't shrunk from him. Instead, she'd clamped her long fingers over his shoulders and held him against her, her body moving, always moving, until he stopped it with his own weight.

Even now with his leg over her and his hands restless on her breasts and belly, he could feel her trembling. A small part of him wanted her to stop, to at least assure himself that she wasn't afraid of him, but a larger part of his mind and heart believed that fear had nothing to do with her reaction. Not once had she taken her hands off him.

Like him, she seemed to need to touch all of him, needed to wipe away mystery and turn it into reality.

The forest was alive with sound this morning. Birds both large and small flitted through the trees, their songs and the rustle of needles a soothing backdrop to the storm inside him. The sky worked its own rhythm, one moment a gentle blue, the next giving way to one dark cloud after another that promised rain but did nothing more than touch the air with its smell.

He felt bonded with the wilderness, so much a part of it that if he'd had a sleeping matt to lie on, he wouldn't use it. How could he? He couldn't leave Twana long enough for that.

Twana. The name flowed through him and gave purpose to his hands. Her waist was smaller than he thought it would be, her hips right for childbearing. She had a woman's breasts, dark at the center, full and heavy, yet erect. The tips felt like small rocks, and he wondered if she knew he was responsible for what had happened to them.

If she did, then she understood she was responsible for his pulsing manhood.

When he rested his weight on an elbow so he could explore her sunken belly, she responded by doing the same to him, her fingertips both cool and hot on his sensitive flesh. Unable to suppress a groan, he lowered his head and lapped his tongue over first one breast and then the other. Her quick, deep moan told him everything he needed to know. Others might call her witch; she might have cast a spell over him today. But she was caught in a spell herself, one he was responsible for.

Pulling her against him, he slid his hand between her legs to the incredibly soft flesh there. She first tried to press her hips into the ground, then lifted herself to accept his teasing massage. Her head had begun to whip from side to side and her exploration of him became more random, sometimes a feather touch, other times her fingers probing with enough force that it almost became painful. Somehow, he managed to concentrate on his exploration of her. She responded to everything he did to her with an abandon that spoke, he told himself, of trust.

When, during a rare moment of sanity, he asked himself how he could be giving himself over to her this way, the question wasn't strong enough and he never waited for the answer. Her flesh was softer than the finest mink, the tiny sounds coming from her throat more compelling than a fawn's soft bleating. She seemed a part of her surroundings, almost as if her body had taken on the essence of lush green growth. The thought that Conrad might have taken her from him filled him with white dread.

Her ceaseless movements, the way she raked her nails over his arms and what she could reach of his back, told him she was ready for him, but although he felt as if he might shatter with wanting her, he drew out the exploration—made her even more his and in turn became much more a part of her.

A clap of thunder rocked the earth, causing him

to glance up. How had the clouds become so much darker and denser in such a few moments?

"Rain?" she whispered. "Is it going to rain?"

"I don't care."

For some reason that made her laugh. When thunder again rolled, she chuckled. "Will you still not care when you are drenched?"

"No. No—not as long as you are here with me."

Through half-closed eyes, Twana caught a flash of light. This prelude to a storm might be nothing, and it might mean that all too soon the clouds would drop their wet loads.

Like Madsaw, she didn't care.

For the third time thunder sent its energy into the earth; she responded to it as she never had before, pulled sound and power in through her pores and sent them racing through her veins. Madsaw was thunder, the strength of a spring-swollen river, heat from a lightning-sparked forest fire. How could she possibly fear Thunderbird when she'd been touched by Madsaw?

Letting emotion take over, she arched up off the ground to nip at Madsaw's chin. When he started to protest, she caught his lower lip between her teeth. She clamped her hands over his shoulders to keep herself from falling back again; her breasts brushed his chest and she pressed herself against him as if by doing so she could bury herself in him.

This wasn't her body; it had never felt like this—on fire.

This couldn't be her mind, not this weak and shattered thing that could only be put back together after he showed it what it was to be a woman.

She could carry his seed. This, her first time, could fill her with his life, and when the child was born, all would know what they had done. She would never be free of him, never have back her heart.

It didn't matter. She needed him too much.

When he again slid his hand between her thighs and the fire he'd created there became almost too much to bear, she spread her legs, muscles jumping, flesh hot and hungry. "Please," she whimpered. "Please."

He pressed his finger against her woman place, hard and insistent, igniting yet another blaze and taking her to the edge of madness. "No doubts, Twana? No doubts?"

A thousand misgivings, didn't he know that? They vanished under a fresh onslaught of thunder and lightning. She felt herself being swept along like a leaf in a torrent of water, whirling, spinning, with no thought of how to escape.

He'd kissed her belly. Startled by the unbelievably tender gesture, she tried to focus on him, but his face remained a blur. There should be something she could say, some words of gratitude, but—but he was now moving over her, spreading her legs with his insistent knees. Again he touched his lips to her breasts, and this time when she moaned, she didn't know whether she was going to cry or shatter.

"Madsaw. Madsaw . . ."

Maybe she hadn't spoken his name aloud;

maybe he was incapable of hearing. It didn't matter because they were going to become one and she would understand—understand—

Pain! She shuddered with it, then forced herself to relax as he withdrew slightly. "Are you all right?"

"I-I don't— My mother said, said . . ."

"That it's like this for a woman her first time. It's all right, Twana. I'll be gentle."

He tried to be. When he again drove himself into her, the pain was much less. Still, she couldn't make herself relax, couldn't reach back into the hungry mist that had claimed her before. Her mind slipped from one half thought to another, listened for the rain to begin, tried—tried to find itself.

He was over her, surrounding her, locked inside her, this magnificent warrior giving himself to her. Gentle and yet urgent, fighting his need so he wouldn't frighten her.

A man like that—this man called Madsaw . . .

Thunder filled her mind, froze her beneath him, made her gasp in fear and confusion. Struggling, she tried to make sense of what had invaded her, but the heavens were rolling with the aftershock of a thunderclap, and she told herself that was what she'd heard.

She didn't have to leave Madsaw and their lovemaking. Could surrender. Surrender.

Feel . . .

The pounding heat that had taken over her body earlier returned. Seeking its source, she buried herself in sensation. Became lost in it.

She'd been struck by lightning, touched by its fiery fingers, burned and yet renewed.

No. It wasn't lightning. Madsaw . . .

For as long as he could stay awake, Madsaw listened to Twana's soft breathing as she lay nestled against him. He'd half covered her with her dress, but although the wind had a bite to it and the threatening rain might come at any moment, he didn't feel chilled.

How could he? Twana had brought him back to life.

Propping himself up on his elbow, he first simply watched her, then gently ran his thumb over her exposed shoulder and arm. Her flesh twitched and a faint smile touched her lips.

Her smile undid him, made him want to scramble to his feet and run into the forest where he would never have to look at her again. Even Vattan had never held his heart like this, never made him willing to give up his life for her.

He shouldn't have touched Twana.

Groaning, he lay back down with his head so close to her throat that he thought he could hear her blood pulsing through the vein there. He had touched her; it was too late for him. She'd crawled under his skin, and he didn't know how to free himself.

Might never again be free.

It was raining when Twana woke. In his sleep, Madsaw had flung his arm over her, and its weight had numbed her side. She carefully slid out from under him, only then realizing he'd draped her dress over her. She stood up and slipped back into what was left of it. If she'd kept some of the rope Conrad used to tie her, she might be able to effect a repair, but she never again wanted to look at what had kept her prisoner to a madman.

With clenched fists and teeth, she fought off thoughts of the trader and focused on Madsaw's sleeping form. Although the trees stopped most of the rain from reaching them, a few heavy drops plopped to the ground not far from his head. Sitting down again, she ran her fingers lightly over his dark, glossy hair.

It seemed as if he'd left her entire body imprinted with him. Her breasts felt sore and roughened, and between her legs she ached. Her mouth was bruised and her flesh tingled. If she bathed, maybe she could wash him off her, but what could she possibly do about his invasion of her heart?

Her heart. The admission that he'd found his way inside her—that she'd let him—only brought a quiet resignation. She could tell herself she wouldn't let it happen again, that he hadn't touched her soul, but if she did, it would be a lie.

And her heart wouldn't listen.

A gust of wind shook the nearby trees and sent a shower of water over her. Because she quickly bent over Madsaw, his head and upper body were spared and he seemed unaware of the rain sliding off his hip and legs.

Off his naked flesh.

She'd just reached out to wipe a drop off the inside of his knee when something dark grabbed her senses and shook them. Frozen, she could only wait for the sensation to subside. When it did, at least enough to allow her to think, she remembered that her mind had been shaken twice while she and Madsaw were making love. She'd told herself she was reacting to his power over her, but maybe it had been something else.

Something dark.

Conrad? She shuddered at the thought that he might have tracked them, but that couldn't be; he'd been too badly wounded and his strength existed only in her mind.

One Ear!

A moan escaped her, a barely audible sound quickly swallowed by the storm. Still, she thought it might wake Madsaw, but although he stirred, his breathing remained deep and quiet. With her fingers now clutching her necklace, she stopped fighting.

He was out there, his great body rolling from side to side as he walked swiftly and surely through the forest. He wasn't coming toward her and Madsaw. Instead, his journey was bringing him closer and closer to the river upstream from them. Touching One Ear's body with her mind, she picked up a sense of thirst but not hunger.

No, not hunger because he'd eaten recently.

"Madsaw." When he didn't respond, she forced herself to release the necklace and shake his shoulder. "Ma—"

He woke quickly, cleanly, as if sleep had never claimed him. His eyes were instantly bright and alert, muscles tense. Instead of demanding an explanation, he simply looked at her, waited.

"One Ear."

"Where?"

She pointed. "He's thirsty. Thirsty and tired."

"You know those things about him?"

She nodded, then forced herself to return to the grizzly. She saw his full belly nearly drag on the ground, even felt the discomfort from his gorging. When the grizzly made his way into the water and began lapping greedily, she told Madsaw that.

"What has he fed on? Can you tell that?"

She started to shake her head, then a horrible thought entered her mind. She could only stare at Madsaw. "Conrad? You think—"

"I don't know, Twana. But maybe."

Maybe.

Madsaw had gotten to his feet without her being aware of that and was holding out his hand to her. She took it and let him help her stand, thought, briefly, about his naked body, then made herself listen to what he was saying.

"If he has tasted human blood, it may change him. He didn't go after Vasilii for reasons we will never understand. Maybe he has been stalking you, but in all that time he didn't attack."

"No."

"If he killed Conrad, he now knows how easy killing a human is."

"Madsaw—" She grabbed his arm and stepped closer, keeping her voice to an unnecessary whisper. "I believe he heard me the night I sent him my gratitude because he did not kill Vasilii."

"Heard? He is a beast; he understands nothing of kindness."

Was Madsaw trying to warn her that her life was in danger? If he believed that, then surely he understood he, too, was at risk. Not bothering to speak, she left him to once again rejoin One Ear. It seemed as if the grizzly would never get enough to drink, but finally, water still streaming from his mouth, he clambered back up the bank and lifted his head to the clouded sky. For several moments he simply watched it rain with a look of dim fascination in his little eyes before shaking his body so that water flew off him. He wiped his mouth almost daintily with a paw large enough to break a man's neck and then stared in the direction he'd come from. Finally, as if remembering something, he began retracing his steps. He hadn't gone far before he walked over to a massive tree and began sniffing its base. She knew he was going to lie down before he tucked his legs under him and rolled over onto his side.

Could he have attacked and killed Conrad? Images of what that had been like were too horrible for her to think about. Not even Conrad deserved to die that way.

"He's sleeping," she told Madsaw. "He won't wake until his belly has finished working."

"And then?"

"I don't know. I will watch him. Not a moment will pass when I won't know what he is doing. If he comes to your village, I will lead him away from it."

"No!"

"I have to," she pressed. "I will *not* let him hurt anyone else."

He didn't say anything, and in his intense stare she read dark resignation.

Although the sun had long been in the sky and was beginning its downward slide, hidden by relentless clouds, there was no warmth to the day, and if his life hadn't been changed by Twana, Madsaw would be glad to see his village. However, he couldn't simply think about stepping inside his warm home, where food to fill his belly waited; today he had to face those he loved and respected and explain why he'd risked everything for this woman.

Three, maybe four times he'd asked Twana to check on One Ear, and although she'd reassured him that the grizzly showed no sign of waking, he knew that when he did, One Ear might try to pick up their scent. If he found it, would he enter the village?

A buzz of voices pulled him from a question without answer. They'd barely broken out of the clearing, but already men, women, and children had stopped what they were doing to watch them approach. The ground was wet from rain, but few deep puddles had formed, and he guessed that most of the children had remained outside. Maybe their parents had gathered in one of the houses to talk about their war chief.

"I'm afraid," Twana whispered.

"No one will touch you; I won't let them."

"No. Not for me. But if they say you defied your chief, what will you do?"

"My chief is also my uncle. The bond between us remains strong."

"I hope it's strong enough. Madsaw, what will they say if they learn what happened between us?"

"They won't know," he told her, "unless you tell them." When she said nothing, he knew their love-making would remain locked within her, but maybe his mother would only have to look at them to know the truth. Would Apenas say anything? Would she hate Twana any more than she already did?

When Madsaw first glanced at his chief's house, he saw no one near it, but a moment later, his uncle emerged to stand with his arms folded, his gaze steady. "I have to speak to him," he told Twana.

"Do you want me with you?"

What he wanted was to keep her safe inside the walls he'd built, but that wouldn't stop tongues from wagging. It was better that everyone know the truth. No matter what they said, he would survive their reaction.

Chief Walkus cocked his head to one side when Madsaw and Twana drew near but did nothing more to acknowledge their presence. "Maybe the trader is dead," Madsaw told him, his voice carrying.

"Maybe? I do not understand."

"Conrad attacked Twana; she defended herself by stabbing him. Twana believes the grizzly was drawn to the scent of the trader's blood."

"You know all this? Did your hostage give you knowing eyes?"

Standing tall, proud because Twana was doing the same, Madsaw told the assembled villagers everything. Without taking his eyes off his chief, he knew when his mother joined them.

"I traded her to the sea-stranger," Chief Walkus said in a voice stripped of emotion. "Why did you defy me?"

Although he'd been expecting the question, it still hit him with the force of a blow. "It was not defiance, my chief. I was ruled by fear for her."

"What happened to her was no longer your concern."

"I believe different. She saved a boy's life; I could not throw her away."

His uncle's lips thinned; still, he knew Walkus was giving his words serious consideration. "You were afraid for her?" he asked. "Why?"

"That man, her father, has always been ruled by anger and the need for power. What he did once, he would do again, even with his daughter."

"What did he do?"

Even though Twana surely didn't want anyone to know this, he repeated what she'd told him about Saha's scars, about a pregnant woman fleeing a man determined to control her. "That is what I thought of when I learned who had taken her."

"You believe your hostage? You are sure she told you the truth?"

Tearing his attention from his uncle, Madsaw glanced down at Twana, who was unnaturally pale but still carried herself with a deep-born pride. "Yes. I believe her."

"What is your wish, Madsaw?" Walkus asked. "You rejected the goods the trader gave for her. Are you saying no debt must be paid for your father's death?"

Before he could begin to put his mind to what he needed to say, he felt a dry hand on his wrist. His mother, who had lost the man she loved, had touched him.

"No," he said, his words guided by memories of being held in a loving man's arms. "I can never forgive what happened to him. It is not the way of the Tillamook, not the way of the Wolf Clan."

Chief Walkus didn't say anything, and in the silence, Madsaw understood that more was expected of him. "My brother will soon return from the Nisqually village. Nothing has changed."

Madsaw's words sliced into Twana's heart; if he said anything more, she might turn and run—run from the reality she'd cast aside while she was discovering what it meant to be a woman. But when he remained silent, she admitted she still stood beside him because she needed to be seen as worthy of having been rescued. No. Nothing had changed. And she would survive as she'd survived Conrad.

"Perhaps you are right," the older man was saying, his focus on Madsaw. "Maybe she would have been treated as less than a slave at Conrad's hands; we will never know. He is dead; his goods are with his companions. It is as if he never happened."

Praying that was true, Twana waited for Madsaw's reply. It was slow in coming. "When Tatooktche's debt has been settled, Twana will return to her village as one of them, return to a man who wants to marry her. That is how it must be."

"You defied me, Madsaw. Went against my decision."

"Not defiance, but yes, I walked my own way." Sober-faced, he met his uncle's gaze. "There wasn't time to discuss this with you; the longer I remained here, the greater her danger. I was right. He would have killed her."

"A man who attacks his daughter; I do not understand such a thing. Listen to me, Madsaw. I must think about what you have said. Then you and I will talk again, alone. Whatever I decide, you will obey."

Whatever he decided. But no matter what Chief Walkus said, Madsaw knew he wouldn't defy his uncle. If he did, he would become an outcast among his people.

When Madsaw ordered her to wait for him inside his house, Twana made the long and lonely walk without him by her side. Aware that everyone's eyes were on her, she kept her head high and did what she could to protect her modesty by holding her neckline together. Only once the now familiar shadows inside Madsaw's house surrounded her did she allow what she'd heard and seen to make an impact. Her future, maybe even her life, was in Chief Walkus's hands.

Dropping to her knees in front of the fire, she

made a brief attempt to tame her hair, but she felt so tired, defeated. Madsaw hadn't defied his uncle; he'd announced to no one that he was willing to give up his position within the tribe for her. But could she really expect him to do that? Did she want him to? So much of what he was was tied up in his role as war chief. He was both wise and brave, a man who put others before himself. That man should one day become chief of the Wolf Clan.

And that man could never openly take her to his bed, never call her wife.

Wife?

An image of old Quahklah pushed its way through her thoughts. When that happened in the past, she'd shaken him off, but she didn't even try this time. She'd given herself to Madsaw and he'd done the same with her. For reasons so complex she couldn't begin to understand them, nothing had mattered more than joining her body with his. She'd never felt that close to anyone in her life, not even her mother. It seemed incredible, impossible even, that no barriers had remained between her and her captor.

That was why she needed to think of Quahklah today; once Tatooktche had paid for her ransom, she would become a wife to a man she'd known all her life, a quiet, slow-moving man who said little except to speak of the finished days when his legs were strong and his eyes keen. She didn't hate Quahklah, not even when the thought of him possessing her body made her shudder. She could never love him, never feel toward him anything like the emotions Madsaw had ignited in her.

It was safer that way.

Married to Quahklah, she would be allowed her own thoughts and emotions, and her heart would remain her own. Quahklah could never make her feel as vulnerable and exposed as Madsaw did simply by looking at her.

She stared into the fire's depths in an almost frantic attempt to bring back Quahklah's image, but it became less than smoke and only the impact Madsaw had made on her body and heart and soul remained. She was left with one question: When Madsaw took his new bride, would she continue to haunt him?

Although she hadn't been given permission to eat, she scooted close to a food basket and picked out a little salmon. As she did, she let go of her dress and the fabric fell away limply. Memories of Conrad's hands on her made her half-sick and she had to breathe deeply several times before she could put her mind to anything else. She would have to ask Apenas if she could make herself another dress; surely Madsaw's mother wouldn't refuse. Surely—

A faint sound spun her around. Apenas said nothing, only slowly walked over to the high shelf where she kept her storage boxes, lowered one to the ground, and opened it. Finding what she wanted, Apenas clutched it to her and carried it over to Twana. When she shook it out, Twana realized she was handing her a winter dress that had seen several seasons but was still serviceable.

"Thank you," she whispered when Apenas remained silent. Apenas muttered something she didn't understand. Still, when her gaze remained on her raw and reddened wrists, she believed Apenas was saying in her own way she hadn't wanted her to be abused by her father. Wanting to show her gratitude for Apenas's gift, she pulled off the dress she was wearing and quickly slipped into the new one.

"It is too big," Apenas observed.

"I don't care. Anything is better than ever wearing the other again."

Once again Apenas muttered under her breath, then returned to the storage shelf, where she selected a small, ornate box filled with whale fat. She dipped her fingers in it, took Twana's forearm, and began rubbing fat on where the ropes had rubbed her flesh raw. When she'd finished with both wrists, she left the box beside Twana and headed toward the door.

"Wait. Please don't go." Twana hurried her words. "I— Thank you."

The deep black of Apenas's eyes seemed to soften a little. "I am a mother, Twana. Nothing matters more to me than my son's happiness. Do not ever forget that."

"I won't; I want him to be happy too."

"Do you? Then let him be free."

"Free?"

"In his heart, allow him freedom."

Incapable of speech, Twana could only watch Apenas turn and walk outside. What she wanted to tell her was that Madsaw wasn't the only one who needed that, but if she did, she would have to tell Madsaw's mother that she'd lain with her son last night and given more than her heart to him.

After eating a little more, she began pacing. The more she walked, the weaker her legs became, but she couldn't bring herself to return to the fire, where memories of lovemaking burned. Twice she walked over to the entrance and looked out, but from where she stood, she couldn't see Chief Walkus's house. She tried to imagine what Madsaw and his uncle were saying to each other, but she didn't know enough about their private relationship. They might argue, but she didn't think so. Instead, she told herself, they would work together toward a solution that would both benefit the village and give closure to Nutlan's murder at Tatooktche's hands.

She'd just thrown her ruined dress into the fire when she heard several children shout. She understood little except that they were calling out Lukstch's name. Her heart gave a painful lurch and she could barely force air into her lungs. Madsaw's brother had returned, bringing with him word of his meeting with Tatooktche.

Heedless of Madsaw's order that she remain inside, she hurried to the opening and watched as Lukstch made his way through the crowd of children toward his uncle's house. When Madsaw stepped forward to extend his hand in greeting to his brother, she saw that Apenas was there as well. The four drew together, Lukstch doing most of the talking. They were quickly surrounded by the children, who pulled at Lukstch's rain cape, searching it for anything he might have brought back from the Nisqually village. Roaring like an angry grizzly, Lukstch charged the children, scattering them. Then the four disappeared into Walkus's house.

Only after she could no longer see Madsaw did she take careful note of her surroundings—and the motionless shaman staring at her. Determined not to let him see how much his presence upset her, she returned his glare until, with a shrug that made his hair shake like a giant clump of seaweed, he turned his back on her and walked toward the forest.

Twana couldn't say how long she continued to lean against the rough boards. Her thoughts were like tangled fibers as she tried to guess what had been on Sokolov's mind and what Lukstch was saying to his brother and uncle. Over and over again she imagined Tatooktche angrily telling Lukstch he wasn't willing to pay a single wooden spoon in exchange for her return, but maybe he'd had time to regret his hasty killing of a powerful Tillamook. Determined to once again hold his head high among his people and equally determined to gain a magnificent bride-price for her, he might be willing to negotiate.

If he was, she would be returned to the man who'd sold her mother to Conrad. Why hadn't she told Madsaw what Tatooktche had done? If she had, surely he'd never want her returned to her stepfather. But she didn't belong here either.

Feeling sick, she pushed away from the house and began walking aimlessly. She couldn't go back inside, not where thoughts of Madsaw waited, where she would feel helpless and trapped. She had to clear her head; otherwise, One Ear might come close without her knowing.

Only, it wasn't One Ear who filled her mind.

Sand from the beach stuck to the bottom of her feet, but she paid little attention to where she was going. How could she when she'd never felt so alone in her life?

"Twana? Twana, wait."

The female voice stopped her in midstep. Kitlote was coming toward her, her hand held out in friendship. Barely aware of what she was doing, Twana stumbled toward her and let the young mother throw her arms around her. Sobs heaved inside her, but she'd spent what tears she had earlier, while Madsaw held her and made her feel safe.

"I'm so glad you're back," Kitlote said. "I do not understand Apenas. To turn you over to that horrible man—"

"She thinks only of her son's happiness. She wants me out of his life."

"But to let you go with the trader without first consulting with Madsaw; I would never dare do such a thing. Is it as they say, that the trader is your father?"

"Was," Twana whispered. "He's dead."

"Dead? How?"

After gripping Kitlote's hands, she told her everything except what had happened between her and Madsaw. "You believe the grizzly found the trader?" Kitlote asked. "You didn't see it, did you?"

"No. But the way he acted, I know he had fed on something." She shuddered. "The thought is so horrible, but it is not a kind world."

"No, it isn't. And neither is what has been forced on you and Madsaw. You love him, don't you?"

"Love? I . . ."

"I see it in your eyes." Kitlote smiled, squeezing Twana's hand. "There are some things one woman cannot hide from another. Maybe that is why Apenas acts the way she does, because she sees the same tenderness in her son and is afraid for his heart."

"You—you believe he loves me?"

"Don't you?"

He'd kissed her, held her, taught her the joys of a woman, fallen asleep with his hand over her and his body turned toward hers. And he'd defied both his uncle and mother to search for her. "He is two men. One is a war chief, the other someone who has slept alone too long."

"Maybe he no longer sleeps alone."

Twana didn't blush. She wasn't ashamed of what she and Madsaw had done; she simply believed it should be kept private.

"Your eyes say a great deal," Kitlote told her. "I see the truth in them. Ah, my friend, it is not always a good thing for a woman to give herself to a man, because even when she again stands alone, her heart remembers what it shared with that man and a part of him is always with her."

Twana ran first one foot and then the other into the sand until she could no longer see her toes. After a moment, she kicked free and continued her aimless walk along the beach. A low and rolling mist clung to the surf some distance from the shore, looking like a lonely and curious creature hoping someone would come out and play with it.

She wished she could. The thought of being a carefree child again briefly filled her with reckless joy, but when she focused on what lay ahead of her, she remembered the weight of her life.

Madsaw's newest canoe was still here, untouched since he went to see Cleaskinch. The hull needed to be sanded and finished before the separate stern piece could be secured with cedar-peg dowels so exact that the seal was watertight. Finally, Madsaw would complete the intricate carvings that said this was a gift from a Wolf Clan man to a Raven Clan woman.

He would never give her a canoe.

Tears she didn't know she had welled in her eyes and blurred the canoe's outline. Reaching out blindly, she ran her fingers over the sides. If she asked, would Madsaw take her out in it just one time? If she could sit in a canoe with him while he put his strong shoulders to the act of rowing, she would be content to live the rest of her life with that experience caught tightly within her.

Only, it would be a lie because she needed more from him than to be taken out into the sea where no one could hear what they said to each other.

She felt hot moisture on her cheeks but didn't bother to brush the tears away because they would only be replaced by more. Turning toward the sea, she lifted her head so the breeze might cool her eyes. Still, she couldn't make herself take her hand off the canoe.

Madsaw's canoe.

Kitlote had been right; her heart would always remember him.

CHAPTER 16

The woman standing beside his canoe was Twana. Even though he was too far away for her to hear him if he called out, he didn't have to see her features to know who it was.

She seemed mesmerized by sea and mist, and if she stood there much longer, she might become part of her surroundings. When he looked into her eyes, he would find their rich color, but now all he could see was the gray of her dress, the gray of her world.

The gray of his heart.

Not caring who might be watching, he continued toward her. The waves made their weary way up and down the shoreline, spitting fine white bubbles along the sand where the breeze could scatter them. He'd been looking at this stretch of water

311

for his entire life, understood that the sea carried within it an endless supply of food—and sometimes brought death. Today he wasn't thinking about death. In fact, if someone asked, he wasn't sure he could say what was on his mind.

Her. The woman called Twana. The woman who'd trusted herself to him.

His legs felt as if someone had tied rocks to them, and there was the dull sound of a drum being beaten inside his head. When he pressed the heel of his hand against his forehead, it took away a little of the pain, but it returned as soon as he stopped. How had he become old in such a short period of time?

A chief's heart comes after the needs of his people. Do not ever forget that.

His uncle had told him that today, but it wasn't the first time he'd heard those words. As if they'd been spoken only moments ago, he heard his father's rough voice as he explained to his eldest son what it meant to be called on to settle disputes, to make the decision whether to trade with another tribe or village, to order men into a rough and dangerous sea in search of whales.

You were born to lead your clan; nothing comes before that.

Nothing, not even loving a woman.

He wanted to turn around and walk into the forest where he would never have to look at Twana again, but even as he waited for his legs to obey his command, they continued toward her. Although he couldn't be sure, he thought he saw her shoulders shake and wondered if she was crying.

He'd heard her sob before and had been happy to give her his strength while she worked her way through her grief at the thought of how her mother's life had ended, but if she was crying because of him—because she'd guessed what his uncle's decision would be—his arms wouldn't be enough.

Maybe he was the one who would need to be held.

Chief, he reminded himself. *Leader of his clan. Married into the Raven Clan. His father's death avenged.*

The woman he loved gone.

Even though his feet made no sound on the sand, she turned toward him, and he wondered if she could now sense his presence as surely as she sensed the wild creatures. He was right; she had been crying. He thought she might try to wipe away proof of her tears, but other than blinking once, she let him see.

"Your brother has returned," she said when his own throat clogged with unspoken words. "He has met with Tatooktche?"

"Yes."

"And?"

He should have come closer before letting his legs rest; he should have kept more distance between them. "Tatooktche first ordered my brother to leave, but the Nisqually chief would not allow that. Another man lifted his voice, told Tatooktche that he must pay for the greed that ended a life."

"Was that man Quahklah?"

"Yes." Fighting to keep emotion out of his voice,

313

he explained that Quahklah had ridiculed Tatooktche, calling him both stupid and selfish. Maybe,
Quahklah had said, he would pay the ransom and
then Tatooktche would be indebted to him. When
he said that, those who had gathered to listen to
Lukstch's demands laughed at Tatooktche.

"Laughed? None have ever dared do that before."

"There is courage in numbers. And he has finally gone too far."

By her short nod, he knew she was absorbing
that. "What did Tatooktche say then?"

How brave she was. "He offered three blankets,
a carved halibut fishing club, and his sister."

"His sister? Madsaw, she has never spoken and
can barely feed herself."

That was what Lukstch had said. "I reject the
offer."

"I see."

"It isn't enough, Twana. A chief's life is worth
more than that."

"I know. What happens now? Lukstch will have
to return to my village?"

Her village. "Tomorrow. He is weary of traveling
and wants to spend what is left of today fishing
with his uncle."

"Walkus is your uncle, too, Madsaw. Don't you
want to be with them?"

A few days ago, standing over the large, sturdy
fishing weir spearing fish alongside his brother
and uncle would have brought him great pleasure,
but things had changed between him and his
uncle—become strained despite the lifelong bond

that held them together. He would not defy his chief; he had made that decision. But neither could he silence his heart and what he felt for Twana. Until that happened—if it ever did—he needed to be alone.

Only he wasn't; he'd sought out Twana.

"You wear a different dress."

She touched the long sleeve but didn't take her eyes off him. "Your mother gave it to me."

"I see. She spoke to you?"

"She said little. Madsaw, I couldn't stay inside. I didn't mean to defy you, but my head pounded and I felt as if I might fly apart. Do you understand why I had to come here?"

Oh yes, he understood because the same restlessness had claimed him. He wanted to walk with her to the shoreline. They would step on the tiny white bubbles until they'd pushed them into the sand. Maybe they'd sit on a rock and watch the tide in its ceaseless journey until the dying sun painted this afternoon's few clouds in brilliant reds and oranges. They'd laughed about how Vasilii was boasting to his friends that he hadn't been afraid all the time he was lost. Not once would he mention Conrad or Sokolov's hatred for her, his mother's mixed emotions. What was even now tearing him apart.

But they couldn't spend the night here.

"Stay as long as you want," he told her. "But when you are done, I want you to go to my mother."

"Where—will you be?"

"I need to return to the village of the Raven Clan."

To see his future bride. With his simple words, Madsaw stripped Twana's mind of every other thought. "Will you go today?" she asked in a voice empty of emotion.

"No, tomorrow."

Then they'd be together tonight. But they wouldn't, she reminded herself. Certainly after everything that had happened, the way the villagers were watching him, he wouldn't touch her. "I can't sleep at your feet," she whispered, her eyes on the safe gray and white waves that would remain long after her life had finished itself. "Don't ask me to do that."

"I don't want this, Twana. Don't you understand?"

Of course she did; hadn't her heart beat in time with his? Still, feeling crushed by heartache, she simply shook her head and tried to imagine the waves lapping over her, pulling her far out to sea where she would join whales and sharks. "You should have left me with Conrad."

"You don't mean that."

"How do you know what I think?" she challenged, because that was the only way she could keep from breaking apart. "You know nothing about me, Madsaw. Nothing." She should walk away from him, but she couldn't remember how to make her legs move, and if she dove into the sea, she would never see him again. Never hear his heart.

316

"I don't believe that. Do you think I can ever forget how you looked when I found you?"

"How did I look? What was I thinking?"

"That if Conrad tried to touch you again, you would kill him."

He was totally and horribly right. She wouldn't tell him he was wrong because if she did, he would see through the lie. Still, there were other things he didn't know, the truth she hadn't told him because at first all she could think about was getting as far from Conrad as possible, and then because only Madsaw mattered.

"Tell me I'm wrong, Twana."

Caught, she wrapped her arms around her middle and began rocking, trying to lose herself in movement. "It doesn't matter; he's dead. When will I be returned to Tatooktche?" she asked.

He looked as if she'd slapped him, but she didn't care—told herself she didn't care.

"Listen to me, Twana." He touched her elbow, but when she stiffened, he let his hand drop back by his side. "If I believed you would be in danger, I would keep you here. Somehow. But my brother assures me that Quahklah wants to make you his wife as soon as you return."

She wanted to laugh; if she wasn't afraid she'd start crying again, she would. So Madsaw thought her capable of killing Conrad. What would he think if he knew what she wanted to do to Tatooktche, the man who'd sent her mother to her death?

"Maybe I will go to Quahklah's house the same day you bring your bride to yours," she whispered.

317

Once again his body jerked, but this time it was all she could do not to beg him for forgiveness. It wasn't Madsaw's fault that Quahklah was willing to pay for her any more than it was his doing that he'd been betrothed to a girl from the Raven Clan. "Why are we fighting?" he asked. "How have you come to hate me?"

"I don't hate you! I don't hate you."

"What I see is a woman who never wants to see me again, who is ready to return to her village."

Only so I can face Tatooktche. Make him pay. "It is as it must be. We have always known that."

"Did we when we made love?"

She swayed, barely catching herself in time. The way he stared at her told her he knew what impact his words had had on her, but she couldn't hate him for his honesty. In three, maybe four days she might be taken back to the Nisqually village, never to see Madsaw again. There would only be memories—and regret if she wasn't honest with him now.

"When we lay together, there was only you and my need for you."

She heard him suck in a deep breath and imagined cool salt air warming as it reached his lungs. "I wanted nothing in life except you," he told her. "When I heard that you'd been given to the trader, I told the others I feared you would meet your death at your father's hands, but that isn't why I defied my chief."

"It wasn't?" She couldn't stop shaking, couldn't remember how to breathe.

"You were inside me. Our bodies were still

strangers to each other and yet you were inside me."

You will always be inside me. "I-I don't know what to say."

"Tell me you no longer want me."

"I can't," she moaned, her body rocking, eyes on the horizon, thoughts going no further than him. "I can't!"

"You want me now?"

He deserved honesty from her. If she said no, she would be lying to both of them. "I'm afraid of how much I want you. I think there might never be an end to how much I need you, and yet I must go through my life without you."

A sound like that of a lost soul traveling through the underworld tore through him. She ached for him, nearly cried because the same emotions swamped her. "The rest of our lives," he whispered in a tortured tone.

He hadn't moved to touch her. She could be the one to reach out for him, but if she did, it might be as if she'd placed her hand in the middle of a fire; she'd be forever burned. "It is how it must be," she told him—told herself really. "You are who you are; nothing can or should change that. I, too, have my place. What I must do."

"Do you want to return to the Nisqually?"

That was her home, the only world she'd ever known. But her mother would never join her there, and she would have to look at the man responsible for her mother's death. "I have never known a true friend there," she told him honestly.

"Here, Kitlote treats me with love. I am going to miss that, but I know what I must do."

For a long time he stood beside her, his eyes fixed on the sea, and yet she knew he wasn't thinking about the great water's riches or the next time he might take a canoe out there in search of what it had to offer. Her thoughts turned to winter, that time of cold and wind and long, dark days and storms one upon the other, the shelter of trees and sturdy houses, the wonderfully clean scents that were part of those storms, sitting around a fire with others while mothers and grandmothers told their clan's stories of wealth, honors, and glorious deeds to eager-eyed children.

Would she ever tell her children of the Tillamook war chief who stole both her body and heart?

"I remember the first time I saw the sea-strangers," Madsaw said. "I was a child still running to my parents for protection when they came in their strange boats wearing clothes made from deer hide that shrank and dried in the rain. I thought the men were wonderful; all the children did. The gifts they bought, their funny words, the hair on their faces. All that seemed so strange to me. Lukstch was only a baby; he cried when he saw them. My father told him to be quiet, but I now know Lukstch was right to cry. Nothing has been the same since the white traders first entered our village. I believe our lives will never again be as it was when my parents were children."

"I've thought the same thing."

"Have you?" He turned his powerfully built body toward her. "We are much alike, Twana. Our thoughts, what we feel."

She could barely see him for the tears that once again blurred her vision. It didn't matter who saw her bold gesture; she had to touch him, feel the strength of his jaw, the vein pulsing in his throat, flesh stretched over muscle. "Maybe we are."

She spread her fingers over his chest to capture as much of him as possible, and although he sucked in his breath and held it for a long time, he didn't move away. Instead, he covered her hand with his and silently led her down the beach away from the village. He didn't ask if she wanted to go with him, but then he didn't need to.

Huge rocks flanked the river where it flowed into the sea, and a few trees had taken root among them, fed by the soil brought down by the river. In that sheltered place, Twana had heard, men and women seeking privacy sometimes came. She didn't have to ask why Madsaw had brought her here, and she would never lie and tell him she didn't want them to be together.

"My brother said he didn't want to leave until tomorrow so he can fish with our uncle today, but I know there is another reason," Madsaw said. "He wants to be with his wife tonight. They are like children who have discovered a new game and cannot get enough of playing it."

"Maybe sometimes it is like that between a man and a woman."

"How simple that must be—to know that making love is right and that no one will say different."

He'd had that once with Vattan; he would have it again with the girl whose name she couldn't remember—didn't want to remember. She tried to tell herself that Quahklah had it in him to be gentle and she would come to enjoy what he did with her, that she would be grateful if he placed his seed inside her and she became a mother. But she would never tremble with wanting Quahklah.

She was trembling now.

"I don't want to say any more about this," Madsaw whispered. "I simply want to reach for you and know you feel the same as I do and that neither of us will speak of tomorrows, only today."

Tomorrow—the end to this brief magic. "There is only today," she told him. A deep blue cloud began spreading itself around and through the other clouds. It might soon drop the rain it carried deep within itself and it might move inland where it would further nourish trees already rich with moisture. She needed to be nourished—by Madsaw. Still, when she tried to lock her arms around his neck, she discovered that they'd become so heavy, she couldn't move them.

He, too, seemed frozen in place. His fingers curled inward toward his naked flanks, and she almost laughed at how little his loin covering hid from her eyes. *I love you,* she wanted to tell him. *I will always love you.* Instead, she watched a seagull swoop and dive and then climb until she lost the large bird in the dark blue cloud. Was that how her love for Madsaw was, forever lost?

No. As long as her heart beat, it would live on.

She didn't realize she'd been fingering her necklace until Madsaw drew her hand away from her throat. He kissed her knuckles as he'd done before, but her flesh felt as if it had never been touched by him. He had said they wouldn't speak of tomorrows; she didn't want to talk about anything—only wanted to feel. To be.

She'd been standing on a small hill made entirely of sand. When she shifted her weight, the sand dislodged and she had to grab Madsaw's arm to keep from losing her balance.

That was all it took. His arms snaked around her, held her with the strength of the sea's powerful undercurrent. She gripped him in turn, arms now tight around his neck, her body trying to become part of his. They breathed together; maybe they both sobbed at the same time—she would never be sure if only she made that little animal sound or if it had been wrenched from him as well.

Then holding wasn't enough and she lifted her face to find his mouth waiting for her. They came together in a rush that was like the river meeting a stormy sea, and her entire world became as dark and filled with energy as the growing cloud overhead. Madsaw was alive with electricity, pulsed with it, fed her in a way she'd never believed possible.

As eager as a fox kit leaving its den for the first time, she explored his body with her hands, mouth, tongue, hip, and belly. But she was no newborn creature of the forest; she'd become a woman with a woman's needs and desires, and they fed her daring.

Madsaw moved constantly. She might have believed him under her spell if his hands and tongue and hip hadn't begun a volcano inside her. She felt herself swell with it, spiraling up and out until he claimed the fragmented pieces and put her back together again. Only, she was no longer the woman she'd once been. Pieces of him were now fused with her—forever part of her.

He yanked off her dress with such force that he caught her hair in it. Hands trembling slightly, he quickly freed her and then clutched her naked body against him. They sank to their knees together. He immediately lowered her onto her back, and she realized he'd somehow spread the dress on the ground so that her back rested on it instead of stone and dirt and sand.

He reached for the tie around his waist, but she pushed his hands away and untied his loin covering for him. For the first time she touched him there, marveling at the exquisite mix of silky flesh and pulsing strength. Already hot and moist, she lifted her hips to him, clutched his arms with fingers that seemed capable of holding a grizzly. When he drove himself into her, she sucked in salt air and closed out the world.

He was everything, everywhere, his powerful body holding her against the ground and yet leaving her feeling utterly free. She rose and fell with him, wrapped her legs around him, bit at his chin and neck, scalding tears coursing down her cheeks.

Giving herself in to both the tears and him, her

mind began to splinter like small clouds touched by a summer sun. She felt the sun's heat—a heat created by the warrior who'd already claimed her heart and was now doing the same to her body. The rhythm that was him increased. It seemed as if he might explode from the movement, and she knew that if he did, she would shatter with him.

He groaned, let out a sound born of the wild. A heartbeat later she heard her own voice rise to be swallowed by the trees. Her body shook and trembled, spasmed in a way she didn't believe possible. He was caught in the same powerful grip, and because she still held him with all her strength, she rode the storm waves with him.

Consciousness came slowly, a spring morning filled with mist. She first became aware of his sweat-slickened body resting half on hers, then her own body began to come back to her. Tears still heated her cheeks, and she didn't dare ask where they came from. Somewhere just beyond them the world waited, but she wasn't ready to join it—might not ever be ready for that.

The river was so close that she could hear its hearty laughter as it rushed toward its end. Thinking of its fragile beginnings and its great power here, she could only make comparisons between the river and what she felt for Madsaw.

Caring had begun that first night when he hadn't forced himself on her but instead sheltered her from her nightmares. She'd had no idea that the gentle stirring would turn into this overpowering emotion. If she had, would she have found a way to escape?

No.

She'd just begun to pull her arm out from under him when the thunder rolled inside her. There'd been no warning, no quiet building of energy as happened during a storm. Instead, the thunder-clap was upon her before she could she could prepare herself—before she could begin to under-stand.

"Madsaw!"

As she'd seen him do before, he put sleep behind him in a single heartbeat. "What is it?"

Her head throbbed, forcing her to press her hands against it to keep it from exploding. She tried to focus on him, but the noise and pain were forcing her inward.

"What is it?" he repeated. "One Ear?"

One Ear! She saw the massive grizzly as it charged through the trees, winced at the thought of the hapless ferns underfoot. The bear's breath came in great woofs of sound that seemed capable of bending the trees themselves. Like a demon from the underground, it followed its nose and en-ergy and primitive desires, mouth open to reveal killing teeth, the masses of fat and muscle swing-ing in rhythm with its running stride.

Ahead of it—

"Madsaw! The fishing weir! He's—"

Madsaw didn't give her time to finish. Bounding to his feet, he grabbed her and pulled her up with him. "He's there?" he demanded as he shoved her dress at her.

"Yes!"

Madsaw had already begun running upriver,

leaving her to keep up as best she could. As she raced after him, trying to pull on her dress at the same time, the horrible scene played itself out in her mind. When One Ear swung his head first in one direction and then another, she guessed he was looking at the men, imagined them pointing their thin fishing spears at him. The pile of salmon briefly held On Ear's attention, and she prayed he would gorge himself while the men escaped. But although she couldn't see One Ear's attacker, she saw a spear hit his shoulder. It may have even penetrated the thick skin, but his lumbering gait pushed it out again. Roaring, One Ear charged. She screamed, stumbled, and sagged against a tree to keep herself from collapsing. Madsaw looked back at her, his face pale. A howl was wrenched from him and he started running again.

The world went momentarily black and she prayed she wouldn't be able to see any more, but the nightmare continued. One Ear lunged after someone, overtook him, knocked him to the ground. She pressed the heels of her hands against her eyes with such force that for a moment she wondered if she'd blinded herself, but that changed nothing.

One Ear picked his victim up by the shoulder and shook him as a dog shakes a stick. She heard a pain-filled masculine scream, screamed herself, forced herself to start running again.

The grizzly released his victim. At first she didn't understand why, but One Ear's stance soon told her that he'd spotted another adversary. The advancing shadow came closer, so close now that little more than the span of a man's arms separated man from bear. Walkus! The shadow— Walkus! Advancing on One Ear, waving a tree branch over his head. One Ear rose onto his hind legs, and Walkus stumbled back a few steps, but when the grizzly dropped down, the Tillamook chief started toward him again. Bellowing, Walkus swung the branch at One Ear's face. If he'd hit his sensitive nose, Walkus might have stopped the grizzly, but at the last moment, One Ear turned his head slightly and the branch struck his jaw. With a swift, silent movement, One Ear batted the branch out of Walkus's hand.

Her vision cleared, expanded, showing her everything that existed in One Ear's world. Lukstch, young, fun-loving Lukstch, lay unmoving on the ground. Other braves pleaded at their chief to run, but Walkus stood his ground, waving his arms and shouting. In answer, the grizzly bounded forward, knocked Walkus off his feet, then lowered his head. She couldn't see Walkus now, but she heard him scream, saw the horror on the other men's faces.

She tripped over a root and fell, but was back on her feet and running again before it registered that she'd hit her knee on a sharp rock. Hobbling with every step, she continued in the direction Madsaw had gone. Her greatest fear was that his concern for his people would outstrip his wisdom. If he was the next to be attacked—

The battle continued. For reasons she didn't at first understand, One Ear had lost interest in

Walkus and was heading toward the three men left standing. When she realized they were between One Ear and the just caught salmon, she begged them to run. If One Ear began eating, maybe the others could grab Lukstch and Walkus and run.

Madsaw!

He burst from the forest, features contorted. Although she begged him to be silent, the moment he spotted his wounded relatives, he began yelling at the grizzly, waving his arms to distract the beast. The other men broke rank, one stumbling into the river, another running into the forest, the third hurrying toward Madsaw. This brave carried a spear, which he handed to Madsaw when Madsaw ordered him to. Looking like a cougar stalking a deer, Madsaw advanced on One Ear.

"No!" she screamed even though only the forest creatures could hear. "Please!"

One Ear lifted his head so that when he bellowed, the treetops themselves shook with the sound, then he focused on Madsaw again. He took several steps, his body rolling with the effort. Madsaw stood his ground, spear poised, and she knew he was aiming at One Ear's eye.

"No!" Didn't he understand? Even blinded, the grizzly could tear him apart. Although every nerve in her screamed with the need to be near Madsaw, she forced herself to slow, not just so her knee wouldn't give out on her, but so—maybe—she could reach the grizzly another way.

He isn't the enemy! You can't hate him; his courage—aren't two men enough? Fish. Think only of filling your belly. Let him go. Let him live, please.

Even with her eyes trained on the forest, she could see One Ear and the others as vividly as if she'd been standing in the opening with them. The grizzly had stopped again and was peering at Madsaw. Instead of charging, Madsaw held his ground, his attention torn between the bear and the two wounded men.

Take me. I sacrifice myself to you. Just spare him.

She heard labored breathing and a pain-filled groan, and knew she was nearly there. In the middle of a step, her legs refused to move. For a moment she thought her knee had given out, then had to face the truth. She was afraid of stepping out from under cover—afraid of presenting herself to One Ear.

But Madsaw had started toward the grizzly, and she had no choice.

CHAPTER 17

Madsaw's attention was so totally focused on the grizzly that he didn't know Twana had arrived until the bear swung toward her. She looked so defenseless that if it hadn't been for her warning to him to remain where he was, he would have charged One Ear in a frantic attempt to save her.

But although she had one hand around her throat in a self-protective gesture, no fear etched her features. He would never understand what passed between her and this killer. At the moment it didn't matter; what did was that two people he loved might be dying and she might be all that stood between him and his own death.

She took another step that brought her out of the shadows so a spray of sunlight glinted off her night hair and filled her eyes with life. The spear he held felt no more substantial than a length of fern root.

Cautiously, measuring his progress in distances a child just learning to crawl could cover, he started toward her. "Madsaw, don't," his uncle hissed. "Don't risk . . ."

The sight of Chief Walkus barely able to lift himself on one elbow hit him like the blow from a dislodged boulder. "I can't let you die."

"If I die, you must take my place. The Wolf Clan cannot be without a leader."

Walkus was right. Still, he would willingly lay down his life if it meant sparing Twana. The grizzly wasn't moving, and yet there was nothing still or quiet about him. His chest heaved from the exertion of his recent run and his mouth hung open, maybe in anticipation of the taste of human flesh. One Ear hadn't attacked the night they found Vasilii. He'd wanted to believe Twana when she said she'd sent the grizzly a message of love and understanding.

How could he have thought that One Ear was anything except what he was, fierce and fearless lord of the forest? Maybe a beast who remembered his mother's death and those responsible.

"Twana," he whispered. "You can't stop him."

"He wants me." Her attention didn't once leave the grizzly. "That's why he's here, why he's stayed around all this time."

He didn't know whether she was right or not and didn't dare take his thoughts from the still heavily breathing grizzly long enough to search for the truth. One Ear stretched out his neck, first toward the pile of fresh salmon and then again in Twana's direction. Her body became as rigid as an aspen untouched by the wind. She kept her full weight off her right leg, and what he could see of her knee looked swollen. She couldn't run. Not that it mattered, for One Ear could easily overtake the swiftest man.

The one brave who hadn't fled took a half step toward his fallen chief but froze when One Ear released a low, rumbling sound. Walkus was still propping himself on one elbow. There was a gash on his side and another on his hip, both of them bleeding freely. Lukstch, who'd wanted to spend the night in his wife's arms, didn't stir. Rage at the monster responsible, maybe even at the woman who might have drawn him here, flooded Madsaw.

"You didn't tell me," he said through taut lips. "He was preparing to attack and you said nothing."

"I was with you. Nothing else—" When she stopped in midsentence, he nearly ordered her to continue. That was before One Ear stepped toward Walkus.

"Stop!" Twana pleaded. "Don't hurt him, please!"

The grizzly had already, maybe, dealt his chief a death blow, but Madsaw didn't tell her that. He watched, paralyzed and fascinated at the same time, as One Ear turned from Walkus and again focused on Twana.

"Please—you don't hate him," she whispered. "It's me—"

She was going to say something else, but he

333

would never know, because One Ear had started toward her and she stared at the grizzly as if he had become a monster rising from the sea's depths. Madsaw clutched his spear until he thought he might snap it in two, and yet he didn't hurtle it because the weapon might only enrage the grizzly more.

One step, two, three, until One Ear and Twana were so close that she must feel his hot breath. Her enormous eyes dominated her face, and the hand clutching her mother's necklace had turned white at the knuckles. She seemed to shrink before the beast.

One Ear was death. Maybe her death.

A scream burst from his lips without his knowing it was inside him. The sound made no sense, had no reason for being. Still, it pulled One Ear's attention from Twana.

And toward him.

Ignoring his wildly beating heart, Madsaw held the spear over his head and tried to gauge whether he could hit an eye at this distance.

"Madsaw!" he heard Twana call out. "Don't!"

Don't? Didn't she know he was acting without conscious thought, that because he wouldn't run, the only thing left to him was trying to kill this monster?

He heard a faint sound and wondered if his brother was trying to speak. His brother. One Ear had—had attacked Lukstch as if the young man were nothing more than a branch that had gotten in his way.

"One Ear. Hear me. It's me you want. Me. Not

him." Twana's voice gained strength with every word. "Take me. I will not fight you. Take me."

Take her? A moment ago he'd hated her because her presence might have brought One Ear here, but now he couldn't find the emotion. Like a puppy flitting from one diversion to the other, One Ear swung back toward Twana. But he was no playfully nipping puppy; his bites were deadly. Again Madsaw counted out each step as One Ear once more closed the distance between him and Twana. She looked so insignificant, a baby about to be battered by a great wave. He called out, his voice hard and urgent, but the grizzly paid him no mind. Finally, frantic, he hurtled the spear. It struck the bear on the shoulder, sticking out of him until he knocked it free with a swipe of his great jaw.

"Twana! Run!"

She still didn't move, continued to stare with eyes so large, they'd left nothing else for him to look at. Releasing her necklace, she lifted both hands as if to ward off the grizzly's approach.

A shout, running feet, more shouts, stopped him from repeating his useless command. Out of the corner of his eye he caught movement, but it wasn't until he heard his uncle cry out that he realized what had happened.

Men from the village, maybe all of them. Some carried bows and arrows while others, like him, were armed with nothing more than a slender spear. Two banished slave killers. The men were yelling like children playing a stick game, their voices clashing with the sound of the river. At an order from one of them, those with bows and arrows stopped and readied their weapons. One Ear spun away from Twana to confront the newcomers. When he roared, the scream echoed against massive tree trunks. Startled, one of the men let fly with his arrow. It hit One Ear's skull and bounced away, blood welling from where it had pierced flesh.

Before the grizzly could take more than a single step, more arrows were loosed. Several missed, but the majority reached their target, one penetrating the loose flesh in One Ear's jowl. He swatted at first one and then another arrow as if they were little more than annoying bee stings. One half-buried near his right shoulder broke off and he licked at what remained inside him.

He roared again; a nearby raven squawked in reply, then fled his tree with a heavy whir of wings. One Ear jumped first in one direction and then another as if trying to decide which of his enemies to attack. He was still rocking furiously back and forth when another volley of arrows hit him. A bellow of confusion, pain, and anger shook the air.

Run! Madsaw wanted to yell at the men, but if they fled, the grizzly might take off after them. Forcing himself to remain silent, he inched closer to his inert brother. He wasn't yet close enough to drop to his knees when One Ear screamed, turned, and all but dove into the river. A great spray of water cascaded out in all directions. The grizzly half swam, half scrambled, his paws finding solid footing on the rock-strewn bottom. The water came up to his neck and in several places turned pink. With an effort, he hoisted himself out of the river and disappeared into the forest.

Madsaw saw only his brother. Although he wanted to clutch Lukstch to him, he laid his hand over Lukstch's chest, not breathing until he felt his hand being lifted.

"Madsaw?" His uncle's voice was weak but urgent. "Is he alive?"

"Yes. So far, alive."

Someone had joined him. Expecting it to be one of the men, maybe Sokolov, he paid no attention until Twana lowered herself beside him. She sucked in her breath and rocked to one side, reminding him that she'd injured her knee, but that wasn't his concern.

Nothing was except learning how badly his brother was hurt.

Twana pushed Lukstch's hair away from his forehead to reveal a large, already purple knot. She next placed her ear against Lukstch's chest, her eyes half-closed in concentration. "His heart beats too fast. Fast and thin. He—" She straightened, her focus now on the torn and bleeding flesh from hip to knee. Her hand closed over Lukstch's limp fingers.

Was his brother dying? If Twana had warned him of One Ear's presence, this wouldn't have happened! But although he wanted to shake her until his pain and heartache disappeared, he knew it wasn't her fault.

He should have walked away when he saw her

standing by his canoe. Should have never touched her.

"Madsaw?" she whispered, her finger a butterfly touch on his arm. "Will he live?"

"I don't know."

"Don't say that! Please, don't—"

"I will kill him!" Madsaw bellowed, fear overwhelming him. "Before I die, I will kill One Ear!"

Twana had no idea how long it took for a panting Sokolov to look the wounded men over before ordering others to carry Lukstch and Walkus back to the village. It seemed to take forever and yet she was glad no one had hurried either wounded man away from where they'd been attacked—from where One Ear might return.

Although Lukstch's wife wanted him carried to Madsaw's house, it was decided that the men should remain together in Chief Walkus's house. Both wives insisted that Sokolov tend to their husbands, and for a moment Twana nearly believed he could heal. His leathery face was hidden by a painted wooden mask carved to resemble a wolf. He wore nothing except a heavy cape made from elk and wolf hides. In his hand he carried a large rattle, which he constantly shook. Those who'd been able to squeeze into the house—fully half of the village—chanted in time with the rattles.

Sokolov began by pacing slowly around his patients, but his stride quickly lengthened until he was running. Finally, thin chest heaving, blowing hard against the confining mask, he started whirling in a tight circle. The cape flew out behind him to reveal his sweat-slickened body. The sounds he made were louder than what came from his rattle and put Twana in mind of what Thunderbird might utter when he flew from his mountaintop home.

But her mother had always said that wounds needed to be cleaned and covered with the moist inner bark from a sumac tree. Sounds and dancing never cooled a fever.

Walking gingerly on her stiff knee, she made her way around the outside of the crowd until she was close enough that she could touch Madsaw. He hadn't once looked at her during the trek back to the village, but he didn't have to for her to sense the concern that knotted his belly. The tender way he'd touched his brother, the pain that haunted his eyes until he saw Lukstch breathe— how could he think of anything except saving a life? Even now Lukstch seemed oblivious to what was going on around him while his uncle struggled to keep his eyes open and occasionally said something either to Madsaw or his wife.

It shouldn't be like this! She'd touched One Ear with her thoughts, given him her love the night he spared Vasilii's life. He'd killed Conrad; wasn't it enough?

Careful to remain where Sokolov couldn't see her, she waited for her chance to get Madsaw's attention. Unlike the others, Madsaw didn't join in the chanting, and when his mother cried, he cradled her in his arms but said little. What were his thoughts? Was she part of them?

How could she not be?

Finally, his breath coming in tortured gasps, Sokolov fell in a heap near Walkus. He sucked in more air, his body shaking, then suddenly became so still that he looked as if he'd died. The chanting stopped, and like the tide rolling over sand, the house became utterly silent. She waited, her knee throbbing, hands aching to touch Madsaw. After a few moments several children began asking whispered questions. Their mothers tried to hush them, but as soon as one quieted, another took his place.

Sokolov's lids spasmed. He opened his eyes, glaring so fixedly at one boy that the youngster began to cry. Ordering the mother to silence her child, he crawled over to Walkus's side and put a hollow tube made from a deer rib bone against the chief's wound. Walkus pulled in a sharp breath but said nothing as Sokolov began sucking on the tube, eyes rolling until little but white showed. Twana knew he was drawing the evil spirit out of Walkus, that if he failed to heal the chief, he would say that Walkus's spirit had deserted him and even a powerful shaman can't save a man when that happens.

The healing sumac bark; that was what both Walkus and Lukstch needed.

When the chanting began again, Twana touched Madsaw's back. He stiffened but didn't turn around. Instead, he reached behind him, grabbed her hand, and began threading his way through the crowd, taking her with him.

Although it was late in the day, enough sunlight

remained that she could see Madsaw's every emotion. There was no warmth to the way he looked at her, no hint of what they'd shared before One Ear's attack. "Quickly, Twana," he ordered. "I am needed inside."

"Chants and rattles won't heal them. They need medicine."

"This is my mother's wish."

"I don't mean to defy her. Surely you understand I want them to live as much as you do."

"Do you?"

His words made her flinch. "Do you hate me?"

By way of answer, he pressed his hand against his forehead, his attention flickering to the house entrance. "My brother may be dying. The same may happen to my chief, and you speak of yourself?"

Struggling for the words to let him know she ached for him and would lay down her life for the two men inside, she reminded him that she'd faced One Ear when she could have remained hidden in the forest. Confusion clouded his features, and she thought he was going to speak, but before he could, she realized they were no longer alone.

"I saw the witch!" Sokolov, his voice muffled by the heavy mask, pointed his rattle at her. "She stood near the men and cursed them with her evil power."

"No! I would never—" She ducked as Sokolov tried to slap her but made no move to hide behind Madsaw. "That's a lie! I want them to live."

"Stop it!" Madsaw stepped between her and the

shaman. "There will be no fighting. Nothing matters except the two men inside."

"I cannot heal them if she is around," Sokolov blustered. "Her evil—"

Madsaw took a menacing step toward the shaman. "How quick you are to give up. What do you want, more gifts?"

"If you were to give me everything you own, it would make no difference. *She* has sealed their death; nothing can save them."

A high-pitched gasp pulled Twana's attention from both Madsaw and Sokolov. Apenas was standing just outside the opening, her slight frame trembling. She looked as if she hadn't slept or eaten in days, and there was a pallor to her that tore at Twana's heart. She desperately wanted to comfort her, but knew better than to touch the older woman. Mouth working, Apenas stared at Sokolov for a long time. "Nothing?" she whimpered. "Do not say that."

"I must speak the truth." Sokolov pulled off his mask and tucked it under his arm. He'd painted his body red but hadn't touched his face, creating a bizarre contrast that another time would have made Twana laugh. "I have given Walkus and Lukstch my best medicine, but it lies on their flesh and cannot enter them. It is *her* doing." He pointed at Twana. "She wants to see them dead. If I remain in her presence, she may destroy my power. I must protect myself from her, must cleanse myself. Only that way can I remain strong."

Although Apenas grabbed Sokolov's arm, he

342

yanked free and stalked away. Twana stared after him, her heart bleeding because Apenas continued to trail after him, her desperate pleas making her sound like an old, old woman.

Finally there was nothing to do except face Madsaw. "Do you believe him?" she asked.

"Do I believe you want my brother dead? No."

She went weak with relief. He had never looked so alone, and yet his eyes warned her that was how he wanted it to be. Maybe she did, too. "They need medicine, not rattles," she told him. "I can give them that."

"Medicine? What kind?"

She told him what she'd learned from her mother. "She said sumac was what she used to stop her wounds from bleeding."

"The wounds Conrad inflicted?"

"And Tatooktche." For a moment she thought he might touch her, but when he didn't, she took several calming breaths and told him she wanted to go into the forest as soon as possible.

"Will you return? Maybe you only want to run."

Anger lashed through her. She tried to tell herself that Madsaw was only speaking out of fear for those he loved, but she'd done nothing to deserve those words. "To run would give me great joy. To never have to face Sokolov again—to never hear you say those things again—but if I did, two good men might die."

"They might anyway."

She couldn't tell him he was wrong. All, really, that mattered was that she do what she could. "I will be back before night," she told him. "If I am not, then you will know One Ear has had his vengeance."

The smell of blood clogged Madsaw's nostrils and made him half-sick, but he couldn't make himself leave his brother's side. Both men's wounds had been cleaned repeatedly and he'd felt encouraged when he saw that his chief's injuries weren't as deep as he initially thought. They would leave scars he would carry to his death, but already Walkus had joked that flaunting them at trading time might make the sea-strangers believe they were dealing with a man blessed by the spirits.

Lukstch said little. Although his eyes hadn't glazed over and he remained cool to the touch, he'd become frightingly pale, and no matter what his wife and Madsaw did, they couldn't stop the wound in his thigh from bleeding. If it continued the way it was, he would bleed to death. Apenas flitted in and out like a butterfly, her features etched with concern. Each time she left, Madsaw knew she'd gone back to Sokolov's house and was pleading with him to make another visit.

Didn't she know the shaman wouldn't change his mind? He'd blamed everything on Twana; if either man died, he would remind everyone that he'd sensed her evil spell, and surely no one would think less of a shaman wise enough to protect himself. And if they recovered, he would take credit for that.

Madsaw leaned close to his brother and spooned a little water into his mouth. Lukstch muttered something, his voice so weak that he sounded like a newborn babe. His eyes remained closed and his breathing had begun to sound labored.

Hurry, Twana. Please hurry. The intensity of his prayer shocked him, and he tried to tell himself he'd been driven by fear, nothing more. He gave Lukstch another drink, carefully wiping away the water that dribbled out of the corner of his mouth. What was it she'd said? That if she didn't return, he'd know One Ear had found her.

His body drooping with fatigue, Madsaw repositioned himself beside his brother. Although he tried to concentrate on the slow rising and falling of Lukstch's chest, his thoughts slipped into the forest—followed Twana, tried to protect her.

It shouldn't take her long to find what she needed. Because he'd given her a knife, she could quickly cut through the hard layers of bark to the moisture-laden skin. She'd work carefully so she'd have enough unbroken bark to lay over the wounds. Then she'd hurry back.

Unless One-Ear wanted her.

Unless she could no longer stand to be around him.

CHAPTER 18

Madsaw was hunched over his brother when she returned. For a moment she stood with the cool night air biting at her back and heat warming her face while she put the peaceful wilderness behind her.

Apenas was the first to notice her, followed by Walkus and Lukstch's wives, who simply stared at her as she approached the wounded men. Madsaw woke in that clean and silent way of his, his eyes glinting red from the firelight. He didn't have to speak for her to understand; he hadn't known whether he'd ever see her again.

Maybe, soon, she'd tell him that for a long time today she hadn't been sure herself.

She dropped to her knees beside Lukstch, unable to suppress a shudder at what she saw. His thigh still oozed. The flesh around it was deeply bruised, his face almost as pale as death. When she touched his cheek, he didn't stir, and the sound of his tortured breathing tore at her heart. *He* was why she'd returned, only him.

Carefully unrolling the thin layer of bark, she cut it into several pieces, laying the largest over Lukstch's thigh. He flinched as the cool moisture touched him, but almost immediately relaxed. She could swear she'd heard him utter a sigh of relief.

Apenas, who'd come closer while she was working, said nothing, and she guessed that Madsaw had convinced her to let his hostage do whatever she wanted. Why Apenas had agreed, Twana couldn't say; maybe only her son's life mattered anymore. She handed several pieces to Walkus's wife and instructed her in how to cover his injuries, then finished with Lukstch.

Taking the young brave's hand, she lifted it to her mouth so she could kiss his knuckles. "It's all right; the medicine will soon help."

"It has—already."

Apenas sobbed, her face contorting, and Twana wondered how long she'd been waiting to hear her son speak. If she dared, she would have embraced the older woman, but although their relationship was no longer what it had once been, now was not the time to explore what it might become—if she remained here, which she wouldn't.

"We won't know until morning if I got help to him in time," she admitted. "The blood loss—"

"He might die?"

Madsaw's anguished question cut into her, but

she had to tell him the truth. Fighting the pull from his cavelike eyes, she admitted she should have tried to find a way to treat him even earlier. "It wasn't my place to confront Sokolov," she admitted. "I told myself I shouldn't do such a thing. But when Lukstch only got worse, I knew I had to do something."

Madsaw nodded, then turned to give his brother a drink. The way he bent his powerful body over the younger, limp man nearly reduced her to tears, but if she surrendered to her heart's need, she would lose the resolve that had come in the wilderness's utter peace.

More tired than she believed possible, she slipped away and curled up near the fire. Neither Madsaw or his mother had moved. He hadn't asked about One Ear, maybe because his mind was totally on his brother—maybe because her welfare no longer meant anything to him.

What was she thinking? Madsaw had done nothing to change what she felt for him. She only had to look into his eyes to believe in his compassion. But she didn't dare, not if . . .

Her thoughts spread out, thinned, became more mist than reality. On the brink of sleep, she pulled herself back. Although she'd been constantly aware of One Ear while in the forest, and been convinced that he was more concerned with licking his superficial wounds than those who'd inflicted them on him, she couldn't rest until she knew for sure that he wasn't now stalking the village. She found him nestled under a tree—not just any tree, but the sumac she'd stripped bark from.

Ice filled her veins; for several moments she forgot to breathe. Yes, he hadn't been that far away while she was working, but she'd been careful to remain as silent as possible, and he'd spent most of the time splashing about in the river, probably because the cold water felt good to him. He'd given no indication that he'd caught her scent in the still air, but could she have been wrong?

Opening her eyes, she made out Madsaw's form, saw how firelight and shadows painted his back and shoulders and arms in eerie lights. He seemed unreal, as if surrounded by the same sense of isolation that had overcome her earlier.

She could tell him—tell him what? That One Ear had found her?

No. He had enough to concern himself with tonight.

If One Ear woke and started toward her, she would sacrifice herself.

Needing to reassure herself that she would at least be safe until morning, she returned to the sleeping grizzly. Not far from him, a doe lifted her head, tested the wind, then bounded away. A rabbit buried underground slept on, oblivious to the potential danger. There was a knot on One Ear's forehead and his right paw looked swollen. The hair near his left flank was pushed back on itself. In her mind she saw herself tiptoe up to the great creature and gently brush his fur until it was once again sleek and smooth. She next "touched" his forehead and learned that an arrowhead remained imbedded in him. The spot would soon begin to itch, and when he rubbed his head, maybe on the sumac tree, he'd dislodge the iron tip—iron that came from sea-strangers such as her father.

Shaking herself free of the thought, she concentrated on the sleeping grizzly. When she "lifted" his paw to see what was wrong with it, it was so heavy that she had to rest it on her thighs. The great paw spread out over her, claws angling toward her flesh.

She felt no fear.

Not questioning her emotion, she ran her hands over the paw, between each toe, even probing at the base of the claws. Finally she convinced herself that he'd simply bruised himself. A bruise was nothing; he would quickly heal. Relief poured through her, and although sleep again sought to claim her, she fought it off.

One Ear was what he was, a wild beast. Maybe he'd deliberately attacked the men today; she couldn't say. And maybe he'd simply been drawn near by the scent of fish and seen Walkus and Lukstch and the others as nothing more than obstacles.

I don't hate you, can never hate you.
Even if you come for me tomorrow.

When she woke, except for the crackling of the fire, the house was silent. For a moment Twana felt disoriented, then remembered that she hadn't gone into Madsaw's sleeping quarters as usual. Looking around, she noted that Walkus and Lukstch's wives were stretched out not far from their husbands. Only Madsaw was awake.

She stood and walked over to him, but he barely

acknowledged her presence. His hand lay on his brother's chest. When she carefully lifted the bark covering from Lukstch's thigh, she saw that it had stopped bleeding. Rocking slightly in an attempt to keep from crying, she waited for Madsaw to say something; he remained silent.

"How long has it been like this?"

"Awhile. His breathing is easier."

"And your uncle?"

"He says he will help me fish tomorrow."

Twana doubted that, but the thought that Walkus had regained his sense of humor lightened the load in her heart. She concentrated on Lukstch's breathing, relieved to see for herself that Madsaw was right.

"Does Apenas know?" she whispered.

He nodded. "I woke her and told her when I was sure."

"And their wives?"

"I told them, too."

But not her. "Did you think it didn't matter to me?" she asked, unable to keep her voice clean of emotion. "Why didn't you tell me, too?"

He didn't answer but only looked at her until she wanted to scream at him to leave her alone, to leave her heart alone. "You are bitter. Why?"

"Not bitter. I have no room in me for that."

"What? There has to be something—"

"I defied the shaman for you. Chose you over him. All will ask how I could have done such a thing."

And maybe everyone would think that he didn't have the wisdom necessary for village chief; she'd already told herself that. "My medicine is working. What will they say to that?"

"Maybe that only a witch could turn sumac bark into healing medicine."

She was too weary to argue with him, too vulnerable to risk sitting this close to him. "I almost didn't return, but maybe that doesn't matter to you."

He brushed a lock of hair off the side of his brother's head. "I couldn't keep my mind on you. Do you understand why?"

Because Lukstch and Walkus had always been part of his life, because what he felt for them went far, far deeper than anything he felt for her. She wanted to tell herself she was wrong, that he'd shown her emotions no one else would ever know about, and only a man who loved a woman could do that, but she couldn't.

She'd risked her life during One Ear's attack and he hadn't said a word.

"Send someone else to Tatooktche," she forced herself to say. "Whatever he offers this time, take it."

"If I do, you will be returned to him."

The room spun, flashed red, then darkened until she could see nothing. "I know."

"And you want that?"

"I want an end to being used. By Tatooktche. By you."

"You hate Tatooktche."

More than you will ever know, for reasons you don't understand. "I want to be married, to have children, to be treated as a woman, not a witch."

"Have I treated you like one?" His voice sounded disembodied, a whisper without substance, a question that slashed at her poor defenses against him.

"I'm your hostage, Madsaw. I will never be anything else. I'm sick of this—sick of not knowing who I am."

The night was a frayed piece of rope, splintered strands spreading out before him, endless and without substance. He knew he dozed, but every time his body drooped, his mind filled with images of what Walkus and Lukstch had looked like when he first saw them, and horror snaked through him, shaking him awake. When he heard the women begin to stir around the fire, he checked his brother and uncle, then went outside for the cool air he hoped would clear his head. He'd barely returned from a moment of privacy in the woods when he was approached by one of the elder men, who asked how long it would be before Walkus could resume his duties. Not for several days, he told the man, then said he would take his uncle's place. The fishing weir would have to be repaired; he wanted to post guards to make sure the grizzly didn't return while the work was being done.

Although the man gave Madsaw a skeptical look, he said nothing, and Madsaw understood that even though the entire village might now question his abilities, there was no one else they could turn to—at least not until they'd discussed his behavior among themselves and come to a decision.

When he checked on it, he discovered that the damage to the weir was far more extensive than he'd first thought. Planning, conferring, organizing, working, filled his mind for most of the day. It wasn't until his mother brought him some smoked fish that he allowed himself to think about those he'd left behind. Apenas assured him that his uncle was stiff but able to move about. Lukstch still slept most of the time, but when he spoke, his words made sense.

"I have never heard of such a thing," she finally said. "To use sumac instead of a shaman's magic."

"Maybe Sokolov has no magic, Mother."

She gave him a look that told him he'd said too much. Still, he guessed she was having the same thoughts and might eventually agree with him. "I spoke to Twana," she said. "Thanked her for what she did."

"What did she say?"

"That she couldn't let a man die."

"She had no other reason?"

"If she did, she didn't tell me. And there is a look about her that says she is restless, unhappy with her world. She only told me to let you know that One Ear is quiet today—that she sees no danger from him. Do you believe that?"

When his mother shuddered and glanced out at the forest, he placed his arm around her. "She knows the grizzly," he told her. "Maybe better than he knows himself."

"She is not like the rest of us. I think I will never understand her."

He could have told her that he'd seen into Twana's heart and mind, but although he'd briefly believed that, he no longer did. She wanted him to return her to Tatooktche. Her explanations had fallen over him like the rain, then sunk into the ground, disappearing so quickly that he couldn't make sense of them. All that mattered was that she wouldn't have said what she did if she loved him.

Although the others returned to their homes as soon as evening shadows chilled the air around the river, Madsaw continued to work until he could no longer see. Then he slowly made his way down the narrow and well-worn path that led him home.

Home?

He'd dispatched a cousin to tell Cleaskinch about the grizzly attack, explaining that until order had been restored to the village, he would be unable to continue marriage preparations. Cleaskinch would understand that a war chief had certain responsibilities. He wouldn't question the delay. What he might never fathom was that Madsaw couldn't call to mind his daughter's face, his daughter's voice, and only wished her the freedom to remain a child a little longer.

Because he'd received frequent updates on his uncle and brother's condition, he wasn't surprised to see his uncle sitting up watching his wife repair a cooking basket. Lukstch remained on his fur bed, but for the first time since the attack, his eyes were open. Madsaw remained with the two until well after dark, telling them about progress on the weir repairs. Then, because Lukstch was showing signs of growing weary, he left.

By now moisture that was more mist than rain drifted around him. There was a chill to the air that kept him from remaining outside surrounded by night's isolation as he wanted. Still, for a long time he simply stared at the deep shadows that were the houses of his village and listened to the sea's soft song. He wanted back the peace he'd known as a child; he also wanted Twana by his side, her warm body and quick mind forever fascinating him.

But she wanted to return to her own village. Said she had no place here.

Maybe she was right.

She didn't look up at him when he entered his house, and he told himself it was easier that way. The children, who'd been ordered to remain close to home all day, clamored at him for information about what the grizzly had done to the weir. They were less interested in the repairs than getting a minute description of the destruction, and when he didn't say enough to satisfy them, they expanded on what it must have been like when the grizzly charged the men. His cousin chided her son for loudly insisting that a grizzly could lift a grown man in his mouth, but Madsaw understood that a child's imagination knew only its own boundaries.

Glancing at Twana, he noticed that she was

smiling at youthful boasts that if One Ear had attacked them, they would have bravely chased him off. He hadn't seen her smile for so long, had seldom seen her smile. She must have done that often, in her own village with her mother.

She didn't have her mother anymore.

Sorrow for her nearly overwhelmed him, but he shook it off. He, too, had known loss and survived. Twana was a survivor who only wanted her life to return to what it had once been.

Apenas sat beside him for a while, then said she wanted to see her injured son one more time before going to bed. As she was leaving, Madsaw saw her look back at Twana, saw Twana meet his mother's quiet gaze, and could only wonder at what was happening between the two women.

Not that it mattered, because Twana would soon be gone and his life would return to what it had been before her.

When he could no longer ignore his tired body, he entered his sleeping quarters and lay down. Although he fought sleep for as long as he could, Twana didn't join him, and her absence told him a great deal. Sometime much later, he sensed a presence. Without opening his eyes, he knew it was Twana.

"Your mother has a message for you," she whispered. "She is spending the night with Lukstch."

"Is he all right? He isn't—"

"He's fine, Madsaw. She is simply a mother."

Was that it, or did Apenas want to leave him and Twana alone? He wanted to touch her; he had every right to hold her against him. Yet his hands remained clutched by his sides. "Is One Ear still near?"

"Yes." She drew out the word until he wasn't sure she was ever going to finish it. "He found some grubs and berries to feed on, but not enough to satisfy him. I thought he might return to the weir; if he came close, I was going to warn you. But he remains deep in the forest—looking."

"Looking at what?"

"Maybe at me."

"What are you talking about? I don't understand."

"I don't either, Madsaw." She sounded unbelievably young and unsure of herself. "I have never seen his eyes like that before. Maybe—maybe I have been so long without sleep that I don't know my own thoughts."

He didn't believe that, but because he sensed she'd said as much as she was capable of, he didn't push her. He waited for her to lie down, and when she stretched beside him instead of at his feet, he accepted the irrevocable change in their relationship.

"Madsaw? I'm sorry."

"For what?" He was aware of nothing except her presence.

"If I hadn't drawn One Ear here, this wouldn't have happened."

Had she been carrying guilt inside her all this time? "No one can say what a grizzly will do."

"One Ear is not like others. He and I—"

"Listen to me. For a long, long time I blamed myself for Vattan's death. If I'd told her the canoe wasn't seaworthy, she wouldn't have tried to escape in it. But I now know those are the words of a man trapped by grief."

"I feel trapped. So trapped."

Even though he couldn't see her, he knew she was staring at the ceiling with the night and her thoughts so closely wrapped around her that maybe she was barely aware of his presence. He wanted the honesty he'd just heard from her, but that didn't stop it from hurting because he was part of the trap—maybe all of it.

"I-I asked your mother if she blamed me. She didn't answer, but I saw no hatred in her eyes."

"You saved Lukstch's life, Twana." He felt the night close down around him and wondered if either of them would reach out for the other. Maybe they'd spend tonight and the rest of their lives separated by fear of how much they'd reveal. "That's all that matters to her."

"But not to me. I'm responsible, Madsaw. *I* brought him here."

"You can't control One Ear. Don't let this tear you apart."

"But I saw—I heard . . ."

She'd started to shiver, but if he touched her now, he'd never be able to let her go. She didn't belong to him; he'd never wanted it like that. They were two separate people who for a few short days had been joined heart and head. But those days were over.

"Sleep, Twana. If you can."

* * *

Sleep, if you can. Madsaw's words mocked Twana for most of the night. She dozed fitfully and might not have found any peace at all if it hadn't been for his comforting if distant presence. With the Wolf Clan war chief beside her, One Ear couldn't touch her thoughts, and images of the attack faded before they could overwhelm her.

Something else kept her awake.

Again and again she reassured herself that One Ear posed no threat. The forest was peaceful with most of the animals sleeping. She saw an owl close his talons around a bat and felt sorrow, but that was the way of the forest. A misting rain continued, sometimes disturbed by an errant breeze, but most of the time she was barely aware of its light tapping overhead. Still, her spine and skin felt as if they were being touched by cold fingers, and nothing she did or thought warmed her.

Madsaw had told her not to blame herself for what had happened to Walkus and Lukstch. She knew he spoke wisdom and didn't condemn her. She was deeply grateful to him for that, but that didn't stop the memory of One Ear standing over a helpless Lukstch.

It had to be that. The lingering nightmare and her inescapable role in it were so deeply tangled inside her that she couldn't find her way to freedom.

Leaving Madsaw, she made her way into the great room, but the air was stale and the walls seemed to have shrunken inward. She stepped outside, shivering at the predawn chill, but if she went back for a cape, she might wake Madsaw, and she needed to be alone with her thoughts—thoughts like small, dark explosions that made her want to scream. She wanted to see how Lukstch was, but Apenas would see her and maybe ask why she wasn't with Madsaw. What would she tell her, that being near him when she knew she would only have to leave him made her heart feel as if it were dying?

The beach waited, the beach that held Madsaw's canoe. She could run her hands over the smooth surface he'd created and maybe cry until there were no more tears left inside her.

"Twana."

The whisper was so soft that at first she wasn't sure she'd heard anything. She stared in the direction the sound had come from, but it was too dark to see anything.

"Twana."

Instantly her body became alert. What was Sokolov doing out here? She nearly ducked back inside, but if she did, he might follow her, and she couldn't stand the thought of him and Madsaw arguing. "What?"

"Ha! You are afraid of me. I hear your voice shake."

"If it does, it is because I am cold."

"I say it is more than that. How unworthy you are of Madsaw. A coward!"

Coward? No. She made out a faint shadow in front of the entrance to his house that she knew had to be him. Although she wanted nothing to do with him, she stepped closer, determined to make a lie of his words.

"What are you doing?" he asked when she was so close that she could smell his greased body. "You aren't in your pleasure slave's arms?"

He was trying to goad her into doing something reckless. Still, it took all her willpower not to strike the shadowed face. *An angry man, nothing more.* "You wouldn't say that to Madsaw's face," she challenged. "Why do you sneak around like some night creature?"

"Because sometimes the night is a friend."

Resisting the impulse to press her hand to her throbbing forehead, she tried to make further sense of her surroundings. Not even the dogs had wakened yet. Nothing should have brought Sokolov outside, unless he'd been waiting for her. The need to run pounded through her; instead, she thought of his twisted, challenging face and met the challenge. "We have nothing to say to each other, shaman."

"Nothing? You're wrong, Twana. Does your evil know no bounds? To command a bear to attack the village chief is a horrible thing."

"How can you say such a thing?"

"How? There are none who do not believe."

That couldn't be true, could it? Neither Madsaw or Apenas had said anything, and even if they'd been too concerned over Walkus and Lukstch to listen to village gossip, surely Kitlote would have told her. She started to lift her hand as if to swat away Sokolov's words, then forced herself not to give in to impulse. "There are many who believe I saved a man's life."

"You?" Sokolov stepped closer, his voice a menacing growl. "You are a fool, Twana."

A fool? If she was, it was only because she'd allowed herself to be drawn into this senseless argument. Spinning so quickly that she nearly twisted her ankle, she turned her back on Sokolov. Instantly she sensed movement, tensed, started to look back at him. Something heavy hit her and knocked her to the ground. Fighting nausea and unconsciousness, she struggled against the weight.

Hands were on her, trying to pin her to the ground. Something—something was wrong, but before it could half register that there were too many hands, she gathered what strength she had and surged upward. She'd reached a sitting position and was trying to struggle to her knees when she heard an oath that sent chills throughout her.

That voice— Nearly undone by senseless terror, she reached for her attacker and buried her nails in his cheeks. He grunted in pain and tried to shake her off, but she held on in blind desperation. Someone struck the side of her face with enough force that her head snapped back. She nearly lost her hold on the man, held on only because to give up was to die.

"Witch! Ogres' daughter!"

"Stop her! Stop her!"

Tatooktche!

Sucking in air through flared nostrils, she gaped at the man she'd been punishing. In her frenzy, it hadn't registered that it hadn't been Sokolov, but now—as if a shaft of lightning had lit the world—it did.

"No! N—" Something had clamped around her throat and was robbing her of breath. Hands. Hands with the power to kill. She released Tatooktche's face and clawed at his fingers, but he'd already stolen too much of her strength. She screamed again, but the sound died inside her.

Tatooktche! How—

The relentless punishment panicked her, made her incapable of thinking of anything except staying alive. But she was a fawn under a cougar's claws—two cougars and the world which was already night faded into nothing.

Madsaw.

CHAPTER 19

The space beside him was cold. Although sleep fought to claim him, Madsaw shook it off and sat up. He could hear people moving about in the great room and told himself Twana was out there. They'd said nothing to each other during the night, not even touched. Still, he didn't want to believe she'd leave him this way. Leave? All she'd done was go in search of something to eat.

When he stepped into the firelit room, it took his eyes a short while to adjust and then even longer to convince himself that she wasn't with the others. She was outside, outside where she could walk and think and dream of when she would be back among the Nisqually, married to an old man who might be incapable of giving her children.

Why should he care? he told himself, then didn't
search for the answer because it already lay
within his heart. Ignoring the greetings directed
at him, he walked out into the morning drizzle.
The moisture felt good on his face and quickly
cleared his head. When he looked around, he was
struck by the sounds and sights that he'd long
taken for granted but this morning were drawn in
sharp detail. True, the children played closer to
the houses than usual, but their laughter and energy were the same. The small menstruating huts,
the houses erected to hold the dead, totem poles
that had been in existence since long before his
birth, the seaworthy canoes down by the beach,
the curtain of clouds—all those things were part
of his world, part of him. He could conceive of no
other place he would want to live.

It was the same for Twana, only in a Nisqually
village.

When he asked Vasilii if he'd seen her, the boy
solemnly shook his head. He sensed that someone
was watching him, and when he looked around,
wasn't surprised to see Sokolov. For several moments the two regarded each other, then Madsaw
turned his back on the shaman and headed toward his uncle's house. Already the village had
lost its sharp edges, become muted and gray. He
didn't have to look further to know that Twana
wasn't here.

Had she left him?

And if she had, what would he do?

Walkus was fixing sea lion whiskers to a bright
red, black, and white wooden ceremonial mask,

his attention so focused on his task that Madsaw was able to watch him without his uncle knowing. A slight movement caught his attention, and he realized his brother was sitting up propped against the house wall. Lukstch pointed at their uncle, shook his head, then made grossly awkward motions. Warmed because Lukstch's sense of humor had returned, Madsaw made the same gestures in return.

"Children who make fun of their elders deserve to be left outside during a snowstorm," Walkus grumbled. "The noses will fall off children who show no respect."

Madsaw couldn't help laughing at the threat his uncle had made times without counting while he was growing up. As a little boy, he sometimes went around with his hand clamped over his nose to reassure himself that he hadn't pushed his uncle's patience too far. "You need to fish, my chief. Spending so much time inside has made you short-tempered."

"I will fish when my lazy nephew completes work on the weir." Walkus set down the mask and indicated he wanted Madsaw to come closer. "Tell me. How much more remains to be done?"

Madsaw had just begun his explanation when Lukstch pushed himself to his feet and made his slow, shaky way over. With Madsaw's help, his brother sat back down. "I hate this weakness," he grumbled. "A man needs his strength."

"Your wife is grateful for a little rest. Relax, little brother. Soon enough you will be dragging her back into the woods."

Lukstch didn't blush. "I can think of no better way of building up the strength I'll need to return to Tatooktche. I have been thinking; maybe I don't dare take a weapon with me. That way I won't be tempted to use it on the man. His arrogance, his greed—"

"Maybe you won't have to go."

Lukstch didn't say anything, and Madsaw wished he could take back his words. "I think she has run away," he finally admitted.

"Run? Why?"

"She's an outsider here. Many hold her responsible for what happened."

Walkus's eyes narrowed. "She defies you, Madsaw. She has forgotten her role as hostage."

He no longer cared about that; she had become more important than his father's memory. He stared at his uncle's mask with its round, wide eyes and beaklike nose. Once the ceremonial masks had both frightened and mesmerized him, but he wasn't a little boy anymore.

He'd become a man who'd given his heart to a woman; that woman had left him, left his world.

"You are sure about this?" his uncle pressed when he couldn't put his mind to what he was expected to say. "She hasn't just gone for a walk?"

Hope flared briefly, then died. None of the children had seen her this morning, which meant she'd left during the night. He told his uncle that, the words feeling wooden. He was wrapped tightly within himself, and the emotions that held him prisoner were too deep and dense for him to fully comprehend them. He wanted to join the children in their play, wished he and his brother and uncle could spend the day fishing—think of nothing except fishing.

"Do you think she is a witch, Madsaw?" his brother asked.

"A witch? No. What happens inside her is a different thing, a gift."

"Then it is not as Sokolov says? She has not cast a spell over you?"

Oh yes, he'd been entrapped by her, but what he felt had nothing to do with a witch's evil powers. He wanted to tell his brother that, but if he did, he would have to admit something else, and the love he felt for Twana needed to remain safe and protected inside him. "She wants to be back where people accept her for what she is, where she belongs."

"With Tatooktche?" Lukstch snorted. "I would rather be tangled in slimy seaweed!"

Madsaw nearly laughed. "No, not with him," he said, then explained that Twana was to be married. Lukstch had seen Quahklah while he was in the Nisqually village and had sat as far as possible from the old man, sickened by the stench that came from his mouth with its three black and rotting teeth. Madsaw's breath caught; Twana hadn't told him about that.

Walkus said nothing, only looked at him with piercing eyes that rivaled those he'd painted on his mask. "You are my chief," Madsaw said. "I will do as you say. It may be that she has decided to live alone in the forest. If she is there, I may never find her, but—"

"Alone?" Lukstch interrupted. He shifted position, wincing and grabbing his thigh as he did. "No one would do that. To be at the mercy of animals and storms—I cannot believe that."

Alone. "She has no fear of animals, not even a grizzly."

"Why not? Does she believe she knows what a grizzly thinks?"

Mired by the realization of how little he knew about the woman who'd left his side, he picked up the mask and held it over his face. Was this how Twana was, the woman hiding behind the mask forever unknown to him?

After a moment, Walkus took the mask from him and set it back down but remained silent. The quiet weighed on Madsaw until he knew he had to return to what he'd said earlier. "I will not defy you, my chief," he whispered. "If your heart can find no peace until your brother's death has been avenged, I will search for her, bring her back."

"Maybe all you will have to do is go to her village."

He tried, again, to imagine her with Quahklah. That was no easier than the thought of her living under Tatooktche's roof until Quahklah claimed her. "I do not think so. Yesterday she told me she belongs with the Nisqually, but I do not believe her. She— Only the forest will give her peace."

He felt a hand on his shoulder, but couldn't pull himself free long enough to acknowledge his uncle. Lukstch said something, but the words floated off before he could make sense of them. *Alone, with nothing but the sound of her own voice for the rest of her life.*

"You love her." Walkus squeezed, then released, Madsaw's shoulder. "It is in your eyes, your voice, what you say. But it is not a wise love."

"I know."

"Do you?"

"Yes," he made himself admit. "What I feel—I want to be free of it. To never think of her again."

"It may happen. It may not. Listen to me." Walkus waited until Madsaw looked at him, then continued. "You asked for my advice. Said you would do what I want. In a few days you will go to the Nisqually village and present yourself to the head chief. If he tells you that no one has seen her, you will know you were right and that she cannot bring herself to look at Tatooktche again, that she has no wish to marry an old man. Instead, she lives with the animals."

He nodded, the rhythm continuing for a long time while he fought to place himself inside Twana's heart. Would she find peace?

"There will be no shame for you. All will understand. Some may believe as Sokolov tells them, that she is using her witch's powers to survive as no one else can, but that does not matter. What does is that you have put her out of your life."

Out of your life. Did he want that? "You are content with this?" he made himself ask. "You can put your brother's death behind you?"

"I want to force Tatooktche to pay for what he did. But how long can I let my heart remain full of bitterness? A chief must lead, not live in the past. Cast her from you; those are my words to you."

Cast her from you. His chief's counsel ringing through him, Madsaw made his way back outside and wandered aimlessly down to his canoe. As soon as he was done with it, he would present it to Cleaskinch and take his daughter as his wife. Only occasionally would he look at the burial house where he'd placed his father's remains and think of the time he'd taken a hostage so he might avenge his father's murder. His days would be filled with fishing and trading, preparing to become chief. At night he'd take his young wife in his arms and wait for their children to fill her belly.

He'd never stare at the forest and think of the woman who lived there, who might have died there.

Who'd touched his heart and left her image there.

Be free, Twana, he thought as restlessness took him back toward the village. *Find the peace you never could with me.*

He tried to imagine her walking through the forest, her senses tuned to the sights and sounds of the world she'd chosen. Unlike everyone else, she wouldn't have to rely on her eyes and ears alone. She could "see" young foxes wrestling with each other, a great bull elk approaching a cow, a quiet pool filled with salmon.

Would she be content with that for the rest of her life? Could she play with foxes and never again need the touch of a human being? Could she watch the elk claim its mate and not want that coupling for herself?

Would she ever think of him? Was she even now telling herself that he was behind her—part of a life that no longer existed?

Spotting Sokolov going into the chief's house, Madsaw nearly hurried after him to stop him. Instead, he continued on the path that would take him past where Sokolov lived and beyond that to the river. Whatever Sokolov said to his uncle and brother wasn't his concern. If either of them decided he needed to know about the conversation, they would tell him. This morning he needed action and work, an end to thoughts of a grizzly-eyed woman who'd let the wilderness swallow her.

Head down, he paid little attention to how close he was getting to Sokolov's house until a flash of color on the ground caught his eye. He paused, squinted, took another step, then stopped and leaned down to pick up the small object.

It was Twana's necklace, the fine links broken in two places.

Rage and fear barely in check, Madsaw stalked after the shaman. He ducked into his uncle's house, then stopped. Sokolov was sitting near Walkus and Lukstch, his strangely high-pitched voice echoing against the walls. "I have done great magic," he said. "I commanded the grizzly to call her to him, and like the fool she is, she believed she would be safe." Sokolov looked up at Madsaw. His eyes narrowed, a faint smile touched his lips. "Hear me, Madsaw. The witch's powers are nothing next to mine. She is dead. Torn apart by great claws and powerful teeth."

"Claws and teeth?" Madsaw threw back at him. Still, a horrible image nearly swamped him. Had Sokolov left her in the forest for One Ear to find? He strode closer and held out the necklace. "What magic is this, shaman? What did you do to her?"

Sokolov blinked rapidly several times, but his voice lost none of its bravado. "What need does a dead woman have for a necklace? Maybe she left it for you to find so you would understand."

Battling the desire to wrap his hands around Sokolov's neck and choke the life out of him, he told his uncle and brother that he'd found the broken necklace in front of Sokolov's house. "Is that where you overpowered her, shaman? What did you do with her? Where is she?"

"You do *not* question me, Madsaw." Sokolov scrambled to his feet and shook his finger under Madsaw's nose. "Do *not* question your shaman's wisdom."

"Wisdom? Cowardice. That is what you are, Sokolov. A coward. If you killed her—"

"I would not soil my hands with her blood. I seek only to protect the village from her evil."

Evil. The woman who'd lain beside him, evil? Never. Madsaw took a menacing step, not surprised to see Sokolov scramble away. He kept after the shaman until if Sokolov backed any more, he would step into the fire. Legs spread, face contorted in what he must believe to be defiance, Sokolov finally stood his ground. "You are unworthy of becoming chief, Madsaw. You are like a man who has eaten too much of fermented berries. No one will follow a drunken man."

"Where is she? What did you do with her?"

"Nothing."

There wasn't any time to argue. With every moment, Twana's danger grew. He grabbed the shaman's shoulders and shook him until his head snapped back and forth and his mouth gaped open. He felt his uncle try to pull him off Sokolov, but all he could think of was Twana. "Tell me!" he ordered. "What did you do with her?"

"Stop it! Stop! I will—you will die, Madsaw. Die!"

"Madsaw!" Walkus ordered. "Release him! Now!" He clamped down on Madsaw's arm. Reacting instinctively, Madsaw struck out and knocked his uncle to his knees.

Instantly horror swamped him. How could he have hit his uncle, his chief? But instead of helping Walkus to his feet, he swung back toward Sokolov and fastened his fingers around the shaman's neck. "Where is she? What have you done with—"

"Not me! Not—"

"Who?"

Sokolov's eyes bulged. He struggled ineffectively in Madsaw's arms. Madsaw glimpsed his uncle trying to stand, glimpsed his brother stumbling toward him, but all he could think about was Twana.

"Who?" he ordered, his face nearly touching Sokolov's. "I will kill—"

"T-Tatooktche."

* * *

Silence far deeper than any the forest had to offer pulsed against Twana's senses until she thought she'd scream, but who would listen?

It had been worse when she first regained consciousness and realized she was with Tatooktche. Listening to him breathe, she'd been able to think of nothing except crying out for Madsaw, but either he or Sokolov had shoved something in her mouth, and both horror and disbelief were caught inside her. Tatooktche had yanked her into a sitting position, and after convincing himself that she wasn't going to pass out again, he'd ordered her to her feet and begun dragging her back to his village.

She'd fought, fought until he struck her with enough force to knock her to her knees. Then he grabbed her hair and she'd had no choice but to follow him. Because Tatooktche was tired from the long walk to the Tillamook village, the journey had taken the better part of two days. He'd given her no more freedom than Conrad had, but at least she'd had enough to drink that thirst didn't make it impossible for her to think beyond that.

Not that thinking did her any good because she was now alone inside Tatooktche's house, her hands bound behind her and roped to a pole. He'd removed her gag after telling her that the entire village had gone to meet with the sea-traders at their good spirit place and wouldn't be back until tomorrow. By then, no one would know she'd been here.

He was gone. Why he'd left her here and where he was going, he hadn't said and she hadn't asked. Instead, she tried to find a comfortable position to sit and listened to the silence.

Listened to the lonely voice inside that called out for Madsaw.

Enough light filtered in through the opening that she knew it was nearing evening. Tatooktche had been gone long enough that if he'd been going to join the rest of his village, he would already be there. Maybe he intended to spend the night with them so he could participate in the trading. Maybe.

She'd been looking at the murky interior for so long that her eyes no longer registered what was there. At first she'd searched for what was familiar, but although she knew these walls as well as she did her own body, nothing calmed her.

If she'd been in Madsaw's house, it might have been different.

As had happened too many times since Tatooktche grabbed her, thoughts of Madsaw washed over her, bringing her dangerously close to tears. He had no idea what had happened to her, no way of knowing where she was and how much she needed him.

Needed. The word pounded through her, filled her lungs. She'd told Madsaw she wanted nothing to do with him, not because that was the truth, but because he deserved the future ordained for him since birth, and he couldn't have that with her.

A whimpering sound escaped her throat, and

she had to listen to it echo and finally fade like rising smoke. Although she'd rocked herself before, she started doing it again. The ropes gave her barely any room in which to move, but remaining motionless allowed desperation and despair to gain the upper hand, and she needed to keep her senses about her if she was going to cope with Tatooktche when he returned.

Tatooktche. She'd just begun the seemingly endless struggle to cast him from her thoughts when a shadow filled the opening and she knew he was back.

"So." Satisfaction and triumph cloaked the word. "You are still here, Twana. Those who call you a powerful witch should see you now."

Breathing deeply to keep calm, she waited for him to approach. He wasn't a big man, certainly not nearly as tall or muscular as Madsaw, but he'd roped her as if she were a slaughtered deer, and in her eyes not even One Ear was larger. "Are you still silent, Twana? I would think you would be demanding an explanation by now. But maybe—" He clamped a hand on her shoulder and shoved her forward so he could check the ropes. "Maybe you have come to your own conclusions."

She had. Somehow, probably through a slave, Sokolov had sent word to Tatooktche that he would help Tatooktche get her back without having to pay ransom. It wouldn't take the shaman long to convince the villagers that his magic was responsible for her disappearance, and he would have back his position of authority and respect. What she didn't understand was what use Tatooktche hoped to make of her. If he offered her to Quahklah, Quahklah and the other villagers would ask how Tatooktche had met Madsaw's demands.

Maybe Tatooktche would kill her.

He squatted before her, grabbed her chin and turned her head first one way, then the other. A wave of nausea nearly overwhelmed her, and although she knew it was hopeless, she couldn't stop herself from trying to escape him.

"Careful, *daughter*," he warned as he gripped her hair. "Before you think to defy me, think how close you are to death."

She knew that. Hadn't she spent her time alone with him nearly paralyzed with fear? Fear and something else even more powerful. "I am worth nothing to you dead, Tatooktche. Alive—"

"Alive, you are indeed valuable." He laughed, the sound far more horrible than the silence she'd had to endure before he returned. "I must not forget that, must not let my anger overwhelm me."

"Anger?" she probed when he released her. Her scalp throbbed, but she vowed not to let him see her discomfort. "What have I done?"

"Robbed me of what is rightfully mine," he said, and then told her that as soon as Quahklah learned that she'd been taken by Madsaw, the old man had approached three families, waving his bridal goods in front of them and telling them he wanted to marry their daughters. "Quahklah grows weary of sleeping alone. None of those girls are as valuable as you. Still, he is willing to give up his wealth for one of them."

"Where is he?"

"Quahklah? With the others."

"He doesn't know you have me?"

Tatooktche didn't answer, and in his smile she discovered an evil she hadn't known existed. It spread over the room and nearly stripped her of her defiance. Calling up Madsaw's image, she fought Tatooktche's power, stared back at her stepfather, let hatred fill her eyes.

"You have no love for me, my *daughter*? After all I've done for you—"

"What have you done? Nothing!"

That earned her a slap. "Free me, Tatooktche," she challenged. "Let me face you as an equal."

"You would like that, wouldn't you? Tell me, if you had a knife, what would you do with it?"

"Drive it into your heart."

"You hate me enough to kill me?"

He was goading her, crouching before her like a hungry mountain lion, tail lashing from side to side, taunting its trapped prey to try to run. Forgetting everything except how much she despised him, she returned his gaze, not like a terror-filled rabbit, but like a woman ready to kill or be killed. "I know what you did," she taunted in turn. "To my mother."

"Tell me, Twana. Tell me everything."

"You sold her," she spat. "Sold her to the man called Conrad. You would have sold me, too, if you hadn't believed you could get more for me from Quahklah. He—Conrad murdered her."

"What he did is not my concern."

"Isn't it?" Even though she knew it was hopeless, she strained against her bonds until they dug into her wrists. Tatooktche wore a long cape under which, she knew, he always carried a knife. If only she could get her hands on it. "Kill me, Tatooktche. Kill me now!"

"Why would I do that?" he asked, his carefully controlled voice a sharp contrast to her emotional one.

"Because—" *Don't say it! Remain silent!* "Because somehow, someway, I will avenge her death."

"How, Twana?" He leaned even closer, his features a dark blur. "The way you did with Conrad? Maybe you'll thrust a knife into my side as you did with him."

"Yes!"

"Leave him bleeding at the mercy of a grizzly?"

How did he know that? The room began to pulse as if it had come alive, and she couldn't breathe. Mind and heart screaming, she could only stare up at Tatooktche. "Have you nothing to say, my *daughter*? No more defiance? If you are so foolish as to think I would risk my life in the same way, that I would let you get your hands on a knife—"

Tatooktche hadn't stopped speaking, but she couldn't concentrate on him. Another shadow filled the opening, another man entered the house and walked across the room. Another man squatted beside Tatooktche.

Conrad. Although Tatooktche continued to smile, what she could see of Conrad's mouth through his beard told her he held it in a grim line. She'd always thought that if she came face-to-face with Thunderbird or an ogre, her heart would stop beating, but she'd seen far worse than that and still her heart thudded so painfully, she thought she might pass out.

"Surprised to see me, Twana?" Conrad asked. His deep, low voice swirled around her like a snake. "Thought you'd killed me, didn't you?"

She'd begun shaking her head, not because she wanted to answer Conrad, but she might explode if she remained still. How he'd survived didn't matter. All that did was that he was here.

He'd come back for her.

Not taking his eyes off her, Conrad jerked his head in Tatooktche's direction. "You wanted your pay for her 'fore you'd let her out of your sight. It's outside, all of it."

"Bring it in here."

"Don't push me, Tatooktche. You know I'm good for it. Didn't I make that clear when I anted up for her mother? It really is funny, Twana." His tone became almost conversational. "What Tatooktche's going to get? That's what I offered Madsaw for you. You ever hear of skinnin' a cat? Probably not, but that's what I've just done."

He clamped his hand over the back of her neck and forced her forward, but instead of simply checking the ropes, he slashed through the strand that held her to the pole. She tried to jerk away from him, but he held her too tightly. "Just skinned a cat, Twana. You're mine. Whatever I tell you to do, you're going to do it. And I ain't going to make the same mistake I did before." Lacing his fingers through her hair, he jerked her head so far back that she could barely see him. "This time you ain't getting loose. Not ever."

CHAPTER 20

His lungs burned from endless running and his legs stung where branches had slapped him. If he'd taken the time to wash the sweat from his body, it might have helped, but Madsaw cared nothing for his own comfort. Tatooktche had Twana; nothing else mattered—not even what he'd done to his chief.

Although he'd pushed himself as fast as he could go, it was evening by the time he reached the Nisqually village. Because the moon lay hidden behind clouds, he had to rely on his memory to identify which house belonged to Tatooktche. The village was so quiet that at first he wondered if everyone was waiting for him and would attack as soon as he revealed himself.

Then, fighting the emotion he'd been trapped

in from the moment Sokolov confessed what he'd done, he reminded himself that this was between Tatooktche and himself. The other villagers wouldn't protect Tatooktche any more than they'd protected Saha and Twana.

Clutching his slave killer, he strode out of the forest. Still, because Tatooktche might be lying in wait for him, he was careful not to reveal himself. What else Tatooktche might be doing stopped his breath in his throat, and once again he had to fight the too familiar fear. If Twana was dead—

A movement to the far side of Tatooktche's totem caught his attention and stopped him with one leg poised for another step. Someone had knelt on the ground and was doing something with a large pile there. Watching, he saw the figure sort through the items. When the person stood, he or she had both arms full.

Dread laced its way through Madsaw, but he forced himself to simply observe and not make judgments. When the figure disappeared into Tatooktche's house, Madsaw slipped forward. Enough firelight spilled out of the opening that he could make out many of the items in the stack. There were knives, cloth, tobacco, a large iron kettle.

Now holding the slave killer with such strength that his fingers started to turn numb, he ducked through the opening and quickly straightened. Senses alert, he hugged the shadows and took in the room. It was little different from the one he lived in, smaller, the stale smoke and fish smell stronger, the walls crammed with storage shelves and a haphazard pile of wood near the fire.

A man knelt behind the fire. He held a large jug in his hand—a jug filled with rum.

The dread that had been threatening to take over Madsaw grew until he could taste it, until it filled his veins and sent his head to pounding. Mindless to any danger, he stalked toward the man—toward Tatooktche. Twana's stepfather surged to his feet, the jug thrust outward in a protective gesture. "What—"

"Where is she, dog dung? Where is she?"

Tatooktche swung the heavy container at his head, but Madsaw easily ducked. "You stole her from me. What did you do with her?"

"I never—get out of here, Madsaw!"

Tatooktche tried to ram the bottle into Madsaw's belly. This time he deflected it with his slave killer. "Where did you get this?" He indicated the jug. "What sea-trader—"

"Leave! This is my house. You have no right!"

Words. They meant nothing to him. "Sokolov admitted everything. Where is she?" When Tatooktche said nothing, he stepped closer, warned himself not to kill the man before he'd told him what he'd done with Twana, took another step. Suddenly Tatooktche turned and sprinted toward the far end of the house. Madsaw guessed he was trying to reach several fishing spears propped against a wall and hurried after him. He overtook Tatooktche before he could grab a true weapon, clamped his hand around the man's arm, and swung him around. In the deep-set black eyes he saw hatred but no fear and guessed Tatooktche had had little to fear in his life.

But Madsaw wasn't a gentle woman or her equally gentle daughter.

"I mean this," he said as Tatooktche struggled and kicked. "Tell me where she is or you will not see the morning."

"You can't—" Tatooktche swung his fist at Madsaw, but Madsaw easily deflected it. He tried again. This time Madsaw captured a bony wrist and jerked Tatooktche toward him. Off balance, Tatooktche tried to butt him with his head, tried to kick at his groin. Tatooktche was a strong man. His long arms and legs made him a formidable opponent, but Madsaw had grown up wrestling with his brother. Once they were too old for play, they'd joined the other young men in mock battles, readying themselves for war.

Tatooktche hadn't done that; probably he'd never expected he would have to fight another man. Concentrating on keeping out of the way of Tatooktche's sharp knees, Madsaw managed to push him back until he'd rammed Tatooktche against the wall. Reaching up, he grabbed the man's throat and squeezed. Tatooktche clamped his hand around Madsaw's wrist and frantically tried to free himself.

"What have you done with her?" He pressed his face as close to Tatooktche's as he could and ordered himself to stop short of choking the life out of Tatooktche. "Where is she? Who—which trader?"

"No—no trader."

"You lie. One of them gave you those goods. Where did he take her?" He squeezed, his thumb digging into the soft part of Tatooktche's throat until the man's face turned red. "Who?"

Tatooktche's eyes bulged as if trying to force themselves out of their sockets. The older man fought and kicked, whipped his head from side to side in a frantic attempt to escape. But his strength had begun to wane; in a few more moments he would pass out.

"Tell me! If you want to see the night again, tell me!"

"C-Conrad!"

"No!"

"Yes. He—he lives."

Conrad. Twana's father. "Where did he take her? Tell me. Now!"

"I don't know, Madsaw. I swear, I don't—know."

Madsaw!
Madsaw!

His name drummed through her; over and over again Twana felt the sound vibrate inside her until it became part of her, until she could hear nothing else, think of nothing else.

If she didn't do that, she might die from shock and horror.

Not far from her, the trader roasted the fish he'd caught just before dark. Whether he gave her any of it or not didn't matter. She wanted nothing from him, nothing except her freedom. But he'd tied her so securely, she knew she couldn't free herself, and that horrible reality kept her chanting Madsaw's name.

"We probably won't meet up with them for another three days," Conrad was saying. "Don't want anyone seeing me until the Nisqually have left, you know. That way, if that crazy war chief comes looking for you, no one's going to be able to tell him anything."

Tatooktche could, she thought, then reminded herself—as if she needed to—that Madsaw had no way of knowing where she was. What had she said to him, that she only wanted to be free of him? That she wanted to spend the rest of her life alone.

Was that what he thought? That she'd run because she didn't love him.

Madsaw!

"It really is funny if you think about it." Conrad sat down without bothering to wipe the leaves and needles off the rotting log he'd pulled next to the fire and regarded her, his head cocked slightly to one side, looking like a hunter trying to decide whether the game he'd spotted was worth the effort. "Madsaw wasn't willing to trade for you. Even went to all the work of bringing everything with him when I had you—when I had you the last time," he said with a laugh that lacked warmth. "I figured, what the hell am I going to do with it except haul it all over creation? At least that's what I thought once I came to."

He turned the stick he was using to cook the fish so that the browned side was now up and its tantalizing aromas seeped into the air. Despite her body's involuntary reaction, she didn't take her eyes off Conrad. Didn't allow herself to be distracted from what he was saying. "You should have finished the job, Twana. Should have made sure you'd hurt me bad enough that I was done for. But you didn't." Again he laughed, the sound both hollow and grating.

"I saw a grizzly not long after you and that brave left," he continued. "Big devil. Liked to scare me to death. I figured that'd be the end of me, but he left me alone."

Why had One Ear let Conrad live? Could it be— Her mind rebelled, but she forced the thought to continue. Maybe Conrad with his hideous bear-claw necklace had frightened One Ear.

"Maybe you don't give a damn what I've been up to." Conrad brought the fish close to him and tore off a hunk of flesh. He chewed loudly, watching her. "But I'm going to tell you anyway. I got hooked back up with my men. I knew they were on their way to see the Nisqually, so it wasn't that hard catching up with them. I'm a tough old bird, Twana. It's going to take more than a knife to kill me. A hell of a lot more. Anyway, I got word to Tatooktche that I was still interested in you. I figured, if the price was right, he'd try to get his hands on you. I was right."

Yes. He was. Despite her aching muscles and the despair that was nearly more than she could battle, she continued to watch him. He'd been in no hurry to put distance between himself and the Nisqually village, which told her he believed he had nothing to fear. And why should he? Madsaw had no way of knowing what Tatooktche and Sokolov had done.

He would think she'd run away.

Mads . . .

Conrad finished eating, wiped his mouth with his sleeve, belched. She'd noted that he carried a jug on his backpack, but although he took a couple of sips, he stopped drinking before the rum could rob him of his senses. He set up his bed on a flat, rockless piece of ground. "A man's got to get his rest," he explained. "Got to keep his wits about him, you know. You, however—well, look at it this way, Twana. I wear you down a little and you ain't going to give me nearly as much trouble."

That seemed to amuse him more than anything else he'd told her tonight. A loud guffaw burst from him. Before it could fade, Twana forced her thoughts into the forest—searching, searching for anything. Conrad's laugh had startled a couple of nearby owls, but the doe she found was so far away that the night breeze covered the sound.

One Ear—

"That Tatooktche's one stupid man," Conrad said in his harsh way. "You ain't going to ask me why I think Tatooktche's stupid? No matter. I'll tell you anyway. He was willing to take anything he could get in trade for you. He should have held out for more; I would have given it to him. You're worth it, *daughter*."

Don't blink, Twana warned herself. Don't blink and don't flinch and don't let him see inside you to the fear.

Madsaw.

* * *

The morning smelled of warmth. Birds had come to life and were singing as if aware that today was going to be one of rare and blessed sunlight. Because there'd been no clouds to hold in the forest's damp heat, the night had been cold, but that wasn't what had kept Twana awake. The ropes had bit into her ankles and wrists and she'd been aware of every rock and root under her, but it had been Conrad who'd robbed her of sleep. Over and over again he reached out to reassure himself that she hadn't somehow freed herself.

Opening her eyes, she stared up at the trees and tried to take comfort in the way the sun brushed the topmost needles with pale yellow fingers. The trees looked clean and fresh and new today, waving lazily in time with the wind's song.

Conrad stirred. His open mouth was so close to her that she could barely hear the wind or birds for his snoring. Tears burned her eyes. She wanted the release that tears would bring, but she was no child disappointed because her puppy had disappeared, and the tears that boiled inside her would change nothing.

Would give her no freedom.

Freedom.

She tried to shift so her shoulders would stop aching, but he'd kept her tightly trussed and there was no escape. Conrad wouldn't make the same mistake twice; this time he'd watch her constantly, give her no chance to run.

Strip her, finally, of the will to live.

Madsaw.

Madsaw.

She'd said his name countless times during the night, and still it wasn't enough. Over and over she'd reminded herself that even if he'd learned the truth from Sokolov and confronted Tatooktche, Tatooktche didn't know where Conrad had taken her. Still, if she didn't hold on to Madsaw's memory, she would have nothing.

As she'd done so many times before, she left her body and entered the forest, insanely searching for Madsaw. But even with the rising sun teasing it with light, she found only darkness. Only a dense and endless fog.

Frightened, she tried to scoot away from Conrad. She felt his fingers slide off her arm and for a moment the fog lifted. Then he claimed her again and night descended. She fought with useless strength, imagined herself slashing at the fog with knives, shooting into it with Conrad's rifle, clubbing it with Madsaw's slave killer.

But the forest had become a massive cave and maybe would stay that way as long as Conrad owned her.

A night of silent battle, fear, despair, and hope no stronger than a spiderweb had left her exhausted, and when her tears began, she didn't try to stop them.

Madsaw.

Madsaw.

She was still crying when Conrad grunted and clamped his hand tightly, briefly, over her waist. Still touching her there, he pushed himself onto his elbow. "Think about it, Twana. Think about what it's like to be owned by me. Whatever I want, I get." He blinked and leaned forward. A smile curled his mouth upward. "Been crying, have you? It won't be the last time, *daughter*. Won't be the last time at all."

He ran his fingers from her throat to her shoulder, then down her side before resting them on her belly. She jumped and squirmed, but her hands and feet were so numb that even if they were free, she wouldn't have been able to use them.

Madsaw! Help!

"Damn, I'm hungry." Conrad grunted. "A man can't think when his stomach's growling. What about you, Twana?" He kneaded her belly. "You hungry, too? Probably got to use the bushes, don't you? Me, too. Can't think of anything else till I get that taken care of. Then—"

He didn't say anything, only pressed down on her belly and stared at her until she thought she was going to be sick. She was unbelievably grateful when he untied her ankles and hauled her to her feet. He steadied her by gripping her elbow, and she realized how quickly she'd become dependent on him. When he stayed with her while she relieved herself, she was too numb to care. She stood beside him, her teeth clamped against the porcupine-quill feeling attacking her legs, while he took care of his morning needs. He didn't say anything, but then he didn't need to.

He owned her.

When he pulled her back toward his camp and her eyes locked on the ropes he used to control her, her mind fled, taking a desperate and panicked journey into the wilderness. But nothing was left, not even the smallest of birds. She could see—see nothing except Conrad.

Madsaw.

"It's a good day for hunting," Conrad said almost conversationally. "Been debating whether I can risk a shot, but what the hell. That damn war chief'd have to be a mind reader to know where I am, and even if he sniffs me out, I'm ready for him." Holding her tethered hands, he leaned down and picked up his rifle. Then he released her and began caressing the sleek wood, his eyes not leaving her. "You're not going to be doing any running this morning, Twana. Not with the way I trussed you up last night. It's going to be a long time before you can walk proper, let alone run."

She didn't bother to speak. Why should she? He was right. Feeling mesmerized, she watched as he emptied black powder into the rifle and packed it down with a metal stick. He said something about it being a smart move to have his weapon primed before doing anything else, but she didn't see as it made any difference since, unless she could clear her mind, she wouldn't be able to led him to game.

Lead him? Had he so stripped her that she would do whatever he ordered?

The thought stopped her, took her from where she stood and back into the trees. It seemed that the fog was less dense, that she could hear more than the rush of blood in her ears. Concentrating, she pushed at the fog with her mind and fought to regain what she'd always taken for granted.

He owned her body; he didn't own her soul.

There. More light. The sound of nearby water, a crow squawking. Daylight filtering down, melting even more shadows, painting trees and ferns and a riot of small white flowers in stark colors.

White flowers like those Madsaw once gave her.

"Damn you, Twana! I speak, you listen to me!"

He'd shoved her so hard that she fell to her knees. Ignoring him, she struggled to stand again. The wilderness remained clear and clean and alive—alive with—

"Did you hear me?" he insisted. "I said, I want me a deer this morning. You take me to him."

No. "First I want water." She was thirsty, but that wasn't what had caused her to stall. Something was out there. Something big and dark and powerful. A few more heartbeats and she would know.

"Water? Why not?" he muttered. Holding the rifle with one hand, he began pulling her toward the creek where he'd caught his fish last night. Not fighting him, she concentrated on making her stiff and aching legs work. She wanted to focus on what had captured her attention but couldn't because walking took so much effort. The wide, shallow creek made a soft laughing sound that soothed her and distracted her from the pain in her ankles.

In one direction, trees grew thick and heavy around the creek, but below them was a rock-strewn area where the evergreens hadn't been able to take hold. As Conrad led her closer, she "saw" a trout leave the shadows to chase a small bug that skipped along the surface. If she could see a fish, surely she could now make sense of the other shape.

She now stood at the creek's edge, felt the dampness on the bottom of her feet, the breeze on her cheeks. Wondering if Conrad would free her hands so she could fill them with water or if he expected her to lap like a dog, she turned to face him. A movement so slight that it might have been nothing more than a wind-tossed branch caught her attention.

Caught it and held it.

"Give me a minute," Conrad grumbled as she thrust her hands at him. "I'm trying to figure—"

"Get away from her!"

Madsaw! Although she'd known the movement belonged to him, Twana nearly screamed when the Tillamook war chief stepped out of the shadows. She felt as if she might explode, might sink to the ground.

"Get away from her!"

"Damn!" With a movement that made a lie of his gray beard, Conrad swung his rifle to his shoulders and quickly aimed at the approaching warrior.

"Stop! Don't risk . . ."

Madsaw continued to stalk Conrad, armed only with his slave killer.

"Get away—"

Conrad was going to fire. Cold understanding registered at the same time she threw herself at the trader. She felt her shoulder hit his arm and heard a sound like the end of the world. Madsaw stopped in midstride, his body taut and strong and beautiful. For a heartbeat she told herself he hadn't been hit, couldn't have possibly been shot. But a red smear coated the side of his head and he lifted his hand and clamped it over his wound and then, graceful as a young buck, slumped to the ground.

"Damnation! Yeah!"

Twana screamed and stumbled toward Madsaw. He lay motionless, still beautiful, and her heart broke. Rage and grief and fear flooded her, stopped her legs just as she reached him. She didn't know what she was going to do, didn't know how to help him, knew only that if he was dead, she was, too.

"Got him! Yeah, got him!"

He was wrong. Even as Conrad grabbed her and threw her to the ground where she couldn't reach Madsaw, she knew her warrior was still alive.

Alive but unconscious.

When Conrad stared down at Madsaw, she realized he'd seen the dark, broad chest rise and fall. She would have given up her life if it meant Madsaw would live, but there was no mercy in Conrad.

Had never been any mercy in him.

He began reloading his rifle, and with an awful certainty, she knew he was going to finish the job he'd begun. "Don't!" she shrieked. "Please—" She managed to wrestle herself into a sitting position and was starting to push herself onto her knees when Conrad swung the wooden end of his rifle at her and caught her across the back. Grunting in pain, she sprawled on the cool ground.

"You don't tell me what to do, Twana. Not today and not ever." He watched her, his stance warning her not to defy him again. "Watch me, Twana," he ordered. "Watch and understand."

Still keeping an eye on her, he stalked closer to Madsaw. He upended his rifle and again rammed his long stick down it, his movements both leisurely and deadly. She tried to stand. He picked up Madsaw's slave killer and started toward her again.

"I'm not going to kill you, Twana. Ain't never going to make that mistake. But there's being alive and there's something else. You don't want to know what that something is."

Breathing heavily, dying inside, hating with a fury that snaked through her, she could only glare at Conrad and wait for him to kill Madsaw.

Kill? No!

As Conrad again turned his attention on Madsaw, she fought off panic and despair. Forced herself to think, to search. To find.

There had been a presence in the wilderness, a shadow, a strength. It hadn't been Madsaw.

One Ear. Not far away, drawn maybe by her presence, maybe by the smell of Madsaw's blood.

Had the grizzly been stalking her since Tatooktche took her? The possibility that he was here to kill her slammed into her, but he was all she had. All that lay between Madsaw and death at her father's hands.

Help! Hear me! Heed me.

Save him! Please, save him.

"You watching this, Twana? I want you to see, want you to understand."

"No! Please—"

"Shut up! Just shut the hell up!"

Hear me, One Ear! Hear my desperate plea.

"You can't—he didn't—"

"Didn't what, *daughter*? He tried to kill me." Conrad glared at her, then stepped over a rock and planted himself beside Madsaw. She concentrated on that magnificent chest as it rose and fell, shut her mind to the blood on his temple, refused to think what would happen when Conrad fired.

Her mind shrieked a message to One Ear, a senseless, wordless plea that the grizzly might never hear or heed, but she couldn't stop Conrad from murdering the man she loved, and One Ear was her only hope. When Conrad steadied the rifle and aimed it at Madsaw's chest, she readied herself to scream.

By screaming, maybe she wouldn't hear the shot.

Only there was another sound. An earth bellow, a rage of noise that split her world and stopped everything else. She saw Conrad's mouth drop open, saw his body jerk.

One Ear emerged from the trees that surrounded the creek as easily as if he were a slender deer. Gloriously brown and silver-tipped, he'd easily hidden himself in the shadows, but now—maybe because he'd heard her silent cry and maybe because he'd come to kill her—he stood in the open.

Conrad dropped to his knees and sighted down

his rifle at the motionless grizzly. One Ear stared back, man and beast regarding each other. Then, as if bored with the trader, One Ear focused on Twana. She looked into eyes that were as dark as Madsaw's, reached beyond them for the primitive mind encased in a powerful body.

You are lord here. Lord and ruler. If you want me—if you cannot forgive what happened to your mother—I can't stop you. But I don't hate you. Can never hate you.

One Ear shook his head, the thick, loose hair on his shoulder moving like a great wave. He planted one foot in front of him and then another, so close now that she thought she could smell him. She heard Conrad breathing. Heard Madsaw moan.

He isn't your enemy, not this wounded war chief who only wants to live in peace with you. I love him, will die loving him. If you kill him, you will kill me.

Little black eyes locked with hers, but she didn't know what, if anything, the grizzly was thinking. He hadn't moved, hadn't attacked or fled, seemed to be waiting for something. Conrad pulled in a deep breath. A heartbeat later, Madsaw did the same.

Be careful! The man with the weapon—he has killed your kind. Killed them and placed their claws around his neck. Stop him. Before he ends you, stop him.

Her throat contracted and she couldn't think how to breathe. She, who had never wanted to harm anyone, wanted Conrad dead.

I hate him. Hate him as maybe you hate me. He

killed my mother. Murdered a good and decent woman. Greed. That's why he did it. The same greed that made him kill your brothers.

Another step, great weight flattening the massive paws and spreading out the deadly claws until they dug into the earth. With every step, Twana believed she felt the ground settle under the grizzly. He was walking toward Conrad, a slow and measured pace that reminded her of how Conrad had stalked Madsaw a few moments before.

Look at the claw necklace. Hate it; hate the man wearing it.

"What the hell is he doing?" Eyes bulging, breath coming in ragged gasps, Conrad stared at the massive shape heading relentlessly toward him. He stumbled awkwardly to one side, the rifle first trembling and then becoming still. Twana guessed that no more distance than the height of a half-grown tree stood between One Ear and Conrad. *Be careful. The rifle—be careful.*

She'd barely finished the thought when One Ear roared and launched himself at the trader. The bellow was still rising when Conrad fired. She waited, waited seemingly forever for One Ear to fall, but he continued, strong and deadly. Became a tearing, killing monster that ripped the rifle from Conrad's grasp, ripped his arm from its socket. Ripped his chest open.

Conrad screamed. Maybe she screamed along with her father. He shrieked again, but the sound was quickly cut off. She wanted to turn from the carnage, but she'd ordered this killing and had to see it through to the end.

Conrad stopped moving, lay limp and helpless, and still One Ear attacked. She sensed the grizzly's fury, his total surrender to the act of killing, and understood that there was nothing left in the bear's mind beyond the primitive compulsion to end a life.

Maybe more than one life.

CHAPTER 21

Staggering to her feet, Twana stumbled toward Madsaw. She stopped only when his sharp warning cry sliced into her. "Don't move! He'll kill you!"

Looking at the enraged bear, Twana nearly believed him. There was so little left of Conrad that he no longer seemed human. Nearby, Madsaw sat with one leg half under him, his hand clamped to his wound, his head seemingly too heavy for him to hold erect. One Ear stopped his savage attack, but his body heaved with unspent energy and he kept swinging his head from side to side as if trying to find something to focus his anger on.

There was one thing. Madsaw.

Peace. Find peace, please.

The grizzly blinked, then settled his weight on his hind legs and rose effortlessly into the air. One

Ear seemed larger than the highest mountain, more powerful than a storm rolling and bucking and blowing in from the sea. His mouth hung open to reveal teeth that could kill with a single bite, and his claws, dangling in front of him, looked more deadly than the weapons of an entire village.

It is done. Listen to me, it is done.

"Twana," Madsaw whispered. "Run. Now, just run."

She couldn't, not because her legs weren't trembling with the need for flight but because if she fled, she would leave Madsaw behind, and she couldn't do that.

"I'm not afraid."

Her voice caught One Ear's attention. His body became corded muscle under the dense coat. He stretched his neck up and out, fighting his eyes' limitations. Learning with ears and nose. "I don't fear you," she told him. "Not anymore. Not after what you have done." With strangely steady hands, she pointed as best she could at the inert body of the man who'd given her life. "He is the enemy. He. Not me and not Madsaw."

Woofing, One Ear lowered himself back down onto all four legs. He took a step and then another, moving slowly and deliberately toward her.

I won't run. If you hate me, if you can't forgive, end me now. Just, please, spare Madsaw.

Madsaw called out another warning. One Ear gave no indication he'd heard, and she couldn't take her thoughts far enough away from the grizzly to try to tell Madsaw that the time for either

peace or death had come. She was dimly aware
that Madsaw had gotten to his feet and had
picked up his slave killer. Half staggering, he
started after the grizzly.

One Ear kept coming toward her, his head nodding in rhythm with the power in his shoulders.
She was becoming mesmerized by unbelievable
strength, by the sheer mass of him. The sun
touched the tips of the hairs on his back with tentative fingers, changing them from silver to a pale
gold that reminded her of her mother's necklace.

A killer. A beast who knows nothing except to
attack, who fears nothing.

*I love you. In all your beauty and courage and
strength, I love you. My mother—she didn't hate
your mother. But she was human and did what a
human must to protect her own children.*

One Ear stopped when he was so close that she
could have reached out and touched him. She
knew Madsaw was behind him, still on his feet,
still ready to lay down his life for her, but the grizzly had become her world.

She watched as he stretched out his heavy head,
saw the moisture that coated his black nose, felt
his hot breath on her cheeks and eyelids and in
her nostrils. Mindless of her roped hands, she
lifted them, not in defense but because in a way
that defied understanding, One Ear was speaking
to her and she knew what he wanted.

His nose was wet, warm and hard like the rest
of him. She felt his strength through her fingers,
saw the questioning in his eyes and knew her eyes
mirrored the same emotion. "I love you." The

words were half reality, half thought. "I love you. I can never hate you."

The grizzly pulled back so she could no longer touch him, but still she held out her half-numb hands and waited. When she realized what he was going to do, an involuntary shudder tore through her, but she forced it into submission. He took her hands into his mouth, half pulled and half sucked them past the great tearing teeth until her fingertips touched his tongue. He held her like that for a moment, then closed his mouth, his teeth pricking the back of her hands.

He'd trapped her, made her his prisoner, and yet she didn't fear him. Felt nothing except an incredible awe that weakened her legs and flooded her with tears.

Madsaw had stopped moving. Even with her sight of him blocked by the grizzly, she knew that and hoped he understood.

Peace. For both of us, peace.

Madsaw untied Twana's hands and began massaging them. His head pounded so that he felt half-sick, but by breathing deeply, he was able to dismiss the pain. She hadn't spoken since the grizzly released her and bounded away, might not have moved if he hadn't pulled her against him and held her until he believed—truly believed—that she was safe.

When she swayed, he helped her sit and went on warming her hands. He'd been careful to position her so she couldn't see what was left of

Conrad, but she seemed oblivious to her surroundings.

Oblivious to everything except him, he thought as, with a childlike sigh, she leaned against him and cried soft, silent tears. He kissed the top of her head, wrapped his arms around her shoulder and let love wash over him.

He loved her. Heart and soul, he loved her. Would never leave her.

The sun beat down on his back and sent prickles of sensation over his flesh. When he again touched his lips to her hair, he felt the sun's warmth radiating out from her and looked up at an utterly cloudless sky.

"Listen to the wind, Twana," he whispered. "Listen to it and find peace."

"It's over," she whispered back. "I'll never see him again."

"You are sure?"

"He has found his peace."

Madsaw no longer cared about the grizzly, not now with her pressed against him and the sun warming both of them. He would later when he told his chief about the woman who had sent a silent plea to him on the wind and made it possible for him to find her, who commanded a grizzly to kill her enemy and then called that same grizzly to her side, but for now all that mattered was that he'd found her again and she was safe. Would always be safe.

"I want you with me, forever." He didn't try to bring his voice above a whisper. "In my village. As my wife."

"Your—wife?"

She hadn't pulled away to look at him, so he didn't know what was in her eyes and could only pray her heart beat with the same rhythm as his.

"Your magic is powerful. Powerful and good."

"I—I told him to kill Conrad."

"The trader deserved to die."

She nodded and he went on. "Listen to me, Twana. I want you to be my wife, to live with me and sleep with me and bear my children."

"I . . ."

"I will tell my chief what is in my heart, what exists between you and me, and he will understand. When I call the village to the council fire and tell them what happened today, all will believe that your magic is good. That will happen if you return with me."

"If?"

"It has to be what you want. If you don't—"

"What I want?"

He could have told her countless things, promised her that she would be welcomed back into his village and accepted as the war chief's wife, but if she trusted him, truly trusted him, she already knew that.

"Will you have me?" he whispered. "That is the only thing, will you have me?"

Sighing, she rested her head against his chest. He felt her hot tears and held his breath. In her answer, she held his heart, and yet he had said all he could.

"As your wife? Your equal?"

"Yes. Forever."

"Forever." She sighed. "This is what you want?"

"I think it is what I have wanted since I first saw you."

"I remember—our first night together when you held me and I stopped fearing you. Maybe that is when I started to fall in love."

"You love me?"

"I will always love you, Madsaw. Always."